About Jude Hayland

Jude Hayland is a writer and tutor. For many years she wrote commercial short fiction for magazines and was published widely in the UK and internationally. After graduating with an M.A. in Creative and Critical Writing with distinction, she began to write full length fiction and has written three novels. A Londoner by birth and upbringing, she now lives in Winchester, but spends part of each year in a village in north-west Crete.

Follow her blog and latest writing news on:
www.judehayland.co.uk
Facebook: Jude Hayland Writer
Twitter: @judehayland

Cover image – from an original painting
by Josephine Chisholm
www.josephinechisholm-artist.co.uk

MILLER STREET SW22

A novel

BY JUDE HAYLAND

Matador
9 Priory Business Park,
Wistow Road, Kibworth Beauchamp,
Leicestershire. LE8 0RX
Tel: 0116 279 2299
Email: books@troubador.co.uk
Web: www.troubador.co.uk/matador
Twitter: @matadorbooks

ISBN 978 1800462 380

British Library Cataloguing in Publication Data.
A catalogue record for this book is available from the British Library.

Printed and bound in the UK by TJ Books Limited, Padstow, Cornwall
Typeset in 11pt Aldine 401 BT by Troubador Publishing Ltd, Leicester, UK

Matador is an imprint of Troubador Publishing Ltd

To my sister, Jane Gaudie
With infinite and inexpressible gratitude and love

Acknowledgements

I am very grateful to 78 Derngate – the Charles Rennie Mackintosh House and Galleries in Northampton – for welcoming me and patiently answering my numerous questions about the day-to-day running of the house in order to make the Harriet Howe House museum sound as authentic as possible. Deborah Sampson and the other guides and volunteers I met provided me with vital details and Liz Jansson, the House Manager, was so generous with the time she gave me in her busy schedule.

Thank you to Josephine Chisholm, artist and teacher, who agreed to take on the commission of designing the cover for Miller Street SW22. It was wonderful to work with someone so sympathetic and responsive to the vague image I had in my mind.

I am indebted to my friends for their continued support – in particular, to Carol Randall, my friend of longest standing with whom I have always shared an obsession with reading novels. Also thanks to Marie Armstrong, Liz Stacy, Linda Gibson, Linda Anderson and Sue Russell – thank you for your perpetual encouragement and interest.

Above all, my family sustains me – they are everything – and my son, George, is the most of that everything.

Thank you.

"Our deeds still travel with us from afar, and what we
have been makes us what we are."
George Eliot – *Middlemarch*

"Dear Lord and Father of mankind,
Forgive our foolish ways!"
John Greenleaf Whittier

AUTUMN
1966

Preface

He is back late.

Later than his rash promise to his parents. And already feels remorse for his selfishness. He could have afforded, after all, some generosity tonight of all nights. There could have been an allowance made for a sort of Last Supper in the bleak back dining room, his father, proprietorial out of habit, at the head of the table, his mother, diffident, sitting opposite. He could have placated so easily the two of them, yielded to the consolation of his mother's undemonstrative, quiet love. His father's brusque pride.

Instead, he had stayed on at the pub near Holborn, bought another round, thrown careless coins and notes in the direction of the barman, moved an hour later to a place in Blackfriars, spent more, drunk more, until he found himself alone, his erstwhile colleagues self-despatched to trains and homes in Sidcup, Surbiton, Penge. He pitied them. And despised them, too, for their willingness to surrender to the shackles of sure, secure and certain futures.

Unlike him. For he was breaking loose. Getting out.

Eventually, he had found his way to the underground, staying awake until Baker Street where he faltered up the escalator, pushed a shilling into a vending machine, rapidly eating a bar of nut chocolate that made him feel faintly nauseous. He knew there would be a plate of stew or shepherd's pie waiting for him in a cooling oven, gravy staining dry into the willow pattern plate, a dish of custard and crumble or tinned fruit his mother would have left on the side. On the next train, he fell asleep, succumbing to the effects of the alcohol before Finchley Road so that the suburban stations slipped unwittingly past, their platforms mostly deserted so late on a Thursday night.

But he wakes up just in time, force of habit, something regulated by years of travelling on the same Metropolitan line so that now he stumbles sleepily down the steps, out of the station, juggles for keys, pats trouser pockets. His car is one of only two remaining in the haphazard parking arrangement that straddles the forecourt. It is nearer midnight than eleven and he feels already the pull of the next day, the early start, and again regrets his extended leave-taking celebrations with those forgettable colleagues. After all, there is no possibility that any of them will keep in touch and it is how he wants it. He is shredding the past few years, the oppressive dullness of it, picking off the detritus to emerge emboldened, freed to a new, uncharted future.

His plane leaves at nine.

Only the second flight he has ever taken (and that weekend trip to Paris with an old school friend hardly counts) and he smiles at the prospect of international travel, even chuckles out loud with the sheer bravado of it. The sophistication. His breath is clear on the late-night October air as he shoves keys into the lock, gets inside. Shivers. The night's close to freezing, he's sure. It has been raining constantly for days, but now the mild, wet air has lifted, replaced by sharp winds as if autumn is shifting prematurely. Avalanches of leaves lie sodden like mulch underfoot. The windscreen wipers on his old car make a stubborn, slow job of shifting the windfall. His fingers are cold and he tries holding them in a fist in front of the inadequate heater, flexes them to restore warmth.

He'll be away from all this in a matter of hours.

Away from these dense, dark days of English winters, the endless wait for signs of a reluctant spring. Over there, sun is mandatory, an obligation, blue skies greeting each dawn as if contracted to the job. He anticipates such a climate, sitting in the darkness of the car's interior, trying to coax the engine, resistant, coughing bronchially into life. His contract is lucrative, audacious, even, given his scant qualifications, his inexperience. But he has youth to his advantage. *It's a young man's world out there,* he has said several times, to his parents, to friends dubious of his decision. He has even said it to himself in moments of doubt and honest reflection. *It's a chance to find a different sort of life. Abroad. New developing lands and territories, emerging industries. That's the future. We're pioneers for a new age.* He revs several times, encouraging the engine's hesitant fire, thinks of that word, *Pioneers.* He likes its suggestion of the frontier spirit, wagons set to forge westward in hope of more. Except he is going east, he reminds himself. To a landscape of sand, new concrete cities being carved out of desert wastes, a place of unrivalled opportunity for the bold. Rapidly, he pulls away from the station forecourt to avoid stalling, heads towards the crossroads to turn left for the short drive home.

Woods of evergreens border one side of the narrow main road. On the other, detached, comfortable houses, heavy curtains tightly drawn against the moonless night, stand discreetly behind cultivated, neat front gardens, high brick walls and picket fencing. This place seems to hover as if confused by its identity, he thinks irritably. As if an absence of decent street lighting and the lack of proper pavements bestow a rural gentility that is entirely at odds with the commuter trains connecting it to its source of income and sustainability. He has grown to despise it. Or at least he used to summon up sufficient cynicism to mock at its sedate, self-satisfied demeanour. Now he is not so sure. His attitude is beginning to slide, he suspects, into a slow acceptance of the insulation it provides and he fears he could slowly be devoured by the ease and complacency of the place, succumb to the prescriptive sort of life it has on offer. And he despairs of that. He glances now to his right, to the row of square and solid houses, built thirty or more years before for people secure in their belief of being kings in their own castles. And he suspects there has been little change. In spite of Nuremberg and Dachau and Dresden, names that now defeat even the power of language to explain, they go on, these houses, these people. This place. Smugness survives against all odds.

But he is getting out.

He is not giving in to the hooks that bind. He glances one way to the dense border of tall evergreens, turns his head for a moment towards those self-satisfied houses. He thinks of the slab of solid sideboard in his parents' front room, the heavy oak dining table in the back, utility furniture acquired with foolish gratitude at the end of the war and is exasperated by knowledge of these objects as if he is implicated simply by living alongside them for so long. His parents are biddable, pleasant people, of course, obliging neighbours, lawful and cautious. And he loves them, inevitably. They give him no particular reason to do otherwise. Except for their lethargy, their compliance with lives that appear to him to offer little more than continuity, survival, ticking off the days, into months, years. Decades.

He speeds up. The road is deserted and he is tired. Besides, a certain recklessness tonight seems appropriate. He is not entirely drunk, but certainly a little affected by the excess of alcohol. And he wants to get back, dispense with his final night at home, fall asleep for the last time in the bedroom that has been his since childhood. He knows this road with a familiarity that allows for risk in spite of its lack of adequate lighting. He takes the slight bend in third gear, accelerates out as he straightens, loses the string of houses on his right as a couple of fields replace them, running down towards the new private housing development under construction. He places his foot down firmly to conjure more speed. Yawns. Leans forward to wipe mist from the windscreen.

And that is when it happens.

The explosion of sound rips through the silence of the night like ferocious gunfire.

And his body reacts, as if the appalling noise has triggered some instinctive electrical impulse that causes his heart to thud uncontrollably, his limbs to tense in anticipation. The impact on the car, the judder as if the metal frame has been picked up and tossed aside by a despotic giant, terrifies. Yet instinctively he does not brake. Instead, he flinches against an inevitable slide, a catastrophic skid into trees, a deep, muddy ditch that must surely be awaiting him. But no.

After a moment, he finds that he is still driving, still pressing his foot firmly on the accelerator, his speed barely interrupted. His forehead sweats in the cold air of the car, his hands shake. He wants to go on, follow his instinct to turn his back on whatever lies behind him. After all, the noise was no doubt caused by something insignificant. A stray, steel dustbin lid, a lost hub cap, a branch from the bordering evergreens.

But eventually, he pulls up.

A couple of hundred yards from the turn to his parents' road, he stops the car, sits for a moment or two to control his breathing, gather resolve, then gets out and starts to walk slowly back the way he has travelled. He tells himself he will find debris from the building site. Carelessly abandoned builders' tools or materials that have found their way into his path on the quiet road. Bricks, bits of masonry, shards of wood, even. Scaffolding perhaps. Objects to explain, to excuse him from any responsibility.

What he finds, however, sitting in the road, is a pair of shoes.

A pair of perfectly ordinary black gentleman's lace up shoes lined up neatly on the left-hand side, as if awaiting their owner's feet. He glances towards the field of new houses, only one or two yet occupied, mere shadowy outlines in the dark night. He looks into the woods, thinks he hears a noise, but knows that it is only in his head, in his body, even, as if the impact on the car, the jar of its framework is reverberating endlessly through every nerve and cell. He starts to shake, tells himself it is the cold and yet even as he begins to walk away from the shoes, heading deliberately back in the direction of his car, he finds his steps laboured, dragging, as if he has temporarily lost the capacity to coordinate movement. When he reaches it, he sits for some moments and has a sudden overwhelming sensation that he is going to cry. Like a young child bewildered by the consequences of his actions and fearful of recrimination. But he is not a child, he tells himself, and switches the strangled sensation at the back of his throat into a cough. He turns the ignition key and is flooded with relief at the sound of the engine, at the car's ability to move him swiftly on, speed him to the turning to his road.

The hall light is on. It is always left on until the last person is home and the front door is locked, bolted against the night. He slips into the narrow driveway and remembers that he is to drop his car at a scrap dealer early the next day. It is worth less than nothing, he knows, and he will be lucky to get a few pounds for a few parts. So no need to inspect for any collision damage, a scar from the night's incident. His first and only car, third or fourth hand when he bought it, it has served him well, but now merits merely relegation to the past.

Like this house, this place and its events.

He is ready to shrug off links and memories, to carve out for himself a new life, unfettered by all that has gone before.

If only he can forget the sight of those shoes sitting neatly, orderly, at the side of the road. The sound of the impact of metal and steel with something indeterminate, defenceless. Undefined.

Early morning, he is away before it is fully light, before his parents are properly awake, hurried farewells in dressing gowns, promises to write, all delivered rapidly on the upstairs landing. He throws his suitcase in the car, backs out into the deserted road, and sees his mother's face peering from the bedroom window, one hand holding back the net curtain, the other waving. And for a moment the sight of her anxious, thin face foolishly hauls him back two decades, to infant school gates, an emptying playground, when the pain of parting was too much for both of them to bear.

Later that morning, 116 children are killed in a welsh village called Aberfan. The radio and television news are haunted for weeks by the tragedy, subsuming all other concerns. A few local people talk briefly of an incident along the main road from the station. Evidently, a dog walker from one of the big detached houses found a man's body when he went into the woods just after dawn. But even gossip in the newsagents by the station is periphery, the subject of the dead welsh school children and their teachers hovering spectre-like over everyone's lips. His mother fills her first letter to him with details of the horrific Welsh event in case he has not heard. In case news of such national disaster does not reach him in his impossibly remote oasis of white concrete.

As an afterthought, she includes a small cutting from the local newspaper. A paragraph or two at best are given over to the unexplained death of a local resident, a man in his late forties found in the woods near the housing development.

Police, the brief article concludes, are investigating.

AUTUMN
2005

1

The key refused to turn. The lock was obdurate.

She pulled it out, stared at it with growing frustration.

"Not having much luck, are you?" The voice came from an elderly man who had stopped to watch. "Sure you're not trying to break in – a forced entry or something along those lines?" He looked mildly amused. A dog sniffed at his side.

"It's the key," she said flatly. "I think they've given me the wrong one. I've just picked it up from the agents."

"Oh, I see," the man said. "New tenant, are you? New blood in the road? So many changes these days, just can't keep up with it." He shifted from one foot to the other as if growing bored with her distraction. The dog made use of the lamppost.

"No," she said. "Or at least not a tenant. It's mine. I mean, I've just bought it. The house. Well, not the whole house, obviously. Just this ground floor flat." She wondered why she sounded so defensive. The elderly man continued to stare as she tried hopelessly yet again to stir metal against metal. Then, muttering under his breath and inexplicably shaking his head, he moved away, catching up with the dog now waiting patiently at the end of the street.

Catherine reluctantly watched him go, even considered calling him back. After all, perhaps he could offer some practical assistance. An elderly man walking a dog somehow suggested reliability and resourcefulness. She tried the key

3

again then gave up, walked round to the front of the house, peered through the window that presented her with a view of the living room, the door open to the hall and the kitchen beyond. Empty rooms, pristine white walls, bare cupboards and shelves, the blankness was unnerving. Even though the initial attraction of the place lay in its newly minted state, the smell of fresh paint, the residue of plasterers' and builders' handiwork, now the need to expend so much energy on laying claim to it as a home, imposing herself upon it, seemed wearying. She wondered if she could conjure the will. But the choice had been hers, she reminded herself. There was no one else to blame for her impulsive step in selling the house in Bevington so swiftly, moving on. Financially inevitable eventually, of course, but she could have delayed a little and then stayed in the town, downsized, as people liked to call it, found herself something more appropriate now that she was alone again.

However, there had been absolutely no desire to stay. Not after the accident.

Instinctively, she had known there was no future for her in Bevington and had soon begun to wonder how she had tolerated the town for so long. It was the anonymity of a city life she needed now, rather than the prurience of a place where she would always be defined by a small paragraph in the local paper: *He leaves a widow, 48-year-old Catherine Wells.* She had been uncomfortable with the inclusion, had felt fraudulent, as if it suggested her appropriation of the tragedy.

Whereas, in truth, it belonged entirely to Edward.

After all, she was still alive. And even in death, especially in such a sudden, dramatic death, Eddie, she knew, would have assumed the right to sole billing.

So she had ignored the advice of inquisitive neighbours, marginal friends, who seemed to paw at her loss, intrude on it self-righteously as if they could offer an indispensable panacea to her grief. *Give in to it, Catherine, let yourself howl from the hilltops. Don't make any swift decisions. We can just imagine how you're feeling … No,* she had thought, *actually you have absolutely no insight at all into my feelings* and she had gone ahead and placed the Bevington house on the market as soon as probate was granted. The first couple who came to view it, alarmingly young with a forthright and radiant manner that Catherine found brazen and faintly embarrassing, had immediately made a satisfactory offer that she had accepted on the same day. She had rung a company for packing cases, speedily began dismantling the contents of the house.

If her response to her husband's death had been considered impulsive and ill-judged by her Bevington neighbours, it had, contrarily, been thought excessive by her few close friends. Her reaction, they hinted delicately, was possibly out of proportion, inappropriately anguished, even. Her sensible older sister, Beth, was more forthright. *You were separated. Still in the same house, of course, but out of love with each other. Otherwise, why were you intending to divorce?* Catherine, too, had been bewildered by the persistence of her distress. Months after Eddie's death, she still found herself waking some mornings to discover her grief as raw as if the event had happened the night before. *We no longer wanted to be married to each other,* she said to her sister in some effort to explain, *but neither of us wished the other dead. And as for being out of love – well …"*

Nothing felt quite so finite as that.

The large bay window at the front of her new flat overlooked a small slab of uncompromising concrete forecourt. Curtains were needed swiftly to soften the space, give her some privacy and protect her from the darkness of the evenings that were already drawing in. She had hoped to be here by mid-summer since the Bevington house had sold so swiftly.

But her solicitor had appeared to dawdle, spending endless weeks trawling through old covenants and concerns over the development and conversion of the large Edwardian house into four flats, querying potential arterial road issues that had proven groundless. Then, just as he had declared the contract fit to sign and exchange, he had disappeared to Tuscany for a month, leaving her in the hands of an excessively cautious junior loath to proceed alone. By now it was late September, any pretence of an Indian summer abandoned, the trees on the common at the end of the road liberally shedding conkers and the early autumn skies fielding flocks of migratory birds, wisely gathering in readiness for their long flight south.

A car pulled abruptly into the kerb, startling Catherine from her position at the window and she pulled away as if guilty of trespass. A young man she vaguely recognised, very white shirt, sharp shoes, leapt out, looking concerned. Agitated.

"Cath – I mean, Mrs Wells?"

"Yes," Catherine said. "Or rather—"

"Keys," the young man interrupted, proffering a small bunch in his hand. "I think we gave you the wrong ones. Actually, it was me. Entirely my fault, in fact. Can't blame anyone else in the office. I muddled things, gave you the keys for a flat in Putney. Not here at all. So sorry about that." He placed the bunch in her palm with a certain slow ceremony. Catherine handed him back the single key that had failed her.

"I was beginning to think it was an omen," she said. The young man looked confused. "You know, denied entry to my new home. Perhaps it's a signifier to what lies ahead." She attempted a laugh, regretted it, and released him back to his Ford Fiesta, his keyless property in Putney. "Thank you," she said, "thank you. I'll be fine now."

"If there's anything else I can help you with?"

"No, really, please. Go. It's all right. Please."

There was a large living room with an open fireplace attractively tiled. She wondered if log fires were allowed and doubted it. The idea of flames and the smell of burning wood was attractive, but no doubt there would be restraints over polluting the south London air. The Bevington house had a gas-effect fire that did the job, as Eddie used to say, but she craved real flames, remembered childhood winter days of toasting thick slices of bread on red embers. The main bedroom, her bedroom, had a fireplace too, but it was blocked up with only a small, neat hearth that invited no more than decorative dried flowers. She walked from room to room, (although, in truth, there were only five) now relishing their emptiness, a kind of pleasing austerity, knowing that within days she would have loaded each one with too many possessions. The van from the storage facility was arriving at nine the following morning so she had a few hours and one night to spend in her monastic-like space. Planning. Preparing. Already she was warming to the task, her initial reservation forgotten. She had sold a lot of the furniture from the previous house, had no wish to take with her the wine-coloured sofa, the leather wing chairs, that oak dining table. They were weighty, heavy pieces that she saw as irrelevant, too portentous for her new home. She would rather exist with very little than lift and impose upon these clean new spaces, elements of the old and outworn. Eddie had loved the wing chairs. He had loved the oak dining table, as if its solidity confirmed his success, his claim to a significant kind of life. And perhaps it had. It had certainly been very, very expensive. Catherine was unsure whether she had ever liked it, had been craven, no doubt, in agreeing to Eddie's purchase.

She opened and closed kitchen cupboards, the fridge, dishwasher, the washing machine like a child inspecting new toys. Their perfectly unused, virgin state was consoling.

Likewise, the toilet, basin and bath. She placed a single bar of soap on the white enamel, tried the taps. She was hungry. Outside, she unpacked a couple of carrier bags from the car and the suitcase that was beginning to look like a weary travelling companion growing tired of the jaunt. Having completed on the Bevington house in late July, she had spent the weeks awaiting her solicitor's return from Tuscany, testing the patience and goodwill of her sister in the Mendip Hills, friends in Croydon, a former colleague in Enfield and had even resorted to a night in a dubious, cheap hotel in Bayswater, followed by another in a serviced room on the Farringdon road. And there had been that one strained night at Alec's house in Hampstead when, finding herself without a bed nearing eleven o'clock at night, she had eventually rung him and begged space on his sofa to sleep. She had stressed the need for his sofa. But she had disliked exploiting his geniality, his steadfast affection and willingness always to provide. One day, finding herself with a week's leave to take from the museum before the end of August, she had headed to a travel agent in Holborn and randomly chosen a seven-day package deal from the list advertised in the window and within twelve hours had arrived at an under-occupied hotel complex in the Algarve. It was only when she had unpacked the faithful suitcase in her small, single room with a precarious balcony arrangement overlooking a trio of swimming pools that she remembered clothing suitable for southern sunshine – swimsuits, shorts, sundresses – were deep in a storage unit in Hertfordshire. It had hardly mattered to her, however. She had felt liberated from dependence upon the kindness of others and wallowed in the solitariness of her simple hotel room. Even the intensity of her confused grief for Eddie had begun to retreat in the hot Portuguese climate as if the constancy of the sun, the insistence of violet-coloured skies greeting her each morning reproved melancholy.

In the kitchen, she unpacked the two carrier bags, placed eggs, a pint of milk, a slab of cheese in the fridge, lining them up with precision as if arranging them for display. She had found a delicatessen in a row of shops three streets away and had managed to spend what seemed an excessive amount of money in gaining very little, but in the absence of plates, of pots and pans, a knife, even, the portions of salad and something resembling a fishy mayonnaise, carefully spooned into small containers, would provide her with a meal of sorts. She tore a rough strip from a loaf of dense brown bread, painstakingly picking up the crumbs it scattered on the spotless kitchen floor and assembled her meal on the tiled worktop where it suddenly appeared paltry, uninviting. Rather like a tray of suspect airline food. There was the wine, at least. Ignoring the food, she opened the bottle she had bought, filled the paper cup she had found in the muddle of rubbish in the boot of her car and drank steadily, touring again her handful of rooms, imagining her books, her pictures on the wall. A particular chair. And sensed suddenly, with considerable relief, a semblance of hopeful anticipation, a feeling that had been absent for so long that it was alien to her, strange.

A dispensation to be happy once more. To begin again.

★★★

The platform was crowded. Sam Gough wished he had insisted on an earlier appointment at the clinic so that they could have left before rush hour. He glanced down at Lydia, tightened his grip on her arm. He felt her flinch, imperceptibly resist his grasp yet at the same time looking around herself with alarm. Like a young child's response, struggling with the dependence she resented. He said something to her about supper, bent his head to her ear so that she might hear his inconsequential words, aiming to distract her from the constant bustle of the platform as the lines of passengers thickened. But she appeared not to notice or at least showed no response. *Smoked Haddock with spinach. A poached egg. The way you like it.* And then risked raising his voice to repeat himself over the thunder of the District line tube train hurtling its way into the station.

There were few free seats. Strap hangers barred their easy route to the two that Sam had spied and a young couple got there first, giggling about something as they claimed the adjacent seats, leaving Sam to take the only remaining pair, not neighbouring, but opposite. He settled Lydia first, wedged her between a man absorbed by his evening paper and a plump woman reading a magazine and took his own seat. He began to breathe more easily, relieved to be on their way, relieved to think of the car that was parked at the station the other end so that the worst of the journey was almost complete. If there was to be another appointment, he would have to drive them the whole way. Or take a taxi although the expense would be prohibitive. Still, money was hardly calculable compared with the distress that Lydia was clearly experiencing today. It was to be expected, of course. He had been warned, had read numerous articles and papers about her condition, the downward spiral, degenerative phases, the trajectory they could anticipate. Yet even so, it was a shock to see her conform quite so obediently to the inevitable. He was aware that he harboured an irrational resentment about such submission as if Lydia should be defying the odds, refuting the experts and rejecting the symptoms of her disease. She had never been a conventional woman, rather one who did things differently, contrarily, almost. Now here she was compliant, acquiescent, as it were, to the terms of the illness. At times, he felt at risk of despising her for it.

More passengers crammed into the carriage at Victoria so that he lost sight of Lydia, able to see only her feet in the flat black sensible shoes that she now wore out of necessity. Petite, narrow feet she had, slim ankles and slender legs. These days, however, such limbs were inadequate to their task, betrayed her too often by allowing her to topple and fall. Her balance was precarious, unpredictable, sudden tumbles sideways, backwards. Sam glanced at the headlines of the paper his neighbour was reading. The century was only a handful of years old and already mired in disaster, marred by appalling acts of terrorism and atrocity. Hardly a clean slate, an age of tolerant, informed enlightenment for the new millennium. At Earls Court, his thoughts were interrupted as a strap-hanging woman, impeding his view of Lydia, started to shift towards the carriage doors so that he could see her again and at the same moment saw also the distaste on the face of the man sitting next to her as her head suddenly slipped sideways onto his shoulder. Rested there heavily. A puppet with strings abruptly cut. Sam sprang towards them, embarrassed, apologetic, retracting Lydia's head from the stranger's dark jacket, realigning it while the man twisted away from her as if to avoid contagion. She smiled, unaware. Sam searched in his trouser pocket for a handkerchief, looked in the other, cursing his disorganisation, his failure to foresee events for there was moisture at the side of Lydia's mouth which was drifting towards her chin, threatening to fall down onto her peacock blue sweater and stain it. He could not bear Lydia to sit in stained clothes. Slowly, with deliberation, she moved her arm, her stronger, better arm as if to reach out to him, then groped her way to the pocket of his navy jacket. Pulling out a clean white handkerchief, she handed it to him, at the same time tilting her face upwards so he could dab her face dry.

Half an hour later, he pulled up outside Willow house, backed carefully into the driveway leading conveniently to their front door. He sat for a moment then looked across the forecourt and saw the car occupying the space for the other ground floor flat.

"Lyddie," he said, taking her hand for a moment, "it seems we're not on our own any longer. Someone's moved in next door. We're not used to that, are we? We've never had immediate, close neighbours. Still, it's to be expected, now we're in London. Let's hope we've acquired some good ones who mainly keep themselves to themselves. Some reserved, quiet neighbours."

"Good," Lydia echoed. "Good … some … some … yes."

Sam looked at her, trying to decide whether her words were more than mere repetition. He liked to believe that she still formed freely her own thoughts and that it was only a lack of adequately functioning speech tools that prevented her from communicating them. A sudden gust of wind tipped leaves across the bonnet of the car. Rain had been threatening all day and the forecast promised a wet night. He always found autumn a tiresome season and disliked the prospect of the next month or two.

"Come on, Lyddie." He urged himself away from introspection, struggled against a profound weariness that was threatening. "Let's get inside and brace ourselves for the evening. Large glass of cheap red for me. And what about a very small sherry for you? Or at least a couple of mouthfuls. Shall we try it? Just to keep me company. Can't do any harm, isn't that what your specialist chap said this afternoon? A little of what you fancy and all that."

Lydia stared ahead at the flock of beech leaves skittering across the windscreen.

"And … all that," she said, "and."

★★★

Monday afternoon and in the back bedroom of flat 3, Willow House, Frances Chater smoothed down the pinch pleats of the new floral curtains she had just hung at her first-floor window, peered out into the garden belonging to flat 1.

There they are again, the two of them. She's clearly an obligation to him. An obstacle to living his life to the full, surely. After all, he's an attractive man. And not old. No, not at all. What – late fifties? Probably more. Mid-sixties, perhaps, and edging northwards from there. One forgets. Older than Andrew, certainly. And she's – well, hard to tell as illness is obviously ageing her. Withering her, clearly. Wonder what it is. Sad, that. Very sad. They've bought the one with the garden, of course. I suppose he wanted that, somewhere for her to sit. No doubt they've moved from somewhere bigger, needing now to be on the one level. Only practical given how she is. I'll ask him in good time. No point in inviting them up for a drink, though, not the two of them. She wouldn't manage the stairs. But perhaps he'd come on his own. Not that I would want to give him the idea of – well, you never know with people. With men. They just assume. Me being a single woman now and living alone. (I won't give anything away about all that, of course – stick to The Plan.) Because I don't suppose she's much use any more in the bedroom department. Don't suppose she could be of any use though it's a vulgar thought, admittedly. But one can't help but consider needs. His needs. A man like that. It's out of his control, dictated by testosterone. Isn't that what they always say about men? That's their excuse, anyway. And vanity, of course. I can certainly vouch for that, more's the pity. It's different for women. After The Change. That's what my mother used to call it. A euphemism if ever I heard one. Not that one is entirely without feelings of that sort. And he certainly has attractions, my neighbour. What you'd call a certain gravitas and an undeniable – well, you can tell that kind of thing even from a distance. That floppy fair hair, more streaked with silver grey now, but a good head of it. He's lucky to have kept it. Like Andrew. It's strange what the genes randomly throw at you. And a good covering of silver grey hair, kept on the long side so he looks a little – louche, is that the word? And it's distinguished too. No doubt about it.

I wonder how long I should wait to introduce myself. They were the first to move in, a month ahead of me. Their apartment, (that's the word they use these days and I much prefer it) theirs was the first to be finished and the most expensive by far, so no doubt the builders had instructions to get on with the place to give the developer some funds. But I've been here myself close on three weeks now so it's about time. And I've got the flyers ready. I'll drop one through their door in a day or two. Or perhaps I'll knock, hand it over in person. Yes, that's the way. Test the lie of the land, see quite how ill the poor wife is. I mean it could just be temporary, a post-operative stage from something or other. Perhaps I should offer my services in some way, sitting with her to give him a break. That would be the appropriate neighbourly thing to do and a way of establishing myself with them. Although I should be hesitant about getting too close. It's probably wise not to risk too much exposure. Not the card I should be playing. Considering.

Look at him, settling her in a chair, walking down to the bottom of the garden and staring down at the soil as if deep in thought. Penny for them. That's what they used to say, isn't it? What my mother used to say, ever interfering busybody that she was, wanting to know even one's personal reflections as if she had some claim on them. Disguising her interest with some pious, sanctimonious claptrap about the soul.

We're nearly complete now. What with the woman downstairs just moved in. She's only been here a couple of days, though, and my flyer through her door while she's still unpacking might not get the notice it deserves. Not that she seemed to have that many things to boast about – certainly not in the way of furniture at any rate. It was a storage company that unloaded, from Hertfordshire. One couldn't help but see. And what did she have beyond a few packing cases, a desk sort of affair, a couple of chairs, that chest of drawers and some pictures? Perhaps it's a post-divorce move and she's had to share out the furniture. Yes, that would be it. I wouldn't be having any of that. What's mine is *mine, after all. Whatever happens with Andrew. I caught a glimpse of her. Slim, definitely the thin sort, not an ounce to spare and that can prove very ageing. And she's about my own age, I'd say. You're kidding yourself, Frances, she's younger than you. (I can just hear my mother saying that. Never one to let a chance go by to put me down.) Not a lot younger, but if I'm honest, I suppose I could give her close on a decade. Of course, it's not clever to be as slim as that in middle age. And far more womanly to have a bit of shape rather than being a strip of string. She seems to be on her own. No sign of a Significant Other or, God forbid, any adolescent children. Children of any sort would be unbearable.*

This centenary business.

Has anyone else in the road even noticed, I wonder? A hundred years since the development of Miller Street which makes us Edwardian through and through. I don't suppose they have. Noticed, that is. It's extraordinary how people are so absorbed in their own lives these days that they don't look around them and see things. A sense of neighbourliness and community spirit has disappeared, no doubt about it. Especially here in London. South London, to be precise, SW22 on the nose.

Well, it looks as if you've arrived just in time to shake things up a bit, Frances Margaret Chater. (My mother again. And a touch of Andrew.)

But if the truth be told, it's self-preservation. I need something to fill my time now, to help the days pass. To occupy my mind.

Otherwise ...

She left the back room, crossed the narrow hall into her living room and the clear view of the substantial semi-detached houses that lined the street. She watched a woman unpacking shopping from the back of a Volvo estate, a small boy skipping around her feet, holding a large box of cereal. In the car, a baby slept, strapped into an infant's seat. Further down, a man skilfully slotted his car in between a motorbike and a Mini, got out, a small case in one hand, a carrier bag that looked as if it contained bottles in the other. The front door of a house opened, a woman holding a little girl dressed in a fairy costume greeted him, a brief kiss, a wriggle from the fairy child and they disappeared inside. She would know them in time, her new neighbours, know some of their houses too, their large family kitchens, conservatories, their loft extensions and infilled side returns. Comfortable, complacent people, leading comfortable, complacent lives, no doubt. And wondered whether any of them ever thought of the fragility of it all, considered the hairline cracks that could appear when least expected, causing the whole fabric to implode.

At the end of Miller Street, Willow House wedged itself conveniently close to the common, a large expanse of open green space that eventually gave way to the busy main road. Even before Frances had moved in, wanting to fill her days with purposeful occupation, she had been to the local history department at the reference library and found out that Willow House had once been the most imposing home in Miller Street. *Once, Frances, don't fool yourself you're moving into a mansion,* her mother's voice carped in her head as the helpful librarian found documents recording the development of the street. By chance, the librarian, Audrey, had a particular affection for Edwardian domestic architecture and was soon sharing relevant census returns with Frances and telling her, over impromptu tea and cake at the new café, all she knew about the history of the street and the uneven fortunes of Willow House. She had greeted Frances' fledgling idea of a centenary street party with considerable enthusiasm, sufficient to seal her plans. *And you must commission a book to mark the event, recording the history of each house and previous owners,* she had urged, aware that the threat of redundancy constantly hovered over her head through lack of footfall in the department, *I would be more than happy to assist!*

Frances watched two boys return from the common with footballs and muddy legs, walking slowly up the street before disappearing down dimly lit front paths. Although it was barely October she already dreaded Christmas and the shift into darker evenings emphatically foreshadowed the season. This year, in particular, Christmas would be intolerable. She watched leaves, caught up by a sudden gust of wind, chase along the road then fall to clog windscreens and gutters. On her walk across the common that morning, she had picked up conkers, choosing only shiny, mahogany, perfectly shaped specimens, discarding the inferior, as if for a specific purpose. Later, hanging up her jacket, she had found them weighing down the pockets and had thrown them away in exasperation, foolish at the sentimentality of the gesture, at the ingrained memory that the conkers provoked.

She turned away from the window, switched on the radio, a low lamp in readiness for the fading light and awaited the six o'clock news. Later, she would mix herself a large gin and sit down at the desk in the window to write the first of the week's two letters. She looked forward to that moment, anticipated it always with pleasure, her pen skimming swiftly over the paper, the phrases, rehearsed countlessly in her head during the day, forming with ease as she wrote. Then she would prop the envelope against the lamp, appropriately addressed in her large, bold handwriting, and glance at it with some satisfaction during the course of the evening:

Ms Charlotte Prideaux, 10 Pilgrim Square, Brighton, Sussex.

She would post it the following morning on her walk across the common.

2

S am Gough, in the garden flat at Willow House, was woken by a noise. Groggily, swimming up into consciousness, he tried to distinguish it. But it seemed to belong to a dream that was fast leaving his mind: something to do with a stack of logs spilling onto the ground and a dog barking loudly. Lydia was asleep at his side. Sleep still seemed to offer her some respite and she slept deeply most nights, although he had been warned that in the later stages of her illness, as movement and control of her limbs declined further, she would need assistance in turning during the night. He pushed the thought away, quietly slipped out of bed and headed for the kitchen, the kettle and tea. He was still unused to living on one level. Both in Scotland then in Cornwall, their homes had been rambling, sprawling places on several floors with rooms that they had used and adapted to their own needs. Here, each space was precisely assigned to a specific use, neat, utilitarian, predictable. He poured water onto a tea bag, splashed in milk and carried his mug into the living room. It was only six o'clock and he resisted drawing the curtains, knowing there was still another half hour or so of darkness, turning instead to yesterday's paper lying unread on the sofa. With luck, Lydia would sleep another hour at least.

They had met in Barcelona. It was a story he always enjoyed telling people, grateful for its inherent romance. He liked to describe how he had seen her sitting sketching at a small pavement café in a side street off Las Ramblas, alone except for the company of Polly, three years of age, a placid, composed, child at her side. He had sat down at the neighbouring table, ordered coffee, drank several before summoning the courage to speak with uncharacteristic caution as if sensing that this encounter was out of the ordinary. They had married simply and quietly six months later. Adopting Polly had followed, a relatively straightforward procedure since her biological father had made it clear, just before he had left Lydia to drift off for a nomadic life, that he had no wish to remain in contact. They had stayed for a while. In Spain, at least. Sam found a temporary contract in Valencia, then another in Madrid. Lydia painted, made some marginal sales, taught a little. Polly played with local children and spoke Spanish with a fluency neither Sam nor Lydia ever remotely mastered. After eighteen months or so they went further south. They both wanted more space than confined city apartments offered them, more proximity to the soil or the sea, a simpler existence, and imagined life in a village in Andalucía. They had talked to a man in a bar one night who claimed to have lived comfortably for next to nothing in the Sierra Nevada and gave them names of several people to contact who could help. But the people had either moved on or had, perhaps, never existed in the first place. Without work, winter proved inhospitable, their idealised lifestyle simply a struggle to stay warm and adequately fed. Polly, now five, had adapted with ease to the local dialect, but they felt inadequate in their dependence on her ability to communicate. Sam knew he could easily get a well-paid job in the burgeoning world of IT somewhere less remote. He had been fortunate in the years before meeting Lydia, had grabbed at opportunities to learn skills for the new industry that now made him valued and prized. He had only to relinquish his foolish ambition for a footloose life, resist a deep instinct to drift untethered, uncounted. And since he had already succumbed to marriage and parenthood, his protest began to seem vacuous. Perhaps he was more conventional than he had always protested. Besides, Lydia wanted to go home. She had only intended being away for six months, a year at the most, when pregnancy and single motherhood had diverted her plans from returning to her censorious family. Meeting Sam had extended her absence by another couple of years, but now she wanted permanence, a home and a sense of a settled future.

Sam had found himself enthralled by Lydia. There had been other women, of course, many women, in fact, in his somewhat careless past although he had always avoided long-term entanglements, considering himself immune to such attachments. But from the moment he had seen her sitting at the pavement café in the scruffy Spanish side street, he had felt an overwhelming desire to protect her, to provide her with a life that shaped itself according to her wishes, knowing that her satisfaction and fulfilment would thus mirror his own. He had never thought of himself as a man given to sentimental gestures. He had few friends, but the casual, transitory acquaintances he had met through work would have described him as a pragmatist, a single-minded man with an eye to the main chance. They would not have recognised the devoted lover, the tender father that he had become overnight. He liked nothing better than to sit watching Lydia while she completed the simplest of tasks; brushing Polly's hair, arranging some grasses in a vase, mixing eggs, cutting bread. She was slight in build with long dark hair that she used to twist into braids or clump loosely together with a clasp so that strands persisted in escaping to hang down her neck. She was not a conventionally beautiful woman, he knew, yet he was overcome by the delicacy of her features, the slight hesitancy of her manner, the graciousness of her movements as if she always considered a gesture, a step, before consciously taking it. Yet in spite of the vulnerability she suggested, the sense of fragility in her bearing, she was resilient and determined, strong minded and resolute. Sam had always been convinced that he was woefully undeserving of her affections and her love. He was simply too inadequate, pitiful even, and he anticipated constantly her discovery of the fact.

So they had looked at the map of the United Kingdom one night, huddling in front of the smoking fire in their rented Andalusian cottage. *Where shall we go?* Lydia had asked. *London? I know London. And there's always work there for you.* Sam had been adamant. *No. Not London. That's not for us. We need somewhere more far-flung. Ireland?* He had pointed vaguely at Belfast. Dublin. Cork. *You need somewhere you can paint. There's space in Ireland.* It was 1978. Ireland seemed unwise. *Yes, space would be good,* Lydia had agreed. *For a studio. And for Polly. Countryside. Animals.* Sam had said, *as long as I can get to a city, not live there, but be able to reach one. I can find work in any city.* They had glided their fingers back across the Irish Sea and Sam had lifted her hand in a northerly direction and placed it on Scotland. *Why not?* Lydia had said. *Scotland,* Sam had said and repeated the word several times as if trying it for size. *I think that will work for us.* It had seemed a remarkably easy decision.

An only child, Sam had inherited some money from the sale of his late parents' house. They were able to buy a large converted schoolhouse with a couple of acres of land in a rural area some forty minutes' drive from a big city. There was space for a studio for Lydia, a light-filled, double-height room that could serve as somewhere to teach, to hold art classes, exhibitions. Polly took the school bus each morning into the nearest small town some three miles away. An adaptable little girl, she made friends easily and soon swapped her fluent command of Spanish for a soft Scottish lilt with vocabulary extracted for a while from both languages. They talked of another child. When Lydia miscarried for the third time, they stopped talking about it and although Sam was bereft at the idea of her suffering, he was ambivalent about their loss. Perhaps he was too selfish to want to see Lydia absorbed by a new life, deflected away from him. Either that or some entrenched sense of his profound unsuitability to father a child hovered insistently at the margins of his mind. Besides, they already had Polly. Gloriously uncomplicated, sensible and reliable Polly.

After ten years in Scotland, they moved several hundred miles south west to Cornwall. A decade in the same place had tested Sam's patience to remain hitched to the same area and the long winter days, when light was so brief it was barely an event, had become increasingly hard to tolerate. Lydia, too, was happy to move to a milder, easier climate. They rented a cottage in a creekside village for the best part of a year before buying an old farmhouse in a remote spot midway between north and south coasts. Polly, now mid-teens, had anticipated seaside, sail boats and surfing and was disappointed with the rambling stone building set at the end of an unmade lane three miles or so from the nearest village. Sam worked increasingly from home, converting one of the outhouses into an office so that he no longer had need of a daily commute. Lydia found a far better market for her art classes and courses and even held several well attended exhibitions in the barn they had partially restored. She began to sell more regularly and built up a modest following, appreciative of her delicate pastels, aquatints and watercolours.

It was Polly, on a visit from London where she was now living, who first noticed a change in Lydia. Sam refused to see it, said she was simply tired and worn out by a long, very wet winter, by tutoring too many untalented, tiresome students.

They both needed a break, that was all. A holiday. A real change of scene for once. In Florence, he continued to push to the back of his mind that she was ill. Her increasing lethargy, her apparent refusal to take interest in her surroundings, her uncharacteristically fractious mood and low spirits were temporary, aberrations caused by excessive fatigue, he reasoned. He chose to ignore her blunt, adamant refusal to spend time sketching when he suggested it. He even tried to joke with her one evening when she had to be cajoled into the idea of going out to dinner, when she had failed to shower, change, stubbornly sitting on the side of the bed in their small hotel room, staring at him rebelliously. *Lyddie, we're both getting older, it's all a bit of an effort, isn't it? But you have to keep on trying. Can't give in to the inevitable, you know.* Except that this was a fabrication for her sake for Sam felt himself to be in essence little changed, only marginally diminished by the passage of years.

Whereas Lydia.

He knew he was being evasive about her condition. Yet it was as if refusing to confront it would, in some way, obliterate it, smudge it out so that he would wake one morning to find her restored to the woman he knew as his wife. Somehow it was so easy to choose to ignore symptoms. If he avoided examining her face too carefully, he could fail to detect the change in her expression, the fixed gaze of her eyes that had replaced their natural vitality. Even the decline of her speech, its cut-glass clarity beginning to lose its definition to the slurring style of someone a little drunk, could somehow be excused, explained away.

It was only when she started to fall soon after their return from Italy, sudden topples caused by no apparent obstacles, that he allowed himself to believe that something was seriously wrong. He noticed with a shock that her handwriting had become close to illegible, that she resisted picking up a paint brush or pencil because she could no longer direct and control them. He saw her fumbling with a fork, protesting lack of appetite to excuse her inability to prepare a meal. Her lassitude, her increasing belligerence towards his suggestions that they go for a walk, drive to the coast, deeply alarmed him. She became more withdrawn as if forgetting how to join spontaneously into conversations and he was aware of a silence between them, the absence of comment from her lively mind. Even so, it was only Polly's insistence that forced him to begin the long, wearying process towards an explanation. Eventually, in a neurologist's clinic in Truro, they received the diagnosis. Lydia sat very still, her gaze fixed immovably on the white wall ahead, her expression unchanged. It was Sam who failed to hold back tears as the consultant quietly outlined the nature of the progressive disease, the inevitable decline that they should anticipate. And afterwards, driving them home, he felt intense anger at what he saw as an inappropriate casting of the dice. At the wrath of the spiteful gods. Lydia, the guileless, should have been left untouched by the ravages of such an appalling condition. If there were any such thing as natural justice or divine intervention, he should have been its victim.

If the weather was dry, Sam took Lydia for a slow walk around the common every day. Its proximity had been part of the attraction of Miller Street. If they were to exchange a married lifetime of rural living for the confines of the city, at least the prospect of grass underfoot, birdsong, an expanse of open land within a few yards of their front door would be some small consolation. He had fought Polly's suggestion at first. He had seen no reason why they should leave Cornwall and their remote stone farmhouse for the practical living arrangement she had in mind. For six months or more, he had obstinately resisted. Then, one day, Lydia fell down the stairs. Her injuries were surprisingly superficial – a twisted ankle, badly grazed legs and bruised arms – but Sam had been alarmed by the potential accident that could have happened. Estate agents were called the next day. By the end of several long phone calls to Polly, he was reluctantly resigned to the idea of moving to London. *It's right for her, for mum,* Polly said repeatedly. *You'll be near me and I can lend a hand with things. And near to excellent health care when you need it. A sensible, practical home on one level close to all amenities. You've got to give up this bucolic, rustic living nonsense now. Be realistic at last, for goodness sake.* He had been surprised by a sense of exasperation in Polly's tone as if she considered their way of life to be self-indulgent, saw them as a couple of ageing hippies. But he had said nothing, allowed her to guide him towards areas of the city where they could afford *a sensible, practical home* and was relieved when they had viewed the new conversion of Willow House to see that the largest of the homes had its own back garden.

"No room for hens," he'd said to Lydia as they had stood amongst the builders' rubble, "no more collecting fresh eggs for breakfast. But I suppose we should be lucky for any green space of our own in a London postal code. And we're only a shake and a whistle from the common. And the river, come to that."

In spite of being close to the main road, from mid-morning to late afternoon, the common was relatively peaceful and Sam and Lydia could walk on the path around it with few interruptions except for a smile or general greeting from a dog walker or someone on their way to the post box. She disliked the imposed exercise. Each time he proposed it, took out her coat, found her shoes, Lydia objected. On days when her speech was less hampered, she would shout at him with surprising belligerence, cling on to the sides of her chair like a young child refusing to go to school. Sam stubbornly refused to give in. He was aware of a battle of wills that he insisted on winning as if there was far more at stake than a simple half hour or so in the fresh air. Rarely before had there been even mild disagreement between them and he found this loss of harmony to be bewildering. On days when speech eluded Lydia beyond slurred, indecipherable syllables, she gave in to his coaxing with clear resentment. By the time they had walked to the end of the road and on to the common, however, she often appeared to have forgotten her resistance and clung to his arm, biddable, dependent.

As October was proving to be a relatively mild month, Sam used the weather to temper his daily persuasion.

"Lyddie, it's a long winter. There will be months ahead when we're hardly able to get out. You don't even need your coat today. Just that jacket of yours, that green thing. Wherever is it? You wore it last week when Polly came over – you know the one."

He knew it would not be long before even slow, supported walking would be impossible and she would have no use of her limbs at all. Even now, Polly considered he was being obstinate. *You've got the wheelchair for mum, use that instead of having a battle every time you want to go out.* But he saw its use as defeatist. He disliked seeing it, tucking it away in the spare bedroom out of sight as if it was an affront to both of them. Always he had found illness, disability, physical impairment hard to confront and was aware of the failings of such an attitude. Now the prospect of living in tandem with Lydia's increasing incapacity terrified him. He looked at her now, her eyes wide with concern as he opened the front door, guided her over the step and onto the path and felt a surge of irrational anger. As if she had chosen such a fate, decided intentionally to inflict premature dotage on both of them. His protest was selfish, he knew. It was Lydia, after all, who was suffering while he was merely the onlooker, the voyeur of the bleak event. They progressed slowly on to the common, taking their usual route along the northern border where the pavement was solid and even. Stout Victorian houses hemmed one side in a semicircle and it had become a habit for Sam to point out details, comment on shabby exteriors in need of attention, newly laid driveways and skips and scaffolding heralding building work. On better days, Lydia attempted to contribute, often random remarks rather than sequential conversation. It had been one of the early changes Polly had pointed out to him, her mother's growing habit of jettisoning herself into a dialogue with no clarifying start so that she had been forced to grope for the gist or subject. Reaching the post box on the corner, they stopped for Sam to find a couple of letters in his pocket, Lydia clinging firmly on to his arm.

"She didn't like it," Lydia said very quietly, almost a whisper. "She ... no. We sent him ..." She stopped, looked at Sam for assistance. He tried.

"Who, Lyddie? Who didn't like what?" She waved one hand in the air as if she found his answer exasperating.

"She didn't ... we thought she ... it went back. Sent it."

Then Sam noticed her attention had been caught by a woman across the common unleashing a large black Labrador and throwing something – a stick, a ball, – for the dog to retrieve. He slipped his letters into the post box and headed them off the pavement onto the grass of the common itself. It was a good day for Lydia, as days went, and he intended to make the most of it.

"Oh, Polly's dog, you mean. Or the one we first got for her. I'd forgotten all about that business. That was – what, over twenty years ago, Lyddie, more like twenty-five." She smiled, gripped his arm a little tighter. Polly had asked for a dog for a birthday present one year, her eighth or ninth, possibly. Living in their remote Scottish glen, the only neighbours distant by a good half mile, they had considered it highly appropriate to acquire a sizeable animal who might bark with ferocity at any chance intruder. Polly, however, had been horrified with the appearance of the German shepherd, flinching at its size although it had still been a puppy. What she had in mind, she had explained patiently to her misguided parents, was a miniature poodle. A Yorkshire terrier at a pinch. She had drawn their attention to her well-thumbed copy of the Observer's Book of Dogs to give them a better idea. The German shepherd had been returned the following day with the intention of finding a suitable substitute that weekend. But somehow, they had procrastinated and a dog had never arrived, a series of cats and the inevitable rabbits and guinea pigs instead running their course until Polly had grown out of pets. They continued their way slowly across the close-cropped grass, Sam recalling the story to distract him from the irritation of their slow progress. He was not a patient man and disliked their sedentary pace. His natural inclination had always been for marathon spurts of exercise: ten or twenty-mile hikes across Scottish moorland, Cornish cross country runs and unseasonable swimming in cold north coast seas. Genteel constitutionals across a south London common seemed habits belonging to another self and one that he was not ready to embrace. Still, he reminded himself, this was for Lyddie. Lydia was his first consideration and, while she was still capable of putting one foot cautiously, reluctantly, ahead of the other, he would insist that she did so. All too soon, the option would not be hers.

A woman approached them.

Sam was aware of someone suddenly altering her direction and hurrying towards them with intention.

"Mr and Mrs Gough! At last, I've caught you! Not that I've been stalking you, exactly, but ... Sam, isn't it? And Lydia? You were the first to arrive, of course, although I was only behind you by a few weeks."

He looked at the woman blankly. Her broad face framed with curly dark hair was too close to his as if she expected some physical greeting. He moved imperceptibly away, disarmed by her knowledge of their names.

"I am sorry to sound rude," he said, "but I have absolutely no ... do we know you?"

The woman laughed loudly. Her smile was expansive, exposing too many teeth. She took a step towards Lydia, placed a hand on her shoulder, a wide, heavy hand with a signet ring on her smallest finger.

"Willow House?" the woman said, stressing the words with deliberation. "I live above you, so to speak. First floor, flat 3. Apartment 3, I mean. Frances Chater. You must have seen me, but of course I can quite understand how things are. You must be very preoccupied. I mean a major move is always disruptive even in the best of circumstances. Let alone when there are obstacles, so to speak." Her hand drifted from Lydia's shoulder, her head inclined in her direction as if it was necessary to clarify her point. "Anyway, I was hoping to see you, naturally. I wanted to welcome you to the road so we could get to know each other a little. And especially now we are nearly complete."

"Complete?" Sam began to lead Lydia away, slowly, but deliberately. She could not be relied upon to stand securely for more than a moment, her balance too precarious. And instinctively he felt a need to detach himself from this woman's interest. There was something prurient in her manner that he disliked. Frances Chater, however, chose to fall into step beside them, impervious. He wished he could hurry, but Lydia's pace was inevitably painstakingly slow.

"Willow House, I mean, we are almost all in residence. There's number 4 next to me, of course, that's still unoccupied, but I did ring the agent to ask and I understand that's a landlord situation. Not that they would tell me much, I might say. But presumably no tenant yet. One can only hope for someone – appropriate." Sam said nothing. He had assumed urban living would offer them a certain isolation, the absence of inquisitive neighbourliness that he saw as the curse of village or small town suburban life. "And of course, there's Catherine in number 2, now, Catherine Wells, I believe it is," she went on, clearly oblivious of his attempt to halt the conversation. "We haven't met yet, but she moved in a week ago, in the flat next to yours. The apartment, I mean. Only, what with your front door being set back with its own porch you might not have noticed her. But perhaps her car? You can't help but have noticed that. It's the small blue one. Sits there most of the day, I believe, as no doubt she's a commuter. Well, there are such good connections here, aren't there? Trains, buses. And the underground, of course. And that keeps the house prices high, inevitably, which is a blessing and a curse, depending on whether you're buying or selling, naturally. Although nothing like those fashionably smart and central areas which are simply prohibitive and out of most people's reach. Still, there's nothing wrong with these parts, I'd say, what with river walks and some good open green spaces on our doorstep. And we've got ourselves a decent investment with Willow House, don't you think? Can't go wrong with a London postcode, after all, whatever the market's doing. Isn't that what the papers always say?"

They had reached the edge of the common and the path that led back to the end of Miller Street. Often, Sam would lead Lydia to the bench conveniently placed under the elm tree to give her a rest before the final short section of their walk home. But today he pressed on, eager to shrug off the woman whose name he had failed to note. Lydia, the normal routine altered, looked up at him anxiously, faltered in her step as if confusing the acquired moves of a dance. He grasped her arm more firmly.

"Excuse me," he said, hoping his abruptness would offend, "but we need to get home, Lyddie and me. In our own way, at our own pace. It's not always easy and delays like this can be confusing for her. So, if you don't mind ..."

Frances Chater took several steps back, one hand flying to her face, covering her mouth as if to inhibit further speech. She shook her head in evident self-admonishment.

"I am so sorry to intrude. Truly, I am. Forgive me. I just wanted to ... but no, quite inappropriate. I see that now."

And she turned and retraced her steps swiftly across the common with the resolve of someone who has suddenly remembered something or has somewhere urgent to go. Sam watched her cross back to the south side, saw her take something from her pocket – a letter – slip it into the post box before heading down to the main road. Gently, he coaxed Lydia along the remaining hundred yards or so of their path home. She muttered something incoherently to herself, sounds more than articulated words and for once he did not attempt to clarify what she was trying to say. He felt weary, suddenly, and regretted his abrasive manner. The woman, their neighbour, whatever her name, was simply being courteous, genial, after all. It was what people did. They made small talk, sought inconsequential conversations, tried out overtures of connection. There was nothing so objectionable about that. He really needed to make more effort to appear affable. Accommodating. To fit in.

That way, Sam Gough reminded himself sternly, attention was deflected rather than drawn.

★★★

On Tuesday morning, in Pilgrim Square, Brighton, Charlotte Prideaux picks up the envelope from the mat, glances at the handwriting, rips it once, twice, then shoves the pieces into her pocket. A pattern appears to have set in. For the past three weeks, the letters have arrived on Tuesdays and Fridays. Fortunate, then, that she is usually there those particular mornings to meet the post, to gather up and discard without Andrew's knowledge. Easier to ride it out that way, resist reaction and see the whole matter diminish to nothing. She regrets reading those early letters now, annoyed with herself for still feeling disturbed by them. Certain phrases lurk and wound. And not so much those of outrage and anger, but the words that sought to direct guilt, culpability. As if the sender was skilfully choosing an attack that was neither hysterical nor histrionic, but measured, seeking subtly to compromise her peace of mind.

Still, Charlotte Prideaux comforts herself as she opens the front door and crosses the square to the litter bin at the edge of the communal garden, she is a strong woman with no tolerance for blackmail or invidious bullying. She knows what she is about and is here, living in this house, which is proof enough of her success. These attempts to undermine her are easily disposed of and the matter despatched to the corner of her mind. Cleanly, she drops the torn, unread contents of the letter into the bin and turns back to the house, swiftly mounting the steps and closing the front door firmly to get on with the business of her day.

3

Harriet Howe House, wedged between Bloomsbury and Clerkenwell, was closed to the public on Tuesdays. Catherine always anticipated the day with relief, a chance to concentrate on the numerous aspects of her job that were neglected when visitors were present. As House Manager at the small museum, her immediate day-to-day responsibilities were focused on the extensive number of volunteer guides and front of house staff that were the backbone of the place. Their loyalty was crucial since budgets were tight, but the very nature of their unpaid positions meant constant shifting of the rotas to accommodate them. On Tuesdays, though, she had a silent house to herself and could turn her attention to work undisturbed on projected special exhibitions, liaise with schools over visits, answer more complex emails that required more than a line or two in reply. Sometimes, she shared the peace with students who came to work in the extensive and ever-growing reference library on the top floor. Or the day would be given over to setting up a temporary exhibition in the flexible display space carved out of a corridor and a couple of box rooms. The narrow stairs of the 18th century house could not be safely relied upon for access once tour groups clogged the landings and stairways. But mostly, Tuesdays at the museum were temperate, measured, without the unpredictability of the visiting public to accommodate.

Even the curator, Robert Knight, rarely appeared. His predecessor, Frank Williams, for whom Catherine had worked for some years before his late retirement, had been a more constant presence who rarely left his desk. But then Frank Williams had held the position for thirty-five years and resisted all change in working methods. Thus he had spurned Catherine's delicate and hesitant prompting in his latter years about the need for a computer system and some sort of cautious inroad into technology.

"Look, I don't want you to think I'm a Luddite by any means," he had said to her constantly, "but really, is this all necessary? After all, we're a museum, not one of those appalling places with amusements and rides. Theme places. I really don't think we need to worry ourselves about gimmicks."

Catherine had sympathised with his attitude, bided her time, but covertly attended several courses to ensure she was computer literate once the concession to modern practice was made. After all, the woman herself, Harriet Howe, had in her time been at the forefront of change and dedicated to shaking off the shackles of habit and patriarchal domination. When Robert Knight, a man nearly forty years younger than Frank Williams, arrived at the museum, the pace of change had been remarkable. Overnight, it sometimes felt, the museum had dispensed with a certain dustiness and gentility of provision to confront the realities and viability of an early 21st century existence. And Catherine's own position shifted. Robert clearly respected her knowledge and invited her ideas and opinions in a way that would have seemed inappropriate to the older man. He even expressed surprise that she had not herself applied for the post of curator which astounded her. She had no academic background, after all, and had never considered herself a potential successor. Of course she knew her subject. At times she felt as if she had lived alongside Harriet Howe, joined her in her campaigns and causes, known her even to the point of feeling that in spite of the woman's magnetism, she might well have been an impossibly insufferable person with whom to spend an entire lifetime.

A little like Eddie, in fact.

As she had told him on more than one occasion. And since the accident had felt only the cruelty of her words, the needless judgement of them.

Tuesday morning slid rapidly into early afternoon. She managed to catch up with one of the duty managers to arrange some weekend cover, completed the copy for the quarterly newsletter and spoke to the secretary of the Friends organisation about the Christmas fundraising evening in early December. Around two o'clock she slipped out for a break away from her screen and walked down to Theobalds Road to sit in the window of a café drinking coffee while heavy queues formed around her for sandwiches and drinks to take back to office desks. Already, the temperatures were deterring people from garden squares yet the city still seemed to hover as if uncertain how to dress. Dark coats and knee length boots vied with the brigade of bare legs and optimistic sandals as if desperate to hold onto a summer legacy. In the past week Catherine had been emptying packing cases and unearthing familiar clothes that she had forgotten since last seeing them in late June. It had been comforting in some abstruse way, to find these dresses and skirts, sweaters and shoes. Just as she had been consoled to see once again her books, a certain lamp, odd pieces of china emerge from their wrapping. Possessions virtually worthless in themselves yet signifiers of a life being lived. Occupied, as it were.

For sometimes – often, in truth – since Eddie's death, Catherine had felt herself undefined, amorphous, as if her sense of an authentic self was doubtful. And she was well aware that others struggled with her situation, groping for appropriate consolation to offer. *There's your work, of course, at least you have that to turn to. And – what is it that you do? Oh yes, that museum place. Well, the routine will help, no doubt. Give you something to hold on to. A sense of purpose.* Whereas what they really wanted to say was, she suspected, *what a pity there are no children. Without a husband or children – or an ex-husband, come to that – where is the focus and resolve of your life?* As if the trappings of adulthood were no longer hers.

Unlike her sister, Beth. Genial, affable Beth, married at nineteen, amazing Catherine with her apparent ability at that young age to settle on a suitable man and predict the continuity of their love and peaceable union. Their mother had applauded Beth's compliance with what she saw as the natural path for a woman. The only choice, to her mind.

Whereas Catherine.

Growing up, she had looked on at her mother's choice of dependence, the way she embraced helplessness and ineptitude as if they were moral virtues and was confused by such an attitude for her mother appeared to view marriage as a chance for delegation that she exercised constantly. She rarely formed an opinion of her own, never made a decision without turning to her cautious, reserved husband for guidance. And hand in hand, as a consequence, she seemed to have a need for constant companionship. It was not a model that Catherine found in the least desirable. Childhood had been tolerable to her, but only in the knowledge of eventually gaining autonomy, the liberty of independence. Her mother would berate her as a child, an adolescent, when Catherine chose her silent bedroom and her books over the conviviality of the living room as if perpetual sociability was a required norm. Always, Catherine had held in her mind the solace of the empty room, the consolingly solitary place in her head and suspected that these would all inevitably be jettisoned if she married. Of course, she had some concern about a consequent lack of love, the absence of a sense of arrival if she did not marry. But when she looked at her parents, she saw so little to envy. To wish to emulate. There was her beloved father, a diffident, shy man living a life that seemed contained, reticent, alongside her mother's loud, declamatory existence. What could either of them gain from such an arrangement? And she knew she resembled her father. She recognised that her excessive shyness as a young girl, her difficulties with forging friendships, her solitary habits were something of a facsimile. When he had died suddenly, too soon, at the age of sixty-two, Catherine felt that she had never entirely known him and had mourned the fact. But when her mother had died nine years later, seemingly inviting premature old age as a token of her widowhood, Catherine had felt no different. Her mother, in spite of her blustering and vociferous manner, remained hidden to her too. She had so little idea of what lay beneath the surface of either of their lives.

She had forgotten to drink her coffee. The queue was thinner now and she stood up to fetch another, but the woman behind the counter indicated she would bring it to her. They exchanged a few words, the weather, the usual convenient exchanges between people who saw each other regularly, most days of the working week, in fact, but knew nothing beyond respective preferences in lattes and sandwich fillings.

Beth's early, conventional marriage had at least given their mother some comfort. And when Catherine herself went to stay in Beth's rural, large and somewhat ramshackle house, she found herself perversely consoled by her sister's perpetual rounds of domesticity; by the endless lists among the clutter of fridge magnets, the odd shoes and trainers in the hall, stray unmatched socks on the stairs, the kitchen table never entirely clear of papers and sticky stains and bits of construction toys perpetually lurking underfoot. Yet at the same time she would find herself anxious to leave such disorder, relieved when it was time to drive away from Beth's kindly, mildly overbearing husband, Henry, the two demanding dogs, the deaf cat with the truncated tail. Only the thought of her nephews and nieces pawed at her heart as she held on to the sweet smell of their frail flesh, the perfection of their small limbs clambering clumsily across her lap, their breath on her cheek, their fresh, guileless faces. Yet at the same time she feared the burden and responsibility of such overwhelming unconditional love. It seemed bewildering to her that Beth and Henry managed to sleep at night, carry out mundane, daily tasks, remain rational and clear headed, all the time in the knowledge that life was absurdly, cruelly precarious and their beloved children as vulnerable as eggshells. And then there was the magnitude of love and endless service a child required that to her appeared to sit unevenly with the demands of marriage. How could she swear allegiance to a man, form a legally binding commitment of love and loyalty when any child that she subsequently produced would require her to revise such an arrangement, entirely prioritise the needs of that child? Maternal love was visceral, she saw, ferocious, a perpetual force of nature that would deride the importance of any other bond. Push it into the wilderness.

Meeting Alec Grey at the age of thirty had further convinced Catherine she would never marry. She was just like him, he told her, and therefore they were ideal for each other. *We will no doubt tire of one another at some stage, Catherine, let's not pretend otherwise. Marriage would be disastrous for people like us. Utterly foolish. That's simply not who we are. What neither of us needs.* She had agreed. He was right about the two of them, of course. Quickly, she became very fond of Alec, enjoyed his easy company on a fairly irregular basis given his constant work commitments abroad, and months turned into several years without Catherine feeling the need to seek or see someone else. This was enough for her. An unfettered relationship with a welcome absence of turbulent troubling feelings. As good, given her nature, given Alec's, as it probably got. They suited each other, were an excellent fit.

But then Eddie Wells.

And her entrenched attitude towards the idea of marriage appeared to dissolve as if it had never existed. Eddie talked of it frequently. He spoke of the house they would buy, the right spot for their honeymoon, stopped by jewellers' windows to look at rings so that even the need for a proposal seemed irrelevant. And Catherine had fallen in love. Unguardedly, irretrievably, it felt, in a way she had never imagined for herself. She suspected she was disregarding good sense, given Eddie's mercurial personality, but at the same time felt exhilarated to be the victim of such passion and powerless to suppress it. His insistence on no children, his categorical resolve that he had no wish to be a father had been easy for her to accept. He was ten years older than her so had clearly considered the matter. And after all, her love for him was absolute. The thought of any dilution was unacceptable.

Robert Knight arrived unexpectedly around four. In his usual frenetic way that sometimes made Catherine feel listless in comparison, he began talking as soon as he came through the front door and into the hallway before reaching her office.

"Not here long, just an hour or so, Kate, then I'm off to some business of Tessa's in the city. But just wanted to check in with you as I'm not in tomorrow." Catherine had met Tessa, an investment banker, just once and had found her remote, hard to engage. Robert was far more affable and easy than his wife appeared. "Everything running smoothly? Any hiccups you anticipate over the coming few weeks?"

"All under control," Catherine said. "There are a couple of requests for outside evening lets that I'd like to run past you and we've been approached for use as a one-day conference – a Tuesday, naturally – by an American university. But nothing that's urgent."

Robert waved his hand as if delegating the matter to her. He balanced on the edge of her desk, retrieving papers from his briefcase and putting them in front of her.

"When you've time perhaps you could give this bid a quick read-through? Just interested to know your opinion. And do we have the fundraising event all in hand? The Christmas one needs to be—"

"Elaborate? Festive?" Catherine asked. "It will be. As always."

"Good, good. Not doubting you, you know that, Kate."

Few people called her Kate. Eddie had called her Cat or Kitty, mostly. Briefly, Caitlin, the year he had become obsessed with Dylan Thomas and had insisted on driving them to Laugharne at dawn on St David's Day. But for Robert, the use of a one syllable name seemed to be an economy suited to his habit of rapid speech. She was aware that he was unlikely to stay long at the museum, that it was a convenient stepping stone to somewhere far more prestigious and esteemed. No doubt he saw himself at the Victoria and Albert, the Ashmolean or possibly sidestepping into a media career, a presenter of popular culture shows. He was still, to Catherine, alarmingly young and clearly ambitious. Now he hovered in her office, looking at one of the pictures on her wall blankly as if trying to recall what he had really intended to say.

"Was there something else?" she prompted. "Only, I'd like to get on with a couple of emails that should go today."

He jumped, as if caught out inappropriately. Looked mildly embarrassed.

"I forgot to ask you when I saw you last week, Kate. Your move. Into your new place. Not an easy move, I imagine. But I hope all went well?"

"Fine," she said briskly. Catherine was aware that his question was out of polite obligation rather than real interest. It had always suited her that they knew little of each other beyond the confines of their work yet inevitably Eddie's accident had breached such distance and Robert had appeared to have difficulty with the appropriate response. The bereaved, it seemed, bore a kind of stigma that bothered people. As if their misfortune made them awkward, disturbing company. "A last-minute hitch over keys, but other than that I am beginning to feel settled."

"Good, good," Robert said, "fresh start for you and all that. Excellent." He looked relieved to have despatched the subject. "Now, you won't see a lot of me early next week. Obviously, I'll keep in touch by email, but I'm off to New York for a few days. Something to do with Tessa, in fact, should be back by Wednesday, Thursday at a pinch."

The day to day running of the museum had little to do with Robert so his unplanned absence was of little concern. It was unusual, however, as his wife worked such a frenetic schedule that holidays were generally brief and organised well in advance.

"No problem," Catherine said, "I've got Val coming in over the weekend, anyway, and I'm sure I can handle anything urgent."

Val Dawson was one of the duty managers who covered for Catherine on alternate weekends and filled numerous roles as needs arose. She took particular pride in the competence and speed of her annual stock take of the gift shop. Having

worked at the museum on a part-time basis for over twenty
years, she was reliable and efficient although her tendency to
talk at considerable length about her complicated home life
meant her company could be wearying to some. Catherine,
however, found her self-absorption something of a relief.
Even in the aftermath of Eddie's death Val had made only a
cursory reference to Catherine's *sad loss* before embarking
on a rambling account of her apathetic son-in-law and her
husband's irascibility. Robert turned to head to the stairs and
his office on the top floor.

"We should have a session when I get back about the
new guide book. Back from New York, I mean. Whether
we're going ahead with the idea, anyway. All right, Kate? I'd
appreciate your thoughts on that."

As always, he took the stairs two or three at a time, his
gangly figure swiftly disappearing out of sight. Catherine
returned to a complicated email request from a Canadian
academic who wanted to know whether a visit to the Harriet
Howe reference library was worth the cost of her airfare across
the Atlantic. Was the woman really as pivotal and significant
as the museum's online information suggested? What about
all the others? Catherine patiently replied that Howe's
contemporaries were certainly not ignored in their collection
and library and that she would find Burdett-Coutts, Octavia
Hill, Henrietta Barnett among other remarkable female
philanthropists well represented.

On Tuesdays the museum café was closed since the public
had no access. It was not run directly by the house, but was
franchised to a small catering company consisting of a mother
and daughter who provided the facility and took the profits.
But the arrangement worked well on the whole. The longer
visitors lingered at the house, the more chance there was that
they would buy from the gift shop and sometimes simply the

lure of a café was enough to encourage people to visit. And it had to be admitted that some of the paying public spent more time over their Earl Grey and fruit scones than amongst the artefacts and evidence of a group of remarkable, pioneering women. Catherine opened the back door that led out into the small courtyard behind the café and sat with a mug of tea in the scant sunshine that had appeared late afternoon. She had ignored a message she had found on her phone after Robert had left and now knew she must ring Elspeth. It was kind of her, of course, the invitation for a meal that evening at her subterranean flat in Southwark where she had lived in some discomfort for many years. Considerate and thoughtful. Although Catherine was aware that there was always a certain self-seeking in such gestures from her older friend. They had not met all year and now it would be inevitable that conversation would dwell on Eddie. Elspeth was a clever woman who nevertheless perpetually cast a bleak, pessimistic aspect upon life and its events so that even another's happiness and good fortune could be greeted with a caustic shrug of the shoulders and a prediction of doom. Men, in particular, received her censure and condemnation after several turbulent relationships in her youth. Catherine knew Elspeth would relish an honest review of Eddie's failings. His loose interpretation of faithfulness, his egocentric conduct and financial excesses, his extremes of activity from frantic to indolent would all seem legitimate reasons to her to see his loss as insignificant.

But here was the thing.

Catherine discarded her tea leaves into a patch of earth surrounding the potted bay tree. She knew she would not be able to offer Elspeth the satisfaction of an accurate recall of her late husband's frailties. For death threw up such a fogged confusion of loss and grief that it prevented honesty. As if, in the wake of its enormity, truths become fluid and less absolute and sentimentalising the deceased appeared to be inevitable. Suddenly their intolerable flaws became mild peccadillos, destructive habits translated into idiosyncrasies with the ability to amuse.

The living, it seemed, had an obligation to recast the past in a more favourable light. Forgiveness was mandatory.

Or so Catherine had found.

And it was not just memories that resisted rational recall.

In the wake of Eddie's death, she had been bewildered by her inability to cope with his abrupt physical disappearance. Despite police, coroners, solicitors, undertakers, running swiftly to her side as confirmation, in the subsequent weeks she could not lose the sensation of constantly searching for him. As if she had lost him, misplaced him, forgotten a rendezvous, confused a meeting. She found herself unconsciously inspecting faces on the station platform, pedestrians on a pavement as if his tall frame and restless gait would suddenly reveal itself. And she longed to see him. In spite of their fractious last few months together, she wanted to find him with an intensity that reduced her to spontaneous tears when a face turned, a figure moved on, and Eddie had remained, inevitably, entirely absent.

No. An evening with Elspeth would be unwise.

She rang her, feigned an excuse, promised to be in touch in a few weeks. She was not yet resilient enough for a visit to that small dank basement flat for a maudlin reflection on life's vicissitudes.

She went back to her office, finished off one or two tasks before checking doors and setting burglar alarms. She still needed to remind herself every evening to head south, down Lamb's Conduit Street and towards Kingsway rather than go north to Euston for the commuter train out to Bevington.

Friends thought she was foolish. *Really? London? Different when you were young. That tiny place of yours in Archway you bought in the eighties. We know you liked it then. But not now. You'll be lonely, surely, living in a big city?* As if loneliness was an integral part of urban living and entirely absent from suburbia.

She cut through Lincoln's Inn Fields, stopped to watch a couple playing a light-hearted game of tennis on the courts in the early evening light. She never lost her love of the city's green spaces, not only the splendid parks and heaths, but the small patches of grass and neat squares and churchyards and playing fields that provided respite to the population, social spaces for strangers to be both together and apart. She could easily forgo a garden if she had such a space at hand and the common at the end of Miller Street provided her with that. Even Beth, initially sceptical about Catherine's apparent random choice of the place, south of the river, had accepted her sister's reason. *I like it – urban, but tree-lined streets and even early morning rowers on the river. Occasional bird song, you'd be surprised. Certainly foraging foxes. And I can afford it. Just.* She did not need to say that she had consciously avoided areas hooked to the past where it would be too easy to stumble constantly across streets and spots redolent of Eddie. Of this early conversation, or that chance encounter of those early days when her world had seemed gilded, metamorphosed by her love for him. In the Aldwych, she joined a long bus queue, changed her mind, crossed Waterloo Bridge and headed to a train. She wanted suddenly the consolation of her silent flat, the welcome of those white-walled rooms, her home, slowly evolving. Of course she would make an effort and find out who else was living in Willow House. She had glimpsed a man over the weekend getting out of his car, a woman – his wife, no doubt – sitting in the passenger seat. And just as she had been about to leave that morning she had heard the door at the side of the house that led to the two upstairs flats opening, saw someone depositing rubbish then going back inside. But there was no need to rush introductions. She wanted to resist new friendships that would inevitably probe, dabble fingers into matters too intricate to explain. Widowhood was something of an albatross for her. It afforded her a status that she was uncertain whether she deserved.

Given the circumstances.

4

Frances Chater sang forcefully, lustily, holding the hymn book at an appropriate angle so that at the same time she could glance over the congregation of All Saints. Inspect. She could not bear people who patently mouthed words or appeared to mutter them through clenched teeth as if embarrassed by the whole notion of singing. Still, not a bad number for a late October Sunday which was too late for the harvest festival enthusiasts and premature for the Advent crowd. Admittedly, she had not been a consistent church attender herself for years, but since moving to Miller Street she had been making good for her long lapse and intended maintaining the habit. It was, after all, one way of filling the blankness of a Sunday morning and seemed to be the sort of thing an unattached woman of her generation might do. The hymn over, she settled herself down for the sermon, shifting her position to catch a little of the late autumn sunlight filtering through the stained glass.

It was never Andrew's kind of thing, of course, churchgoing, so she had stayed in step. He was all for a good carol service and had quite an interest in the architectural side of things: gothic buttresses and gargoyles and intricate carvings on pew ends. Even effigies seemed to fascinate him. But not faith. Not the idea of an almighty power, immortal souls and sins and redemption and reckoning on the day of judgement. Too much a man of science for all that, he once

47

said to her, although she had hardly been trying to convert him, her own belief probably little more than a custom learnt in childhood, an inherited form of obedience never fully examined or relinquished. Her mother had been the religious stalwart of the family who had insisted upon all the rituals with something of the zealot about her: grace before meals, prayers before bed, fish on Fridays, church twice a day on Sundays. And the samplers on the walls of most rooms with a corrective and coercive message from the bible, tracts and liturgical verses flowing freely from her mother's lips as a substitute for maternal endearments. Yet for all her avowed Christian values, her pursuit of Goodness, Grace and Truth, as she termed it, she was a sour and morose woman who seemed never happier than when depriving others of joy. Inevitable, really, Frances thought, that she had rebelled against it all once she had left home, siding with Andrew's secular attitude.

But now, of course, she was finding herself indebted to some of that early indoctrination. For dormant in the back of her mind, she had discovered a wealth, a buried treasure trove of gospel texts that spoke to her situation as if composed for the precise purpose. She had been floundering, trying to fill the letters twice a week – The Correspondence, as she thought of it – without resort to repetitive rants and ugly expletives. And that was not the way she wanted it to be at all. That was never going to be her style. Reason at all costs, she had decided, rational arguments and sense were all that was required. Selecting a biblical verse or phrase as a focus for each letter was therefore proving invaluable. And regular attendance at All Saints was serving as a sort of revision class, a form of regressive therapy allowing her to unlock the learnt lessons of the past. Frances tried now to follow the train of the vicar's sermon and pick up on its message. *Do unto others as you would have them do unto you.* Highly relevant to her purpose and she would make use of it in good time, but she lost the man in his analogy with corporate greed and focused instead on the elaborate flower arrangement at the altar.

There had been a wedding the day before.

She had caught sight of bridesmaids in peach, a busying photographer, groups by the lychgate as she had walked across the common and had felt suddenly inordinately sad. As if the whole business, the satin-ribboned cars and confetti, absurd top hats and tails, the vows and prayers and blessings were all a pathetic charade, the seeds of slow destruction already sown indelibly into the proceedings. She stared at the flame-coloured gladioli, tawny gerbera, bronze chrysanthemums, golden roses and amaryllis that tumbled artfully out of white vases. How hard it was at times to remain positive, constant to her task and convinced of its success. She held no illusions that the matter would be settled swiftly and without a degree of unpleasantness on all sides yet surely, she would see victory. For right, moral right, no less, was on her side and she was doing what had to be done, waging a just war and therefore success was ensured. The thought consoled her.

She abandoned any attempts to listen to the vicar's meandering message and switched her mind to more practical matters. Later in the week, she would deliver the invitations for the initial meeting to Sam and Lydia Gough at number 1, Catherine Wells in number 2 and even drop one through the door of flat 4 next to hers although she had not yet caught sight of anyone there. Give them all a week's notice, that would be best. Long enough to confirm – she would insist upon an RSVP – not too long to forget. And she would serve wine, of course. Decent wine. To set the tone. Always important to set the tone from the start. By the time she was standing with the rest of the congregation to sing the last hymn – *Lord of all Hopefulness* – Frances felt cheered, invigorated. A project underway was all it took, she told herself. She closed her hymn book with some affectation and sang the words out strongly with no need of a prompt: *Be there at our labours and give us, we pray, your strength in our hearts, Lord, at the noon of the day.*

★★★

Catherine arrived late. Ten minutes only, but she knew Alec would already be there. Alec Grey unfailingly arrived early. In all the years she had known him, she had never managed to shake his habit, catch him out, and for some indefinable reason she found his predictability a mild annoyance. From the door of the restaurant she could see him sitting at a small table at the back of the room, reading the evening paper which he put aside the moment she caught his eye. She sat down opposite him, apologising, explaining, blaming impossible crowds at Russell Square, her resort to walking.

"You're here, Catherine," Alec said mildly, letting one hand rest for just a moment on hers, as if wary of the gesture. He filled her empty wine glass from the bottle on the table. "That's all that matters. We have all evening. And I can drive you home. The car's just around the corner."

She drank gratefully, picked up the menu, put it down again. She was aware of a certain awkwardness in their exchange as if each was testing what was now appropriate.

"You don't want to do that. Drive me home, I mean. I can so easily get the train. Or the bus, come to that. It's miles out of your way."

"I know," he said, "whatever made you rashly move south of the river?"

"It wasn't rash. I like it," Catherine said defensively. "Besides, I can afford it. Whereas you, Alec, are somewhat more fortunate when it comes to homes."

Alec smiled, refilled his own glass. It was a barb too familiar to pursue or challenge. Alec lived in the large house he had inherited from his mother in Hampstead. Not a particularly attractive or painstakingly preserved and maintained house, but nevertheless: Hampstead. Just off Flask Walk. NW6. In fact, apart from years at university in Durham, a brief flat share in Highgate, he seemed to have lived there his entire life. The idea of a home south of the river appeared to Alec to be an ill-advised act of rebellion. Catherine looked around at the low-lit room, the handful of discreetly isolated tables and biddable, vaguely obsequious waiters.

"What's happened to this place? When we first used to come here it was so ordinary. Cheerful. Italian. Decades ago, I know, but even so …"

"It's still Italian," Alec said reasonably, "we're drinking Italian wine from – somewhere near – north of Siena, it seems." He peered closely at the label.

"Exactly," Catherine said. "That's my point. It's possible to know precisely where the wine comes from. The provenance of the grapes, no doubt. This place used to serve house red or house white. I seem to remember chianti baskets although maybe that's stretching things. Anyway, it's got very fancy. And very expensive."

"My treat," Alec said. "Don't worry about it."

"I'm not worrying, but it's just … oh, I don't know. I just wish everywhere hadn't become quite so smart these days. So self-consciously affluent." She stared back at the menu. "Do I sound very old and cantankerous?"

"A little," Alec said smiling, "but it's allowed. We are both older, after all."

"But you are never cantankerous. Never that."

He shrugged as if seeing the lack of the trait a deficiency of sorts. Blandness, a tendency towards complacency and contentment could be viewed as weaknesses, he had once suggested to Catherine. Neither of them spoke for a few moments, studying the extensive menu, the intricacies of description that marred clarity. A waiter hovered, retreated, returned too soon. Somewhat randomly, they ordered. Alec shook out a large highly starched white napkin, leant his elbows on the table.

"So, all settled in? Put down roots, met the neighbours, feeling at home, all that sort of thing?"

"Getting there," Catherine said cautiously. "And I really find I like it. The flat is fine. Surprisingly spacious. I was worried that, after the house in Bevington, it would seem – but, no, this suits me. The area too. As for neighbours, I've not met any yet, although I've caught sight of the woman who lives upstairs. And there's a couple who appear to have the big flat at the back. That's an extension, of course, from the original house, part of the development. It's the one with the garden leading down to the railway."

Catherine sensed he had stopped listening. Alec was a man who tended to dismiss detail, required only a precis in answer. At times, the habit could be convenient, when Catherine wished to divulge little of a situation, avoid too much disclosure, but tonight she would have been grateful for a more narrative response. Still, it had always been the nature of their friendship, their erstwhile relationship, to respect a certain detachment and disinterest. She could hardly expect Alec to indulge her now in convivial conversation about curtains and scatter cushions, the convenience of the late-night corner shop merely minutes away from the flat, the ease of her daily commute. And such topics were, she knew, her own form of evasion, a tactic to avoid far more complex matters that lay between them. Even this dinner, extravagant, pleasant, was an occasion she was unsure how to negotiate as if there were terms she did not fully understand.

In the months after Eddie's death, Alec had been delicately solicitous; initially, an appropriate letter of condolence, the offer of advice on practicalities followed by an occasional phone call. The actions of a close friend, a kindly acquaintance. He had been a discreet presence at the funeral on that very wet December day, sitting at the back of the church during the service and silently handing her an umbrella as she had hovered in the porch, helpless in the unremitting rain. Catherine had been grateful for his evident support yet had been wary, on the whole, of accepting or presuming too much. Alec had loathed Eddie. On the one awkward occasion soon after their engagement when the three of them had met over an early evening drink, the two men's mutual dislike had been tangible. Catherine, with the blinkered, naïve vision of the newly in love, could not understand their animosity towards each other. Eddie, for once, had relinquished his habitual manner of easy charm and Alec's instinctive cordiality had been strained. Her sister, Beth, had considered she was ingenuous. *What did you expect? You agreed with Alec that you'd never marry, that you were alike in that way, no permanent ties or commitments. The man feels betrayed. Although such a strange arrangement, I always thought. (after all, what else is there? What else are you supposed to do with a life?) And then along comes Eddie and all your convictions are instantly thrown out of the window. You change your tune drastically and expect Alec to understand.* Catherine had insisted to Beth that there had never been any kind of arrangement with Alec, that an absence of one had been, in fact, rather the point. But she could see that, tacitly, an assumption had grown up of the other one always being there. Like a certain sum of money in a safe, unspectacular savings account. A reliable fall back for diversion. As for Eddie's disdain for Alec, his dismissal had been absolute. *Whatever did you see in such a dull character, Kitty? Typical boring lawyer. It makes me doubt your judgement, darling. No more introductions to old friends like that, for the love of God!* It ensured they had never met again. And for the first few years of their marriage, Catherine had made little attempt to keep in contact with Alec beyond Christmas cards. Then they had met by chance in the bookshop in Piccadilly, shared an innocuous coffee, news, met once more just before Alec was heading for a complex legal case that was likely to keep him out of the country for months. Easy and insignificant occasions that were neither, as Catherine told herself at the time, here nor there.

Now she looked across the table of the Italian restaurant in Weymouth Street, over full plates and glasses, listening as Alec talked of a recent business trip to Marseilles, of a possible problem with the roof tiles at the Hampstead house, and wondered, inevitably, whether Eddie had been right about Alec. And by association, since she might still find some comfort in his predictable company, a degree of solace in his steady companionship, perhaps she, too, had always been too dull, too tedious to complement Eddie. No doubt Eddie had raged about her in later years to eager, credulous ears (young women's ears, in particular) in a similar vein to the way he had condemned Alec. *Too dull, too boring beyond belief.* And if that was indeed the case, it was inevitable that Catherine saw herself as culpable, the principal catalyst for the disintegration of their marriage which no doubt had been ill-founded on her unreasonable belief and expectation that Eddie would mellow. Change. From there, it took her little time to adopt a certain responsibility for his very foolish, fast drive along a narrow road sheer with early December ice and a catastrophic collision with a high, unforgiving brick wall.

Alec refilled her glass.

"You have to finish the bottle for the two of us," he said, "I'm driving you back to Clapham, remember, so no more for me."

"Not quite Clapham. Clapham's too pricey these days." She drank, gratefully. "But we still get a common. And the river. Which is rather the point of south London, I'd say. Early morning mists over the Thames and pubs along the towpath. No river walks in Hampstead, Alec."

"There's the round pond," he said. "Will that do? I seem to remember you were rather fond of that in the days when you used to come and stay with me most weekends."

"You're a fantasist," Catherine said. "I rarely if ever spent an entire weekend with you."

"Really? Why ever was that? I seem to have distorted memory, then." Alec looked genuinely disappointed.

"But we did spend quite a bit of time around Hampstead. Restaurants and book shops and walks on the heath, of course. That Viennese café with the strudel. And I seem to remember a concert at Kenwood once and a picnic. More than once, in fact. Years and years ago now, of course. When I was living in Archway before I was working at the museum and before … well, everything that happened next."

Alec put down his fork, pushed his plate away as if appetite had suddenly eluded him.

"So where does that leave us now, Catherine? Now that Eddie – sorry, tactless of me. I was wondering whether you had any thoughts for your future. Plans, shall we say, for how you see yourself living. The shape of your life if you like."

"I've just sold a house and bought a flat, Alec. I think I've had my quota of plans for the foreseeable future." She attempted a light tone, a broad smile to disguise her understanding of his words. She picked up her fork and attended unnecessarily to a pool of oily pesto. Suddenly, she felt overwhelmingly tired as if her words of evasion to Alec bore in them more truth than she had known.

"Of course," he said quietly. "Forgive me. That was unnecessary of me." He brushed away a breadcrumb that appeared to have attached itself to his tie, drank from a glass of water. "But work – tell me about that. The museum is thriving, I hope. Visitor numbers buoyant?"

They stepped carefully and with relief onto safe ground. Alec travelled frequently, spent extended time abroad both for his legal commitments as a partner in a firm that specialised in maritime law and for various business enterprises that Catherine had never quite grasped. His frequent absences had dictated in part the nature of the relationship they had once had. Or perhaps had been the reason it had flourished at all for Catherine had often wondered if they could have sustained a more conventional arrangement. There had been, after all, a measure of attraction in the unpredictability of their meetings. A friend had once said that they behaved more like illicit lovers than a regular couple in their pattern of rendezvous and snatched dates, but the parallel had been inaccurate. They had simply suited each other, Catherine had always believed. Until Alec's return one day after a five-month absence abroad dealing with complicated, drawn-out litigation when their reunion, warmly anticipated by Catherine, had felt pedestrian, unacceptably pragmatic and functional. She had allowed herself then to think that perhaps, whatever she and Alec had pursued, had run its course.

Soon after, she had met Eddie.

Alec drove her home. She was relieved when he resisted her invitation to see the flat, suggesting another occasion instead. Dinner, he had said, an invitation to dinner or Sunday lunch at one of the pubs along the river followed by a long walk along a towpath or through the park. Inside, she kicked off her shoes in the hall, picked up post, mostly mailshot, carried it through to the living room, thought about making tea or coffee and gave up on the idea of both. Standing in the bay window overlooking the street, she saw some remaining lights in the house opposite, watched a figure crossing one room then moving on to another, hands reaching out to draw the house firmly into darkness. The road where they had lived in Bevington had been wide with deep front lawns so houses opposite had felt remote, out of reach. Here, the narrowness of Miller Street, the proximity of her neighbours encouraged a certain voyeurism and she imagined couples, low voices, young children calling out from their beds, hushed tones coaxing them back into sleep. And wondered whether she felt envy for such intimacy, if, now that she lived alone again, she would become aware of loneliness: a noted absence of human company, that consolation of warm limbs at her side as she fell asleep each night. She thought of Alec, driving back to his cold, austere house in Hampstead, listening to Stockhausen or Schoenberg as he crossed Putney Bridge with considerable relief, breathing more evenly as he made his way across the quietening city, skirting Regent's Park and criss-crossing the cushioned empty streets towards comfortably familiar territory. Before Eddie, she had matched Alec's self-sufficiency, felt an ease with her blithe choice. Now she questioned it. Her initial desire for Eddie, that visceral need of him, the overwhelming hunger to be constantly with him in those early years had startled her into a way of being that had shocked her yet had so swiftly become familiar. Even in the last year or so of his life when they had lived alongside one another incompatibly, when she had yearned to be free of such domestic tension, she had been uncertain whether she wanted to return to the detachment she had known before they had met. Alec had seen her marriage to Eddie as foolish, unwise. He had never believed in her ability to maintain it since he saw her as too independent and incapable of change. Years ago, Catherine would have agreed with him.

But now?

Now such selfishness, the idea of a life devoid of responsibility, of hooks, seemed vacuous, untenable, for as the years stacked up their deeds stuck. Memories of error and failure attached themselves leech-like and it simply was not possible to shrug off actions and words to some convenient incinerator of the mind. Even her intention to revert to her maiden name after Eddie's death had eluded her, her tongue no longer quite mastering the sounds as if it had become an empty husk, inappropriate for her to claim any more as her own. Her marriage persisted in clinging on, impossible entirely to erase.

But for now, there was a relief to be found in her silent, still rooms. For the moment, at least. She drew the curtains, went into the bedroom, undressed, hung up her clothes. In the bathroom, she stared at the mirror, ran her hands through her mid-length hair given to unpredictable waves, wondered whether to cut it shorter or let it grow long again. Uncertain any more what suited her, insecure in her own opinion.

Then she remembered the letter.

Partially lost between the gaggle of leaflets and flyers from the pizza parlours and Chinese restaurants that she had gathered up from the hall, she found the white envelope with *By Hand,* printed boldly in the top left corner. Clear, large rounded writing in navy ink took up the rest of the space.

For Catherine Wells, Apartment 2, Willow House.

5

Polly Gough stood at the window of her parents' living room, peering out into the back garden, darkening in the twilight.

"It's a good size. Not too small, but far more sensible than eight acres."

"Six. And four of those were leased to local farmers in recent years. It was in Scotland that we had eight."

"Even so. It's been a good move. A sensible move. You have to admit that." She took the mug of coffee from her father, sat down wearily in the large armchair and yawned. Across the room, Lydia smiled, attempted to say something and waved her hands as if in substitute for words. "Sorry," Polly said, yawning again. "A long week. As always. Don't worry, I'll stay awake long enough to keep mum company. You go. Enjoy yourself."

"I don't have to go," Sam said, sitting down again, "I'm really not at all interested in meeting the neighbours. Can't think why I agreed in the first place. It wouldn't matter in the slightest if I just didn't turn up." He had accepted the invitation rashly, he thought now, out of shame for his brusque attitude towards Frances Chater when they had met on the common, eager to make some sort of amends. But he had no wish to become sociable and perhaps it was better to establish detachment from the start. "Besides, your mother would prefer me to stay in, wouldn't you, Lyddie?"

He attempted to take her hand, but she resisted, held hers firmly in her lap.

"She has me this evening," Polly said firmly. "I've driven over in appalling south circular traffic just to be here. So, go. Now. And try to be charming. You know you can be if you want to. Very charming. You're still not half bad-looking for someone of your age. Besides, it might be good to ..." She nodded obliquely towards her mother. "Explain. How things are. Good, understanding neighbours are invaluable, you know."

"We have you now," Sam said. "We don't need good neighbours. That's why we moved to London, after all."

"I'm in Deptford. Near enough and willing, but not next door."

He stood up, partially relieved by Polly's persuasion. It had been a difficult day, raining the entire morning, and he had not felt able to insist on their routine walk around the common. He had tried to settle Lydia with some music, playing a few of her old records that usually calmed her. He had found some of the illustrated art books that she generally enjoyed browsing, even dug out one or two of her old sketch pads. But she had been restless, irritable, unappeasable. He had work to do, he explained somewhat curtly, picking up the Matisse volume she had discarded to the floor, the spilled sketches of wild flowers she had made years before. He had a report to write, copy to submit, deadlines to meet. In truth, the very few freelance assignments he now undertook were more for his own fulfilment than the scant financial reward, but he was anxious to maintain some semblance of a working life. Today, however, each time he tried to leave the room to go to the computer, Lydia had called him back in a voice of wild desperation. Yet having gained his company once more, she had then seemed exasperated by it, as if he was failing to understand her needs in some way. Which, he conceded, considering her difficulties in communicating, he no doubt was. Finally, by early afternoon, he gave in to television, finding a channel showing an old film which appeared to hold Lydia's attention for an hour or so. He disliked using this as a solution, protesting to Polly that daytime television was an opiate and a pacifier that would do nothing to stimulate Lydia's mind. In truth, his objections to its use lay in the confirmation it gave of her declining state: Lydia had rarely watched television before her illness, had been intolerant of it as a form of entertainment. Now she could sit for hours apparently mesmerised by what Sam saw as trivial, banal content.

"Have you eaten?" Sam said, shrugging into the jacket hanging on the back of the chair.

"There's some food – a casserole in the kitchen – I made it this afternoon and it just needs warming up. Or you could wait until I'm back if you like. We could eat together." He hoped his suggestion did not sound too pleading. They had left Cornwall and moved to London to be nearer Polly for Lydia's sake, not his own. Yet it had begun to feel that he was the one constantly anxious for her company, in need of her positive practicality to assuage his darker moods. Polly had been a sensible, level-headed little girl who had proceeded to maintain a calm, unwavering focus as she had negotiated childhood and adolescence alongside her less pragmatic parents. Now, at the age of 35, as a deputy head teacher of a large inner-city primary school with its fair share of social deprivation and challenging educational needs, she retained an admirable if bewildering level of equilibrium and steadiness. Sam often wondered if her lack of a permanent male partner lay with her intolerance of what she claimed she always found in men: a certain spinelessness, chronic self-obsession, a tendency to vanity. There had been two or three boyfriends over the years that they had met, but all had been temporary rather than long-term features. Yet he and Lydia would have liked to see her settled, as he had once unwisely said to her. *Settled?* she had retorted. *Settled! Like some 19th century woman in want of an eligible suitor, I suppose. I am settled. In a job, a career. In a heftily mortgaged, miniscule, but very decent flat. Even Deptford is considered desirable and respectable these days, you'd be surprised.* And as always, Sam had found himself envying her certainty, her conviction for the life she had devised clearly and carefully for herself.

Catherine's initial reaction was to refuse. *Please come up to apartment 3 for wine and nibbles, a chance to get to know one another and a discussion on the imminent, exciting centenary of our street!* She had been instantly wary of the tone, the assumption of Frances Chater's message. Yet she also tried to censure her reaction. It was no more than a harmless gesture at neighbourliness, after all. Besides, at some point, they would all inevitably meet and delaying the event for too long would seem to inflate its significance. So she found herself ringing the bell of the side door a little after seven o'clock, wondering whether the bottle of wine she was clutching was appropriate and was instantly summoned up via the intercom to a narrow landing and a second open door. Frances Chater, dressed rather formally in a dark blue skirt and white blouse with an elaborate bow tied at the neck, ushered her in warmly as if a friendship was already established. The sitting room, although of a good size, was overstuffed with furniture, so appeared cramped. A floral-covered three-piece suite dominated the dark expanse of fitted carpet and in addition two armchairs hugged the sides of the room as if elbowing for space. A writing desk, antique in appearance, sat in the window that overlooked Miller Street; a coffee table, heavily laden with platters of small sandwiches, curls of smoked salmon, ham and salami sufficient for close to a dozen, sat in the centre of the room. In spite of the clutter, there was somehow a sense of extraordinary order and control about the room as if nothing was allowed to be left to chance: cushions were uniformly angled, glasses lined up with precision, books arranged on a shelf as if selected for identical size rather than content. Dense ink-blue velvet curtains hung from floor to ceiling at the front window, somewhat insistent and oppressive. Frances held out a glass of wine to her and, feeling clumsy and awkward, Catherine proffered her bottle in return.

"Oh, there's no need for that," Frances said, swiftly pushing Catherine's bottle to the back of a substantial sideboard as if dismissing it as inferior. "Besides, I'm sure we'll all be reciprocating with entertainment over the next few months, taking turns, as it were, although you're always most welcome here, of course. We can think of it as Headquarters! I've assumed white for you? Or would you prefer red? I have a good bottle of Côte du Rhône if you'd prefer. Everyone swears by Australian Shiraz these days, but I prefer to stay with what you can rely upon. Tried and tested, as it were!" She giggled in a high pitch that sounded unnatural and strained. Catherine watched as she smoothed down her skirt, adjusted the bow of her blouse and fiddled with her watch strap, her hands restless. "Sit!" It seemed to be an order. "Make yourself at home and do tuck in. I've made far too much food as always. My mother always mocked me for my lavishness when it came to catering. There's side plates there and napkins too, of course. How's the wine? Not too dry? I see you're only sipping. That one's a decent French, but I've an Italian Pinot if you prefer."

Catherine sat down on the sofa, drank more wine to reassure, but Frances had already darted from the room to the kitchen opposite and was saying something about a temperamental oven and charred pastry and the difficulties of adjusting to gas after electric. She appeared to be the sort of person who found silence, even for a moment, unnerving and was compelled to fill it. Reappearing with a plate of small savoury tartlets, she placed a heatproof mat with some deliberation on the table and positioned the dish. Catherine glanced at the large carriage clock on the sideboard and noted that only a few minutes had gone by since she had arrived. Already she wanted to feign an excuse and leave, retreat from the stuffed room, from Frances Chater's persistent chatter and the sense of entrapment she felt. Within moments, however, the woman had disappeared again, speaking into the intercom in the hall in a voice loud enough to travel down the stairs and out the front door without its aid. Catherine heard swift steps on the staircase, another voice, and Frances ushered into the sitting room the man she recognised from the garden flat.

"Now, we are complete, I think," she said, her face flushed, her voice still unnecessarily loud, "at least for this evening. Sam, meet Catherine Wells. Sam's wife, Lydia, can't be here, of course, but I'm sure Sam will admirably report back to her. You will keep her in the loop, won't you, Sam? I wouldn't want her to think we were choosing to ignore her. That's so important with people who are ill. Incapacitated, I mean. But now, no more of that. Red, no doubt, for you, Sam. I'm sure you'll want red."

He hesitated for a moment as if about to disagree, but Frances was already pouring from an opened bottle and he took the glass willingly enough, sat down in one of the large armchairs opposite Catherine.

"I suppose I should know you already, at least by sight. Lyddie would have done in the past. But I'm appallingly blinkered, I'm afraid, wander around with tunnel vision most of the time." He smiled warmly at her, and ignored Frances' attempts to fuss with the cushion he had dislodged from his chair. "My wife, Lydia, is seriously ill, you see, and no longer mobile or capable of conversation. But you'll meet her in time, I'm sure."

"I'm so sorry," Catherine said, inadequately, wanting to say more, but unable to conjure anything she felt appropriate. She liked his directness. He picked up a couple of small sandwiches, swiftly ate them, then one of the mildly charred pastries while drinking steadily from his glass. Frances had left the room again, saying something about papers to fetch, keeping up a constant, but inaudible stream of conversation from somewhere along the hall. Outside, the rain had returned after a brief lull, but Catherine resisted talking of the weather. It would seem trivial in the circumstance, as if she was choosing to be intentionally evasive; she had become too familiar in the past year with people who seemed at pains to pursue desultory topics in order to avoid more potent matter.

Frances soon returned and handed them a single typed sheet of paper rather in the manner of an invigilator for a formal exam and took the remaining armchair.

"Now," she said, her voice lowered so that she sounded faintly conspiratorial, "I wonder how much either of you know about the history of Miller Street."

She looked from one to the other, clearly anticipating their ignorance and she was not disappointed. Neither Catherine nor Sam Gough were aware that the centenary of the road was to fall the following year. If information about the original construction of the houses in Miller Street had filtered through to them from estate agents or deeds, they had not remembered. Now they both found themselves sitting silently while she spoke at considerable length, listening to her plans for a street party to celebrate the event, rather like, Catherine felt, biddable children who found it easier to appease than oppose a coercive parent. Already, it appeared, Frances had leafleted all the other houses in the road, made tentative enquiries about neighbours willing to serve on a committee, sought out any expertise in catering, accounting, publicity, sponsorship, in provision of music and entertainment. She drew their attention to the form she had handed out, to the space left for them to fill in their own area of proficiency and interest. For their cooperation was assumed, Catherine saw. Obligatory. Mandated. Frances Chater was clearly a woman who did not brook opposition. Sam Gough accepted a refill of his glass.

"Well, I have to admire your initiative," he said eventually when it was evident that a response was expected from them. He picked up another sandwich, ignored Frances' attempt to give him a plate. "Really quite remarkable. No objections from the long-time residents of the road, presumably? That you might be stealing their thunder so to speak?"

If the question was heard, it was ignored. Frances opened a large purple notebook and turned to a clean page.

"Now, we have only eight months before the proposed date which is the middle Saturday in July. And there's Christmas in between which these days seems to occupy two or three weeks – although really, for most people, it just seems an excuse for excessive socialising. Nothing to do with the true value and meaning of the Christian religious festival. For some of us, anyway. So it means time with a capital T is of some urgency. I've already pencilled in the first meeting of the committee in two weeks and I am presuming that …?" She let the question hover in the air like an irresistible temptation, looked from Catherine to Sam with a broad smile that seemed to assume their fortune and collaboration. Sam leant forward to scoop up salami and smoked salmon nestling on slivers of toast.

"This is all delicious," he said, "did you buy it from the

delicatessen near the newsagents? Lyddie and I have been meaning to try the place. Someone told us the owner's from Bologna. Do you know Italy, Frances? Lyddie and I were last there just a couple of years ago."

Frances began to speak as if with the intention of steering things back on course, but then, with some deliberation and a hint of self-deprecation on her broad face, closed the large purple notebook and put it firmly down on the table next to the untouched side plates and paper napkins.

"I have, of course, been intolerably rude," she said then paused, picked up her glass of wine that she had not begun to drink. "Or at least I have behaved inappropriately. I see that now. Just grabbed the baton and headed for the tape, so to speak. It's my enthusiasm, you see. Always my downfall as my mother would have pointed out. Let her grasp the nettle and there's no stopping her." She turned to Catherine as if seeking propitiation. The woman's eyes were fierce, unyielding, Catherine saw, although there was also a sense of nervousness in her manner. "We should simply be getting to know each other on this first occasion rather than me using it to rally the troops. I have put things in the wrong order and for that, I apologise. Shall we spend a bit of time now simply introducing ourselves?"

Catherine looked at Sam, hoping he would once more skilfully divert the conversation. But instead he appeared to be waiting for her to speak, sitting back in the large armchair, cradling his wine glass in both hands and watching her with apparent interest. She fervently wished now that she had not come, yearned for the solitariness of her flat, those undemanding white walls. Frances Chater coughed twice as if to prompt one of them then broached the silence herself.

"Well, shall I start us off? My move to Willow House is something of a new start for me. From Worthing, actually. My mother died about a year ago and although I could have stayed on in the house – I'd been living there as her main carer for some time, you see – I decided that my moment had come. For London, I mean. Of course, I'm a little mature to be hitting the high lights of city living – a single woman in her mid-fifties – or even nudging a little past that, if the truth be told! – but there's still life in me yet, I'd say. And what a lovely part of our capital city we've all chosen for ourselves. As I said to my cousin on the phone last night, it's like living a village life within a cultural gold mine. Such a setting what with transport and local shops and the parish church only a stone's throw away. Do either of you worship there?" Catherine shook her head. Sam grunted a few words about it not really being their kind of thing. "It can be a support, you know. Spiritually. Some words of wisdom to lift the heart and the mind and the soul. You'd be surprised. And with your wife so ill, Sam. There are times when – anyway, enough about me! Whose turn next?"

Sam made an extravagant gesture of looking at his watch, aped surprise and shifted in his chair.

"Actually, I really need to be going. Our daughter is kindly sitting with Lyddie and I don't want to wear out her patience. Said I'd be less than an hour and already I've outstayed that. Besides, I'd rather like some time with Polly myself while she's here. I'm sure you understand, Frances."

"So soon?" Frances said, "what a pity, but naturally, family always come first. And having a daughter must be such a blessing with your wife as she is. I can see quite how things are and you have my huge sympathies. But just before you go, perhaps you might like to complete this." She held out a pen, picked up the form that he had placed dismissively on the floor by his chair. "Just so that I can know what your strengths are when I'm allocating tasks. For the centenary street party," she added as if suspecting he might have already forgotten. Sam stood up, carelessly brushed breadcrumbs and pastry flakes that had collected on his shirt onto the dark blue carpet where they seemed to gather conspicuously like pale flecks of dust and sand. He placed his empty wine glass on a small mahogany table between a cactus plant and an African violet, avoiding a protective coaster.

"I'm an IT man, myself," he said, staring squarely at Frances, "that's all I know, really. Still do a bit, working from home, some consultancy stuff and a bit of copy for a couple of charities. But, of course, what with my wife and her needs, I don't have time for committees such as yours. Sorry. You've got the wrong man if you think you can rely on me. Very sorry about that." He smiled wanly, made for the door then turned as if suddenly remembering Catherine was still there. "Apologies to be in something of a hurry, tonight. It has been very good to meet you, Catherine Wells from Flat 2. Or do people call you Katy?"

"Some call me Kate," Catherine said, "although mostly—"

Sam interrupted. "Kate it is, then. You must come and meet Lyddie soon. Lydia Brook is her professional name as an artist, in fact. Although, of course, she's not had so much use for it of late, sadly. Not able to paint or draw any more. As you'll see. And we're not terribly sociable these days, you will have to forgive us. We've always tended to be rather solitary people, in fact, but now circumstance dictates and all that."

"Of course," Catherine said.

"We've just moved from rather a wild bit of Cornwall, so all this city living is a bit of a shock, I can tell you. A lack of endless horizons and hares nipping through the long grass."

"A big adjustment, I can imagine. But a practical choice. And there are still good places for walks and fresh air, by the river. And the common, of course."

"Hard to get lost, though."

"Well, yes. I suppose so."

"And hard to be lost to others."

"I'm not sure about that. Cities can accommodate solitariness very well."

He looked at her for a moment before turning and heading through the front door and swiftly down the stairs. Catherine grasped at her chance to leave and stood up, but found herself blocked by Frances who was standing at the threshold of the living room effectively trapping her.

"Now it would be inhospitable of me not to offer you coffee, Catherine. Or more wine, of course? And do eat some more of this food or I'll be scoffing it all night. I know Sam's had to leave, but at least he's shared something of his talents with us. I already have some essential jobs in mind for him. Even a title – Communications? Technical Coordinator? I'm sure he's marvellous with spreadsheets."

"I thought he said he wouldn't be able to help," Catherine said weakly and turned away from Frances' arresting stare to look at a cluster of framed photographs on the wall. "Family?" she said as a diversion. Frances followed her eye.

"Oh, something like that," she said vaguely, staring at the photographs as if she had forgotten they were there. "Nephews. Godchildren. Long-time acquaintances. And my mother, of course. My late mother, I should say. Now what is it to be, Catherine – coffee or wine? Or tea? I have Early Grey and Peppermint which is excellent for the digestion at this time of the day. Or would you prefer me to call you Kate? Although, personally, I think abbreviated names are unwise. Not what was intended when your parents named you, after all."

"Nothing, thank you. And I really do have to go. I have work to do. My job, you see. I—"

Frances caught Catherine's arm, propelled her lightly but firmly back towards the sofa.

"At least fill in your sheet before you leave so I know who

I have on board. Interests, strengths and so forth. And contact details as well, of course. Email, mobile as well as landline. Of course, you can't escape me, living downstairs, but it's as well to have the full picture! I will put both you and Sam down as our first confirmed committee members, you see. How's that?" She spoke as if bestowing some kind of honour. Mechanically, Catherine took the pen, sketchily filled out the form, handed it back to Frances who ran a swift eye over it as if checking for inconsistencies, omissions.

"I'm not sure about being on a committee, though," she hedged, "like Sam, I'm not really the type of person who's any good in such situations." Already she dreaded the thought of countless similar evenings in Frances' cluttered sitting room, of the place filled with the comfortable, complacent residents of Miller Street, compelled to become part of their settled, sociable lives. She had left the house in Bevington, she had thought, to avoid such intrusion.

"Oh, Sam and his protests," Frances said, as if there was an established familiarity between them. "Of course, he wants to be involved. Just feigned modesty on his part, I assure you. And it will do him the world of good, get him out of himself, living with an invalid the way he does. Now let's have a look if you have anything useful to offer." She looked down at the space for *Occupation/Line of work* and tapped the words Catherine had written with an index finger, her nails neat, manicured and varnished pale pink. "House Manager at the Harriet Howe museum so social history is your speciality! Well, that's fortuitous, wouldn't you say? Serendipity, I believe the word is. Your historical expertise will certainly be needed, Catherine."

"I'm not an expert by any means," Catherine protested. "Not a historian at all. My knowledge is restricted to Harriet Howe and the house, I can assure you."

Frances waved a hand as if dismissing her claim as misplaced humility.

"Nonsense, you'll be just the person to write up the history of Miller Street for some sort of centenary booklet I have in mind. Of course, I'll be happy to pass on all the research notes I've already gathered. But feel free to use your own access to resources. I can see you are going to be very useful to the committee!" She took one final glance at Catherine's form, her pen hovering over a space beside her name. "Title?" she said. "People are so fussy these days. Myself, I am quite happy with Miss, but if you are one of those who insist on Ms—?"

"Actually," Catherine said, "it's Mrs."

Frances paused for a moment as if expecting her to say more, but when Catherine did not elaborate, she wrote the information down with precision.

"I see, thank you," she said, "Mrs Catherine Wells. Most helpful."

6

F rances Chater was prurient.

Inevitably, she would probe for more, but at least she had been stalled, an explanation of Eddie's accident conveniently delayed. For Catherine felt fraudulent in her claim to widowhood and the ensuing sympathies and condolences that the status wrought. Aware that, if Eddie had died just a few months later, they would no doubt have been living apart, their separation evident, and Catherine considered less worthy of such consolation. They had already begun to talk intermittently about arrangements although such conversations had always been terse, as if both had been floundering towards the idea of a future that neither could quite grasp.

It had taken a while for her sense of culpability to surface.

Rather, like a dull, dormant ache that takes time to register fully, she had woken up one morning a month after his death to be aware of a sense of direct responsibility for the accident. The facts, of course, clearly laid the blame elsewhere. Presented unequivocally by the coroner, Eddie had driven at excessive speed late on an icy winter's night while under the influence of an excessive alcoholic intake, had lost control of the car and collided with that high, unyielding brick wall with catastrophic results. *Death by Misadventure.* Case swiftly concluded and closed. But to Catherine, the facts were bald, superficial, skimming the surface of truth rather than delving for clarity. Beth had been scathing when she had tried to explain her sense of guilt. *Eddie was irresponsible, thought he could get away with driving too fast, drinking too much. You know that, Cat. It wasn't your fault, for goodness sake. He was always a law unto himself. Lord of his own universe where he made up the rules.* But Beth had not been there in the house that night, did not understand how events had climaxed into that fatal drive of his. Nor had she seen the way Catherine had behaved in the months leading up to that December day, accepting too passively the failure of their marriage and doing nothing to rescue it from a painful impasse. If only she had been more willing to compromise, willing to subdue a certain pride and accept his inconsistent idea of faithfulness, he would still be alive. *Henry says you're just suffering from survivor's guilt, that's all,* Beth said again and again. *Ridiculous, really, you weren't even in the car. Now you need to forget all this nonsense, Cat, and just get on with your life. You're not even fifty yet. You might even marry again.*

She realised that she was hungry, had hardly eaten all day and for some reason had resisted the numerous sandwiches and savoury snacks that had been pressed upon her earlier. In the kitchen, she opened the fridge, piled a plate with leftovers and went through to the front room, listening to its silence. She did not warm to Frances Chater. She was always wary of people who assumed a friendship, felt it betrayed a certain arrogance and insensitivity. But then in turn, her own reticence could no doubt be seen as defensive, cold. The woman was assertive and undeniably productive, hardly qualities to mock although there seemed something feverish about her, as if her behaviour was learnt, acquired rather than natural. She liked Sam Gough. He appeared forthright, amiable, charming, even, and she detected in his handling of Frances a habit of self-preservation, discretion. She saw him as an ally, a sympathetic voice in Willow House, and

perversely hoped Frances would be able to convince him
to be a fellow presence on the centenary committee if she
herself could not escape. She ate a curling slice of smoked
cheese, the scant cold remains of some fish pie. Half a pot
of yogurt. Four walnuts. Then curled up on the chair by the
window and flicked through television channels.

Catherine had, in fact, noticed the parish church on the
common that Frances had mentioned. As children, she and
Beth had been sent to Sunday school for an hour or so of
informal activities, a story with a loosely moral content and a
couple of cheerful hymns while the adults sat in stiff church
pews or stayed at home to mow lawns, wash cars. Somehow
the habit had waned in early teens although she could not
remember any rebellion from either of them. Simply there
were other things to do that filled Sunday mornings and
then they both left home and church became a matter for
other people's weddings, Beth's wedding, her children's
christenings, events observed more as social gatherings than for
their spiritual significance. Of course, there were the funerals.
Catherine had been too bewildered by the loss of her father to
recall much of that service. Her mother had been dismissive
of the prospect of her own and had set strict instructions for a
swift and unsentimental despatch.

But then Eddie.

For a man given to subversive gestures and a generally
flippant attitude to the observance of common law, Eddie
could be contrarily conventional. He would expect,
Catherine had been sure, the formalities of religious ritual
to mark his death. A brief cold crematorium departure by
the serving vicar of the day would not be to his taste at
all. So there had been a service. There had been hymns,
thoughtful prayers, readings, an address by an old friend of
Eddie's in the church in Bevington and Catherine, numbed

by the swiftness of events, had been not so much comforted by the vicar when she went to see him in the days after the accident, as sustained by his refusal to offer platitudes. *But where is he?* she found herself asking for although she knew the question was absurd there was a persistent clamour to understand. Clinically, categorically, there was the evidence of his physical death, but this did not stop her instinct to delve for more. A generation used to clear cut answers, rational explanations, surely the information could be sourced from somewhere. The vicar had listened with patience, said little, but had nodded his head as if similarly confounded. Then he had said something about Eddie no doubt having his own relationship and path to his God and switched swiftly to examining the choice of music. Catherine had attended two or three services at the Bevington church after the funeral, feeling some obligation towards the vicar, but had found little to hold or compel her. She had no grasp of what she expected – hardly a sudden conversion to religious devotion or profound spiritual awakening – but the experience had been too neutral, formulaic. Bland. Yet from time to time, she found herself drawn into empty city churches, the sort now inconspicuously wedged between sandwich bars and retail outlets, survivors of the London blitz, but betrayed by 20th century street planners, no doubt only their listed building status preventing their complete destruction. There, in the strange stillness of those places, smelling of dust and dying flowers and burning candles and fading incense, she liked to sit on an unforgiving pew and try to think. Of anything. Of Eddie. Her father, her mother. Of the nature of love. And try to see some sort of pattern or shape or direction in it all, a lodestar, even, to follow. But after ten minutes or so, she would glance at her watch, remember a phone call she needed to make, something she needed to buy and would swiftly stand up, make a hasty retreat from the place as if suddenly ashamed of her self-indulgence, the banality of her thoughts. Yet months later she would be pulled back, another dusty city church devoid of its birth right of fields and yew tree, another uncompromising pew.

And sit again and think. Or at least try to think.

Polly picked up the plates, piled them by the sink. She could hear her father settling her mother in the sitting room, a patient tone of voice that she knew was not natural to him. If Lydia had changed irrevocably from the mother she had known, Sam's temperament had mutated in order to cope. She had seen them too infrequently in the past year, the journey to rural Cornwall difficult to fit easily into a weekend, particularly in winter. The demands of her job were not restricted to weekdays and too often she found herself in school on Saturdays, producing reports, sorting documentation, catching up with endless matters. Now that only a few miles along the south circular separated them, she was able to visit regularly and, inevitably, absorb fully the level of her mother's decline. He came back into the kitchen, pulled out a chair and sat down. Polly glanced at the clock.

"Thanks, Polly, for staying, I mean. Your mother eats so little now, but I like to make a proper meal each night. Try to keep some semblance of normality going."

"You never cooked more than a boiled egg in the past. Actually, if that. I'm very impressed," Polly said, indicating the emptied casserole dish that she had set to soak. He shrugged.

"It gives a point to the day, I find. Something to discuss with her in the morning. What to eat for dinner. Not that she's interested, anymore. It was one of the things I first noticed, the way she stopped caring. About what we ate, what she wore. What we did. It was as if something had switched off in her. She'd abandoned being herself."

Polly sat down next to him. Briefly, she placed a hand on his arm then pulled the bowl of grapes towards them, broke several off and ate them slowly.

"It's all a bit of a bloody nightmare, isn't it?" she said, "not what you saw for your old age, I'm sure."

"We're not old, Polly," Sam said wearily. "And there were all the plans for the next stage. You know how we'd talked about eventually selling up in Cornwall and going to live abroad? Back to the beginning, like when I first met the two of you. Only we weren't thinking of Spain. It was going to be Greece, we'd decided. One of the islands, probably. Long, assured hot summers, marvellous light. Wonderful place for your mother to paint. And for me to grow things. Have a vine. Chickens. A bit of land. That was the idea. And then suddenly this."

"I know," Polly said. "You lost her. I've lost her too, you know, the mother I had. And I miss her terribly. All the time. Every day I think of something that I want to tell her about – something silly that happened with one of the kids at school or that one of the littlest ones said and I'm just about to pick up the phone – and I remember. She's absent now, isn't she? Here, but not here."

"I'm not sure," Sam said, getting up from the table, filling the kettle. "She can't communicate with us, most of her speech is now gone, but how can we know what's going on in her mind? We have no idea whether she feels the frustration of being able to do so little. Can you imagine what that must be like for her? Watching herself lose ever more control every day. No wonder she can be so difficult. It's not her fault, of course, I'm not saying that. But it's not easy."

"You're doing your best," Polly said gently. "Not just the cooking, but all the other stuff. Personal things in particular. I'm sure Mum must appreciate all that, even if she can't show it. You're being heroic, you know."

"No, Polly, I'm not," Sam said firmly. "I resent it. I am raging inside all the time at the injustice of it. And do you know the worst thing about that? It's not even Lyddie I am feeling sorry for. Not really when it comes down to it. Or at least not all the time. If I'm absolutely honest, it's my own suffering, my own forced change in lifestyle that I begrudge."

"That's natural," Polly said. "It's a form of grief, isn't it?"

"Grief?"

"Premature mourning, then, for the woman you loved. Because she's someone else now. She's your patient. Your entirely dependent, needy relation that you can't abandon. Out of duty. Responsibility. Out of love."

"Is it?" Sam said. The kettle had boiled. He ignored it, sat down next to Polly again. "Love, I mean? I suppose so. Yes, it has to be that, doesn't it? Otherwise, it would all be simply intolerable. And yet looking at the months ahead, knowing the prognosis of this ghastly disease, I wonder how ever we'll cope."

"Don't think ahead," Polly said. "Not now. What's the point?" She stood up, began to gather her large, cumbersome bag that had partly spilled contents onto the kitchen floor.

"Coffee. You'll have some coffee before you leave? Or tea?" Sam tried not to sound in need. Polly shook her head.

"I've got an even earlier start than normal," she said, "got some tricky parents coming in before school and there's still some paperwork I need to do for another meeting at the end of the day. Social worker stuff, care order business. I'll pop in and say goodbye to mum before I go."

He waited in the hall, looking out through the side window at the dark street, empty apart from a lone dog walker. He envied the solitary walker, his freedom to leave his house spontaneously and spend time alone. Only in the past month or so had he found it impossible to go out and leave Lydia entirely on her own. Until then he had managed to snatch half an hour or so for a quick drive to a shop, even a solitary pint at the corner pub, confident that she would cope with his brief absence. But on the last occasion, he had returned to find her so distressed and alarmed that it had taken him much of the rest of the day to calm her. Like an infant who has lost sight of the adult in charge, she had appeared incapable of rationalising his temporary disappearance from her side. Polly kissed him on the cheek.

"Take heart," she said encouragingly, fishing for car keys, "you're being amazing, however self-deprecating you choose to sound. I wouldn't have believed it of you."

Sam smiled. "Thank you. I presume that's a compliment."

"Of course," Polly said. "And you know what? There's time for Greece. All that talk about olive groves and vine leaves and endless months of strong sunshine. For you, at least."

"Not without Lydia. It wouldn't be fair," he said, opening the front door onto the night.

"By the way," Polly called as she walked to her car. "I forgot to ask. How was your meeting? Neighbours nice?"

She looked back at her father, standing in the doorway, the light of the porch illuminating him. Sam pulled a face, slowly tipped a hand one way then the other as if to indicate a precarious balance.

Frances Chater hovered at the edge of the ink-blue velvet curtains, watched the small car drive away. *That will be the daughter. Not so much in a hurry to get away as you suggested, Sam. Still, I don't grudge him a little licence on that. She must be a comfort to him, considering. Adult children can be, after all. Catherine seems pleasant enough if a little quiet. I suppose that comes with the territory, stuck in museums and negotiating with the past for a living. I'll have to reserve judgement until I know her a bit better, of course, but she seems a little on the distant side. Still, better than having a wild, socialising type living underneath me, entertaining every hour of the day and night. Clearly no husband in residence although obviously an ex. She was noticeably vague about that, I have to say. Still, can't expect to know everything on a first acquaintance. And the response from the rest of the road is quite encouraging. Ten replies so far and all positive about a party. Others are no doubt hanging back to see how their neighbours respond. What sheep we all are! Someone has to lead though, or we'd find ourselves sleepwalking through life, out the other end without even living it. Wonder what they made of me – Frances Chater, spinster of this parish so to speak.*

If only they knew.

She brushed down the twitched curtain, went to her writing desk, opened the notebook sitting on top. It was the wrong time in the week to begin the next letter, but she could select the theme. That way, ideas flooded her mind and sentences and phrases came fully formed when she eventually sat down to write. It was a good scheme. Soon, she would make her first visit.

Or rather, as she preferred to think of it, stage her first vigil.

She would need a new coat with the colder weather coming on. Her current pale camel was inappropriate for purpose. Far too bland and apologetic. Something more confident was required, bold yet not brassy. Olive green or terracotta, perhaps, or even burgundy. And a mackintosh and large umbrella. Or should she cancel if the chosen day proved wet? No, come rain or come shine should be her motto. In fact, the more inclement the weather, the more her case was strengthened. Frances was not sure how she could rationalise that conclusion, but no doubt it was something to do with endurance and suffering. In the kitchen, she rinsed the wine glasses, drained them, dried them with a clean linen cloth and put them straight back in the cupboard. Good cut glass, those three were. The last remaining of the original eight inherited from someone on Andrew's side of the family. She was surprised neither Catherine nor Sam had commented on them as they clearly had the weight of quality and she was ready to explain they came from her mother's house in Worthing. Oh yes, she had her story entirely prepared down to the smallest detail.

Although that business with Catherine over the photos had nearly caught her out.

Still, she had covered up, not skipped a beat, she was sure.

She would have to review her catering for whole committee meetings. Couldn't turn every one into a virtual wine tasting and run up excessive bills. After all, economies were required short term if she was going to manage for months without finding a job. Perhaps she should shift things to later in the evening and make the meetings coffee and cake affairs? That would be the way. Good, freshly ground coffee and decent cups – and there were plenty of those genuinely from the Worthing house – and her walnut coffee cake. Or the lemon layer that had turned out so well for her mother's wake (although that day was now inevitably hitched to more searing matters than citron butter cream). Anyway, either would serve their purpose well. *All in all, a good day's work, Frances Rosemary Hodges, as my mother always insisted on calling me, even after thirty years of marriage to Andrew. Just to annoy me and show she never really approved of a dentist.*

***

A week later, a day following a night of strong winds and heavy rain so that the trees on the common had been suddenly stripped of any remaining leaves, Catherine arrived back from the museum to see a taxi pulling up outside Willow House.

A young woman, long black coat, heavy dark hair streaked with blonde hanging almost to her waist, took some time to pull herself and several overloaded carrier bags from the cab. Catherine approached her front door, opened it then paused, aware that the taxi had not driven away. There seemed some bother with payment, the young woman searching a purse, pockets, the crowded carrier bags, saying something about being short of just a couple of pounds, but certain that she had more change somewhere.

"Can I help?" Catherine said, stepping forward. The young woman, no more than twenty-two or three, turned around, stared at her for a moment then held out her hand as if expectant of such gestures.

"Thanks, yes. If you could lend me a fiver. Or a tenner would be better, just to be on the safe side. That would be great. I'll pay you back as soon as I'm sorted." She smiled broadly, passed Catherine's note to the driver. "Keep the change," she said to him and watched him drive to the end of the street then turned to the assortment of bags seeping their contents onto the forecourt. "You couldn't give me a hand, could you?" she said to Catherine. "Just to carry this stuff up to my flat. It's number 4, on the first floor." She picked up one of the smaller bags, began to head towards the house then stopped and turned again towards Catherine who was rescuing spilling clothes, some books, several shoes, a couple of mugs, attempting to restrain them from toppling on to the kerb. The young woman held out her spare hand. "Pleased to meet you. I'm Violet, by the way," she said, "kind of a new neighbour, I suppose. Violet Lawrence. You know, a bit like the author."

WINTER
2005/6

7

*T*he Harriet Howe House Museum in London presents an unparalleled collection of correspondence, books, pictures, documents, artefacts, curiosities and costumes reflecting the extraordinary life and achievements of a remarkable woman. Set within a four-storey late 18th century town house where Harriet Howe lived for many years, the museum provides a unique insight into her life and times. Philanthropist, suffragist, female rights activist, social reformer and political campaigner, Harriet Howe – 1850 to 1940 – was married four times and lived a long and admirable life that touched many. Her legacy lives on into the 21st century.

Catherine saw Sam Gough standing in the entrance hall, guidebook in hand, as she was on her way upstairs to replace a volunteer who needed to leave early. He looked up from his reading, inclined his head.

"I thought it was time to come and find out about this woman, Harriet Howe," he said. "See if she's everything you've claimed for her." Catherine, recalling only a brief conversation about where she worked when she saw Sam and Lydia in the newsagents one Sunday, was surprised. He had given no indication of his intention to visit or shown any particular interest in the house. Swiftly, he went on to explain himself. "Actually, the Chater woman sparked my interest in this place if I'm honest. Said you were the historical advisor for this centenary business she's getting us all into and that surely I knew about the museum and must have visited it and if not wasn't it about time. I have a feeling she wants you checked out to see if you're the genuine article, but decided to delegate the job to me." He smiled engagingly, pulled at his scarf, unbuttoned his heavy overcoat adjusting to the warmth of the building. The day was bitterly cold, a sharp frost, the first of the season in the city, had arrived overnight and although the temperature had risen marginally during the morning, the wind was penetrating and the possibility of light snow forecast for the late evening. "So here I am, Kate!" he went on, arms in a gesture of mock surrender. "Here at the harridan's bidding. Can you prove your historian's credentials by giving me a personal guided tour?" He smiled expectantly.

"Absolutely not," Catherine said, "at least not right now. Although you're welcome to join one I'm about to give to a couple who've turned up late and missed their earlier scheduled slot."

Sam shrugged as if unimpressed by the suggestion. She glanced up at the face of the grandfather clock – *circa 1850 mahogany longcase clock, from the family home of Harriet Howe* – "or you can wait an hour or so when I'll be entirely free. We usually close at 5, but I can keep the house open late for you if you would like. Or just roam on your own. We're only a town house on four floors, everything is well labelled and the guidebook is pretty informative, you'll find."

"Ah yes," he said, pushing his glasses into place and reading from it aloud. *Amongst her contemporaries and friends was the social reformer Henrietta Barnett as well as –*" He broke off as if mildly bored. "Actually, I was hoping to be spoiled with some personal attention. Just one to one, as it were. I'm not really the museum type and will probably give up if left to my own resources or just one of a group. But of course, I've no right to expect special treatment just because we're neighbours and somehow both been press-ganged into this street party business. On the other hand, I wouldn't dream of asking you to stay late on a Saturday evening just for me." He waved her away as if despatching her to other concerns and turned towards the gilt-edged framed portrait of a very young Harriet Howe, – *painted on the occasion of her first marriage in 1873 to Charles Henry Kerslake (died 1880)* – hanging next to the clock. Catherine paused on the bottom stair.

"It's fine, staying late, I mean. I'm often here well after closing time to get up to date with things especially if it's been a busy day. Like today, in fact. Besides, I usually stay until the cleaners have finished and that won't be much before 6."

Sam smiled broadly. "I like the sound of that," he said. "Tell you what, I'll just slip away for an hour or so, find something else to do until you're free for me." Rapidly, he buttoned up his coat again, his hand already on the door to leave. "A personal Saturday evening tour with the museum's expert sounds just the job."

"I am not an expert, I can assure you."

"We'll find out later, shall we? Five o'clock it is, Kate. In the meantime, I'll go and find myself some coffee. And thank you."

Catherine watched him leave, taking the three steps down to the pavement in one go, pausing by the railings for a moment to tie a shoelace. The streetlights were already on, the early December afternoon shifting slickly into the premature darkness of the winter's evening. She turned and swiftly climbed the stairs to find the couple waiting for her.

They spent an hour touring the house. Sam was a rewarding visitor, commenting constantly on items displayed, examining correspondence, books, furniture, asking pertinent questions that suggested a genuine interest. Catherine felt both flattered and relieved although was unsure why his opinion should matter to her.

"Please tell me if I'm boring you," she said as he examined the copy of a letter Harriet Howe had written to The Times concerning the urgent need for better housing for London's poor at the end of the 19th century. "I can be rather obsessive, assume everyone finds her life story as fascinating as I do. But of course, she was remarkable."

Sam said, "Four marriages did you say? She sounds most remarkable."

"Unlucky too. She was widowed four times. But at least each marriage made her progressively richer so you could say she was pragmatic in the choices she made. She came from a relatively modest background – her father was some sort of middle-ranking clerk in the city so she certainly was not born into money – but she was a very wealthy woman by the time she died in 1940."

"And no children?"

"No children. Although you can see in her letters references to numerous nephews and nieces and godchildren. Perhaps she married mainly for the purpose of enriching herself for the sake of her philanthropic passions and causes. She clearly didn't wallow in the state of widowhood and seemed to reinvent herself every decade or so, took up a new concern, and embraced whatever that happened to be."

"She sounds formidable," Sam said, "yet I'm ashamed to say I'd never heard of her before. Should I have done?" He followed Catherine up the stairs to the top floor and the library and reading room.

Catherine shrugged. "She was a woman for a start. So not an obvious candidate for the history books or even a statue, come to that. And it's true that she allied herself with so many causes, a finger in every needy pie, as it were, so perhaps was not easily defined. There's clear evidence that she fell out with a lot of people, wasn't the easiest to please and grew impatient if progress wasn't swift enough on one of her campaigns. And without doubt she gained some notoriety from her numerous marriages."

"Hardly fair. Not exactly living a decadent life, after all. She clearly spent her husbands' money philanthropically."

Sam sat down at one of the tables in the reading room, pulled out a chair for Catherine.

"But she failed to embrace the ideal of the Angel in the House so considered close to scandalous in some quarters. She had formidable ambition and courage, of course, when you think of the opposition she found. And she's an important figure for social historians, involved in so many reforming movements. Prisons, housing, suffrage, you name it. Even the way she lost her husbands is relevant because it highlights for us—" Catherine stopped abruptly, self-conscious of her manner. "Now I am being a complete bore. Far too serious and intense. I've lectured you endlessly for one day. I'm so sorry."

Sam shook his head. He leaned forward, resting elbows on the table, hands under his chin as if to concentrate more fully on what she had to tell him then just as swiftly stood up, started to roam the small room as if suddenly restlessness.

"Not at all, Kate. Quite the opposite, in fact. It's all fascinating. Although you've probably exhausted the capacity of my brain to remember anything more for today. Shall we save the rest for another time?" He placed the guidebook in his jacket pocket with some deliberation. "Bedtime reading for me for a week, I promise. Because I do intend to come back for another visit." They headed for the steep staircase linking the four floors of the house. "And you probably have no idea how refreshing it is to attach my mind to something different for a day. I can feel rather overwhelmed at times by – shall we say domestic concerns? Responsibilities? As if there is no world beyond the demands and indignities of my poor beloved patient. Not that I would have it any other way, naturally. It's not as if Lyddie has chosen to be as she is. She was always the most independent and self-sufficient woman so to find herself trapped in this way by – sorry, now it's my turn to apologise for going on and on." He touched Catherine's shoulder as they reached the second-floor landing, looking embarrassed as if regretting the confidence. Rapidly, he changed the subject. How long had she worked at the house? Were finances a constant problem, maintaining such a building in central London? How many people did the museum employ? Catherine answered, at the same time wondering if his interest was genuine or merely conjured as a suitable distraction from the weight of his daily concerns. He was dressed casually yet carefully as if there was a certain consciousness in his choice of black polo neck sweater, dark trousers, grey scarf. A satchel type leather bag over one shoulder. She watched him as he took his time studying the extensive charts on the wall placing the events of Harriet Howe's life within a historical context. The place was deserted now, even the cleaners finished, and their voices echoed back at them in the stillness of the house. Catherine collected her coat and bag from her office, checked locked doors and alarms and came back to find Sam standing staring out at the dark, dank winter's evening as if loathe to leave. Suddenly aware of her, he swiftly shrugged his arms into his coat and wrenched open the door, holding it while she turned out lights, set a final alarm.

"Do you have to rush off anywhere right now, Kate?" he said as they began to walk through side streets towards the main road. "I'm sure you have all sort of plans for Saturday night so please don't feel at all obliged to keep me company any longer." He looked a little uncertain as if expecting a reproach from her.

"Actually, I was thinking about a film," she said tentatively, "there's one I've been meaning to see. But it isn't important. Nothing booked. Not important at all."

He stopped abruptly in his stride, turned to her.

"Only I was wondering if you'd keep me company for just a little while longer. If you wouldn't mind, that is. A cup of coffee for half an hour or so, perhaps? No, not coffee, it's too late for that. What am I thinking? A drink. A much better idea. Of course. A drink. Is there anywhere close by we could go?"

There was a pub two streets away that Catherine knew, tucked into one of the side roads between Clerkenwell and Holborn that was rarely busy until later on Saturday evenings. Sam carried two glasses of wine over to their table in the corner. The only other occupants of the place were solitary drinkers absorbed, apparently, by their thoughts.

"This is very good of you, joining an old man for a drink like this. Our daughter, Polly, has taken Lyddie to Kingston to do some shopping today. Christmas and all that, I think. And she said she'd stay on for a couple of hours, cook her a meal, to give me a break. Seems a pity not to make the most of my freedom. But I have to admit to being something of a stranger in London these days. My memories of it are so long in the past."

"You used to live here?" Catherine asked.

"Oh, not really," Sam said dismissively, turning to his glass. "No, never, in fact. But I did work here for a while, as a young man. Briefly. All a very long time ago now, of course, and places change so, don't they?"

"Perhaps. Although what I find comforting about London is how little it changes in essential ways. At least that's how it seems to me. Of course, there's constant reinvention, an area has a new face, tries to shed its previous identity in pursuit of improvement. But the original is still there if you look for it.

The essential bones of the place. It's like layers and layers of wallpaper stuck over the supportive plasterwork of the room."

"I don't even recognise some places now. No memory of them at all."

"There has been massive development over the past decade or two," Catherine conceded. "Canary Wharf for a start. Docklands. And the building never stops, it's true. More high office blocks, new shopping centres, regeneration – and of course now with the Olympic Games coming to London in 2012 – but I still like the thought that Harriet Howe would be able to find her way home if you put her down in the middle of Gray's Inn Road or Great James Street. Still find her way to what was once her own front door."

Sam traced the rim of his glass with one finger.

"Lyddie and I have always been rural creatures. We turned our backs on city life a very long time ago. But now, well, needs must. Proximity to doctors, hospitals. And Polly, of course. Most of all Polly." He drank steadily and seemed so deep in thought that Catherine was surprised when he suddenly asked, "But you, Kate, you've always lived in London?"

"Mostly," she said. "I grew up in the suburbs."

"Where?"

"South East," she said, "half an hour or so out of Victoria."

"Sorry," Sam said, "I interrupted. A bad habit of mine, as Lyddie used to point out." He smiled ruefully.

"I've always worked here too and had a flat in Archway at one time. Although for the last few years I've lived out in Hertfordshire. A place called Bevington." She paused, anticipating Sam's next question. Inevitably, he asked,

"And what's brought you to Miller Street?"

She delivered the facts to him. Baldly, as free of embellishment as she could, adding simply,

"So then I left Bevington. There seemed no reason to stay."

She had become used to a range of reactions when she spoke of Eddie, at one end of the scale excessive, claustrophobic sympathy whilst at the other something closer to resentment as if the tragedy impinged unfairly on people's composure and equilibrium. Sam, however, said nothing, then shook his head, touched her hand for a moment, picked up his glass and drank until it was nearly empty. She was overwhelmingly grateful for his silence.

Eventually, he said, "I should have bought a bottle," indicating the dregs in their two glasses. "But you'll let me get you another glass at least? You're not in a hurry to go somewhere, I hope. That film you mentioned?"

He was on his feet before Catherine had a chance to protest or reach for her bag to pay her round. She watched him at the bar, aware of feeling gratified by his desire for her company, although initially she had intended to use her planned film as an excuse for a brief drink, a swift departure. She knew her ingrained habits, her instinctive response to spontaneous gestures, the residual retreat of the painfully shy child, the self-conscious adolescent. Sam returned with two more glasses. Nuts. Crisps.

"I don't think I had lunch," he said in explanation, beginning to break into packets. "I suppose we could have had dinner instead of just a drink, but it simply didn't occur to me. I'm a bit out of touch with social niceties, perhaps."

"No, really," Catherine said, "it's still early – a drink is fine."

"Of course. Good." He ate steadily through the packet of crisps, most of the bag of peanuts and Catherine waited for the conversation to return to Eddie. Curiosity about a fatal car accident, she had found, was rarely swiftly satisfied. But instead Sam began to talk of Miller Street's centenary celebrations, of two further meetings at Frances Chater's flat that he had failed to attend. Catherine had been to one of them and had met a few of the other residents of the road who had agreed to be co-opted onto the committee.

"They were all a little frightening, if I'm honest," she said, thinking of the group gathered in Frances' flat, offering their expertise. Each had appeared confidently emphatic as if their value to the whole enterprise was indisputable. She had felt invisible, had said little, but at the same time had been grateful for the sense of anonymity. "Friendly enough, but I rather got the feeling of the event being lifted from our hands. Or it could have been if Frances was not quite so ..."

"Indomitable. Insistent," Sam offered, "overbearing."

"Possibly. Yes, I'm sure you're right. Even so, she knows how to stand her ground, you have to give her that. She was careful to remind everyone several times that she was the one who came up with the idea of the street party in the first place."

"Lyddie and I have done our best to avoid her."

"I'm sure she's well-meaning if in rather an insensitive and intrusive kind of way."

"Self-righteous, more like. But take no notice of me, Kate. Lyddie and I have always been rather wrapped up in each other and our own lives, I suppose, mutually sufficient or something and always so busy. Lydia had her art and there was a smallholding, both in Scotland and then in Cornwall as well as my day job doing various tech things at various times. Living so close to a big community has been an alarming change for us. Or at least for me. I can no longer be clear on what anything is like for Lyddie, of course." Catherine, wishing to reflect his reticence over Eddie, said nothing, but Sam seemed to want to talk. "Losing the ability to communicate the way she has – her speech has slowly declined and now there's virtually nothing left of it – it's appallingly cruel. Both for her and for me. I no longer know what she's feeling. Not in any real sense. I see her anger, sometimes, or perhaps it's frustration, and occasionally she still smiles. At Polly, in particular. Yes, she always smiles at Polly. But there's no way of telling if she can think anymore. How do I know if she's even thinking? It's a disease you wouldn't invent even for your worst enemy. Possibly for the tyrants of the world, child murderers, leaders of genocides, but for normal, law-abiding, loving, passionate people like my wife? No. It's too absurd." He fished a final crisp from the near-empty packet, screwed it up in one fist and found a smile. "I am so sorry, Catherine, this is hardly providing you with a genial Saturday night post-work drink. Forgive my outpouring. No doubt it sounds far too much like self-pity."

"Not at all," she said inadequately.

"And part of it is, of course. Self-pity, I mean. That's a terrible admission when you think of my wife's suffering, but there you are. I'm not a good man. The flaws are legion." He broke off, picked up his glass. "But actually," he went on after a moment or so, "I find I've settled into city living quicker than I expected. Much to my considerable surprise. It was a bit of a shock at first, swapping endless rural views for bricks and mortar, but it has its compensations, I'm finding. Plenty of places to go for some distraction. Decent pubs everywhere you look instead of having to trek miles to find a half reasonable one. And there are the galleries, of course. I'm still hoping there's time to take Lyddie to a few before it becomes too difficult. She was an art student in London, you see. Before I knew her, but nevertheless, the place is firmly in her past and we thought it might help, me and Polly. Stimulate something, some memories."

"And you? Where did you grow up?"

Sam shifted in his seat, glanced at the large clock on the wall.

"Oh, that was too long ago to remember. I'm terribly old, you see. And it was just a place, really. A dull, anonymous place where nothing ever happened. That's the best that can be said about all that. It's Spain, then Scotland and Cornwall that hold my past. Our past."

"I know Cornwall a little – Scotland, hardly at all."

"We were in the north-east. Remote, very beautiful, but unforgiving, long winters."

"And Cornwall? Eddie – my late husband – loved Cornwall so we had several brief holidays there, long weekends, that sort of thing. Usually, Eddie would suddenly have a desperate urge to be beside the sea and we'd pile into the car on a Friday night after work and drive like crazy to get there by midnight. We took a cottage a couple of times, somewhere near Fowey, I think. Another time it was The Lizard. But all a while ago now." Catherine's recall was partial, censored, she knew. In truth, such impromptu weekend trips had been qualified by Friday night traffic jams on the M4, squabbles over his excessive speed followed by a disregard for a punctual return on Monday morning when they had argued about the need to be responsible to work commitments.

Still.

There had undoubtedly been snatched moments of joy, forceful markers of intense happiness that clung on in memory, refused to disappear. Perhaps that was all that mattered, the ability to recollect such evidence of love.

Sam went on. "We were inland, not far from Helston, but our place was somewhere that only an ordnance survey map makes clear. A hamlet of a hamlet. I doubt you'd know it."

"Eddie was very keen on ordnance survey maps," Catherine said. "Always insisted we stopped and bought the relevant ones for the area so we could probably have tracked you down if we'd had you in our sights!"

Sam looked alarmed for a moment and Catherine wished she had not started to talk of Eddie. Perhaps people found it inappropriate. She wondered why she found it so hard to resist his appearance, her albatross in every tale.

The pub had become more crowded since they had arrived, the bar now dense with drinkers, people scanning the room for available tables, and they had to raise their voices to be heard. Had Sam met Violet Lawrence, the young woman living upstairs in Flat 4, she asked. No, he certainly hadn't met her although he suspected that he might have caught a glimpse of someone that could have been Violet getting into a car outside Willow House one morning. Long dark hair or was it fair? Auburn, even? Catherine related her brief meeting at the kerb side, omitting the detail of the taxi fare loan that Violet had apparently forgotten. Frances Chater, however, appeared to have befriended her and had suggested to Catherine that the young woman would bring a youthful aspect to the centenary committee if she could be persuaded to join.

Outside, the evening had grown swiftly colder, a sharp night frost already setting in.

"Heading straight home?" Sam said as they walked briskly along Theobalds Road and cut down towards Kingsway. "No, of course not," he said, "there's that film of yours you're off to see."

Catherine hesitated. Suddenly, the prospect of buying a solitary ticket to the cinema seemed bleak. Yet the return to her quiet flat felt equally unattractive and she was surprised by her sudden thirst for company. It was the wine, no doubt, the ease of Sam's conversation, the Saturday evening crowds that made her desire something she could not quite define and was unfamiliar to her. In the final months of Eddie's life, tensions between them had grown to such an extent that she had rarely spent time at home with him at weekends. She had found being alone peaceable in comparison, a respite from what she saw as the sad detritus of their disintegrating marriage. Yet unwittingly her choice of such solitary behaviour had further fuelled antagonism between them as if he viewed her tacit retreat as spineless, a further lack of commitment to him if she refused to parry and spar.

After his death, she had begun to see his point.

They might, after all, have resolved matters sufficiently, patched up, mended and darned in an acceptable sort of way if she had been more combative. Who knew?

They reached the Aldwych.

Catherine said, "I think I will stay on a little longer. Before going home, I mean. I might ring a friend or see that film, perhaps. But thank you for the drink. And for enduring my lecture on Harriet Howe."

He touched her arm. For a moment, he looked as if he was going to lean forward and kiss her cheek, but then appeared to check himself as if regretting even the thought of such a gesture.

"Not at all, I enjoyed it all immensely, I can assure you. And your company, Kate, thank you so much for that," he said with some formality, "enjoy the rest of your evening."

He turned away, to be immediately swallowed by the density of pavement traffic.

Catherine thought suddenly of Alec.

If he was in London, he was unlikely to be doing anything on a Saturday night. She knew his irritation with thronging restaurants, elusive taxis and teeming cinemas and theatres that marked weekends in the capital. And it was months since they had met, since that meal at the Italian restaurant. She had intended being in touch several times to ask him over for the promised visit to her flat, one Sunday, possibly, lunch at a pub by the river, a long walk by the towpath or in one of the south London parks that she intended displaying as equal to anything his Hampstead had to offer. She wedged herself against the dark façade of a bank and found her phone at the bottom of her bag. His landline rang and rang and she imagined it resonating round his cold cavernous house. She tried his mobile which went swiftly to a messaging service. She ignored its request to leave her name, knowing Alec would recognise her missed call if he chose to do so, crossed the main road and headed somewhere without clear direction.

On the train home to Miller Street, Sam remembered his phone. He had switched it off at the museum, had chosen to forget to turn it back on at the pub and now did so with a certain reluctance.

There were four missed calls from Polly.

He closed his eyes, the sense of a mild, pleasing inebriation from two large glasses of wine drunk on an empty stomach instantly leaving him. He heard the sound as soon as he opened the front door, stepped into the hall, a kind of keening, almost musical in its drift up and down a random scale. And Polly's voice, attempting to calm, console.

"Where have you been?" she said as he appeared in the doorway of the living room, agitated, accusing. "I've been calling and calling you."

Lydia looked up at him, slowly lifted her arms towards him, like a young child, a toddler, reaching towards the safe embrace of a parent. He sank down next to her on the sofa. Gradually, her noises stilled to barely audible sounds.

"I'm sorry," he said, focusing on Lydia's face, dried tears, profound confusion in her wide-eyed stare. Her hair, he noticed now as if for the first time, was thinning so that pale lines of scalp were visible. He took her hand. She clung on fiercely although continued to look at him with bewilderment as if uncertain whether to trust.

"It was disastrous," Polly said quietly, sitting down

opposite them in the armchair. "The shopping trip, I mean. It was all fine at first, we parked easily and I got Mum in her wheelchair and she seemed happy, enjoying herself, seeing all the Christmas lights and decorations. There were carol singers in the street, by the tree, and we listened to them for a while. She was smiling, recognising the tunes, I think. Then suddenly it was as if it all became too much. We were in one of the shops, Bentall's, and of course it was quite crowded and noisy and there were a lot of people and she started—" She broke off suddenly, a catch in her voice that surprised Sam. He was unused to seeing Polly overwhelmed. She stood up, went to the window and drew the curtains rapidly against the winter night. "Sorry, didn't realise I hadn't even drawn them – I should have done it when we came in. We've been back ages. I didn't mean to snap at you, Dad. So sorry. Did you have a good day? I wanted you to. I thought we'd have a good time too. I'd looked forward to it so much, just me and Mum, but I suppose I hadn't allowed myself to realise quite how far things had changed. I felt so ashamed that I couldn't cope. Everyone was staring at us as if Mum was some freak or that I was ill-treating her in some way. She was making these strange noises, waving her hands and – well, she wanted you. At least I think she did. For reassurance. She was crying out and nothing I said or did was any good. I just couldn't calm her down."

"Too much sensory stimulation," Sam said wearily. "I believe that's the phrase. I've been told to expect it at some stage. The brain can't process so much input or something like that. Inability to handle it. I just didn't know we were quite there yet." He looked over at Polly, pale, her hands now stuffed deep into her overgrown cardigan, her feet encased in heavy boots that she would normally shed in their hall and had clearly forgotten in her distress so that her appearance looked unnaturally weighted. "I'm so sorry it had to be with you, Pol. The first time. I suppose it was testing for her, a new environment like that. She doesn't know Kingston and the unfamiliar was obviously all too much. And the crowds and artificial lighting in the shops – I should have anticipated it."

Lydia was silent now, her eyes closing every now and again as if she was close to sleep. Sam shifted a cushion behind her head and she turned her face into it away from the light. Within moments, it appeared, she was asleep. Polly went into the hall, found her coat and car keys on the floor where she had clearly dropped them in her anxiety to settle Lydia. Sam followed her out.

"Won't you stay a bit, Polly? The least I can do is cook you something to eat. To make up for being so irresponsible."

She shook her head, shrugged into her coat. She looked exhausted, her face dulled by the strain of the afternoon.

"What about your day?" she said to her father, "after all, the idea was to give you a break from all of this rather than make things far worse." She glanced back at the living room, lowered her voice although Lydia seemed settled in sleep. "The trouble is I haven't really adjusted, have I? I mean, rationally, I acknowledge she's got this ghastly disease, done my research into the progression of it. But knowing the facts is one thing. What I haven't let myself do until now is to think of its features as attaching themselves to her. To my mother. To Lydia Florence Gough. She was supposed to be immune, somehow, the miraculous exception to the rule. So, I took her to Kingston, to the shops. I wanted to have our day out, mother and daughter, and pretend that nothing had changed. Pretend at least for a few hours and behave the way we used to behave. Claw back some of those habits. Those ordinary, normal habits that you don't think about until they're gone. A ham sandwich and a coffee in some small café. A mooch around the department stores, a bit of trying on of unsuitable clothes and a pot of tea and cream slices afterwards. But I was caught out. And I felt so stupid and so cruel. To mum. For putting her in that situation, for exposing her, if you like. And do you know the worse part of it? When mum started getting distressed and making those awful noises and people were staring at us in disgust? I felt acutely embarrassed by her. Ashamed, if I'm honest."

"It's understandable," Sam said, "you mustn't blame yourself for what's only a natural reaction."

"But it's not, is it?" Polly said, moving towards the front door, "I mean, being ashamed of your sick mother is hardly a compassionate gesture."

"You were thinking of her, Pol. Or at least you were thinking of how she would have felt in the past, drawing unwanted attention to herself in that way. In fact, she might still have been feeling that, for all we know."

Sam kissed the top of her head, held her in a gruff, rough gesture of affection. She pulled away after a moment, smiled as if attempting a return to equilibrium.

"What about your day out? You had a good time?"

Sam looked vague, as if trying to recall earlier events that now felt entirely unhitched and irrelevant to the day.

"Oh yes, I suppose so. I just wandered, really. London streets and a few sights. Nothing of any importance or consequence."

Mechanically, he helped Lydia to bed. Tonight, she was biddable, submissive to his attentions when so often she resisted. She was asleep again within minutes. He had not eaten yet felt disinclined to bother with food and instead found the remains of a bottle of wine and emptied it into a large glass. Carrying it into the small room at the front of the flat, he sat in darkness for some time, staring out at the street, into the windows of the houses opposite, bright with enormous, garishly lit Christmas trees brazenly declaring festive cheer. He drew the curtains to shut it out. And then thought that maybe he should make more of an effort. Perhaps it would make Lydia happy to help him dress a tree. Or to watch him, at least. The old decorations must be somewhere, no doubt. Surely, they hadn't been thrown out in one of the culls he'd made on their possessions in the rambling Cornish house. It had always been something that Lydia had done, the tree, the decorations. He'd shifted some soil into the bottom of a bucket, wedged the fir with a stone, a log, until it was unwavering then unthinkingly left the rest to Lydia. Of course, in the past couple of years he'd taken over the cards, her handwriting increasingly illegible as her control regressed. Not that there were ever many cards to write: a couple of friends from Scotland, a few more recent Cornish acquaintances, a distant cousin on Lydia's side. He turned on the computer, gulped down the wine and sat staring blankly at the screen, the cool blue light suffusing the dark room with a strange glow. Outside, a car drew up, doors opened and slammed on a conversation that he strained to hear as if drawn to the vitality of voices. Then the car drove away and there were only footsteps on the forecourt round to the side of the house, a door opening and closing, before silence again.

Frances Chater glanced at the clock. Just gone ten. A neat pile of Christmas cards ready to be written and addressed sat on the desk in front of her yet she had no idea whether she intended sending them. After all, something signed with only her name would raise suspicion, but adding Andrew's would be inaccurate. And how many people even knew? She had told no one. His absurd dalliance with a woman some twenty-five years his junior was too humiliating to share with even the closest of acquaintances. And she was not someone who possessed the sort of confessional, female friendships so many women seemed to boast. No, silence was the best way of dealing with such a temporary, specious scenario, one that would be soon swept away and normal service resumed.

But of course she could not count on such a discreet response from Andrew.

Let alone the brazen Charlotte Prideaux. The woman was blatantly manipulative and Andrew sadly in thrall. She picked up her pen then swiftly put it down again. Perhaps she should give the whole idea of cards more consideration. After all, who would notice if theirs failed to arrive? She felt the shadow of a headache begin to throb and thought of going to bed early. There was that rather good psychological thriller from the library she was halfway through with perhaps some peppermint tea. A car pulled up outside, an engine kept running and she marginally tweaked the navy velvet curtains to see Violet Lawrence talking through the open passenger door which was soon slammed, the driver revving and disappearing rapidly down the street. Frances moved quickly to her hall, waited until she heard quick footsteps on the stairs and then opened her front door.

"Violet? Could you do with a bit of company? I don't seem to have caught up with you all week. I've got the kettle on. Or a glass of something, perhaps? As it's nearly Christmas."

Violet seemed to ignore her at first, ferreting for keys in deep pockets, then suddenly stopped, turned towards her as if considering the idea.

"Oh well, all right, Fran. Why not? If you insist. Got any Whisky? No? Gin, then, I could do with a large Gin. I've had such a terrible evening. You wouldn't believe it."

Frances smiled. "Come and pour it all out to me, Violet. I'm a late bird and never in bed before the small hours."

"And if by chance you've got anything at all to eat," Violet said, already heading through the open front door and into Frances' kitchen, "just, you know, a bit of cheese. And some bread – cheese on toast, maybe, the way you did it before with those pickles and mustard and stuff. That was really good. It's hours and hours since I've eaten and I really should have something to soak up the alcohol, you know."

She started to open cupboards, marshalled glasses, found the Gin. Frances retrieved Violet's large bag from the floor, her long black scarf, coat and shoes, tidied them into the hall cupboard.

"You'll find a new bottle of tonic in the fridge, Violet. And some lemons. Now, Cheddar or Gruyere? With a poached egg on top? I always think that adds an extra touch."

8

Catherine drove out of London on a road that was a ghost of its normal self.

Midday on December 25th, a time when most people who were going to travel for the holiday had already done exactly that. Beth has taken considerable persuasion.

"Come the day before. You don't want to wake up alone on what won't be the easiest of Christmases."

"Better than last year," Catherine had reminded her. "Eddie had only just—"

"Even so. We've got people coming in for drinks on Christmas Eve, neighbours from the village, and it would be nice for you to meet them."

"No. It won't. I'll be an embarrassment."

"Of course you won't. That's ridiculous."

"Well, if not an embarrassment, an awkwardness. An aberration."

"Only if you think of yourself in that way."

"Because it's true. I am."

Beth had reluctantly agreed to her plan to drive down the next day.

Eddie had adored Christmas. For a man who had always shunned the idea of a family, children, his transition into a convivial, generous host for the season was surprising, Catherine had always thought. His planning would begin in early December and the enormous tree he always insisted upon brought home from the local garden centre with a certain ceremony and dressed with lavish care. Gifts were extravagant, both in cost and in reach, behaving like a benevolent lord of the manor rewarding annual service to the underlings. Culinary traditions were scrupulously observed and Midnight service had been obligatory although more as a social than a sacramental event. In the first few years of their marriage, Catherine had allowed herself to be swayed from her mildly cynical view of the season to a more wholehearted indulgence and watched the kitchen fill up with bottles of champagne, Burgundy, Brandy, Tawny Port, maturing stilton. At the time, Eddie's salary from the advertising agency had been adequate to meet the hefty credit card bills that had duly arrived in the New Year and Catherine had felt it unnecessary to point out the excess of his gestures. Once he had parted from the agency, in the acrimonious way that she was to learn he always severed connections with viable sources of income, she had become less acquiescent. For Eddie had seen no need to curb Christmas habits simply on the grounds that his choice to go freelance and pursue random, spontaneous ventures had rendered his income at best minimal, at worst, entirely absent. Catherine's salary from the museum had barely coped with their average month to month living expenses and certainly could not tolerate the pressure of Eddie's feckless festive spending. She had urged restraint. They had argued. He had accused her of being mercenary. A Scrooge figure ruled by the head rather than the heart. He was being ostentatious, she claimed. Each became entrenched. And, inevitably, began to occupy positions more extreme than either had ever intended: Catherine, parsimonious in her corner, ever more distant from spendthrift Eddie in his.

But still. Memory can be selective.

And now, switching lanes for no other reason than boredom

with the empty stretch of dull motorway ahead, Catherine selects. And there is Eddie, clutching a bottle, a green carrier bag, arriving on her doorstep on Christmas Eve, that narrow slab of pavement in Archway and the red front door leading up the narrow stairs to her flat, the floor of the square living room scattered with wrapping paper and unwrapped gifts and ribbons and tags that he manages to step around, find a chair. They have known each other less than a week. Already she is convinced that she is in love with this mildly raffish looking man, has tried vainly, in fact, to persuade herself otherwise since instinctively she senses he is an irrational, unwise choice for anyone seeking stability. Which, after all, perhaps, she is. For there is nothing like Christmas to alert the doggedly single, childless woman to her state, claw and nibble away at her choice, force her to examine the strength of her resolve.

"I'm surprised to find you here," he says, looking around her room, picking up cards from her mantelpiece and reading them as if they are displayed for his inspection. "Thought you'd be off with extensive friends and family by now."

"Tomorrow," Catherine says, "my sister's house in the Mendip Hills. I go tomorrow morning."

"Good," Eddie says. "That means you can spend this evening with me."

He finds her kitchen, her fridge, puts the bottle of champagne to chill, arranges slices of the smoked salmon he ferrets from his bag, conjures an exotic fresh fruit salad from mango, papaya, guava. By the time he leaves the next day, he appears to have accommodated himself to her small flat so that it does not seem strange to see him opening the cupboard to find the tea in the morning, seeking out her pale blue mugs, sitting opposite her at the table.

"No tree," he says censoriously, glancing into the sitting room as he pulls on his coat, takes his scarf from the hook in the hall, "everyone should have a tree at Christmas." And she finds herself apologising, promising to do better another year. "I'll make sure you do," he says as he rapidly takes the stairs down to the front door. "If a thing's worth doing ..."

And he runs back, takes her hand and kisses it with absurd formality given the intimacy of the previous night, the early morning. "Thank you, Catherine. Cat? Kate? We'll have to see. I haven't decided what to call you yet."

She left the motorway early, felt in need of slower, mud-encrusted roads, sodden fields, rabbits and perhaps a partridge or two. The landscape swiftly became rural as she diverted onto back routes she had found on previous journeys. In the past year she had seen more of Beth than in the last five when their lives had been very separate. Several weekends she had driven down to Somerset in need of respite from house clearance and the implosion that a sudden death brings. Henry, her brother-in-law, had been practical, helpful, and she had been grateful for his steady, sensible approach.

Eddie again.

Catherine slows down to gingerly pass two riders and their horses in the narrow road and he is there once more. Eddie at Beth and Henry's festive dining table eight or nine years before, at his most exuberant, endearing, enchanting the younger children with his games, his performance as a kind of genial Christmas spirit. Even Henry, in general patently irritated by Eddie's mercurial behaviour, is amused. And their mother, Catherine sees her now, dressed in her dark maroon velvet with a string of jet black beads at her neck, laughs at some foolishness of his, lets him top up her glass from one of the bottles of expensive claret that he's pressed on Henry. And Beth's words as the two of them fiddle with a steaming pudding and whipped cream in the kitchen, warm the mince pies and search for the brandy butter that no one will eat. *Surely he'd like children? Eddie's so good with ours. He's a natural. It's not too late, you know, for the two of you to become parents.* But Eddie is adamant, has always been resolute. And Catherine tries to explain to her sister that she understands his reasons, has accepted his stance from the very start. Yet privately she is unable to comprehend fully his rejection of the idea of fatherhood for he is never willing to articulate it with any clarity.

And she remembers now why the horses trawled Eddie back again.

That year, or another possibly, for they went to Beth two or three times for Christmas, Eddie decides he wants to try riding. He sees Annabel's riding boots, the only child who has taken up the hobby, and wants to go to the stables with her on Boxing Day and find a horse to ride. They try to curb his enthusiasm, tell him it is not possible simply to turn up and expect to find a convenient mount, but Annabel is pliable and the stable owner is charmed. She lets Eddie ride her own horse around the paddock for twenty minutes, but Eddie is soon bored and wants to go out on the road, across the fields. He grows exasperated and difficult when he is refused and spends the evening insulting the stables for its cautious attitude. The next morning, he can hardly get out of bed for stiff limbs, but he is able to joke about it and, his temper restored, challenges them all to a five-mile cross country walk to a local village pub. They oblige him. Toby, only three or four years of age, frets in his pushchair; Eddie releases him, lifts him high onto his shoulders and the two of them stride ahead, Toby's scarlet woollen hat an indelible, robin redbreast-like marker in the distance.

★★★

Frances woke late. She consoled herself that already it was eleven o'clock so that a portion of the day was conveniently spent. Midnight service, followed by a pointless exercise of cleaning the kitchen then a determined hour or two of reading, meant that she had not been in bed before three. Or close on. She made herself coffee, toast, and sat by the window overlooking Miller Street to eat breakfast. She saw Catherine Wells leave, first filling her car with wrapped presents, a large holdall, heavy coat, boots, stowing them all in the boot before driving off towards midday. That was clearly her gone for a few days, then. Ten minutes later, it was Sam Gough's turn and that invalid wife of his, Lydia, getting into their car, Sam taking ages fiddling with things. Her seat belt, her scarf, taking off her coat, arranging something at her feet. Looking as if his patience was only just being held in check. Poor woman, it wasn't as if she chose to be so dependent. Back to their apartment he went, just to the hall, probably, because within a few seconds he was out again, putting in a couple of carrier bags, bottles probably, judging by the care he took in positioning them. Then they were off, to the daughter, no doubt, a short drive for them around the south circular to spend the day. Violet had left three days before. Her parents' place, she'd told Frances, somewhere near Hereford, she'd been vague on the details. She'd pulled a face that spoke boredom, resentment, even. Family stuff, she'd added, rolling her eyes. Frances had sympathised, listened to Violet's complaints about her strange, unsociable brother, her over solicitous mother, sitting in Frances' kitchen eating the sandwich she'd made her, accepting a second to carry back to her own flat. *Why not stay in London?* Frances had suggested as she layered gammon and Gouda into slices of wholemeal bread, *you're a grown woman, Violet, and have a right to your own Christmas plans, surely. You have so many friends. And there's no need to be alone here because, by chance, I am planning to stay at home over the holiday just for a change so you're most welcome to join me. I could cook for us, even, and—* Violet had stood up at that point as if she had not been listening, shrugged, yawned. Held her hand out for the sandwich Frances was placing on one of her pink plates. *Oh, it'll be a bit of a laugh, really. Loads to eat and drink. Too much bother making a fuss about it. It's just Christmas, after all. Who cares?*

Now Willow House was empty, the fabric of the place felt hollow and Frances moved quickly to the bathroom, to throw herself into activity to deflect reflection on the matter.

The brief vigil two days before had been a mistake.

Almost too much for her to bear.

The train at Victoria had been predictably crowded, luggage racks dense with suitcases and parcels and loaded bags and she had felt close to a sense of panic, sitting among people whose excitement and anticipation felt tangible. She had not stayed long. Once she had seen the tree, set in its annual position in the front window of the house, facing onto Pilgrim square, noted that the usual decorations were in place – those expensive gold baubles they'd bought at that interiors shop several years before, the silver glass-like trinkets, the angel figures she had found at a place in the Lanes – she had walked down to the seafront, sat on one of the hard benches and had waited until the biting wind off the sea, the rain that threatened sleet in its menace, had driven her back up the hill to the station again. One last glimpse at the house and she saw that the tree lights were now on. A new set, she noted, not the muted, ivory lights they had used for years, but brighter, multi-coloured little bulbs, garish and insistent in their glare. She had not been surprised.

Charlotte Prideaux was, after all, a very garish and insistent sort of woman.

She had the day planned. A walk, a very long walk until it began to get dark then home to cook the meal she had planned, that good bottle of wine and perhaps some television. In the end, the cards had been signed as usual from both of them in case circumstances had changed: a last-minute coming to his senses, an emergence from his folly, breaking free from *La Belle Dame Sans Merci*. She had stacked them neatly on her desk, awaiting a late posting so that friends would remain entirely unaware of the disruptions of the past year. They would open the card from Frances and Andrew, read the message she always liked to include along the lines of *Andrew still working hard with the dental practice, refusing even to consider slowing down and I'm still holding the fort as his practice manager – planning on Provence for next summer – hope all well and we really must do something about meeting in the new year!* But the thought of even referring to her mother's death in April had been intolerable. And not because she particularly grieved for the elderly woman who had lingered impatiently in her dank house in Worthing, claiming to the string of carers and district nurses that she was *well past her sell-by date* and an unnecessary drain on the health service. No. It was not the memory of her death that pained Frances, but the funeral service that had followed it on that windy and wet spring day, windswept, downtrodden daffodils in the cemetery, enormous black umbrellas attempting to shield the scattering of mourners. And Andrew, supposedly there in support of her, but hovering at the edge of the group, needlessly checking his phone. Then suddenly that other car pulling up and Andrew moving towards it, towards the woman getting out, thinking himself unobserved, hidden by the black hearse, his own self-absorption.

Frances was surprised to find so many others out walking. Many with dogs, of course, a large collection of parents with small children trying out new tricycles, dawdling family groups slowly crossing the common as if anxious to spin out time until the next meal. But there were also people simply alone, like her. And not just the homeless huddled into the shelter of shop doorways along the high street or curled up beneath contraptions of cardboard near the river. There was, evidently, no shame or stigma in choosing to be alone on Christmas Day and she began to relax, to attempt festive greetings with anyone who willingly caught her eye. She avoided as far as she could the residential streets that felt treacherous with their holly wreathed front doors and well-lit rooms redolent with complacent happiness. She snaked from one south London common or bit of green to the next, striding out, determined to stall her mind from darker reflections, running through the carols from the midnight service the night before, and even humming aloud in a subdued voice. *Hark the herald ... How still we see thee ... Stood a lowly cattle shed ... Angels from the realms ...* By the time she reached the ultimate point of her planned walk, she was tired, very tired, and wished she had been less ambitious in her route. For now there was no option but to retrace her steps and her attempts to remain positive, to resist self-pity, swiftly waned. Inevitably, it was growing dark and the lack of any sun since midday was hastening an early dusk. She wanted only to be back at Willow House, however unwelcoming its emptiness, wanted only to give in to the sense of profound loneliness that suddenly overwhelmed her.

Then she remembered her present.

And she allows herself, walking back along main roads, the commons and the parks seeming unwise in the dulling light, to think of Andrew unwittingly opening the carefully packaged gift. She pictures Charlotte Prideaux handing Andrew the brown paper parcel with a Brighton postmark and *A CHRISTMAS GIFT FROM A PATIENT* printed in capitals. No doubt Charlotte watches him with mild interest when he finds the red box tied with festive ribbon and opens it to delve down through layers of tissue paper, eventually revealing the exquisite extravagance and softness of pale grey cashmere.

A sweater in his size, his preferred style.

Frances imagines Andrew's face as he spies the small gift card she has hidden in the folds of wool, bearing her simple message. *From Frances. With love. With the love that endures and forgives.* She tries to take the scene further, compels him to look harshly at Charlotte Prideaux, to curse her presence in his living room.

Their living room, in the matrimonial home of Andrew and Frances Chater.

She propels him into the hall, urges him to pick up the phone, to reach out to her in her first-floor apartment in Willow House. *It's all a dreadful mistake,* he will say, *I love you. Come home immediately. I am so sorry. So terribly, terribly sorry. How can you possibly forgive me? How can I have been such a fool?* And her charade is so intense that when she reaches the top of Miller Street, she finds herself rushing to the end of it, fumbling for her keys so she can race up the staircase, open her front door onto the phone that will, no doubt, be ringing for her.

But of course, it is not.

And the darkness of the flat, its silence, puncture her fantasy, her grasp of hopeful expectation. The neat pile of unposted Christmas cards glares at her from her desk. All she can do is sweep them carelessly to the floor, slide into a chair and weep like a lost child.

***

Polly stands in the middle of her small living room in Deptford, her feet deep in discarded wrapping paper and torn ribbons and bows.

"I have something to tell you," she says, "an announcement, as it were." Her broad smile is reassuring. Sam looks at her

117

expectantly then glances at Lydia who is settled in the armchair by the Christmas tree.

"Well?" he says cheerfully, "good news, I hope?" Promotion, he thinks, she's gone for a headship somewhere. A new boyfriend, perhaps. "We only want to hear cheerful news today."

Polly nods her head then pauses for calculated dramatic effect. Her blue woollen dress, matching blue woollen tights remind Sam of the child of ten, hair always wavy, never entirely neat, and he feels overwhelming tenderness for the memory.

"I am going to have a baby," Polly says and moves swiftly to sit by Lydia's side. She cups her face in her hands. "Mum, do you understand me? There's going to be a baby."

★★★

They sat at the table in Beth's big kitchen amongst the remains of the day: crumbled mince pies, naked slices of Christmas cake stripped of their icing and marzipan coats, bowls of half-eaten plum pudding. In one of the other rooms, Henry was insisting on a game. The younger children complied. The older retreated to their phones, repossessed their childhood bedrooms. Henry's great aunt was asleep by the log fire in the living room, a cat on her lap. Beth poured pale tea.

"I forgot to tell you," Catherine said, "Robert's leaving. Robert at the museum? The curator. Off to New York with his wife for a couple of years at least – she's got a two-year contract over there, I believe, some prestigious offer she couldn't or didn't want to turn down. And I suspect he's making the most of the chance. I'm sure there could be all sorts of opportunities for him to advance his career over there."

Catherine had not been surprised when Robert had eventually told her about his resignation just before they closed for Christmas. He had been uncommunicative about a couple of trips he had made to New York and had resisted talking about development plans for the following year as if his interest was engaged elsewhere. Beth sipped hot tea, steam clouding the reading glasses she had forgotten to remove.

"Will you apply for his job? You should, you know. It would give you a new purpose. Something to—"

Catherine interrupted. "Something to fill a vacuum in my life, you mean. A new direction?" and immediately regretted her sarcasm. Beth was simply thoughtful, concerned. She tried again. "Robert says I should apply. He's been very kind and says that in his view I'm the right person for the job, that there's nothing he does that I couldn't handle and he'll put my name forward if I agree. But of course, the trustees will have in mind someone far more high flying with impressive academic credentials. Although in truth, the salary is too low to attract someone like that and we're not a particularly glamorous or dynamic outfit as far as museums go."

"But it's ideal for you, surely," Beth said, "I can't see why these trustees would even look elsewhere. It's an obvious solution just staring them in the face."

Beth had the habit of removing obstacles from situations. She encountered potential conflict with a clear if simplistic vision that did not even notice the quarrel and therefore as a result lived blithely. Catherine envied her sister's disposition and told her as much. Beth shrugged her shoulders, poured more tea, picked up a chocolate that had strayed from its box onto the table, ate it.

"I'll think about it," Catherine said cautiously, "applying, I mean. Definitely consider the idea."

And some hours later, she wakes in the night in the small spare bedroom that never quite loses its shades of the nursery and thinks that Beth is probably right. She knows she is attached to the Harriet Howe museum in a way that she would deny to anyone who might suggest it. She has always disapproved of people who allow themselves to be defined by their job, considering it at best vain, at worse, desperate. Yet she finds consolation in the place, a sense of solace in perpetuating the woman, her commendable aims and purpose as she negotiated her way through the entrenched attitudes and oppression she found during her life. The absolute darkness of the room suddenly feels claustrophobic. Catherine is unused to the obscurity of the countryside and Beth and Henry's house is detached, set well back from a quiet lane in land of an acre or more. She sits up, grapples for a light and studies the frieze of nursery rhymes that still decorates the wall: little Miss Muffet on her tuffet, Jack Horner in his corner, Humpty Dumpty having his great fall. She stares long and hard at Jack and Jill rushing up their hill with an empty pail. And she wonders if she is clutching at this promotion out of cowardice rather than genuine ambition. If it is simply a ruse to disguise a lack of direction, an uncertainty about what she really wants now. But even if it is just that, does it really matter? Most actions in any life are no doubt propelled not so much by profound conviction as by expediency, convenience.

At least for people not as admirable and compelled by moral outrage as Harriet Howe and her like.

The cow is jumping over a huge yellow moon next to Miss Muffet's spider. She pulls back the curtain a little so that any slight light in the night sky can relieve the darkness of the room, turns off the light and attempts to sleep again.

9

On Boxing Day, Sam gave in to the wheelchair sitting in the hall.

"It's part of our lives now, Lyddie, if we want to go out, no more trying to make those reluctant legs of yours work," he said as he helped her into her warmest coat, shuffled her feet into sensible, sturdy boots and settled her in the chair. "And at least we can go further with this contraption. What about the river this afternoon? Always something going on there to watch."

Lydia nodded compliantly. Her mood was affable, or at least not hostile. He was grateful. Signs of any affection from her were increasingly rare and although he knew that her inflexible glacial stare was involuntary, her facial muscles now too stubborn to respond to impulse, it was hard not to be hurt by it. As if she were at best indifferent to him, at worst, repelled.

He headed them cautiously down Miller Street, aiming to feel positive rather than seeing the use of the wheelchair as a sign of bleak inevitability. The day was overcast, but dry and there was no reason for them not to spend at least an hour out in the air. The casual company of strangers, on the common, by the river, was welcome on a day which promised little other diversion than the inevitable screen. Even leaving Lydia alone in a room for more than a few moments to go to the kitchen or the small front room he thought of as his office became tense

121

since he was made equally anxious by her silence as by her slightest sound, her dependence so absolute. At least outside, with Lydia in her chair, his thoughts could roam with greater ease. He skirted the north side of the common, halted them for a few moments to watch a father with a child negotiate the complexities of a new two-wheeler, a sibling experiment with a scooter, then pushed on in the direction of the river.

He was unsure whether Lydia had absorbed Polly's news. Perhaps her relative calm today signalled that she had and, unlike Sam, was able to focus entirely on its joy rather than dissect the implications. It was what, after all, he would expect of Lydia.

There's going to be a baby, Polly had said, and immediately he had badgered her with questions, explanations, rather than focusing on her obvious delight. Lydia, if she had still been capable of speech, would have quietly silenced Sam, placed her arm on his and insisted that they listen to Polly. He had tried to check himself, suppress his disquiet. No, there was no partner involved, Polly had told them both evenly, equably. The decision to have a child was reasoned and long considered rather than a chance event and she hoped that her parents would understand and support her in that choice. Sam had been astounded, not so much by her announcement – although that, too, he had to admit, had initially confounded him – but by Polly's composure, her certainty and capability that were so superior to his own. She had explained at length her careful, methodical planning for the pregnancy and subsequent birth as if she had anticipated his objections and was forestalling them. He had shied away from details of sperm banks and donor choice that she had appeared willing to share, asking only whether her future child might feel deprived, cheated by the lack of a named, natural father. Polly had paused long enough for him to realise his error and he had been humbled by her response. *You have always been my father,* she had said simply, *not some man mum knew fleetingly and swiftly disappeared from our lives before I was even born.* Later that evening, driving home to Miller Street, Sam had felt bereft. Lydia sat beside him, incapable of responding to his need to talk. He had managed a kind of monologue for a while as they drove along the south circular, something along the lines of *Well, Polly's always known her own mind. It's not what we would have wanted for her, of course, what we had in mind, but we're a different generation, Lyddie, we must admit that.* And he had even taken her part, voiced the sort of things he knew she would have said in return if she had been able. *If it's what she wants, what will make her happy, we will support her, won't we? And a child. New life. That's wonderful. Absolutely wonderful.* But soon he had given up the conversation, had switched on the radio to smother thought, found some easy music and before they had pulled up outside Willow House, Lydia had fallen asleep. He had sat outside for ten or fifteen minutes before he had managed to summon sufficient spur to get out of the car, lift her sleeping weight inside, thinking fleetingly of the number of times he had carried Polly as a young child, deeply asleep in her car seat in Spain, in Scotland. The past had the habit of lying glibly, at playing with time, for these occasions seemed hitched only to a handful of years ago as if intervening decades had been spent slumbering rather than living. They should have done so much more with their time when they were unconstrained, able. Polly had the right attitude. She was not waiting passively for chance to play its hand, but was reaching out, manipulating circumstance, event.

He managed an hour's walk before Lydia began to show signs of discomfort. The wind had picked up and although he was warm from the exertion of pushing her, the air was clearly biting into her skin, disturbing her. With some reluctance, he turned round, found a swifter route back to Miller Street. In another hour, the light would be gone. He had never been particularly bothered before by the short days of the season. Of course, like everyone else he would look forward to the spring, to first snowdrops, crocuses and early daffodils in Cornish hedgerows. But he had also enjoyed the darkness of winter, the permission it granted to give in to a certain hibernation. Even in Scotland, with scant hours of light for several months of the year, there had been some solace to be found as if darkness was his natural habitat. Now, however, the lack of daylight was oppressive to him. Urban streets did not even offer real obscurity, but hovered in a kind of unsatisfactory twilight that was enervating.

"Sam? And Lydia, too. How nice. A happy Christmas to the two of you!"

Self-absorbed, he was startled by the greeting as he turned the wheelchair into the forecourt of Willow House. Frances Chater swiftly deposited a black sack in the rubbish bin and came to stand close by his side so that he found it hard to continue to their front door. "A good day yesterday? I saw you go off late morning. To your daughter's, I presume. It must be a comfort to have her nearby, things being as they are."

"Thank you, yes," Sam said and concentrated on finding the door key. Frances placed her hand on Lydia's arm, patted it, the way, he thought, one might pat a Labrador.

"Good to get some air after all the festivities," she went on. "I'm just back from a walk myself as I didn't have a chance for any exercise yesterday. With friends in Twickenham all day, quite a gathering, actually. In fact, I was only home just before you were last night. I couldn't help noticing your car as my friends – well, to be exact, Charles, the husband of my close friend, insisted on dropping me home. And picking me up, you see, what with no transport on Christmas Day. Which was so kind. One appreciates it. Season of goodwill and all that, of course."

She stopped, breathless, as if there had been some compulsion for her to speak with great speed. He muttered something about needing to get Lydia inside, wielded more energy than was required to push the chair towards the front door.

Frances said, "I quite understand. Of course, I would invite you both up to my apartment for tea, it seems so un-neighbourly not to, what with it being Boxing Day. I've rather a good Christmas cake on the go that needs sharing as it happens. But there are the stairs so with Lydia's incapacity – well, it just isn't feasible, is it?"

He knew he was being manipulated yet it was hard to resist her skilful trap. Besides, however much Frances Chater irritated him, the prospect of conversation with someone, with anyone, would relieve the long afternoon, stave off the evening.

Within a few minutes, she had fetched her cake and installed herself on the sofa next to Lydia. As he waited for the kettle to boil in the kitchen, he heard her relentless voice, adopting a stressed manner of speech as if this would make it easier for Lydia to understand. When he carried the tray of tea into the living room, he saw that she had drawn the curtains and immediately regretted his invitation.

"I hope you don't mind?" Frances said, gesturing towards the window. "I know it's not yet four, but I think it's so much cosier on these winter days to shut the darkness out."

"I rather like to see the garden," he said curtly, "for as long as possible. Until it's entirely dark."

"I was only thinking of Lydia," she said, looking at her somewhat conspiratorially as if preferences had been expressed while he had been in the kitchen. "I do know a bit about such situations as you have here. I looked after my mother for years, you see, and there was definitely a bit of dementia there at the end."

Sam handed over a mug of tea, slopped some onto the rug by her feet.

"Lydia's illness is not dementia," he said coldly, "it's a progressive neurological condition that I imagine you don't know a great deal about. If anything at all. Few people do."

Frances' hand rushed to her face for a moment, fingers spread over her lips as if to retrieve words already spoken. Then she sat and stared into her mug, slowly sipped at her tea.

"Apologies," she said eventually, "I am so very sorry. And I wasn't assuming, I assure you. I was simply trying to help. Now do have some cake. I've cut small pieces as it's quite rich, but it really is an excellent recipe."

Sam willed the phone to ring, even for Lydia to grow distressed so that there would be some reason for sending Frances home. But Lydia seemed unusually content, her mood of the morning still evident. Frances began to talk again, inconsequential comments about the room, the furniture. She noticed the pictures.

"Cornwall, I take it? And Scotland, perhaps. All your work, Lydia?"

Sam had no memory of telling Frances where they used to live. Or did it slip out at that ghastly first meeting in her flat? He supposed he might have mentioned that Lydia had been an artist although his habit of discretion was so ingrained that he doubted it. To Catherine he had spoken in more detail. That day when he had gone to the museum and they'd had a drink. When he'd even been tempted to ask her out to dinner, so grateful for her company, before reminding himself of the impropriety of such a gesture, at the embarrassment it would have caused. He was disarmed by Frances Chater.

He disliked her instinctively, even inexplicably distrusted her, yet there was something chameleon about the woman that cheated him of a clear opinion. He watched her as she stood up, moved from picture to picture, pointing, complimenting, all the time looking at Lydia as if to engage her, encourage her involvement. At such moments, she made it hard for him to despise her entirely.

"I take it you have no family to spend Christmas with?" he asked abruptly. "These friends in Twickenham you mentioned, they are …"

She turned away from the watercolour of Constantine Bay, returned to Lydia's side.

"Friends, yes, old friends. In fact, I used to work with Jennifer. Many years ago now, of course, in our nursing days, but we've always kept in touch. Well, one likes to, doesn't one? But family – well, it's the first Christmas without my mother and so no, certainly no one else close by. Relations, that is. But Jennifer and I are very close. And they have a splendid house. Do you know Twickenham? No? Well, I won't bother to tell you where exactly. But just imagine somewhere with a perfect river view. They've done awfully well, you see. Her husband – goodness, I'm being very boring, aren't I? Just like some ghastly Jane Austen spinster going on and on. But what about the two of you? I do hope your Christmas day was successful."

Sam shifted in his chair. His tea was cold. He had forgotten to drink it, too busy parrying with this woman. He did not want to eat her dense fruit cake. He grunted something meaningless, looked at Lydia for support and felt grieved by her inability to offer it. In the past, he had never been particularly aware of any reliance on her, but these days he felt increasingly vacuous, susceptible, as if without her voice, her endorsement, he was exposed in all his inadequacy. They were no longer a partnership and he felt abandoned into an involuntary freedom.

"We spent the day with Polly, our daughter," Sam said unnecessarily since their movements had obviously been monitored from her upstairs flat. And he found himself pushed to declare Polly's news as if it gave him significance, a status of some kind. Frances appeared interested, enthusiastic even, taking Lydia's hand as if in congratulation. Suddenly, he felt unexpectedly consoled by sharing the fact of Polly's pregnancy as if he had not until this moment allowed himself unqualified joy at the prospect of the child. As if the habit of pessimism stemming from Lydia's prognosis had become his default position that he found hard to shift. "Yes, it's good to have something to look forward to, isn't it Lyddie?" he said firmly, shaping the sentiment of it into a conviction.

Eventually, Frances stood up, began to show signs of leaving although delayed longer in the hall, talking of the street party arrangements.

"Less than seven months away now," she said, "of course I do appreciate that it's difficult for you to get to all our meetings. But perhaps just briefly – we have our next one early in the New Year and it would be so good if you could join us as your input would be invaluable, I'm sure. I have a very efficient woman from number 20 – that smart detached white house with the monkey puzzle tree in the garden? – who's a professional caterer for the highest class of events so she's taken over that side of things which is an absolute boon, I can tell you. But of course, you'll have read the minutes I popped through your door so I really don't need to go on and on. Talk the hind legs off a donkey, that's what Andrew would – I mean, my father, of course, my father always used to say that." Sam opened the front door firmly, said something about needing to get a meal for Lydia. She began to walk away then stopped and hurried back just as he was on the point of closing his door on the late afternoon. "I knew there was something else I meant to mention. Your front door key."

"Key?"

"I was thinking it would be a good idea if I held a spare one for you. Just in case of emergencies. Even without your situation with Lydia, we all have our forgetful moments, locking ourselves out, and it would be comforting for you, surely, if you knew I had the means of—"

"No," Sam said, "there's no need for that."

"Oh well," she said, pausing as if granting him the chance to change his mind. "If you are absolutely sure."

"I am. Thank you, Frances, but I am quite sure."

Frances stood in Violet's sitting room, a space that always managed to look both untidy yet sparsely furnished: a couple of upright chairs, a small wicker sofa covered with a batik patterned throw, large cushions propped against the wall. She had collected the stained coffee mugs, the plate – her pink plate – several glasses the day before, washed them, lined them up on the shelf in the kitchen. She had picked up the tea towel from the floor, tidied towels in the bathroom, checked the fridge. Thrown away half a carton of curdling milk. A single sprouting potato. The stub of a weeping cucumber.

There was nothing for her to do today.

She had already checked windows several times, sought for carelessly running taps, chance hazards that might have been overlooked when Violet left. She had straightened her duvet, plumped pillows, resisted the impulse to remove all bedlinen to take back to her own flat to launder. Yet probably Violet would not mind. The girl seemed to possess a docile nature, as if disposed always to agree with whatever caused her least effort. At first, Frances had thought her withdrawn, depressed, even, for there was an apathy about her, a lack of vitality. But after knowing her a few weeks, she concluded that Violet's disposition was simply indolent. No more nor no less. She spoke quietly, slowly, as if a more energetic tone was too demanding. Her movements too, the almost slothful way she walked, lowered herself into a chair, opened a door, lifted a cup, suggested a required effort with which she was uneasy. She was twenty-three years old. Yet Frances thought of her as little more than an adolescent in need of guidance. Violet had blithely handed over her spare front door key to Frances the moment she had raised the matter, no doubt finding it easier to concede than to protest and eager at the chance to despatch some responsibility.

Back in her own flat, Frances opened a bottle of chilled wine, began to drink steadily. It was only seven, but there was the latest letter to write and she always found the words flowed more easily, the phrases took on more bite if she wrote whilst not entirely sober. There was a post the next day. No doubt there would be a delay with some deliveries, overlap from the pre-Christmas rush, but as long as her letter arrived before New Year's Eve it would serve its purpose to see out the detritus and damage of the old year, hasten in the recovery of the new. *Charlotte Prideaux,* Frances declared out loud to the walls of her living room, to the print of a Parisian street hanging above her mother's rosewood side table, *your days are numbered. Have no illusion that your spell as mistress in my husband's bed will last beyond the early spring. Make plans, arrangements to repossess that flat of yours in – Peacehaven? Shoreham?* She turned the television on, but failed to find anything of interest. She knew music was unwise. Still, an excess of sentiment could surely be permitted tonight of all nights. For whilst she had managed to trudge through Christmas Day with comparative equanimity, considering, December 26th had proved far more challenging.

The date was simply too significant. Irrevocably hitched to potent recollection.

Perhaps she shouldn't have chosen Rachmaninov. *Rhapsody on a theme of Paganini.* But then her collection of CDs was scant, a handful of popular classics bought cheaply for the small portable player she had brought to the flat. She settled herself on the sofa, arranged the cushions, sat back as the opening notes, the insistent, recurring theme played. Neither she nor Andrew knew anything about music. There had been a few concert visits over the years, well-known concertos, programmes of light music and for a while even a piano in Pilgrim Square, inherited from one of Andrew's relatives. But it had failed to justify house room through neglect and eventually had been bequeathed to a local church hall. A pity, Frances had said at the time, and had nagged, claimed to notice some sort of potential talent when in truth she had been ignorant of the signs of such aptitude. If only life could be lived in retrospect. Informed by hindsight so woefully lacking at the time. She rubbed a fingertip around the rim of the glass, removing the stain of lipstick.

And thought that only the very young are devoid of guilt and self-recrimination, living lives unshadowed by regret. Remorse.

She refilled her glass, aware that she was growing mildly drunk, closed her eyes and gave herself solely to the music. But within moments she abandoned the idea. Stood up, moved to the tinny CD player and abruptly switched it off. It was entirely unwise, she knew, to invite unguarded emotion, the sort provoked by intense beauty or sensual pleasure. Survival depended upon rationality, a tight control over events and muddying the waters with indulgent sentiment was pure folly.

She went to the kitchen, opened the fridge, faced the single pork chop, the watercress and orange salad sitting expectantly on the middle shelf. She was not hungry. Or at least not for a solitary chop and a dose of chilled iron. There was still a third of the bottle remaining and she emptied it into her glass, ferreted for the packet of cashew nuts, snacks and crisps kept for Violet's visits, and carried them back to the sitting room.

She was amazed by her blithe ability to lie.

The fluency of her account to Sam Gough, the ease with which she had slipped into her account of the day she had spent with Jennifer and Charles Osborne in Twickenham had been impressive. If pushed, she could have described their tree, the elaborate table decorations, the silver sixpence extracted from her piece of pudding sitting in their resplendent dining room.

It was over twenty years since she had spoken to Jennifer.

She had no idea whether the two of them were even still alive, but she imagined they were. There had always been something indestructible about Jennifer, even more so about Charles. An arrogant man, opinionated, dogmatic, she had never liked him. But it was Jennifer who had been her close friend until the two of them had fallen out, not just grown apart, but argued, rowed over a matter that Frances now confused in her mind and could hardly remember. There had been the suggestion of a rapprochement a few years later, the proverbial olive branch extended by Jennifer in an unexpected phone call that Frances had rebuffed. Perhaps she had been unwise, her attitude too censorious and ill-judged. Still. It was all so long ago, events and emotions hitched to other selves that were now scarcely recognisable. Like looking at strangers who loved and loathed with passions that were now faintly embarrassing. She was tempted to trace them, Jennifer and Charles Osborne, thumb through the phone directory in case they still lived in their substantial house within spitting distance of the Thames. But then what? She had no desire to call them, to hear the complacent tones of Charles or the exaggerated inflections of the preciously-educated Jennifer, gloating in their smug, self-satisfaction. For what would she receive from them, in her present situation, but pity? No. She'd used them, exploited them for her own purposes in her fabricated tale to Sam Gough.

Lying, of course, had become an essential part of coping, the only way to manage and accommodate her temporary situation.

And she should know a thing or two about the dark art after months of living alongside pernicious liars. But theirs were heinous rather than pragmatic. And whilst Andrew was certainly culpable, it was Charlotte Prideaux who had master managed, initiated matters, no doubt. A Lady Macbeth of a woman, a ruthless manipulator of his affections. Frances thought of her pale oval face, opaque, closer to plain than pretty, her seamless, thirty-six-year-old complexion, her slim, rather white hands.

And she hears Charlotte Prideaux's controlled yet resolute voice on that bleak April afternoon, the scant sunshine giving way frequently to heavy rain that beats and runs down windowpanes. She sees her looking at Andrew as they stand in the kitchen in Pilgrim Square, the three of them, fussing over pots of tea for the funeral guests, crustless small sandwiches and slices of lemon layer cake. *You might as well tell her now,* Charlotte Prideaux says, taking his arm so that the tray of bone china tea cups he holds are endangered, *there's no point in delaying things any longer. Now's as good a time as ever, Andy.* (Andy. No one had ever called her husband Andy. He had never tolerated it.) And Andrew turns to Frances, his face craven with guilt, like a young boy seeking clemency for some petty misdemeanour. Frances has already spent some hours absorbing the blatant evidence of his infidelity – that sudden catching of one of those slim white hands, the not quite so covert kiss and embrace in the crematorium car park behind her mother's hearse – and has sat through the service comatose, not with the supposed grief others suspect, but with her own blind foolishness for failing to suspect. Andrew's betrayal cruelly wounds yet it is the knowledge of her gullibility and her consequent humiliation that truly overwhelms.

Briefly, at least.

Like a rider tossed from her mount, fleetingly dazed, she soon regains her stride, adjusts her path. She leaves the kitchen, circulates with plates of egg and cress on white and ham on wholemeal, encourages Andrew to check on empty cups, talks appropriately to her mother's few cantankerous friends. At the same time, she keeps an eye on Charlotte Prideaux, having at least the discretion to remain out of sight, filling kettles in the kitchen, rinsing cups, rather than fraternising with the bereaved. When the last mourner has departed, Frances sits down on the sofa in the front drawing room that overlooks the square and faces the two of them. Charlotte, opposite her, tense in the armchair that has only recently returned from the upholsterer, is the first to speak. Frances barely absorbs her words. *She is brazen,* she thinks, flinching at her clichéd protestations of love for Andrew. For *Andy.* She is a spoilt child who spies the prize she wants and pouts and sulks if she does not receive it. And Andrew, inordinately flattered, fawns, placates, behaves as if a tawdry eight-month love affair is conclusive proof of the end of their long marriage. He lacks, Frances sees, resources to resist her desire. She is not even beautiful. But she is young, driven, ruthless even, and he is too inadequate to resist. Frances fiddles with the hang nail at the base of her index finger, feels the sag of the sofa cushion beneath her thigh; no one speaks for some moments. Outside, a car cruises Pilgrim

Square, searching for a parking space. They are expecting a scene, she is sure. They have their defence ready for when she inevitably explodes into a vituperative rage or hysterical tears. She notices that Andrew's black funereal tie has a small stain on it, mayonnaise from the egg and cress, possibly, or lemon cream from the sponge. Charlotte turns to him now as if urging some sort of action, that pale, seamless oval face of hers suddenly impatient, slim fingers touching his wrist. *I'm sorry, Frances,* he says quietly as if his voice is strangled with a cold, *but you have only yourself to blame, you know.* And she stands, Frances stands, moves swiftly to the door of the living room, goes upstairs and pulls out a suitcase from the cupboard on the landing, packs it mindlessly in the bedroom, as an afterthought takes the carriage clock – their silver wedding anniversary present – from the mantelpiece and goes back downstairs to the hall. Andrew is standing there now. He looks frightened. *Not now, Frances,* he says in little more than a whisper, *don't go right now, not today. There's no need.* Frances glances past him into the living room where Charlotte Prideaux is standing, inspecting titles on the bookshelves, her slim arms folded around her petite frame, until one pale hand reaches out for a book, takes it with a proprietorial air. *Oh, but there is,* Frances says firmly, *you have made that absolutely clear. Both of you. I shall go to my mother's house. Which is, of course, now mine. Yes, for the time being I shall be in Worthing.* And just before she closes the front door behind her, she shakes her head at him and says, *How unoriginal, Andrew. Really. The dental nurse. At your own practice. How entirely crass.*

She did not cry, she remembers now, until later, hours later, in her dead mother's cold house when exhaustion and the effects of several slugs of brandy from the bottle always kept in the bathroom cabinet for medicinal purposes broke her resolve.

But only temporarily.

For crying is pointless, she has always believed, tears are a messy and tiresome business that speak only of weakness and sentimentality. All quite unnecessary, Frances thinks, and has said as much to Andrew in the past on occasions when he has questioned her lack of visible emotion. She remembers him now on one particular day over two years ago now, when her failure to weep propelled them into an argument of foolish proportions. There was nothing wrong, she had told him then, in exercising control and restraint in a situation where hysteria would be futile.

Not hysteria, he had said curtly, *but a little evidence of natural human feeling would be appropriate.*

She wrote her letter before she went to bed. *Render unto Caesar,* she headed the single sheet of notepaper and after half a dozen lines signed off *What God has joined together, let no man put asunder.* She placed the envelope on the hall table, ready to post first thing the next day. She had been asleep some hours when the sound of the phone ringing in the sitting room shocked her suddenly awake. Inclined to ignore it since it was no doubt a mistaken number, she eventually groped her way towards the light switch, stubbing her toe, shivering in the cold air, propelled by a remote fantasy of Andrew's voice at the other end of the phone greeting her.

It was not Andrew.

The caller was hesitant, brief. She too, in reply, found little to say, unprepared, entirely overcome. *You rang. Today of all days, you rang,* she managed to stutter, her voice dry, strangled. Afterwards, she wished she had said so much more to the caller than merely repeating surprise at knowing how to find her. Where to find her. But no words would shape what she had needed to express. Not at the time. Retreating to her bed, still warm, the phrases came easily, fluently, lodged in her head when it was too late to deliver them, when there was no longer anyone there to hear what she had not realised until that moment needed so very much to be said.

10

atherine liked the days between Christmas and New Year, the sense of suspension in the capital, a hiatus from normal life. The museum would attract a few visitors, spontaneous rather than organised tours, and it was never difficult to organise a rota for this period as if some volunteers welcomed the excuse for a productive occupation away from turkey trimmings and long-stay relations. Eddie had always resented Catherine's need to work for the final days of December. It was absurd, he used to argue, demanding anyone to work during the festive period. Everyone should be entitled to take off the 12 days of Christmas as some sort of human right. He always refused even to consider Catherine's point that the Christian religious holiday was an irrelevance to vast swathes of the country's population, countering it only with mutterings about ancient saturnalia celebrations. She often felt that Eddie had been born out of his time. His tendency to absolute views, to reject rationality in favour of unconditional judgements would have suited the rule of some medieval baron or potentate. Compromise was entirely absent from his personality. As a young man, she imagined his attitude must have played to his advantage, imbuing him with an air of confidence rare in anyone under the age of thirty-five. And the spirit of the time had without doubt suited him, the prevailing temper matching his somewhat maverick qualities, his audacity.

So he had got on. He advanced. He had prospered.

By the time Catherine met him, however, the tone had shifted, the mood more sombre. People like Eddie needed to reinvent themselves, subdue and tame their natures to fit in with a new sensibility. Money was no longer a loose commodity to treat flippantly. Eddie's disregard for restraint and caution in claiming excessive expenses was only the start of his swift decline in a world that had become far more corporate and prescribed. He was still widely liked, admired even, for his originality, his undoubted creative talents, but his stubborn resistance to fit in, to concede, were viewed as unwise.

And he was no longer young.

The arrogance and audacity of his youth had lost its appeal in the middle-aged man.

Yet his perpetual self-belief could still be endearing. In their early years together, Catherine had found her own diffidence had been diluted by Eddie's exuberant nerve as if some of his certainty had found its way to lodge under her skin. He had a few loyal friends and went into partnership first with one, then another, the next scheme, the new project on the horizon always engaging his ruthless enthusiasm. The disintegration and failure of each idea, one by one, was, on the surface, borne by diverting the blame as Eddie was adept at avoiding culpability. For it was never his notions or concepts that were at fault, he would take trouble to explain, but the cowardly and unimaginative nature of the markets for which they were intended.

There were fewer visitors than Catherine expected. By twelve she had sent one of the volunteers home to nurse a heavy cold and went to join the other, Ailsa, their only intransigent and rather intractable guide who had worked at the museum since retirement from the civil service some ten years before. They hovered by the admissions desk, waiting for custom.

"Very quiet," she said, in a reproving tone, "it really is very empty, hardly worth my while coming in from Harrow. Or even to open the place up and heat it in the first place. Now last year on the same day, we had a good crowd, I remember. Large party of Australians and quite a few passers-by who just took a fancy to the place. Looking for something more cultural than the winter sales at the stores, I expect. Do you remember that Catherine? Perhaps you were sharper on the publicity last December."

"I wasn't here last year," Catherine said.

"Not here? Surely it wasn't Robert. Prerogative of the top man to take the entire holiday off, I thought."

"I was still on – what is it called?" Catherine groped for the phrase which Ailsa supplied with no sign of awkwardness.

"Compassionate leave, yes, of course. You weren't back until January, were you? Awful business, that, with your husband. I'd quite forgotten." She screwed up her face as if at a disagreeable smell, a tasteless topic unsuited to polite discourse. Catherine suggested Ailsa could leave early, given the absence of visitors, but she was not a woman who liked to divert from a plan. "I've said I won't be back until six so let's leave things as they are, if you don't mind. No point in upsetting arrangements. He's driving the cousins to catch their train from Watford so we'll give him time to strip their beds and get the washing on before I'm home." Ailsa generally referred to her husband by a pronoun as if his individuality was of little consequence. A highly intelligent woman, well informed on all matters pertaining to the house and Harriet Howe, she was a knowledgeable and efficient guide yet a cold individual. Catherine pitied her anonymous spouse. "So Robert's off in the New Year, I hear? Got his successor lined up yet?" Ailsa tidied the rack of postcards, straightened the piles of house guides lying on the desk.

"I wasn't aware," Catherine said cautiously, "that it was public knowledge about him leaving. I mean, does everyone know? I think Robert was hoping to tell you all once his successor was in place. That would be what the trustees wanted, I'm sure."

Ailsa turned her attention to the stock of bookmarks on display, made a swift count and opened a drawer in search of more. Catherine waited patiently. Ailsa was a woman uneasy with conversation, preferring statement to any sense of exchange. Eventually, she turned to Catherine and said,

"Well, of course, it's nothing to do with us volunteers, anyway. We're an invaluable commodity yet without status. But you know how people talk. Inevitable, really, when we have time on our hands on a quiet shift. So the word's gone round. And yes, naturally, there's concern."

"Concern?"

"About the viability of the museum. About the chances of Harriet Howe house surviving in the current market. Surely it's only practical to think of the future."

"I don't see how Robert's departure changes anything," Catherine said. "We are a thriving concern, our numbers are buoyant and we offer something unique to the general visitor as well as to research students and social historians." She sounded too defensive, she knew. Ailsa shrugged her shoulders, adjusted the brooch at the neck of her bottle green sweater, fiddled with the waistband of her tweed skirt.

"All I'm suggesting, Catherine, is that the museum might be better served by being part of something bigger. A department in one of the larger concerns. There's enough of them. When you think of the upkeep of the house alone. And this building on the open market would reach a tidy sum, I can tell you. Property prices in this area? Well, the sky's the limit, as they say."

"But the building is part of the point," Catherine said. "Somewhere Harriet Howe actually lived."

"Briefly," Ailsa said crisply.

"For over fifteen years."

"Hardly a lifetime."

"And the place associated with so much of her campaigning work. If you consider the number of social reforms discussed and argued over in these very rooms and the people who saw this building as the hub of – well, you do the tours, Ailsa. I don't need to tell you the significance of the house."

Ailsa took her time to reply. She opened another drawer, brought out some greetings cards to add to the depleted stack, counting them out with deliberation.

"Of course, in an ideal world, one wouldn't want to see small museums like this disappear. But it's no good becoming sentimental, Catherine. And it has to be admitted that we are rather quaint, shall we say? Stuck in our ways? When you think of the way things are going. I mean it's all interactive stuff now, isn't it? Visitor participation. As a matter of fact, he was only reading about that the other day in his paper and showed me a whole section about people's expectations these days when they pay out good money for a visit. Of course, it's not to my personal taste, all this button pushing and authentic experience stuff. But I'm only saying, Catherine. We could be considered a little outmoded."

Catherine was saved the need to reply by the front door opening onto a party of five and Ailsa turned away from her, swiftly moved to greet them.

Irritated, Catherine went back to her office. Clearly, Ailsa would not consider her a suitable successor to Robert, a figure she appeared to revere and such opinion would possibly be widespread among the other staff. But it was more Ailsa's doubts about the future of Harriet Howe House that disturbed her. Surely, the woman was being provocative, an attitude she displayed with ease, although normally her focus for confrontation was on more domestic matters such as inadequate supplies of milk in the staff kitchen or a pile of unwashed mugs on the draining board. She sat at her desk for some time, checked volunteer rotas for the following week then went through the diary of school visits and group tours booked for January. Considering the time of year, the numbers were satisfactory. Sufficient. It was inevitably always a low month for admissions. But it was true that Robert's zest for future planning had waned since his resignation and as a consequence perhaps a complacency had settled over the place that she had done little to shift. Ailsa's barbed comments about the direction of the museum were mischievous, no doubt, but there was a core of truth in them that she found hard to ignore. She watched the darkness of the winter afternoon envelop the narrow street outside her office, lights in the houses opposite illuminating front rooms until drawn curtains reclaimed them.

She had done nothing about applying for Robert's position despite his encouragement and Beth's automatic support.

Such resolve had swiftly waned as if her custom of compliance was too ingrained to defy. And it stemmed not from apathy, but from a habit of fulfilling others' expectations rather than attempting to exceed them. The conscientious, biddable yet unremarkable child had carried similar traits into adulthood where her competence and efficiency were noted, accommodated. She had set her own limitations by believing in them. Besides, she had never been ambitious in any real sense, fulfilled by the nature of a job rather than its status. And during her marriage to Eddie it had never occurred to her to seek promotion, advancement, finding a consolation in the routine of the work, her easy familiarity with it that allowed her to devote time elsewhere: to Eddie, his sudden schemes and projects and notions, his madcap ventures.

But now.

For the past year, she had felt fettered by his death as if a form of obligatory mourning had been required of her. A period for recrimination and reproach. It was only once she had left Bevington, moved away from the place with its potent associations, that she had felt the possibility of purposeful activity once again. After all, she no longer woke every morning thinking of that final conversation, that rash and meaningless exchange of futile comments that appeared to have propelled Eddie to grab his car keys from the hall table, stick in his pocket the remains of the bottle of whisky he had been drinking from all evening and slam the front door in a gesture that she had woefully misjudged as hollow melodrama. Eddie could be reckless, rash in his actions, she knew. But his own sense of self-importance had always protected him for wilful physical risk.

Until that December night.

Catherine was pulled back by Ailsa coming into her office, buttoning up her coat. She glanced at the clock and realised that over an hour had gone by with her achieving very little.

"I'll be off now, Catherine," Ailsa said, "it's time to close, anyway. Not the most interesting of days, I have to say. Shame the café isn't operating over the holiday. Those last visitors were most critical of that and they do have a point, I had to agree with them." She pulled on her leather gloves with slow deliberation.

"It's out of my hands," Catherine said, "as you know the café operates entirely separately from us so make their own hours."

"Even so," Ailsa said, "someone should speak to them about it. After all, they are dependent on the house for the concession of being here."

Catherine, about to argue, realised she had a valid point. She thanked her, said she would make a note of raising the matter with Robert who would, she knew, immediately delegate the matter to her to handle.

"Happy New Year," she said as Ailsa pulled on a severe woollen hat and headed for the front door. "I won't be seeing you again until 2006."

"Indeed," Ailsa said, "let's just hope it's a reasonable one for all of us. 2005 has hardly been plain sailing."

Catherine agreed then, impulsively, before she had a chance to check herself, said,

"By the way, Ailsa, I wanted you to know. I am going to apply for the curator position. To succeed Robert when he leaves."

Ailsa stopped, turned and looked at Catherine as if she needed clarification for what she had heard. When Catherine said nothing, she eventually said,

"Well. That's a surprise, I must say. I wouldn't have thought it of you. But good luck. And when you think about it, it's about time a woman held the reins at this place. Yes, good luck with that, Catherine."

★★★

Sam Gough stared at the chopping board, at the items he had laid out neatly as if for a cookery demonstration: a red pepper, an onion, several carrots, garlic, leeks. For a moment, his mind was blank as if these were objects that formed some part of a childhood memory game and all that was required of him was to recall them in a few minutes, note when one had been surreptitiously removed. Then he heard Polly's voice from the other room, picked up the sharp knife and started chopping methodically. He could not remember cooking a meal before Lydia became ill. Not consciously taking charge of an entire meal for the two of them where he was required to plan, shop, prepare. It was simply what Lydia had done. She had always taken pleasure in it and had been a good, adventurous cook. Of course, he had always been capable of pushing some food together if required, combining bits and pieces from the fridge, opening a couple of tins, frying some eggs. But in truth he had only become aware of his dependency on her for meals when her ability to prepare them had gone. It had reminded him of his own father's inadequacy in the kitchen, a boast rather than an apology, and his mother's insistence upon wholesome, traditional meals. Once, when she had been ill with flu, the two of them, father and young son, had eaten at the local fish and chip shop three nights running until she had abandoned her bed in exasperation and struggled downstairs to cook. His parents had been living in the bungalow in Deal when his mother had died. Visiting once, Sam had watched his widowed father producing mashed potato from the dried contents of a packet, pouring boiled water onto the white pellets, and pronouncing the results to be pleasing. His father, a man who had always been fastidious about his food, relying now on instant convenience packs and sweet snacks to satisfy a diminishing appetite. Such signals of a life reduced to the acceptance of so little had upset Sam more than the clinical evidence of his father's ageing body. The memory had stirred him into unearthing Lydia's neglected cookery books, enduring the sudden cult of TV personality chefs.

Lydia's ability to eat freely was already compromised by muscular failure and Sam was aware that before long she would not be able to tolerate anything other than a pureed, thickened substance. He remembered now, as he concentrated on shredding the thin, papery wrapping from a garlic clove, the first time he had needed to cut up Lydia's food. He had attempted to joke about it, as if the pain of seeing her inadequacy could be masked by humour, saying something feeble about his extended household duties. Pretence, he realised now, moving on to the leeks, rinsing mud from their roots, had become an essential part of his ability to cope and he was ashamed of it. He had no idea why he edged the two of them through each and every day by recourse to a form of deception. In fact, looking back over the past couple of years of her illness, he could not recall ever confronting her with the reality of it. Perhaps the slow dawning of knowledge, the delay in obtaining a clear diagnosis, meant that they had never had an entirely open and frank discussion, never truly shared their feelings about its cruel descent into their lives.

And after all, what was the point?

There was no treatment, little respite, no cure: only an inevitable downward trajectory towards paralysis and silence. Yet Sam suspected it was his own cowardice that prevented him from talking honestly to Lydia. He had always known himself to be, at heart, essentially spineless, weak. And now he was aware of talking to her, caring for her in a manner that was cordial, faintly kind, but lacked intimacy. He relied, in fact, upon a false persona of cheerful practicality to ease him through the inevitable indignities that the illness thrust upon her. As if it was all a temporary erosion of regular life, a suspension, like an unfortunate holiday, a brief yet insistent bout of bad weather, and that normality would soon be thankfully restored.

Polly came into the kitchen. Hovered at his shoulder.

"Looks good. For tonight?"

"In your honour. Must feed you up. Now you're eating for two."

Polly smiled, picked up a stick of raw carrot, perched on a stool and watched as he carefully lifted ingredients into the large casserole dish.

"That's rather an outmoded way of treating pregnant women, but never mind. I like to think Mum understands, but it's hard to tell. I've been going on and on about it, how many weeks I am and stuff. And she smiles at me, but then she always does. Do you think she does? Does she understand about the baby?"

Sam opened the oven, slid the heavy dish inside and turned to face her. She needed confirmation.

"Of course. I'm sure she does. Mothers and daughters have a bond, don't they?"

"It was part of the reason, you see. I mean it wasn't a sudden decision, this pregnancy, it's something that I've been thinking about for a long time. But all the same it became the right thing to do now. Before it's too late to share it all with her."

"It is," he said. "It's absolutely the right thing." He pulled her towards him, wrapped her closely in his arms so that she could not see his tears.

★★★

Charlotte Prideaux looks at the parcels under the tree. There are still several to unwrap. Spending Christmas in the Italian Alps meant that they only took their main gift for each other and those were hardly surprises. For her, the antique ring she had seen in The Lanes and hinted heavily for Andrew to buy. For Andrew, the extravagant watch intended to replace the cheap, tawdry one she disliked him wearing. There are a couple of small additional tokens from each to the other, of course. She picks up the small, rectangular, gift-wrapped box bearing her name, guesses perfume. There's a flat, soft shape less expertly folded into tissue paper, awkwardly bound with a ribbon. A silk scarf, she thinks, and hopes he has played safe with a plain rather than patterned design. She has also bought him a couple of books, a tie. The watch was, after all, a particularly extravagant gesture. Then there are a few presents from grateful patients or possibly patients who anticipate troublesome teeth and see a bottle of spirits as sensible forward planning, a form of private insurance. She notices the parcel that had arrived just as they were leaving for the Alps, another apparently from a patient that she had tossed carelessly beneath the tree and had forgotten to mention to Andrew. Now she looks more carefully at the handwriting, turns it over to look in vain for a sender's address. Swiftly, suspiciously, she tears the brown paper wrapping and does not stop there. She splits decorative ribbon with her teeth, opens the box, discards layers of tissue and penetrates to the contents: a pale grey cashmere sweater with a small gift card slipped into the V of the neck. *From Frances. With love. With the love that endures and forgives.* Charlotte Prideaux twists the soft, delicate wool of the sweater, contorts it as if attempting to demonstrate how to wring out dirty water from a dishcloth. She can hear Andrew in the kitchen, the sound of glasses, the fridge door opening and she gets up, goes into the hall and runs up the stairs, the debris of wrapping and contents under her arm. *Anything the matter?* she hears him call. *I was just opening a bottle of something.* She stands on the first-floor landing, calls back down the stairwell. *Nothing,* she says, *go ahead, I'll be with you in a moment. The fire could do with another log.* She bounds up the second staircase, finds one of the suitcases in the spare room that she brought with her the morning she moved into the house with Andrew, the day after that appalling funeral. She shoves the pale grey cashmere sweater into one of the cases, pushes it under the bed. Tomorrow, she thinks, or the next day or the next, she will take it to one of the many charity shops in the town. A brand new, unworn, expensive cashmere sweater: she will be lauded for her generosity, her thoughtful gesture. She smiles at the irony. Quickly, she goes down to the main bedroom, changes her jeans and shirt for a dress, applies a bit of make-up, some perfume, as if this is the reason for her sudden foray upstairs. Andrew is standing with his back to the room, staring, apparently, into the fire. She goes up to him, slides her arms around his waist, presses herself close. He does not move for a moment then turns, holds her at arm's length. *You've changed,* he says. *You look ... that dress.* She breaks away, stands in the middle of the room and turns a circle as if in slow motion, drops an elaborate curtsey. *For you, Andy,* she says, *always and forever, all for you.*

★★★

Violet stretched herself out fully across the carpet of Frances' sitting room.

"Sorry, it's my back. Do you mind? Sitting in the train all that time."

"A good Christmas?" Frances asked, removing the coffee mug from Violet's hand where it threatened to spill. Violet made a face of sorts. Edged off purple socks.

"All right, I suppose. Usual stuff. Relations. Too much eating. People nagging you to go on country walks. My mother worries about me too much, though."

"Mothers do."

"She can't understand why I haven't got a job yet. She thinks I'm not even trying."

Frances drank her coffee, watching the shape of Violet as she alternated between foetal curls and full-length stretches, her black T-shirt and jeans parting in the middle to reveal an abdomen that seemed too inadequately concave to house essential components of liver, kidney, heart.

"And are you?" she said, immediately regretting her mildly censorious tone.

"Sort of," Violet said and sprang suddenly to her feet as if the floor had propelled her. Youth, Frances thought, was both the cruellest and the kindest of times. Violet collected her coffee mug from the table, sat down in the armchair by the window. "There's not a lot around to interest me right now, actually. And I don't want to get into something dull and then this absolutely perfect job turns up and ..." She waved her hand as if in pursuit of that perfect, elusive job that was looming just out of reach. "And I know what you're going to say, Fran. That I'm just a spoilt overindulged child of the rich who should be ashamed of themselves for not needing to do a decent day's work to survive. And that's just not true. My parents are just, well, quite comfortably off, really. That's not my fault, is it? And actually, I'm incredibly hard up at the moment. I mean, the cash flow is not exactly healthy, I can tell you." She stretched out her hand for the plate of toast that Frances had made. "What with Christmas and all that."

"But your home, the flat," Frances said, "that belongs to your father so you live rent free, I suppose?"

Violet shrugged carelessly. "Sort of. I suppose you could call it that. I'm more of a caretaker, really, as he bought it as an investment. And it's not as if he needs the money right now. Rent, that is."

"No, but you do need a job, Violet. Surely. You are a highly intelligent young woman, after all. Don't you get bored?"

"Do you, Fran? You don't seem to have a job."

Frances drained her mug of coffee, thought of the excuse of going to make some more.

"Not at the moment," she said evasively. "With all the aftermath of my mother's death and selling her house and moving here it has been impossible to focus on anything new.

151

You see, I nursed her for so long that I found I was quite worn out by it." She paused, preparing to elaborate, but Violet had clearly stopped listening and returned to her position on the floor.

"My mother worries that I'm getting depressed," she said. "She's always looking out for it. She's a bit obsessed about all that kind of stuff. Mental health. There's a bit of it in the family, you see, going back a generation or so."

"I see," Frances said. "Well, I can't claim to know you very well, Violet, but I wouldn't have thought you were the sort prone to depression."

"No, I'm not. My mother makes it up, I expect, as an excuse. Something she can say to her friends as the reason why I haven't got a job yet. Why I didn't do the whole university thing. *Poor Violet, she finds it hard to cope with the day to day. It's a family thing, you know.* But the truth is, I'm lazy. Just really, really lazy. But that doesn't hurt anyone, does it? I mean it's not as if it's a crime or anything."

Frances said, "Would you like to stay for some dinner, Violet? I don't suppose you have anything in your fridge to eat as you've just got back from your parents. And I have some very nice fish. Or meat if you'd prefer. Some steak, actually."

Violet sat up and took the last piece of toast, picking it up cautiously from the pool of butter that had melted onto the plate. She licked her fingers, a cat tending to its paws, inspected ovals of dark varnish on her evenly shaped nails.

"That's really kind, Fran. Really kind. But no. Didn't I say? Am sure I did. I've only come back today because we're going skiing tomorrow. To someone's chalet thing in – you know, one of those places where people go to ski. Austria, maybe? Yes, Austria. At least I think it is. A God-early start, in fact, so I'm staying over at Sophie's tonight in Greenwich. You've met Sophie? Maybe not. Anyway, it's a friend of hers or the family of this friend who owns the place. Or rents it. Or something like that. So I've got to get all my stuff together. All my ski and cold weather stuff, you know? Though heaven knows where it is. Actually, I don't even know I've got anything decent here, but it's too late to go shopping now. Or is it? What do you think?"

She stood up, looked out of the window then at her watch, parcelling her long hair into one hand, holding it on top of her head as if it helped her to think. Then swiftly she dropped it, picked up her socks from the floor and found her door key sitting next to the buttery plate.

"See you next week or the one after. Not sure exactly how long I'm staying, you see. Until we all start driving each other mad, probably. Or run out of money. There's always that, of course. Thanks for the toast and stuff, Fran."

Frances stood at her front door, unnecessarily watching Violet let herself into her neighbouring flat. The poinsettia plant she had placed on a stand on the small landing in a brief fit of seasonal appropriation looked forlorn, one scarlet leaf drooping in spite of regular watering. No doubt it had suffered through lack of light. With sudden resolution, she picked it up, carried it back inside and deposited it in the rubbish bin. Christmas, she concluded, was over. She had survived. And now only a couple of days of the old year remained before she could bid it good riddance, label it as one best despatched to oblivion.

And move on.

★★★

Catherine removed the cards from the sitting room, the few scattered around the kitchen, her bedroom. She felt too impatient to wait until the obligatory Twelfth Night, wondered why she had bothered decorating the windowsill with sprigs of holly that were now dried and devoid of red berries. But then she had intended doing more. She had thought of inviting her neighbours in Willow House, extending a festive gesture to Frances Chater, however mildly alarming she found the woman, suggesting Sam and Lydia Gough come round for tea. And Violet, of course. Possibly Violet Lawrence. But she had managed to sidestep any such invitations, each time the thought occurred, justifying to herself its inappropriateness. Lydia might be too ill, Sam diffident to come alone. Frances could pounce upon the idea with too much alacrity, judging it as a signal that her company was needed on a more regular basis. *Thus,* she thought, *I gravitate more and more to being unsociable, self-contained. As if I am fulfilling some prescribed, assigned role of the lonely, grieving widow. When I am not. Absolutely not. After all, if Eddie had not died, I would still, in all likelihood, be alone at the end of 2005.* In truth, she suspected her reluctance stemmed more from an uncertainty about how to behave in such situations. The previous year, Christmas had occurred too soon after Eddie's accident for her to feel obliged to deal with it. This year she had planned to embrace it more willingly. She flicked through the cards quickly, reread any brief messages: *We really must catch up in the New Year. Hope you are settled in your new home. We think of you often and wish you well after such a difficult time.* And so on. Messages that were sincere and kindly meant yet undoubtedly would not lead to any concrete gestures and similar sentiments would be echoed in similar cards the following year. It was, inevitably, the way of things. There were people acquired, ripple-like, simply from having been alive for a certain number of years, bumping up against them on a fairly involuntary basis so that a loose connection was made. Only the truly solitary, those with a recluse mentality, could claim to be friendless, immune to the desire for any form of companionship. And Catherine knew she was far from that. Yet if she was being entirely honest, she was unsure how many of these Christmas well-wishers could really be classed as friends. After all, she could go for years – and usually did – without seeing any of them and knew only about the warp and weft of their lives from these condensed messages, a few scrawled lines inside a seasonal card.

The phone rang. Beth, she thought, or possibly Elspeth, from her dank semi-subterranean flat in Southwark, inviting her to dinner. Or even Alec. It would be good to see Alec again soon. Really, she should have rung him to arrange something.

"Hallo? Mrs Wells? Catherine?" The voice was hesitant. "I'm not sure if I've reached the right—"

"Yes?"

"Ah good. It is you. I wasn't at all certain I had the number down correctly. It's Gillian March. From Bevington?"

"Of course," Catherine said. Their immediate neighbour from the house in Bevington. A woman she had hardly known, spoken to on only a handful of occasions about the weather, the local traffic, until the night of Eddie's death and the police car outside the house for hours. She had been very kind, solicitous in an unobtrusive way. Pots of tea or perhaps coffee, brandy, certainly, and an offer to stay the night so Catherine would not be alone.

"I'm sorry to intrude on you like this, but it's just that someone was looking for you the other day. In fact, the other week, just before Christmas, and what with one thing and the other, the holiday and visitors and so on, I just haven't got around to ringing."

"Looking for me?"

"Actually, for your husband. It was Mr Wells who was wanted. This person went next door to your old house, you see, and Tanya and Greg – the people who bought your house – well, they sent him my way. You see, I think they were a bit unsure. About what to say. An awkward situation for them."

"Of course," Catherine said.

"And so was I, really. I mean, I didn't like to – well, I didn't think it was for me to tell a stranger about the accident. About what happened to your husband. After all, I had no idea what sort of connection this person had with him. And it's not the sort of thing you want to announce on the doorstep just like that, is it? But then neither did I want to hand out your contact details just like that. So I asked for his."

Catherine noticed a car pulling up in Miller Street. Doors banging, loud voices and then Violet Lawrence, picked out by the security light at the front of Willow House, coming out from the side entrance with a suitcase, hefting it into the boot of the car. Gillian March began to give details, a name, a number, email address. Carelessly, Catherine wrote them down on the back of one of the cards lying in a pile. She doubted she would do anything with them.

"Thank you, it's probably an old friend of Eddie's. Perhaps someone who's been abroad and hasn't heard."

"Very pleasant, he was, and very personable Not at all insistent, I have to say. Most polite. As are the people who bought your house, thank goodness – Tanya and Greg. Lovely young couple. And you were so sensible to move, Catherine, after your loss. Memories and all that. But brave, nevertheless. Always good to have a fresh start with no connections with the past, though, isn't that what people say?"

For ease, Catherine agreed. As if the past could be uncoupled from one's life simply by selling a house, switching post codes. How convenient if the manacles of memory could so easily be dismissed.

The phone call from Gillian March in Bevington over, she

went to the window to draw the curtains, saw Sam Gough placing rubbish in the bins at the side of the house, tightly enclosed in strong black plastic sacks and tied with string in an attempt to deter the intrepid urban foxes. She smiled, waved, but he failed to respond, heading back to the garden flat no doubt too preoccupied even to notice. Foolishly, Catherine felt a moment of rejection as if the offer of a handshake had been ignored, a cheek turned to deflect a kiss.

11

Frances sat in the back pew of the church on the right-hand side, a place she had begun to think of as her own. She liked the sense that from here she could view proceedings, join in the parts that appealed yet permit herself distractions since few would notice. Thus she was now familiar with the names on the wall memorial plaque that edged her shoulder: *To the glory of God and in loving memory of Arthur Henry Larkins, servant and benefactor of this parish 1812 – 1884 and of Evelyn Maud, dutiful, loyal wife and their infant son, Edmund Walter. The souls of the righteous are in the hands of God.* Arthur Henry was, no doubt, a Victorian patriarch, munificent in parish circles, despotic and tyrannical at home. Poor Evelyn Maud. No dates for her. Perhaps she died giving birth to infant Edmund Walter or to another, subsequent child, Arthur so intent on prolonging the Larkins line that he would have done his best to secure her a state of perpetual pregnancy. Yet here he is, *servant and benefactor of this parish,* forever immortalised for his selflessness. Which, of course, would have been the point of him ensuring funds were supplied for such a memorial. Frances turned back to the pulpit, tried to concentrate on the words of the visiting vicar who had not been able to hide her surprise at the diminished congregation. In January, only the stalwarts, for whom Sunday would be an arid space without a church service, were in attendance. After a rich December diet of carol singing, nativity plays and Midnight Mass most would consider their vague allegiance to the church fulfilled until at least Lent. She gave up trying to follow the sermon's interpretation of the Good Samaritan, anticipated instead her plans for the week ahead.

It was time, perhaps, for some change in strategy. Despite her vigils in Pilgrim Square, her twice weekly letters, Charlotte Prideaux was still *in situ*, Andrew, evidently, still in thrall. She had held hopes for Christmas. New Year's Day had been a possibility. Both were times, after all, for sentiment, re-evaluation.

Remorse.

She thought of Andrew now, wearing the expensive pale grey cashmere sweater she had sent, thought of his arms shifting into the softness of the fabric, his shoulders shrugging into it and had a rare and visceral desire for the feel of his flesh close to hers. She knew she was not a particularly tactile woman, had always found displays of open affection something of an embarrassment. Only in death had she embraced her mother, briefly, and then as a required obligation to the nurse hovering, insisting on a gesture of farewell. Her commitment to retrieve Andrew, to unshackle him from the machinations of Charlotte Prideaux, had been from the start a matter of moral right. Andrew was her husband, for better for worse, in sickness and in health. He belonged to her. He was hers to claim. Now, though, sitting in her chilled corner of the church, her fingers fumbling with the torn spine of the hymn book resting in her lap, it was a desire for physical touch, for the fold of intimately familiar limbs around hers, that possessed her. Some general shuffling, an excess of coughing and searching for tissues and glasses suggested the sermon was at an end, the final hymn announced. Relieved by the distraction, Frances stood up, stirred frozen toes in her ankle boots, and joined in some painfully thin singing of *Immortal, Invisible God Only Wise.*

Across the common, she saw Catherine Wells, heading in the direction of Miller Street, a wedge of newspapers under one arm, and felt relieved by the possibility of distraction. She quickened her pace. There was something elusive about Catherine that Frances found irritating. She had hoped for more from the woman, not quite friendship, but some form of companionship manageable even within the constraints of her deception. But so far there had been an air of distance from her that Frances saw as hostile. Sam Gough, troubled and burdened with his wife's illness, could be excused a certain remoteness in his manner although it was clear he appreciated her gestures of neighbourliness. She quickened her pace, called Catherine's name and was rewarded when she stopped just as the path reached the turn into the street.

"So glad to catch up with you," Frances projected loudly from ten yards or so, "I haven't really had a chance to – well, would you say it's too late to wish you a happy new year? Of course, it is, we're almost into February. Even so. Better late than never, I always say. Good Christmas? But then that's all forgotten now, isn't it? Onwards and upwards, that's the way." Catherine smiled opaquely at her, said something about cold weather, scant daylight. "Oh, but spring's only just around the corner, you have to remember that! And I always find spirits lift at the sight of the first crocus." She waited for agreement, received a faint smile and decided to abandon restraint. The consolation of company was required. "You look as if you could do with coffee, Catherine. And we're both of us cold, I can tell. How about we treat ourselves to something warming at that smart café that's just opened in South Street? You know the place, less than a five-minute walk from here and definitely open on Sundays."

Catherine hesitated. She had intended going to the café herself, needing some time away from the flat and her endless preparations for the following week's interview with the trustees. A quiet hour or so devoted to the Sunday papers would be a respite. Yet she could not see how to avoid Frances' invitation without appearing unfriendly. Swiftly she agreed.

The place was crowded, but Frances hovered over a couple who were sitting with empty cups and plates and soon the table was theirs. They ordered.

"Nothing to eat. The pastries are excellent, you know. Particularly the apple Danish. No? That's obviously how you keep yourself so thin, Catherine. Deprivation. Whereas me …" She laughed shrilly, slipped off her burgundy winter coat, took a moment to arrange it around the back of her chair. Catherine concentrated on the coffee, agreed that it was excellent. Grappling for something to say, she asked about the progress of the street party arrangements which conveniently occupied Frances for some time without the need for her to contribute. She glanced at the woman and man at the table next to them, quietly enjoying the Sunday papers without the apparent need to talk and found herself envious of such ease and compatibility. Frances was reminding her about the date of the next meeting, assuming her attendance.

"Of course," Catherine said, "it's on the calendar," wondering why she always capitulated quite so easily to this woman. She had intended avoiding such meetings, simply producing the material concerning the history of the street that she had promised.

"As long as we meet the deadlines, we should be fine," Frances went on. "Just five months to go now. All the groundwork is done, the foundations, as it were. I have that very resourceful woman, Sylvia, at number 20 in charge of catering and Adam Featherston – you know him? – a lawyer, evidently, at number 52, the place that's just had the loft conversion. Anyway, he's dealing with all the regulations, closing the street to traffic, informing the police, all that sort of thing. And entertainment is safely in the hands of that family at the end house. The one with the big extension? No doubt a recording studio or something along those lines. They definitely have media connections, anyway, I'm assured." She lowered her voice as if the information was covert.

"There's the weather," Catherine said, putting down her cup, "no way of ensuring that. It could pour with rain all day."

There was a pause. Frances looked down at her plate, pushed the few crumbs that had escaped the apple Danish into a neat pile with her pastry fork.

"We'll meet all contingencies," she said eventually. "But really, I don't think there is any need for pessimism of that kind."

Catherine felt duly reprimanded, attempted conciliation.

"Of course, a Saturday in mid-July should be fine. Hot, even. I was just meaning that there's always the possibility of rain, English summers being unreliable."

"Quite. But no need to dwell. Dwelling does no one any good."

"No. Of course not. I'm sure it will all be a huge success. And so enterprising of you to find the time to devote to the organisation of it."

Frances smiled. She pushed her plate and cup to one side, leaned forward across the table. She was wearing a neat navy dress and a string of pearls that looked out of place among the casual Sunday morning dress of the café's customers.

"Well, I'm not working at the moment so I do have time on my side. My mother's long illness meant I had to give up my job, you see, and after I lost her, I felt I deserved a little break. Before going back to work." Her answer was only a partial fabrication, Frances thought. As manager for Andrew's dental practice, her job had naturally been abandoned the moment she had left the house in Pilgrim Square to head for her mother's bleak semi in Worthing. Eventually, of course, the remaining funds from her mother's estate after buying the flat would run out and she would be compelled to find some sort of work. But she refused even to think of that outcome. The humiliation of seeking a reference from Andrew as her last employer would be unbearable. "Admin," she added unnecessarily to Catherine. "I was always in admin of one sort or another. In offices, you know. An office manager. So you could say that arranging events like the street party plays to my strengths. Just like you, Catherine."

"Sorry? I don't quite follow."

"The social history you're doing for us, for the residents of Miller Street to mark the centenary."

"Oh, right. Yes, I see. Well, I'm sure anyone else could have gone along to the local history section of the library and checked records and—"

"Yes," Frances said baldly, "they could. But nonetheless, it will look better to have the suggestion of an expert's name attached. *Miller Street – a hundred years of History by Miss Catherine Wells*. That's the title page I have in mind for the little booklet."

Catherine said, "Mrs."

"What?"

"It's Mrs Catherine Wells. Not that it's necessary to add that – or even give my name, come to think of it."

Frances leaned further forward over the narrow table, her face intense in expression.

"Oh, of course, I'd forgotten. Apologies. Divorced, I presume? Not that it's a problem anymore since most people are these days, aren't they? Apart from the Catholics. And even then, there appear to be ways round, as it were. Annulments, I believe they like to call it."

"No," Catherine said, wondering why she felt such a need to clarify, to placate this woman's intrusive curiosity. "I am not divorced. My husband died. He was killed, in fact."

Part of her, unkindly, relished the shock on Frances Chater's face, swiftly followed by a certain annoyance at being wrong-footed. She listened to the apologies, the pity and sympathies which flowed copiously for some minutes.

"At least you have your work," Frances was saying. "I always think when there is a profound loss, a grief like yours to endure, Catherine, work can be a refuge. It's the routine, I should imagine."

Most people had expressed similar sentiments to her. *Thank goodness you have your job* as if it provided a panacea to tragedy. Yet in many ways it had felt entirely inappropriate returning to the museum, attending to matters that before the accident had seemed of upmost importance and now struck her as trivial. Perversely, it had been like falling in love, the same difficulty with focus and concentration, every sense acute and critically attuned to feeling. But unlike love, loss dulls and wearies. It exhausts rather than enlivens. And rather than finding routine a supportive tool, it had felt crass, insensitive.

"Yes," Catherine said, "You are absolutely right, Frances. Work really helped."

★★★

Polly knelt on the floor and held the cake out close to Lydia's face. Her brown eyes stared in alarm at the flames of the six candles.

"It's all right, Mum," Polly said, "just candles on your birthday cake. And it's chocolate because I know it's your favourite. Me and Dad would sing for you, but you know how tone deaf we both are."

"Nonsense, Polly," Sam said, "I always thought you had rather a nice singing voice. You were in that musical years ago when you were at school."

"Everyone was in that musical, Dad. Anyone who wanted to be. In the chorus at least. And it was just a way of trying to get to know Steven Masters who was playing the lead. We all fancied Steven."

"I didn't know that," Sam said sounding shocked as if the event of Polly's adolescent crush was a recent matter. Polly rolled her eyes indulgently.

"I wonder if you'll be as possessive about your grandchild as you have been about me."

"Possessive?" Sam retorted in surprise. "Surely, neither of us were ever that. Or not overly so."

"Oh, not Mum," Polly said, looking back at Lydia who continued to stare at the cake and candles as if trying to decipher their significance. "She's always been very liberal and understanding, haven't you, Mum? Don't you remember the time I wanted to go to that party in Falmouth and the two of you had a row about letting me?"

Sam did not remember or at least had forgotten too many of the details to bother to dredge them up. Whatever Polly claimed, he could recall only ever minor disagreements over the years that now felt as insubstantial as dreams. He sat down next to Lydia, took her hand. She was wearing the black trousers with the elasticated waist that he tended to dress her in each morning as it was easier than coping with fastenings, with the challenge of tights. He wished now he had made more of an effort or changed her clothes before Polly had arrived for the attempt at a birthday tea.

"Shall we blow out the candles, Lyddie?" he said, slipping

an arm around her shoulder. "And remember to make a wish."
Lydia seemed to smile at him, but then suddenly she jerked
her head away, looked down into her lap.

"This time next year, Mum, when it's your birthday again,
there will be a baby with us. My baby. That's something to
look forward to, isn't it? Something to wish for." Polly blew
out the candles, cut substantial slices for Sam, for herself.
Carefully, she divided a third piece into small mouthful
portions and broke each again into a size no bigger than a
fingernail and watched as Sam patiently offered teaspoons to
Lydia. "I've something to show you both," she said suddenly,
reaching into her large, untidy bag. "It's the scan picture. I
went to the hospital last Friday and – well, it does make it all
seem so much more real."

Sam took the rough grainy image from her hand, held
it with some awkwardness, uncertain. As if viewing a foetus
inside Polly's womb was intrusive, inappropriate.

"Should I know what I'm seeing?" He attempted humour
to cover a sense of embarrassment. Polly laughed and went
over and sat down next to him, explained the shape of emerging
limbs, growing organs, the trace of a spine. She repeated the
explanations directly to Lydia, took her hand and attempted to
guide it over the image. Sam watched, heartened.

"The hospital said they could tell me the gender – you
know, whether I'm having a boy or a girl."

"And?"

Polly stood up, replaced the scan picture with particular
care in her bag and curled up in the big armchair. Her growing
stomach was hidden in a mound of loose cream clothing and
she cradled it extravagantly.

"I said I didn't want to know," she said, "it's all been quite
calculating so far, inevitably, getting pregnant this way. So I've
decided on at least a bit of mystery. You'll simply have to make

wild guesses about your grandchild and wait until the summer to see."

"You went on your own? For the scan, I mean."

Sam looked at his daughter's radiant face, at her composure and self-possession. As always, he envied her guileless honesty, the clarity of her understanding.

"Why not? It's what I want, Dad, remember. It's my choice, how I've planned it."

***

Catherine said, "This week is just the first round. They'll draw up a short list, I expect, and then arrange final interviews."

"But they know you," Beth said, "surely you should go straight to the final session. In fact, I can't think why they are bothering interviewing anyone else at all when you are clearly the best person for the job."

"It's not how it works. The trustees have to follow procedure."

"Yes, yes, I know they must be seen to be impartial, advertise externally, Henry's said all that to me already. Even so, seems ridiculous to me."

"I'm surprised at how nervous I am," Catherine admitted. "At first, I wasn't even sure I wanted the job, but now it seems to be the only thing I know I do want. I mean I know I don't have the typical profile for such a post, but—"

"Just a sec, someone's screaming for me. Back in a moment." Beth broke off, called out to a son, a daughter, saying that surely it was possible to find whatever appeared to be lost without involving her. Catherine imagined Beth's warm kitchen, its large table permanently cluttered, the comforting smell of food cooking or recently eaten that was never entirely absent. She glanced around at her own room, the silence of its order, its appearance to any stranger walking into the place that this had all been entirely her choice, what she had consciously controlled and selected for herself. Whereas in truth it felt far more like pure chance, the roll of the dice. It was Beth whose direction had always been faithful and firm, consciously embracing a life that secured her the large, muddled kitchen, school bags and books and permanent piles of ironing and washing, sudden disputes with stubborn children, the reward of a temporary truce. Beth picked up the phone again, sounding rushed now.

"Let me know, anyway. How it goes, I mean. The interview. I need to go and sort out lost homework and football boots and we've got Henry's aunt here, of course, and he really should be taking her home by now. Except it needs me to remind him because she'll have fallen asleep and Henry will be in front of the computer looking up stuff and lost to the world. Good luck, anyway, Cat. Thinking of you."

Catherine picked up her folder of notes for her presentation, her *Vision for Harriet Howe House Museum – the next five years* and put them on the hall table ready to take with her the next morning.

She must ring Alec.

He had rung her just after New Year, apologising for being away, out of contact for so long. A prolonged business trip, a case that had kept him out of the country for longer than planned. Now he was back and would like to see her. *Lovely,* she had said, distracted at the time by the application for the job, by Robert's increasing absences which were causing her workload to increase. Yet at the same time genuinely wanting to see Alec. Even missing the ease of his undemanding company. *How about at the end of the month? There's just so much going on at the moment.* He would be away again then, he'd said. *And it will be nearly spring by then.* She had wondered if there had been a note of irritation in his voice, but had told herself that was unlikely. It was Alec, after all, who was perpetually transient, inaccessible. She went into the kitchen, opened the fridge, wondering what to eat.

And remembered suddenly the phone call from Gillian March in Bevington.

That person anxious to get in touch with Eddie, unaware, apparently, of his death. She had scrawled down a name, a number, and now felt negligent for not having made contact. He might – or was it a she? – return to Bevington, to Gillian March and blame her for not passing on the message. Catherine looked around her kitchen, opened the drawer that contained random pens, notepads, the minutes from Miller Street party meetings that Frances Chater unfailingly posted through her door. In the living room she checked the bookshelves, the small table in the window. But there was no sign of the scrap of paper or the card – yes, that's right, she wrote the details on the back of a Christmas card – and suspected that it had long been consigned to waste.

It was probably insignificant, anyway.

No doubt the anonymous caller would forget all about a need to reach Eddie, that it had just been a visit made on a whim when in the area and he or she would be entirely unconcerned about hearing nothing more.

SPRING
2006

12

Frances felt too warm. She unbuttoned her burgundy coat, decided to replace it with something thinner, lighter, for future visits. Already there was slight warmth in the thin sun, the suggestion that the year was turning and for the first time she had noticed clutches of daffodils and primroses in the well-tended front gardens around Pilgrim Square. Soon, in the garden of number 10, there would be tulips and the small, fragrant narcissi she had asked Andrew to plant some years ago. And the magnolia tree would not be far behind.

The day had been productive as far as these kinds of days went.

She had seen Charlotte Prideaux arriving at the house, leaving her car double parked while she unloaded shopping, carrying it up the steps and inside, failing to notice both Frances and the vigilant traffic warden fixing a parking fine under her windscreen wiper. A petty triumph, Frances knew, but nevertheless valued. When Charlotte came out of the house again, she had snatched the penalty ticket, thrown it inside the car with exasperation and driven off. Swiftly, assuming the woman would be back once her car was more legally parked, Frances had slipped her latest letter through the box. She had been unable to resist holding open the flap to peer for a moment inside, onto the familiar narrow hallway, the first run of the stairs that led up to the half landing. A woman's black leather jacket hung from a rack of brass coat hooks on the wall. An addition, the clothes rack, cumbersome and intrusive and tangible evidence of Charlotte's impact upon the fabric of the house. Her letter lay neatly in a pool of sunlight on the oak flooring, *Delivered by Hand* clearly written under Charlotte's name. This time, Frances was particularly pleased with her chosen text: *Here I am – I stand at the door and knock* which she had come across some weeks before and had been saving for a personal delivery. She stared for a few moments down the length of the hall towards the closed door that led to the kitchen then turned abruptly away, retraced her steps down the path, out of the square and up the road towards the station. A yellow raincoat, perhaps, Frances thought. A sensible spring purchase in a bold and assertive colour suggesting neither cowardice nor surrender.

Violet saw her first. The train was already pulling out from the platform and Frances, staring mindlessly through the window, was recalling the absurd height of Charlotte Prideaux's heels.

"Hey, this is a coincidence!" Violet sat down opposite, depositing a tumble of carrier bags at her feet. "I thought I saw you at the station, but then I was buying some stuff to eat and nearly missed the train. Have you been away, staying here or something?"

Frances said something about visiting a friend. Lunch with a friend, she added, and began to elaborate about a neighbour from Worthing who had been good to her mother in her final years. But Violet seemed to have stopped listening. She took out a box of fast food from one of the bags, the cloying smell of cheap oil invading the carriage, and steadily ate through the contents, precariously balancing a disposable cup of tea between her knees until Frances relieved her of it.

"What about you, Violet? What's brought you to Brighton?"

She skilfully shifted the conversation, holding fast to the cup while two sachets of sugar were emptied and the liquid swirled with a fingertip. Invention and subterfuge were necessary, of course, but this constant resort to lying was draining. And Violet's company at that moment was unwelcome. She felt weary, uncommunicative, and inconsequential conversation pointlessly tiring. Besides, she was not used to seeing Violet away from Miller Street. Always it was at her invitation, in her flat, on her own terms. Here she resented the sense that Violet had engineered their meeting and consequently held the upper hand. But at least it was only Violet, someone so given to self-absorption that she was unlikely to ask probing questions. She finished the final French fry, took the disposable cup of sweet, stewed tea from Frances.

"Me? What was I doing here? I've been staying for a few days with friends of my brother, actually. Having a bit of a break from the flat which I certainly needed, I can tell you that. Waking to the same walls every day can get you down, you know. Just so routine. And well, anyway, I've been helping them out, these friends of Arthur – that's my brother – with a new business of theirs. Like they really needed me, you know how people do? Even without realising it. They were just so out of their depth, I can tell you." She delved into the cluster of bags at her feet, found a packet of biscuits and tore it open. Crumbs shot over her jeans, her heavy boots, and over Frances' burgundy coat. She brushed them away elaborately, offered Frances a chocolate digestive, working her way down the packet until she could find one that was not broken. "It's Alternative, you see," she went on, "their business."

Frances said, "Alternative?" The biscuit tasted dry and strangely of soap. But also, mildly comforting.

"Arthur's friend's business. Well, they're now my friends

too, I suppose. Having slept on their sofa for several nights. And walked their dogs. It's Alternative Therapies. Although I've said to call them Complementary. Goes down much better, you know. Funny that, just the one word. Anyway, I helped them out with some branding, you could say. Offered them much-needed support, I can tell you."

"And you can assist these friends of yours because – you're some sort of expert in all this? You are entirely knowledgeable of the field, are you, Violet?" Frances knew she sounded acerbic, imitative of her mother's default tone that had so crushed her when she was growing up. It was that clothes rack in the hall of 10 Pilgrim Square that was causing her mood, she knew. Andrew had once suggested that one would be useful, functional, and she had instantly dismissed the idea. *Unnecessary,* she had said firmly, *intrusive, such a foolish idea, Andrew, really,* and had reminded him at some length of the substantial understairs cupboard with its provision of hooks for coats and scarves, a shelf for the neat storage of gloves and hats. She wished now she had not been quite so adamant.

It was, after all, simply a request for a clothes rack.

Violet, however, pooling shards of broken chocolate digestives into her hand and emptying them into her mouth, blithely went on.

"Knowledgeable? Absolutely! You could certainly say that. Well, not an entire expert, of course. Not actually qualified with diplomas to my name or anything. But I've been on the receiving end of so much of this stuff, these therapies, over the years and I have actually thought of going into it all, you know, like professionally, studying and setting myself up as one. A therapist. Possibly, anyway. But I just haven't got going with it all, really. Not yet. But my mother has. Decided to train a while back. And she used me to practise on. Her model, you could say. Her case study for her assignments. I've had the lot. Reflexology, Reiki, head massage, in depth tissue stuff. All the business with the essential oils. So, you see, I am as good as. Expert, that is. Or at least almost. Just a few steps removed, you could say."

Frances had no interest in hearing about the fledgling business of Violet's friends yet neither did she want to make the effort of any other conversation that distracted from thinking of her visit to the Square. Her vigil. Always she spent her train journey home anticipating her next move, calculating her progress and she kept a notebook in her bag for jotting down random thoughts and plans, drafts for subsequent letters. Violet's perpetual chatter was an irritation. Yet when she broke off abruptly and simply stared out of the window as the train edged into Horsham, the silence lay too heavily between them and Frances made some attempt to be amenable. Violet, after all, appeared to welcome her practical support and she grudgingly admitted that the girl provided her with a temporary repository for her affections.

"So, you and your mother have a shared interest in these complementary therapies," she began. "That must be a great bond for the two of you. I've always thought it would be such a consolation to have a daughter who shared a similar vision, as it were. You must be very close."

"Well, I suppose so," Violet said, her expression unconvinced. "Most of the time, though, I seem to be more of a worry to her. At least that's the way she behaves."

"Parents do worry, that's their job. A lifetime sentence of anxiety that the children rarely appreciate."

"Fortunate for you not to have any then, Fran."

"Pardon? What do you mean?"

"Well, you've never married or done the whole family thing, have you?"

"Ah, yes. I mean no, you're quite right, Violet. But one can't help noticing the anxieties of friends. Other people. And how their children never seem to realise that their judgements are only driven by superior knowledge. By the maturity and wisdom acquired over the years. And love, of course. Unconditional love must be at the centre of it all.

"My family's always been a bit troubled," Violet said. She took out a brush from one of her bags, began to work it slowly, rhythmically, through her long strands of hair. "Or at least on Mum's side of things. Her father messed up big time when she was really young and her mother never really got over it, she says. Saw it as shaming the rest of the family, giving them a bit of a stigma or some nonsense. Attitudes being what they were back then. For that generation, anyway. Of course, he couldn't help it."

"Who couldn't?"

Frances often found Violet's conversation hard to follow with its habit of vague and muddled allusions.

"My grandfather. Mum's dad. Not that he was ever really my grandfather as he was dead decades before I was born. To me, he's just a random name in the dodgy family history. One of those dark skeletons as it were."

"I see," Frances said neutrally.

"My mum was only twelve or so when he killed himself. Terrible, of course. But clearly, he knew what he was doing. He'd tried twice before, evidently, so it was a case of third time lucky. Lucky for him, that is. My grandmother was less than impressed as you can imagine. Evidently, she never really got over it."

"What a dreadful thing to happen," Frances said, shocked and disarmed by Violet's succinct account of a family tragedy. "And your poor mother. She must feel burdened by such a past."

Violet stopped brushing her hair mid stroke, stared back as if the thought had never occurred to her.

"But it's the past, isn't it? That's the point. And that's what gets me, all this trailing literally dead events into the present when there's absolutely no point. No point at all."

The train had pulled into the station for Gatwick airport and immediately the carriage became crowded with passengers and heavy loads of luggage clogged the aisles. As if prompted by the sight of suitcases, Violet switched subjects to her plans for a working summer abroad. By the time they reached Croydon, Frances had heard about the possibilities of her working in a club in Ibiza, as a holiday rep in Corfu or waitressing on a cruise ship in the Mediterranean. Each idea seemed to captivate her enthusiasm for some ten minutes or so before negative issues began to nudge, cloud her face and she moved onto the next option.

"What a pity you won't be at home in July to celebrate the centenary with us," Frances said, interrupting Violet's mild interest in working as a supervisor at a children's beach club in Corsica. "You seemed so interested when I first told you about the plans for our street party." Violet looked at her blankly. Frances began to search for her rail ticket slipped into the side pocket of her navy handbag. The train felt unbearably stuffy to her by now and her tolerance for Violet's perpetual conversation was strained. "I thought you seemed quite keen on offering some face-painting sessions for the children of the road. We do want to provide some entertainment for everyone, after all."

Violet said, "Oh that!" She rolled her eyes as if exasperated by her own forgetfulness. "I've been meaning to tell you. I just knew there was something as soon as I saw you sitting here in the carriage. Immediately, I thought, well, that's all very convenient because I can tell Fran now and it will be something to talk about on the way back to London."

Frances waited. Violet smiled expectantly as if the matter in her mind had been communicated by some sort of osmosis.

"Tell me what?" Frances said eventually. She buttoned up her coat, brushed away the last of Violet's chocolate digestive biscuit crumbs.

"My parents," Violet said, "didn't I say? They want to come. To the Miller Street party thing. After all, my dad does own the flat. He's every right to invite himself when you think about it. And they both seem to think it's a good idea to get to know the neighbours and all that stuff in case they ever want to use it. Or even live there for a while. At the flat. Once I've moved on somewhere else which I could do. Any time." She gathered up her bags as the train pulled into Clapham Junction. "Are you getting off here? My ticket only takes me this far and we can get the bus back to Miller Street. Oh, and all that business about the summer. I don't suppose I'll be going anywhere until August, actually. At the earliest. I don't really want a working summer, after all. The summer's too good to spend it working. So, count us all in, Fran. For the street party thing, I mean. I might as well come along."

★★★

Andrew Chater gets back later than usual. The day has been frustrating, disorganised, thanks to the inadequacy of the latest receptionist. She has double-booked patients, allocated inappropriate length appointments so that he has been presented with a mere ten minutes for a complicated extraction and thirty for a routine filling. Her resignation, offered just after lunch when he confronted the chaos of her patient record-keeping, has been the only high point of his day. Still, it means a string of incurious temporary staff before a satisfactory replacement can be found and the prospect is wearying. He pulls his car into the only remaining residents' parking space in Pilgrim Square, wonders whether Charlotte is home. She left the surgery early, a hair appointment that he had forgotten and greeted irritably even though her absence for the afternoon is clearly down in the practice diary. He sits for a few moments at the wheel of the car, inordinately tired, suddenly, with the idea even of getting out of the car, finding keys and letting himself into the house. He checks his phone. A text message from Charlotte. *Delayed! Highlights take forever! Get things going, will u? Table? Check wine. God, any allergies? Forgot 2 ask! XX.* For a few moments, the message makes no sense and he wonders if he has mistakenly taken the departing receptionist's mobile instead of his own since the day has already been one of chronic confusion. Then he remembers. Groans audibly. Ted and Flora are coming to dinner. He likes Ted, tolerates Flora with relative ease since, in spite of her habit of talking too much, she is a clever woman who appreciates good wine. Besides, he has known them both a long time. But tonight, he wishes only to go into his house, shower and change into shabby clothes and succumb to an evening of banal television and bland food. Macaroni cheese, baked beans on toast, fried up fridge leftovers coated in commercial mayonnaise. Charlotte is a good cook, an impressive and original cook, and he knows already that she will view the success of the evening as dependent upon her culinary skills. He has glimpsed the signs over the past couple of days. An excess of marinating, deboning, maturing, stuffing and skimming, a gradual gelling of gelatine, a slow and delicate flavouring of nutmeg, allspice and cloves to custards and creams. He feels nauseous at the prospect of such clever food. Then there's Ted and Flora themselves. For despite their good manners, their tolerance and discretion – or perhaps because of all these things – the absence of Frances hovers over such occasions as these. The inevitable elephant in her own front room. The first time Ted and Flora had invited them to their house, Andrew had been engulfed with gratitude. Frances had only left the month before and their gesture seemed to be an acknowledgement of their approval of Charlotte, of his actions in discarding his wife of nearly thirty years for this vibrant, attractive and intense young woman. He remembered watching Charlotte getting ready for the evening, choosing between a skin-tight, low-cut black dress and narrow, tapering velvet trousers and high heels and thinking how successful, how strong and admirable it made him appear with her at his side. He had driven to their house in Rottingdean feeling invigorated, a man who had ruthlessly shed the shadows of compromise and conciliation, broken free of chains that bind. He had kissed Charlotte passionately outside Ted and Flora's house, slipping his hand down the front of her silk shirt – she had decided on the tapering trousers – and softly fondled her breasts like an adolescent experimenting with the act. But once inside their neat, spotlessly tidy Rottingdean home, sitting opposite Charlotte on one of their comfortable chintz chairs, he had felt awkward. Diffident. Gauche. As if he no longer knew exactly who he was or how he was meant to behave. To his old friends in Charlotte's company, to his young lover in theirs. Suddenly, all skills of easy social intercourse seemed to elude him and he had spent the evening feeling guarded, tense.

A neighbour hovers in his car, parallel to his parking, raises a hand as if to question whether Andrew is about to pull away. He shakes his head, resolutely gathers his jacket, his bag, crosses Pilgrim Square and swiftly mounts the steps to his front door. He throws keys onto the hall table, drops his bag on the floor, hooks his jacket over the end of the banister then remembers, moves it next to Charlotte's on the new coat rack, trying to nudge himself into the habit. In the kitchen he opens the fridge door, hungry yet inhibited by the number of dishes expertly cling-film wrapped and sealed. He has a sudden absurd desire for a plate of porridge, brown sugar oozing over the surface to meet a pool of chilled milk yet he is unsure whether they even have the ingredients in the house and certainly scant knowledge of how to make it. From the bread crock he grabs a loaf, hunks off a chunk with deliberate carelessness so that crumbs shoot across the worktop, onto the pale ceramic floor. Spreading it liberally with marmalade, he goes back to the hall, heading for the stairs, intending to lie down for half an hour or so to prepare for a long evening ahead.

A letter lies on the floor.

He noticed it when he came in, but neglected to pick it up in his hurry to find some food. Seeing Charlotte's name handwritten on the envelope, he puts it on the console table next to his keys, starts to turn away when something familiar catches him, pulls at him dully. Even when he has gone upstairs, abandoning the idea of a rest to stand instead for several minutes under a hot shower, he cannot dismiss that handwriting as a coincidence. He stands on the half landing wrapped in a towel, his wet feet making dark imprints on the soft carpet, staring down at the letter.

And suddenly, he is not surprised.

When Frances had appeared so compliant about leaving the house, acknowledging his relationship with Charlotte, he had been relieved by her apparent acquiescence, the dignity with which she had behaved. Defeated, she had shown remarkable composure as if she had long anticipated such an event and was prepared to accept the dramatic change in her status. It had absolved him, he had liked to think, of all guilt in the matter for she, too, had clearly viewed their separation as inevitable.

But Frances, by nature, was not a biddable woman.

Combative, she had always been loath to lose even insignificant disagreements for her need for control was instinctive. And standing now, bath towel looped around his waist, his hair still wet against his head, the firm curve of Frances' letters, looping and swirling confidently around the C and P of Charlotte's name seem to lift off the beige envelope, rise up and imprint themselves on his bare skin, tattoo-like.

The front door swings open. Charlotte, hair newly streaked, highlighted, cropped into the nape of her neck, stands in the hall. She looks up, sees Andrew and bounds the stairs towards him, scattering her flat black shoes as she goes. How impossibly young she is, so energetically vibrant and alive, and he lets her pull his towel away from him, bury her face in his chest. He kisses the top of her head, smells the artificial scent of lacquer and lotions.

"Do you like it?" she says, "the new style, I mean." She places her head on one side, slowly swivels it and the fringe falls over her eyes. She flicks it aside.

"Of course," he says. She steps away from him, takes his hand and leads him upstairs to the main landing. "Flora and Ted – they're not here for another hour."

Andrew follows in her wake, feeling helpless and incapable of any resistance. As if the conviction and brazen certainty of this extraordinary woman precludes any choice.

"By the way," he says, letting her push him down onto the bed, watching as if from some curious distance while she slips out of her clothes, swiftly discards her watch, a silver bracelet. "There's a letter for you downstairs. Delivered by hand. I think it's from Frances."

She brings her face close to his, momentarily shrugs a bare shoulder.

"Oh, that business. It's not the first, you know, Andy. I just tear them up."

"You mean there have been others? Why didn't you tell me – how many?"

"I've lost count," Charlotte says indifferently. "Some sent by post, some hand-delivered."

"You mean she's been here? To the house?" Andrew is appalled.

"Oh, your ex is quite the stalker. Stands at the end of the square or under the lamp post at the top. Perhaps we should get the police involved."

"You really think we should?"

Charlotte places a finger over his lips, whispers close to his ear.

"No, of course not. Don't be ridiculous. She's just trying to scare me off. And she's no chance of doing that. Just forget about her, Andy. I do. She'll go away soon enough. And once the divorce is all through – well, she'll no longer be our problem."

Andrew closes his eyes. He feels bewildered, lost, as if his capacity to understand his own feelings, even his own desire, has been removed from him and he has to rely on the instructions of others for an appropriate response.

"You're right," he says, "of course you are. Once all the ghastly legal details are sorted and we've moved on. Properly moved on, I mean. The situation will right itself." He has no idea what his vague phrases mean, but the words seem to satisfy Charlotte. He lies back, trying to lose himself in the moment, trying to detach himself from the shadow of culpability that has appeared in the form of that neat, white envelope sitting expectantly, accusingly, on the console table in the hall downstairs.

13

Catherine finally rang Beth on Sunday morning.

"That's ridiculous!" Her sister's reaction had been predictable. "When did you hear?"

"Earlier in the week," Catherine hedged. She had felt unable to face Beth's supportive outrage when she had first heard from the trustees and had delayed the call by nearly a week. Now she tried to diffuse it. "But it's not all that surprising, really. I knew it was a long shot going for it in the first place. In fact, I'm not even sure why I bothered to apply."

Her disappointment was still too acute for her to admit. It was easier to feign indifference.

"It's crazy," Beth said sharply. "You're clearly the ideal person for the job. It's such an insult. I can't believe it. Will you stay?"

"Will I stay? At the museum? Of course, I will. It hadn't even occurred to me to leave."

It was entirely untrue. Catherine's failure to be appointed as Robert's successor had disillusioned her deeply. And the news that the trustees were suspending an appointment in the immediate future, the first trawl of candidates presumably too inadequate, was of no comfort. She had spoken only briefly to Robert Knight who was now firmly, enthusiastically, entrenched in New York and although he sympathised with her, she could tell he now considered the matter to be beyond his concern or even his interest. He had moved on, his focus now shifted definitively from the museum to Manhattan. For two or three days, she had scanned newspapers and websites for other job opportunities, had rung to enquire about a couple, had even considered a radical move. Her flat would be easy and profitable to let, she had reasoned at four o'clock one morning, unable to sleep. The position as the development manager at a small museum in York had seemed inviting. The marketing officer at a stately home in Derbyshire with a particularly notable collection of Victorian and Edwardian arts and crafts, accommodation provided, had been briefly of interest. But she knew she was simply playing out her reaction like a petulant child deprived of the prize. She had no intention of leaving the flat in Miller Street, of handing it over even temporarily to someone else for the place now reflected her back in a way that offered her confirmation. A sense of arrival. And although she loathed to admit it, the museum had become intrinsic to her too, rather like a family firm that, however infuriating at times, could always be forgiven since it provided the stability and continuity she required. It was useless to protest otherwise.

"In the meantime," Beth went on, her tone still irascible as if Catherine herself bore some guilt for the situation, "you are doing your own job as well as Robert's, I suppose. Until the trustees find someone who does come up to their so-called expectations. And that could be months away."

"It's inevitable, really," Catherine said, "I can't possibly do everything, of course, and I can call on one of the duty managers when things become too overwhelming. I've been told there's a budget for that. But it feels like all long-term planning is simply on hold which is frustrating as there's so much that I would like to develop and I simply don't have the authority to implement anything radical."

"You're being exploited," Beth said firmly, "paying you for one job whilst you're doing two."

"It does feel like that right now," Catherine admitted, "I'm doing very long hours, trying to cover everything. But Beth, I'm clearly not what the trustees think is needed. I have the experience and knowledge, naturally, but I'm not an academic with a high-flying university degree and the right sort of connections." Catherine spoke with a rationality she did not particularly feel. "Not like Robert at all with his string of articles published in scholarly journals. That kind of thing."

Beth said, "Why don't you come down and see us next weekend? It's definitely beginning to feel like spring, lambs in the fields, all that sort of thing. Drive down Friday night, why don't you? We've got nothing on and I'm sure you could do with getting away and you can bore me and Henry to your heart's content with all this nonsense about the job. We'd all love to see you."

"It's tempting," Catherine said, "although to be honest I think I'd prefer to put the whole thing out of my head for a while. And anyway, I'm needed at the museum next Saturday as the volunteer rota is a bit thin at the moment. Somehow, with Robert's office being empty – well, let's just say I feel I need to be there to convince the staff that we're still a going concern. It could be months before they make an appointment at this rate."

"You're overdoing it," Beth said. "Working far too hard with no rewards, it seems to me. And what about a bit of a social life? What's the point in living in London if you never go out anywhere?"

"I do go out to places," Catherine protested, "plays sometimes. And films. Last week, in fact."

"Alone," Beth said sternly. "You went on your own?"

"It's hardly a crime."

"No, but it sounds so …"

"Pathetic? Lonely? Desperate?"

"Of course not. I only meant – I mean, it must be well over eighteen months since all that awfulness and you could begin to be thinking of moving on."

"Actually, it's just fifteen months since Eddie's death if we're counting." Catherine knew it was pointless to grow exasperated with Beth. Her sister spoke out of a misplaced sensitivity, resorting frequently to euphemisms as if it removed the brutality of the event. She was also in the habit of seeing others only in her own likeness. Her intolerance of solitude, her natural antipathy to the idea of a single life, was thus transferred to other people whose needs she viewed through the prism of her own requirements.

"Even so," Beth said, "surely you want to begin to plan ahead. Not exactly start again, but begin to think about the future and how you see yourself. What you really want. And now there's not going to be any new job to concentrate on."

"There's the centenary party," Catherine said suddenly and managed to distract Beth from what could so easily become a tiresome dispute between them and Beth, always reluctant to focus for too long on anything that required disagreement, was diverted. At least temporarily. She asked appropriate questions, wanted to know who was involved on Frances' committee and Catherine, somewhat elevating her role and enthusiasm for the event, supplied answers that appeared to satisfy.

"So, a chance really to get to know your neighbours at last," she said. "And you say this woman, Frances, is organising it all? How enterprising of her."

"Or controlling," Catherine said and immediately regretted it. "No, you're right. I suppose every road needs someone who's the opposite of a social pariah. Even so, Frances can be—"

"Bossy? Or full of initiative? Or possibly she's just someone with a lot of time on her hands and wants to put it to good use."

"You're so much nicer than me, Beth. Always charitable. Whereas I find her overbearing. Is that the word? Somewhat domineering. But it's true she doesn't go out to work or have any particular dependents."

"And Alec?" Beth said.

"Alec? What makes you think of Alec?"

"I've been meaning to ask. If you've seen anything of him."

"No, not for months. I've told you, Beth, I've been so busy since Robert left the museum. Besides, he's no doubt abroad."

"Will you ask him? To this street party, I mean. I suppose people on their own, single people, will be expected to bring a partner."

There seemed an inevitable circularity in Beth's conversation.

Catherine looked out of the bay window of the sitting room, saw the early morning sunshine had shifted to cool, overcast skies that threatened rain by the afternoon. She had planned a long walk later, to the river or a park, in need of air and exercise after a week of extended days at the museum. But the prospects suddenly looked dispiriting. She did not want to fight brisk winds, find her feet damp, her hair strung, seaweed like, into wet strands against her face. Beth had begun to talk about Toby, her youngest child, something about singing and a competition, or was that bit about Posy who had always been musical whereas Toby always struggled to stay in tune? Sometimes it seemed to Catherine that her sister had been the mother of small children for most of her adult life. She listened, commented here and there and outside saw Sam Gough with Lydia, attempting to help her into their car. He looked clumsy as if he had not quite mastered the manoeuvre, moving his hands firmly under her arms then pausing, the two of them suspended as if uncertain of the next required move. Lydia's face looked bewildered, as if she was confused by the failure of her limbs to follow instructions, a colt whose legs splayed helplessly beneath the weight of its body. Sam appeared to be coaxing her into leaning onto the frame of the car door, hanging on in some way, then suddenly seemed to change his mind as if in exasperation and took heavy hold of her in a firm lock instead, propelled her back towards the house. A few moments passed then they appeared again, this time with Lydia in her wheelchair, Sam pausing to fasten her coat, shrugging on an old anorak himself, before setting off towards the end of the road in the direction of the common. For a moment, she thought of hurrying out to join them, then immediately rejected the idea, thinking of the awkwardness for Sam if he did not want her company, but felt compelled to accept it. Thus the sensibilities of negotiating friendships that Catherine felt had always hampered her, but never troubled Beth. Their call finally ended, Beth pulled back to the business of her family Sunday, Catherine went to get her coat for an hour or two of solitary walking.

The phone again.

She dropped her bag, peeled off gloves to grab it just before it stopped ringing.

"Catherine? Gillian March again. From Bevington. You remember?"

"Of course I do. Naturally." Immediately, she felt wrong-footed. Someone had been looking for Eddie and Gillian had asked her to respond. She had done nothing. Other than losing the caller's details.

"I really wouldn't bother you a second time and it's no concern of mine at all. I mean whether you follow this up. But the thing is he's been here again. Yesterday, in fact. Come all the way once more, looking for your husband. Or rather looking for a way to contact him. And it's put me in rather a difficult situation, not knowing whether to tell him about what happened. So once more, I just took down his contact details. Promised to pass them on."

Catherine apologised several times, blamed work, her own incompetence. She grabbed a pencil, paper, and carefully wrote down a phone number, a name. An email address. Promised to make contact straight away.

"So you didn't say anything about the accident? This person doesn't know what happened?"

"No, I didn't tell him in so many words, but possibly he might have suspected a certain evasion on my part." Cowardly, Catherine wished Gillian March had been less circumspect and therefore sidestep the need for her to be in contact with Eddie's pursuer. Clearly, whoever was looking for him was not willing simply to go away. There was always a chance that Eddie had owed this person money, possibly even a substantial sum. His lack of caution, the ease with which he had borrowed and expected lenience on the part of his benefactor had been established habits. Gillian went on. "Such a nice young man and I felt so sorry for him, having to make a second journey out to Bevington that this time I invited him in. Gave him coffee. Some of my homemade shortbread fresh from the oven. My husband was here so it seemed quite safe, you see. I mean he'd come such a – well, I have no idea how far he'd travelled, actually, didn't think to ask, but he said something about a train so he'd gone to considerable bother. So if you could be in touch, Catherine, I really wouldn't want him disappointed again."

Catherine felt reprimanded. Suitably cautioned. As soon as the call was over, she went straight to her computer in the spare room, typed the email address Gillian March had given her and *Dear Mr Taylor.* Then sat for some time, trying to think of words both succinct yet comprehensive. After all, she wanted this to be a brief, finite communication between the two of them. Yet reducing a man's death to a few terse words was unacceptable.

But what to say.

There was always the bald truth, of course.

Dear Mr Taylor, I am sorry to say that one winter's night when the driving conditions were appalling, sleet threatening and roads livid with ice, Eddie, already far from sober, grabbed his keys from the hall table and drove off in his car with half a bottle of whisky for company. We had been quarrelling, sparring, scrapping for hours, exchanging barbed insults over matters that now entirely elude me. It was unusual for me to meet him in verbal combat and I think my willingness to take him on for once fuelled his temper.

I failed to stop him leaving.

I failed to grab the keys and keep them from him, throwing only vague remarks about his unsuitability to drive considering his drunkenness in his direction.

I could have driven off myself in his car for I was stone cold sober that night, antibiotics for a dental abscess preventing me from drinking. It would have enraged him, but saved his life. Some compensation there.

In my defence, and I appreciate it's weak, I didn't think he would really drive. At least no further than the end of the road where I expected him to pull into the kerb, to sit and sulk and curse for a while, endure hours in the cold before eventually shrugging home to fall into a deep, lengthy alcohol-fuelled sleep.

Sadly, however, my passive response to his flight that night coupled with his flagrant abandonment of sense resulted in a life ended in a moment. In a matter of mere seconds.

No. The truth, Catherine saw, could be too raw to tolerate.

Poor Mr Taylor, whoever he was, did not deserve such disclosure.

So instead, a compromise.

Dear Mr Taylor, My husband, Eddie, was tragically killed while driving some 15 months ago. I am so sorry to have to deliver such news. No one else was involved in the accident.

She pressed *send,* relieved to have despatched Barnaby Taylor from her concern and went to find coat, boots, for her delayed walk.

★★★

Sam placed plates in the sink, idly ran a tap over them and left them to soak. There was a chance Polly might call in later after visiting friends in Richmond. She had said as much when they had spoken the day before and he wished now he had been more encouraging of the idea, pinned her down to a time, instead of implying it would make little difference to his day. Their day. Sometimes he had to remind himself that Lydia was still a part of that. That the woman sharing his bed, sitting opposite him at breakfast, dinner, was his wife and not some distant and vague relation thrust upon him for care and safekeeping. And he still loved her, of course he did. Just as he had always loved her, without compromise or doubt. What he found hard to accept, even to himself, was that now he so often felt paralysed by loneliness in her company. By a sense of rejection as if she had wilfully chosen to exclude him, to subject him to a form of cruel separation. He walked back to the living room, sat down opposite her in one of the pair of armchairs he had recently moved to the end of the room so that they overlooked the garden. Soon after they had moved in, one day in early autumn, he had pushed some spring bulbs into the borders of the newly turfed patch of lawn so that now there was sign of some life emerging from the dark soil. He had never tended a small urban garden before and had only distant memories of one from his suburban upbringing. He had cultivated land in Scotland and Cornwall, vegetable patches, kitchen gardens, fruit trees, even hens with an attempt at some self-sufficiency. Now he felt constrained by matters such as herbaceous borders, perennials, annuals and bedding plants. Still, such a garden might give Lydia some pleasure although her vision was now increasingly compromised so it was hard to know how far her sight travelled. But at least he was trying. Offering her more than a television screen or a magnolia wall to stare at all day. People could see the effort, note the gesture.

As if it actually mattered what anyone else thought.

He had pushed their walk too long, taken them too far along the tow path, distracting himself with river views on one side, a substantial development of an old brewery site on the other until he realised she was becoming restless, showing some discomfort of sorts. He had turned back straight away, but it had taken them too long to reach home by which time Lydia was deeply distressed and passers-by were glaring at them as if there was something antisocial in their behaviour. Sam had glared back with hostility. But she was calm again now, her expression peaceful and he leant forward, took one of her hands, cradled it in both of his. It was not a gesture he used to make before she became ill and now he wondered why. Perhaps he simply presumed too much, thought his affections too profound for such easy signals.

And all those things he had failed to say.

Presuming there were endless, infinite years strung out ahead of them, boundless time at their disposal. He pulled his chair closer, tried to engage Lydia's unflinching gaze.

"So Lyddie," he began. "All the things we didn't talk about. Didn't tell each other. Have never shared. The things I suppose I thought we'd get around to one day. I always meant to tell you everything. The dark secrets of the soul, is that what they're called? Shouldn't die still holding on to those.

But let's not get too far ahead. I'm not sure I'm ready for the full confessional yet because at heart I'm a coward and always have been. Always too anxious for your good opinion of me. Too terrified that if you knew the truth about the man you'd married in good faith, you'd abandon me, disappear into the mist without a backward glance, taking Polly with you.

But let's start with you, my darling Lyddie.

Because I've always wanted to know something and never quite managed to find the voice to ask. Was going to get around to it one day and now, as a result of my poor timing, you have the upper hand in the matter and won't be able to tell me the truth anyway.

But here goes.

Have you always been as faithful to me as I assumed you were? That young student of yours, do you remember? All those years ago. What was his name – Jez? Josh? Something along those lines and really it doesn't matter now. None of it matters. But I used to wonder as he so clearly adored you. Was in love with you, no doubt, the way he used to look at you. It was a couple of years before we left Scotland, wasn't it? You held that exhibition at the house one summer and he came to it, admired your work and asked you for a bit of help. Some tuition in – I don't know. I didn't take much notice at the start. But he wanted some help in getting a portfolio together. In fact, he always seemed to be there that summer. Hanging around. Then we even put him up for a week or two, didn't we? Maybe it was longer. Something about a bit of trouble with his landlady and we had spare rooms in that cavernous place of ours. I remember he used to play with Polly as well. Or amuse her somehow. Bike rides or something like that. Any excuse to get close to you, I used to say. Jokingly. I know I used to laugh about him. All that earnest talk of his about his Art and what he called His Vision. And you were always so kind and encouraging. Was there more to it, Lyddie? Was I being very naïve? I was away a lot, of course. There was that big contractor job I was doing in Glasgow at the time and it used to make sense to stay over in the week. Then the same kind of thing turned up in Dundee. Good money, couldn't afford to turn it down and you agreed. Said you and Polly would be fine. Long summer days and all that. I remember admiring how resilient you were, and how I'd look forward all week to driving home to the two of you on a Friday night. Was there more to it, Lyddie, with you and that man? Josh? Jezz?

Not that I'd want to know now, Lyddie. Not that I need to know.

In fact, even back then I think I would have chosen ignorance. Head in the sand sort of reaction. Knowledge of that sort can hurt, can't it? The act can be insignificant, but awareness of it does the damage. Haunts and takes away peace of mind."

Sam released Lydia's hand to her lap. Her head slid sideways from the cushion where it was resting and he leant forward, adjusted it for better support. He kissed her lightly on the cheek.

"There's so much more, Lyddie, that I want to ask. And, of course, it's only fair to take my turn. You can't ask the questions, any more, but I know what there is to tell. What I've always been meaning to tell. But enough for now. All getting a bit deep, isn't it?"

He kissed her again, this time on her lips which felt dry. As if parched by too much sun.

The doorbell rang. Polly stood there in a vibrant, billowing crimson dress.

"Sorry!" she said, stepping into the hall. "Is the dress too much? Just felt it was time at last that I revealed to the world the truth of the matter. Don't want people assuming I'm simply getting fat."

Sam looked at her and smiled broadly. Instantly shredded the introspection of his day.

"You look ..."

"Like a ripening strawberry. A radiant raspberry. Or something like that. Blooming, isn't that the word people always use about pregnant women? Although to be honest, I'm knackered. It's been a crazy week, parents' meetings, governors' meeting – in other words, school life as normal." She kicked off her shoes, dropped her bag and keys. "Come on, put the kettle on, I'm desperate for tea. How are things? Had a good week?"

"Fine," Sam said, "absolutely fine. Tea. Yes, of course. Tea."

14

Alec Grey was predictably early. Catherine saw him park the car across the street, sit for a minute or two checking his phone. He looked tanned, rested, in spite of his protest to her on the phone of working hard for months on a protracted case abroad.

He had rung early in the week and Catherine had been comforted to hear his voice. As always he was direct and brief on the phone.

"This coming Friday evening, are you free by any chance? I've been given some tickets for something. A play, I think. Some former clients of mine have a connection with a place just starting up. Not exactly a theatre, I understand, but some sort of performance space. Probably be horribly experimental, but anyway, it's in your neck of the woods, south of the river, so I thought I could come and pick you up around seven? Earlier, if you can make it so we can get a drink beforehand. We'll eat after if that's all right."

She had agreed immediately. And found herself looking forward to seeing Alec in a way that surprised her. As if she had been unaware of a vacuum of need that his invitation confirmed. And not only because it would pacify Beth, satisfy the absurd drive of the younger sibling always to appease the older. Alec, gratified, had checked her address, swiftly rung off and she had begun to anticipate Friday. She was overdue leave at the museum, would take the afternoon off, get her hair cut, perhaps buy something new to wear, minor indulgences that had recently felt remote. She had never loved Alec. Not in the way she had loved Eddie. But she held for him a grateful, residual fondness that came, perhaps, from the simple fact of the survival of their friendship. A kind of loyalty that endured whereas more intense passions so often spent themselves, wore each participant down with the demands of such ardour.

Like Eddie, perhaps.

Yet for the first few years, she had embraced his audaciousness, his constant need to flout convention, choosing to see such qualities as complements to her biddable, cautious nature. Her admiration for him had been unqualified. Her defence of his sometimes outrageous behaviour absolute. It had been hard to remember the moment when a slow slipping away of such conviction had begun. Perhaps it was the move to Bevington that had prompted it although initially Eddie had seemed more content, affable, as if freed from the constraint of perpetuating an image among the wine bars of Covent Garden and Camden that he had grown too old to sustain. He had seemed to adapt, dug the garden, planted apple trees, worked steadily, sensibly, on a promising business venture. Catherine had watched him, relieved, loved him, saw the richness and goodness of the man she had married. But the respite had been brief. The apple trees took too long to flourish, the business idea required too much caution. It was as if Eddie had grown bored with being level-headed, needed to break from such restraint and expected Catherine to concur. She urged patience. He wanted to see in her only a reflection of his own carelessness. Gradually, there had been a slow ebbing away of spontaneous affection between them, of familiarity and warmth to be replaced by polite, but guarded exchanges, not hostile, but checked, qualified. Later, much too late, Catherine saw that the loneliness she had felt at the time of their estrangement had been in Eddie too. It had not been as she had imagined her predicament alone. And she had wondered why neither of them had been able to see the sadness of each other's loss and instead had turned away from the possibility of salvaging what once they had found so dear in each other.

Now Alec stood at her door, holding an enormous bouquet of flowers that masked his face.

"Rather a belated moving in gesture, I know," he said. "Sorry, am I annoyingly early? Wasn't sure how bad the traffic would be as it's Friday."

"They're beautiful," Catherine said. Violet Lawrence was hovering on the forecourt, taking an inordinate amount of time to place plastic bags in the rubbish bins with her focus blatantly on Alec and his floral offering. Catherine, clutching the flamboyant flowers, ushered Alec into the hall. Violet turned back to her rubbish, clearly disappointed with the lack of an introduction.

"Your neighbour?" Alec said.

"One of them. We're quite a community here in Willow House. Just as well it wasn't Frances Chater, though. She would have been more difficult to shrug off. You'd have ended up with a role in the centenary street party, no doubt." Alec looked curious, but she waved her hand, led the way to the kitchen to place the bouquet in the sink. The room immediately filled with the heady sweetness of oriental lilies, orchids, peonies. White roses. "I think I'll leave them here in water until later. It'll take me ages to arrange them." The flowers surprised her. A generous man, he was nevertheless not given to gifts he would consider extravagant and of only transient value. Catherine could never remember him buying her flowers in the past and the gesture touched her deeply. "Thank you, Alec, they really are lovely."

He shrugged dismissively, glanced at his watch.

"There's just time for a tour," he said, "before we go off to whatever this performance offers us. Lead the way." Yet Alec had already left the kitchen and was wandering from room to room, rather like a conscientious surveyor, calmly assessing, staring, noting detail. She watched his careful progress then joined him in the sitting room where he was looking out of the large bay window onto Miller Street.

"Well?" she said, "do you approve?"

"Very pleasant," he said, "yes, I like it very much. Peaceful too, I should imagine. Apart from being on the flight path to Heathrow."

"I've got used to that now. In fact, I hardly notice the planes. Besides, city living isn't supposed to be exactly tranquil. It's silence that I find unnerving."

"That's true," he agreed. "We're alike in that way, Catherine. No good trying to sell either of us the merits of rural living."

"It really is very good to see you again, Alec," she said and kissed him lightly on the cheek. "That's for the flowers. Uncharacteristic, but much appreciated!" He laughed, placed a hand on her shoulder for a moment then broke away, moved to a shelf on the far wall where she had displayed a few framed photographs. He picked up one then another with some deliberation. There were several of Beth, Henry and the children at various ages. An old black and white picture of her mother and father, gauche in awkward deckchairs on a bleak beach. Bognor, possibly. Perhaps Clacton. Carefully, he replaced each one, then picked up the remaining frame that was positioned a little behind the others as if recessed. He turned to Catherine, photo in hand.

"Eddie," he said somewhat curtly, "still flying the flag for him, I see."

Defensively, she said, "I don't know what you mean. It's just – he was my husband, Alec." She had forgotten the photo was even displayed, had hardly intended it to take on shrine-like significance when she had found it in one of the packing cases soon after moving in. But equally, she had felt a need to acknowledge Eddie, his place in her recent past that had brought her to the flat in Miller Street. Alec replaced the photo, neglecting to return it to the same discreet spot so that now it seemed to dominate over the others.

"Quite an Icarus, wasn't he?" he said, still looking at the full-length image of Eddie, a cream sweater, flying jacket, standing in a ploughed field staring at something apparently remarkable beyond the photographer's shoulder. "He chose to fly too close to the sun."

Catherine thought of how Eddie would have approved Alec's analogy, affording him such mythical status. She could see his amused smile, a slight nod of his head in a gesture of feigned self-deprecation. Aloud she said,

"Shouldn't we be going? We don't want to be late."

They drove to the venue, a large room above a pub in Richmond that had been loosely adapted into a performing space so that the division between actors and audience was ill defined. Alec carried a couple of glasses of wine for them from the bar up the narrow staircase. "I'm not even sure what we're going to be watching, but am not filled with optimism."

"It might be very good," Catherine said, peering at the programme which gave little detail beyond an alphabetical list of cast and contributors. They took two unnumbered seats as remote from the front as they could find. "As long as they don't demand audience participation."

"I shall refuse if they do, loudly and vehemently," Alec said. "I am only attending at all out of a sense of kindness and misplaced loyalty. The young man who's producing this thing is the son of one of my oldest and most faithful clients. I believe I'm his godfather too," he added as if recalling the fact from the depths of his memory. "I was certainly at the Christening a couple of decades ago."

The room filled up steadily and soon every seat was taken and latecomers were being encouraged to sit cross-legged on the floor.

"I think we're the oldest here by any reckoning," Catherine said, sipping steadily at her wine as lights began to dim and actors emerged from behind a black curtain and took up freeze frame positions. Alec leant towards her, whispered into her ear, held her hand for a moment.

"I'm ever indebted, dear Catherine! I don't think I could have endured it without you."

He had booked them a table at a Lebanese restaurant close to the pub. Once, Catherine remembered, walking swiftly at his side after the performance as they tried to avoid the sudden rain shower, she had found Alec's tendency to manage, to assume her consent to his arrangements, a considerable irritation. Now she found herself grateful. She wondered whether she had grown more pliant, more appreciative of behaviour that had felt oppressive in the past. Or if ten years of living with Eddie's volatility had caused her now to value the prospect of steady equilibrium.

"It was an intriguing production," she said as they sat down at their table by the window. Alec pulled a face.

"That's kind," he said, "indulgent of you."

"Well, it was entirely original," she went on, trying harder, to offer something that Alec could relay to his friend and erstwhile godchild. "And contextually, there were all sorts of interesting references."

"Were there?" Alec said, swiftly eating bread from the basket the waiter placed between them. "If that was the case,

I'm afraid they all passed me by. Couldn't make head or tail of it although the saxophonist was good. There should have been more of her. Really, Catherine, be honest, wasn't it all absolute nonsense?"

"No," she said firmly, "at least not entire, utter nonsense. At times you could see the idea was to recreate a Chekhovian sense of hopelessness, combined with the wit of Wilde. Perhaps."

"Wit?" Alec said, raising his eyebrows, "I must have missed that bit. No doubt too busy yawning and looking at my watch. You see, I was quite right to bring you as you've furnished me with sufficient material to report back and prove I actually came to the wretched thing. Chekhov and Wilde with a touch of …?"

"An attempt at Stoppard, I'd say. If you want to be very generous. Maybe even Beckett."

"Utterly derivative and pretentious, then."

"Maybe there was the suggestion of sending those up as stereotypes, even. Perhaps that was the idea."

"An idea that failed to entertain."

"It was experimental. Different. And a very young cast. You have to allow them that."

"Is that an excuse?"

"Oh, I think so," Catherine said.

Alec grasped both her hands in his across the table.

"You have come to my rescue yet again. The way you used to. Do you remember? I can't tell you how grateful I am. My knowledge of anything artistic is so woefully inadequate compared with yours."

She felt absurdly complimented. Alec's approbation suddenly seemed of enormous importance and his company reassuring. Their previous meeting in the autumn had been inevitably strained, neither any more secure in how to behave with each other. But now she felt at ease, content with the convenience of a measured affection between the two of them. Several small dishes were placed on the table. The waiter retreated and they began to eat.

"So tell me, Catherine, how's life at the museum?"

She told him. With an honesty that she had failed to share even with Beth, she talked of her deep disappointment, a feeling close to humiliation at failing to gain Robert's job. She mentioned her fleeting consideration of leaving the museum entirely. Alec went on eating steadily, at the same time encouraging her to try more of the dishes. Eventually, he said,

"But you're happy enough with what you are doing now? If this position hadn't come up you wouldn't even have thought of leaving?"

"That's true," Catherine said, "I've always felt a deep attachment to the place – Harriet Howe House, I mean. And to be honest, I wouldn't stand a chance of a curator or director post in one of the really eminent institutions."

"You mean you haven't published in obscure journals stowed away in university libraries where no one ever read them. Nothing to be ashamed of there."

"No, it's just that I am not sure if it's enough anymore. If I should allow it to be enough. The job I'm doing, I mean. Am I am being too complacent simply staying with what is comfortable? Perhaps I should be more restless? Ambitious?"

Alec shrugged.

"That's hardly a question for someone else to answer. And surely, now you're settled here in …" He waved his hand towards the window, to the street now windswept and wet, traffic stalling. "You've made a sensible move, I'd say. A new start after a very difficult time. Why not be content with what you have?"

Sense and sobriety had always sat effortlessly with Alec and thus he was inhabiting middle age as if he had at last reached his natural state. As a younger man, he had often seemed dully sedate, predictable, traits that had felt inappropriate in someone under forty. Now, however, such qualities could be seen as admirable, a source of strength and reliability.

"Tell me about this prolonged case of yours," she said, wanting to change the subject, picking up a fork and turning to her neglected plate, "the one that's kept you out of the country for so long. Is it all over now?"

He talked at some length, expanding on legal loopholes, flawed evidence, complicated case law that she only half grasped or understood. She was enjoying his company too much to notice the lateness of the hour, but the restaurant was now empty and the waiter hovering with the bill. Alec glanced at his watch.

"I must get you home, Catherine, it's late. Or perhaps you'd like coffee?"

"Why don't you come back to the flat? I could make us coffee."

"No, I don't think so," he said somewhat abruptly, briefly scanning the bill. "I've got phone calls to make tonight and some emails I should send."

"Tonight? But it's so late."

"Different time zones. For some people it's early morning. Singapore, for example."

"Of course," she said, feeling foolish. Wrong-footed.

"And, actually, I have a very busy weekend," he went on, fiddling with a credit card, searching in a pocket for loose change as if suddenly in a hurry to leave. "There's so much to see to while I'm back. It's only a brief visit, of course, more of a stopover, really."

"I see. I thought that …" She was defeated. She had no idea what she wanted to say or what she expected from Alec. Not this, however. A certain brusqueness, detachment, the suggestion of indifference. She looked for her coat that had slipped from the back of her chair onto the floor, gathering crumbs, curiously embarrassed by his sudden change in manner. "Actually, I'm working tomorrow too. Saturdays have become essential with the current state of affairs at the museum. It's the volunteers, you see, I think they're feeling rather insecure and if I'm there it's a show of strength. Or that's how I see it."

Alec, shrugging into his jacket, looked up at her for a moment and said, "Don't overdo things, Catherine. Don't let yourself be exploited."

"Fine words," Catherine said, but then realised that Alec was not listening, saying instead something about the rain, an umbrella needed. The convenience that the car was not far away.

Negotiating his way out of Richmond's one-way system, pulling up abruptly at a crossing to let a couple cross, Alec said,

"I'm selling the Hampstead house."

"Selling it?"

"Well, it's far too big and I've only held onto it this long for sentiment's sake, I suppose. Or possibly simply out of inertia. I can't say it means a great deal to me."

"You're buying something smaller?" Catherine stared at the couple as they crossed slowly, their hands and arms entwined like a hybrid creature of sorts.

"Eventually, perhaps. I suppose I will need a base here of some sort."

"A base? So you'll be spending even more time abroad? Well, that's nothing new, I suppose, you've always been constantly in transit."

Alec said, "I'm getting married."

Catherine turned to him and in the darkness of the car's interior, saw him smile.

"Married?" she said flatly.

"Yes. Very soon, in fact. Next month. It's someone – well, we've known each other for years, off and on, and suddenly, it seemed to be the right moment. No point in waiting any longer."

"I see," Catherine said. And as if assuming her need for more detail he went rapidly on.

"She lives in Singapore so that's where I'll have my main home. She's – Alyssa, that is – she has a son, you see, a son of ten and we don't want to disrupt his life, naturally. Not good for a child to lose his sense of security."

"No. Absolutely not. I can see that," Catherine said mechanically. And at the same time remembered her scarf. It was no longer around her neck. She was sure she had been wearing it at the start of the evening and concentrated now on that small room over the pub, then on the Lebanese restaurant, trying to locate it. The scarf with the olive green and beige shapes that someone once said resembled seahorses, her youngest nephew, she thought, trying to focus on Toby's fresh face, freckles on the tip of his nose. As if it would help.

"And of course, the climate is good," Alec was saying. "Reliably hot all the year round. Rainy seasons, of course. And a lot of humidity, it has to be admitted."

"Humidity?"

"But you can't have everything. No winters at least. And the Far East is a useful location for me when you think about it. Easy access to Australia, Japan, the Middle East. So it all makes sense. Perfect sense. Couldn't have worked out better, really."

"Yes," Catherine said, aware that she was contributing very little to the conversation, although Alec seemed not to notice.

"Of course there's endless paperwork to sort out, becoming a resident there. You know how things are. But once we're married – she's half Sinhalese, half American, did I say? Alyssa. But she's lived there most of her life. Singapore, that is. She's in banking."

"I see."

Perhaps it had fallen off into the road, the seahorse scarf. When they scampered back through the wet streets to find Alec's car. She would ring the restaurant the next day, though. Just in case. Suddenly, losing the scarf that had been a Christmas present from Beth one year seemed to have taken on distressing proportions. She started to fumble in her bag for front door keys although they were still a couple of miles from Miller Street. The need for the stillness of her flat, its quiet, undemanding walls, was overwhelming. Alec, seemingly unaware of her silence, had moved on to talk about Hampstead estate agents and surveys and solicitors. About auction houses and disposal of furniture and surplus possessions. He pulled up outside Willow House, left the engine running.

"Thanks again for coming this evening, Catherine. I think I would have walked out half way through without your company to keep me in my seat." He placed his hand lightly on her knee, an avuncular gesture, she saw now. "And it was good to see you again, of course. Seeing you settled after all you've been through."

She thanked him for dinner. The way she would thank a vaguely known acquaintance for an obligatory occasion. He leant towards her as if to kiss her cheek, but she pretended not to notice, turned swiftly away to open the car door. Then she stopped abruptly, turned back to face him.

"Tell me one thing, Alec. I'm confused. Why now? You've always said you would never marry. You must have had so many chances in the past. And why take on someone else's child when you have always rejected the idea of a family life? Why do it all now? I'm at a loss to understand."

Alec said nothing at first, as if taken aback by her question. Then he shrugged, lifted his arms up from the steering wheel, a gesture of capitulation, and turned off the car's engine, staring ahead through the windscreen at the darkened street.

"I'm not sure I know the answer to that myself," he said quietly. "It's a compromise, I suppose. Wise words of independence at thirty or even forty suddenly seem hollow and pointless a decade or so on. Arrogant even. What was so special about me to think I needed something different from the vast hordes of the populace who seem to find marriage the most comfortable arrangement? And I found myself thinking that I wanted more. More of what others seem to have. At least I think I do. I don't know if I am brave enough to grow old alone."

Catherine said nothing. She touched one of Alec's hands for a moment as if in some sort of acknowledgement. Acceptance. "I don't expect you to understand," he went on. "And, of course, I might be making a terrible mistake." He attempted a comical face that in the darkness looked sinister, bizarre. "It's just that suddenly everything seems very – brief. Fleeting. There's so little time."

Catherine nodded or shook her head. Later, she could not remember which, but she knew she had said,

"Good luck, Alec. I hope it all works out for you. Good luck," and hoped that she had meant it. Or at least that she had sounded as if she did.

Inside her flat, the overpowering sweetness of Alec's flowers flooded her head as soon as she stepped into the hall, filled, it seemed, every room. The following morning on her way into work, she took a vase round to the garden flat, handed it to Sam Gough.

"Could you give these a home? A gift from a friend and I find I'm allergic to oriental lilies. They seem to make me sneeze. And there are simply too many roses to count. Lydia, perhaps, would enjoy them."

15

Frances brought an upright chair from the kitchen, placed it in the open doorway of her living room and sat down squarely on it. The floor was already accommodating latecomers, sitting cross-legged as if infants at school assembly.

"No easy escape for any of us!" Sam whispered to Catherine who sat close to him on the large sofa, attempting to seat four. "A truly captive audience."

"I think it's the way she likes it. Or expects it. And I have to admire her. She behaves as if she's lived in Miller Street forever. Look how she's persuaded all these others to get involved."

"A manipulative woman."

"That's a bit harsh – perhaps simply managerial by nature."

"I'm sticking with manipulative," Sam said. "Those flowers, by the way. Thank you so much. Lydia really noticed them. I must try and make more of an effort, remember to buy fresh flowers for her since they seem to be something she can still take pleasure in. There's so little for her now."

Catherine, about to reply, was silenced by Frances calling everyone to attention, her voice forcefully projected. The room quietened, faces turned towards her as she reminded them of how much they needed to discuss. She passed round spare copies of the agenda she had drawn up and posted through doors, just in case, she added with a certain censure, anyone had forgotten to bring their own.

"For once, every member of the street party committee is here. Congratulations, everyone!" she said with satisfaction before adding, "apart from Violet Lawrence who, strictly speaking, is not really committee, but a sort of ad hoc member I myself have co-opted for specific duties.

She's my immediate neighbour, you see," Frances added as if justification was required. "In fact, I often feel almost *in loco parentis* towards her as she's very young. Compared with the rest of us here in Willow House." She indicated Sam and Catherine as if in evidence. Catherine stared fixedly into her lap, Sam muttered something incoherently. "Well, one can't help it, really. Her youth, you know. Any of you would do the same, I'm sure."

An elderly man with a persistent, hacking cough sitting on the desk chair by the window waved his agenda at the room.

"Perhaps we could get on? As you say, there is a lot to cover tonight and I'm sure we'd all like to be home well before midnight."

"Of course," Frances said somewhat sharply, "I was just about to call on Henry, our treasurer, so to speak, or would you prefer to be called our accountant? Anyway, please take us through current costings and funds."

Further pieces of paper were handed out, columns of figures referred to and an energetic discussion about charges for tickets to the street party followed. The figure suggested seemed exorbitant to Catherine. She raised her eyebrows in Sam's direction, but she was unsure whether he was even listening. The woman in charge of catering, Sylvia Stratton, joined in, arguing that an extensive evening barbecue with locally sourced organic meats and a selection of salads were included and was hotly challenged by someone called Rowena who had already drawn attention to herself when she had first arrived by sitting on the floor, upright against the wall, to support, as she put it, her *tricksy back.* It was all absolute nonsense, talking about such charges, Rowena said in a small, but penetratingly high voice, claiming that most people in the street would prefer to bring their own food, sausage rolls and sandwiches and cheese straws and the like, and what about the vegetarians, like her, who objected to the presence of meat altogether, let alone those on special diets and that not everyone in the street had surplus cash to splash on the event anyway. There was an awkward silence as Rowena ran out of breath and sat massaging her lower back with one hand. Eventually, Sylvia Stratton filled the void, muttering something about Sunday school outing fare and that not every resident of the street need feel obliged to attend if it really was not their kind of event. Then a young man Catherine recognised from walking a friendly golden retriever on the common joined in, wanting to know if there was going to be a cash or a free bar as he had a friend in the wine trade who could give them a good deal on New World wines if anyone was interested and could be bothered to ask him. Frances, looking bewildered by the sudden velocity of opinion, informed him sharply that his non-attendance at the past two meetings had made it impossible for his suggestion to be considered and that commitment was to be expected from committee members or their inclusion on it would be terminated. The young man stared at Frances, as if ready to counter her attack, but then simply sank back down into sulky indifference on the low chair by the bookcase. Swiftly, she resumed control of the discussion although nearly an hour passed before agreement on cost of tickets was reached. Frances suggested a break for coffee before they went onto the next agenda item. The room immediately broke into noisy conversation like children released for playtime.

"Did I miss anything?" Sam said, standing up and stretching as Catherine handed him a cup from the tray Frances was carrying round. "Everyone seemed irate about something, but I'm afraid I was a bit too self-absorbed to follow. I've just noticed the date, you see."

"The date?"

"Of the street party. I don't suppose we'll be coming. Not that Lyddie could really manage it, but I might have turned up for a couple of hours just to show neighbourly spirit."

"You have to come," Catherine said. She drank the coffee too swiftly, burning her tongue. "You must have realised the date before now, surely." She wondered whether she sounded like Frances, adamant, insistent.

"I'm not good on detail, Lyddie would tell you. Or she would have done in the past when she could. No, you see it's the 15th , isn't it? 15th July. That's the date Polly's baby is expected. Our daughter, Polly."

"Congratulations," Catherine said, "that must be very welcome news."

"Sorry, I thought you knew. But then why would you? I have to admit it was a bit of a surprise when she told us. More than a bit, if I'm honest. No partner involved, you see. Polly has simply decided she wants a baby and has gone ahead and sorted matters to suit her. It's typical of Polly to know what she wants, of course, and to do something about it. She's always had a very resolved and practical way of looking at things."

Catherine felt an instinctive envy of Polly that confused her. She had never known herself to be someone who coveted another's good fortune, had watched the course of friends' pregnancies in the past without a qualm. Sam went on.

"Of course we're all creatures of our own generation. What is perfectly acceptable and sensible to Polly and her friends would have sounded like something either out of science fiction or the sad tale of a fallen woman to mine. But I have to say I've quickly adjusted to the idea and it's marvellous to have something to look forward to. New life and all that." He stared into the contents of his coffee cup as if seeing significance.

"I admire Polly's certainty," Catherine said. "Taking control rather than waiting for chances and choices to present themselves and then even when they do, failing to see them for what they offer."

"Polly's the most level-headed person I know, Kate. Entirely unlike me, I have to say. And her mother. Lyddie and I are – or were before this ghastly illness of hers took over the driving seat and began dictating the terms of our curtailed lives – rather fly-by-nights in comparison." He swallowed his coffee, put his cup down on a small table where it was quickly removed by Frances circling with her tray. "Anyway, it takes us back to the due date and all that. I understand babies don't always arrive according to plan, but you never know. And although I believe Polly's got some friend of hers lined up to be at the hospital with her, I'd want to be on hand. For the first glimpse of this grandchild of ours."

"Of course. Still, I don't think Frances will see even an imminent birth reason enough to get out of your street party obligations," Catherine said.

"Probably not," Sam smiled. "Hardly the maternal sort, I'd say."

"She seems to be very fond of Violet, though."

Frances was making clear signs of wishing to resume the meeting and chairs were swiftly seized, spots on the carpet retaken with a sense of prior ownership.

"Now," she began, "we still have Entertainment, Road Closure, First Aid and Trestle Tables to cover – points 5 to 8 on your agendas, so some brevity from people speaking would be appreciated. Catherine, perhaps we could leave your item for another evening?"

"I wasn't aware that I was expected to speak about it tonight?"

"Good. No one's really interested in hearing about your social history research and the booklet, anyway. Not to any great extent."

"Fine."

"Charmless," Sam whispered to Catherine. "The woman has the diplomatic skills of a large rodent."

Frances turned to someone called Rufus and asked him to elaborate on his contacts with jazz bands.

After Alec had dropped her the previous Friday evening, driven off to his Hampstead home soon to be emptied and despatched for a quick sale, Catherine had gone to bed, tried to read a book, attempted to sleep and had inevitably lain wide awake in the darkness of the room, allowing Alec's news to flood her mind. She had, she knew, no right to feel betrayed. After all, she had married Eddie and even before that, the nature of their relationship had been essentially casual, pragmatic. Yet she was hurt by something that felt akin to disloyalty, treachery almost, as if all the time they had known each other, Alec had been protesting one choice whilst aspiring tacitly to something very different. But that was unfair. He had been honest, after all, admitted that he had changed his mind about marriage. Even children. Perhaps part of Alec's reasoning lay in a subliminal desire for fatherhood, for posterity, and his fiancée was no doubt young enough to provide him with his own child. Unlike her. The incongruity of fertility, man versus woman, was one of Nature's cruellest gibes, of course. Now she thought shamefully of how, after Eddie's accident, Alec had been quietly solicitous, helpful, a crutch that she had accepted with assumption rather than profound gratitude. She could hardly blame him for seeing this as a sign of rejection. And if she was entirely honest with herself, the idea of Alec's presence in her life was little more than as a convenience, a pleasant and undemanding diversion from time to time. No wonder he had sought someone who wanted to offer him so much more since he appeared, against expectation, to have discovered a need for a way of life that was remarkably normal. Distinct and commonplace. No doubt he viewed her as pursuing something of a husk of an existence without definition or direction. Eventually, she had slept, but only fitfully, vivid, grotesque dreams of Eddie, his hand always slipping just out of reach of hers, disturbing her. She had been relieved to be working the next day and after unloading Alec's flowers on Sam, had arrived early at the museum an hour before opening and stayed late. Mary, the most affable and sympathetic of the volunteer guides, had brought her some tea around five.

"You look exhausted, Catherine," she said, misinterpreting her dulled eyes as a product of her work load. "They really can't expect you to keep doing two jobs, you know. Any idea when the new boss will be in place? Not that you aren't more than adequate to the position, in the opinion of most of us here, but it's not fair on you."

Catherine had thanked her, sent her home to her husband in Rayners Lane and had unnecessarily devoted another couple of hours to developing ideas for a potential future exhibition. *Unsung Heroines,* she tapped out on her keyboard, before turning off her computer. Outside, the mildness of the early spring evening had been encouraging and she had walked slowly, standing for some minutes on Waterloo Bridge to stare at the skyline, ever-changing and evolving, centuries rubbing up against centuries. It had helped. She had consciously discarded her despondency as fleeting self-indulgence, handed a generous amount of change to a homeless woman and headed on home to Miller Street to find relief in her quiet freedom.

Trawling herself back to the committee meeting, to Frances' overheated sitting room, Catherine realised a vote was going on for an item she had entirely failed to follow. Tentatively, she raised her hand, following the lead of most of the room. People were shifting, coughing, stretching cramped limbs as more pieces of paper were being handed out by Frances. Already it was ten o'clock. Sam interrupted as she began to speak.

"Frances, perhaps this is a subcommittee concern – children's activities – and could be discussed separately? Possibly this is something for you and Violet to sort between you, in fact. I, for one, really must go now. My wife, you understand."

Frances said, "Of course! An excellent idea, Sam, and you must go home to Lydia. And you are quite right, Violet and I can handle this as a team. Just the two of us."

"This is all a little irregular," Rowena, still cross-legged on the floor, complained amidst the sudden movement around the room as people grabbed bags and jackets and the chance to leave. "I mean the full committee should really approve any decisions."

"You haven't approved anything yet," Sylvia, the catering woman said, "you've vetoed anything the rest of us have agreed."

"And as chairman of the committee," Frances said swiftly, "I can make the decision to treat this as a delegated matter. And I can assure you, Rowena, all is in hand, and I'm keeping a close eye on things there. Violet being my neighbour, you see. So I don't think we need detain anyone any longer."

She stood up, moving her chair from the doorway to allow escape and there was a rapid exodus into the hallway, down the staircase and out into Miller Street.

"That was skilfully handled," Catherine said to Sam as they reached the forecourt of Willow House.

"There's only so much I can take of polite company," he said. "Can't think why I got myself mixed up with this nonsense in the first place."

"Frances Chater's manipulative skills, remember."

He smiled then turned towards his front door, staring at it for a moment as if reluctant to go in.

"It's a pack of lies about needing to get back to Lyddie, by the way. Polly's here as well as an old friend from Lyddie's art school days. Think they're talking babies and breathing exercises and labour pains all evening. At least Polly and Vivian are. I'm surplus company, in fact. Well, for half an hour or so, at any rate."

Catherine said, "A drink? Or more coffee?"

"You don't have to be gracious, Catherine. I was thinking of taking myself off to the local for half a pint, but if you're offering ..."

He stood in her kitchen as she opened a bottle of wine.

"I always seem to be using you for respite," he said, "sorry." He took a glass, followed her into the front room, looking around. "They did a good job on the restoration, I'll give them that, the developers. Kept all the original features. Our place is a bit ad hoc, really, a couple of original rooms at the back of the house then a modern extension added on. Still, it gives us easy access to the garden which is ideal for Lyddie. Why we bought the place, of course. For her needs. It's not my kind of thing at all. Sorry – that sounds uncharitable. She can't help it. Just as she can't help these mood swings of hers. It's the illness speaking, not her. And when I think how placid Lyddie has always been, so gentle – sorry, here I go again being boring. You must be a good listener, Catherine, bringing out my confessional side. But that probably sounds rude. Does it?"

He smiled as if expectant of a denial. She gave it.

"At least you have Polly's baby to look forward to."

Sam sat down in an armchair, leaned forward, cradling his glass in both hands and paused as if his answer needed considering. The lace of one of his shoes was untied and Catherine wondered whether to point it out. She felt grateful, flattered even, that Sam appeared to seek out her company although she was equally aware that she was no doubt little more than a convenience to him. A sympathetic single neighbour moved by his situation and available to provide some social relief. As she was, of course, she reminded herself, noting the ragged edge of one of the sleeves of his sweater. And wondered whether, if their roles were reversed and Lydia was the carer for her sick husband, she too would receive such gestures of empathy and concern. Catherine doubted it. The prerogative of men seemed to be to provoke general admiration and support as if it was an aberration for them to behave with compassion towards their partner. In a woman, it was assumed to be a given response that necessitated no comment. She refilled Sam's swiftly emptying glass, asked whether he had eaten, if she could make him a sandwich. Again, he hesitated and she saw now that this was a long-ingrained, even cultivated habit of speech rather than a genuine hiatus of uncertainty. He smiled sheepishly and said something about forgetting to eat before the meeting and followed her back into her kitchen, watched as she found bread, smoked cheese. Apologised for a lack of ham.

"The truth is, Kate – you don't mind me calling you Kate? – no, you said not." He turned to stare out of the back door onto the darkness of her slab of courtyard garden. "The real thing about all this, Lyddie's illness and now this baby business, however welcome that is … well, I find it's forced me to confront an awful lot that has been comfortably buried.

And no one likes confrontation, do they? Especially not with themselves. In fact, it's the worst possible kind."

Catherine waited. Put the substantial sandwich on a white plate, placed it on her small kitchen table and sat down. After a few moments he turned, looking as if he had forgotten she was even in the room then joined her at the table. He picked up one half of the sandwich then swiftly put it down again.

"I've reached the stage when I can no longer pretend. That's probably what it's all about, this feeling of hopelessness at times. All those aspirations and plans that came to nothing. That I failed to fulfil either because I was too cowardly and too scared or because I was simply not good enough. Inept, you could say. Didn't have what it takes."

Catherine said, "I'm sure most people have failed ambitions. Things they regret not achieving in their lives."

"Do they?" Sam said. He stared at the sandwich on its white plate for a moment then began to eat rapidly as if suddenly remembering his hunger. "I don't mean outrageous aims like becoming extraordinarily rich or the latest talk of Hollywood, but simply …"

Again, that pause. Catherine noticed a crust had escaped to the floor.

"Satisfaction. Fulfilment. Is that what I mean? I don't know any more. I'm not sure I've ever lost my young man's view of thinking it's all ahead of me. Never accepted that the future is finite. And very, very limited in scope. It's such a ghastly reality, you know. And reality has never been one of my strengths."

"But there's so much ahead, surely."

"Not for us, me and Lyddie."

"I'm sorry. That was tactless of me."

He said nothing for a moment and she wondered if she had offended him. But eventually he went on.

"Well, of course there's Polly with this child of hers. And yes, naturally there's a certain anticipation in that. For me, at least. Something beyond my life with Lyddie. But do you know, it all feels a bit passive. Does that make sense? Vicarious pleasure from other people's achievements. You get to an age when you retreat inevitably and become the backdrop to other people's lives. I'm finding that hard to accept."

He finished the sandwich, drained the last from his glass of wine. Outside, the sound of a door closing, a car's engine starting made them both glance at the clock on the wall and Sam stood up abruptly.

"As usual, I've taken up far too much of your time, Kate. Polly needs to get home and Lyddie will be tired. Worn out, I should think, from her evening listening to female chatter."

"Of course," Catherine said, swiftly moving ahead of him into the hall to the front door as if guilty of delaying him. He moved more slowly, however, stopped to look at two prints that were hanging on the wall.

"Like these," he said, indicating the abstract sea scenes. "I noticed a couple you had in the living room too. Perhaps I could bring Lyddie in one day."

"Any time, please. You're very welcome."

"And, of course, you must pop round to us. I can't pretend to be up to your standards in sandwich making, Kate, but ..."

"I'd like that," she said.

"We've never been very good at neighbourliness, never needed to be before. But I'm sure we can make an exception for you, Kate."

Catherine watched him turn to the garden flat, disappear through his front door. Just as she was about to close her own, her attention was caught by a figure at the window of the flat above, defined by the bright street light. Frances Chater darted back from the curtain, but not before she had looked directly at Catherine, appearing to note with interest Sam Gough leaving her flat.

★★★

Barnaby Taylor sees the sign for the internet café at the end of the street.

"Give me twenty minutes or so. Just need to check stuff. See you at that bar?"

The others nod, move on. He finds a free computer, pays the woman at the counter for half an hour and buys a coffee. He swiftly scrolls down messages, reads a couple, is about to delete one from an address he does not recognise when he stops. Curious. He clicks on it, reads.

My husband, Eddie, was tragically killed while driving some 15 months ago. I am so sorry to have to deliver such news.

And reads the message again as if the sense is ambiguous when, in fact, the meaning is all too clear and it is his feelings that are clouded. Undefined. He is unsure whether the content is highly significant to him or of no relevance at all. He clicks *Reply,* then changes his mind, logs off. Swallows his cooling cup of densely black bitter coffee. Stares at the darkening screen. Outside, the spring evening is warm, the Prague pavements crowded with visitors and tourists like him, exploring with guide books and maps, searching the old city for authentic sites before they are swallowed up by developers. By progress. Barnaby stands up abruptly, returns his cup to the counter, to the woman who expresses her surprise that he has used only fifteen minutes of his time. But Barnaby hardly hears her, anxious to leave, to find his friends in that bar in the square where he can try Slivovice, drink quantities of the local beer.

Drink with a desire to dismiss, to obliterate entirely the impact and consequence of that email from Catherine Wells.

16

F rances considered the options.

The card with the large heart was appropriate, but vulgar, she thought. Besides, the message inside was too long, leaving little space for her own. In the end, she bought the one she had first picked out, a peaceful country scene with *To my darling husband* in italics the only greeting. It had been one of their early discoveries soon after they had met. Shared birthdays were significant, Frances had claimed, birth twins even, though Andrew was two years older. And once they were married they had agreed always on a joint present, something for the house, the garden, occasionally a special weekend away. Even when Andrew had tried to spoil her with a surprise gift over the years – that silver chain, the watch, a fine wool shawl – she had rejected them, insisted he return them to the shop, reminding him that he was failing to play by the rules. Their rules. Individual presents were for Christmas, not for their fortuitously dated birthdays.

Except for this year, of course. This year would have to be the one exception.

Back at her flat, she sat down and wrote her selected text inside the card: *Love is patient. It keeps no record of wrongs* and then, thinking that the First Letter to the Corinthians might sound a little clichéd, she turned over and wrote on the back: *A wife of noble character, who can find her? She is worth far more than rubies.* Frances was grateful to the lay preacher, standing in for the vicar who had succumbed to food poisoning on Easter Sunday, for introducing her to the verse from Proverbs even if she found his interpretation to be somewhat contrary. Now there was simply the matter of delivery to decide. She was due a visit to Pilgrim Square so it would be easy enough to substitute her usual letter to Charlotte Prideaux with the card for Andrew. That way, she could discreetly leave a small carrier bag in the corner of the porch with the bottle of single malt whisky she intended to buy. On the other hand, there was a risk it might disappear before Andrew found it, vanishing down the throats of the some of the characters who clustered near the station or, even worse, be discovered by Charlotte who would no doubt take delight in pouring it down the kitchen sink along with the dregs from her morning coffee. A postal delivery was the solution, of course, and no doubt Fortnum & Mason or Harrods could assist. The cost, she knew, would be prohibitive, but the impact of the gesture well worth it. As for the card, she would take it with her to Brighton the following Monday and risk its fate through the letter box of number 10.

The afternoon hung. From next door she could hear Violet's music and felt unequal to the task of knocking at her door, suggesting a snack, a walk across the common. Even the offer of taking some washing off her hands which Violet usually obliged was unappealing. Street party matters were all up to date. In fact, she now regretted delegating so many jobs to neighbours since it left her with inadequate concerns. A certain lack of control. Resolutely, she went into the bedroom, changed out of clothes she considered too casual for a trip to Knightsbridge, possibly Piccadilly. Dithering between her navy suit and the newer olive-green dress and jacket, she heard her mother's sarcastic tone, *so who do you think will be looking at you, anyway, Frances? It's all wasted vanity, you know.* And firmly thought of her mother's ashes, scattered liberally and no doubt illegally under the disintegrating West Pier, discarded the caustic voice in her head along with them and walked across the common to catch the bus.

Harrods overwhelmed her. She stood at the bottom of the escalators, forged her way to the Food Hall, but felt inadequate to the task of attracting attention and gaining service amongst such a crowd of customers. Outside, she decided to walk to Piccadilly, determined to muster her assertiveness that appeared to have temporarily eluded her. Perhaps she was unwell. Nothing serious, but simply a virus or a bug of some sort that was affecting her strength. She disliked feeling insufficient, floored by a situation when she had always relied, boasted even, of her resilience. The day had grown warm, a precursor to summer, and Green Park was full of impromptu picnickers, discarding coats and jackets, unwisely stretching out onto grass which was no doubt still damp from recent rain. Frances stopped and stared for a moment, trying to catch a memory that would not come fully into focus then pressed on, past the Ritz hotel, past a coffee shop that she hesitated outside, but then thought too hectic. She was thirsty, suddenly worn out as if she had walked all the way from Willow House instead of simply from the top of Sloane Street. Really, she told herself, it was no distance at all, for someone who in the past had walked miles along the front at Brighton, at Devil's Dyke, always insisting to Andrew that they take their exercise regime seriously especially once they had both passed fifty. She reached Fortnum & Mason's, pushed her way through the revolving doors as if at the end of a strenuous mission, and stood in the carpeted interior, again haunted by an echo of another time. In the Fountain restaurant she was told to wait to be seated even though it was nowhere close to full, but she obliged until a woman with a severe, unsmiling face led her wordlessly to a table. She ordered tea then called the waitress back and added a round of toast. Perhaps she needed to eat for in addition to her sudden tiredness she felt now a sense of dislocation. A detachment from the reality of the moment. Suddenly, the events of the past year seemed like the stuff of fiction, merely the plot of a sad story she had read so that once she had finished her solitary pot of tea she would, in fact, be heading back to Brighton, to her house in Pilgrim Square.

To her life with Andrew.

There would be no bus journey back to Miller Street, shrinking back into her adopted carapace, hitching herself once more to the identity she had created as a shield, to avoid shame, humiliation.

The pretence, she thought, was at last beginning to muddle her.

She ate her toast slowly, cutting each piece into small squares as if she was frail, her appetite diminished by illness or great age.

And suddenly, it came to her.

The memory that had stirred remotely as she had stood looking over Green Park, came into sharp focus and she was trawled back, hooked to another day entirely. *I know a chap,* Andrew had said, *at least I know his reputation. For these sorts of problems. Only about my age, but already got an impressive list of private patients. And we wouldn't have to spend heaven knows how long on a waiting list. It won't be cheap, but it might be money well spent.* She had refused at first. She remembered objecting, suggesting they give it more time, but eventually, growing more and more desolate each month, she had given in. She had worn a purple dress, a black woollen coat. How foolish to remember such detail all these years later, but it had seemed important to her at the time, to dress appropriately for an appointment in Wimpole Street. Afterwards, she had wanted to walk, persuaded Andrew that they needed air, not the confinement of a tube train or

the extravagance of a taxi when the consultation had already
cost them the equivalent of a week of groceries. So they had
walked south towards Henrietta Place, crossed Oxford Street
and headed down Bond Street, sharing the pavements with
discreet shoppers, neither of them speaking except when
Andrew made a tentative suggestion of lunch. But Frances was
not hungry and neither, in truth, was Andrew, but he was at
a loss to know exactly what he could do to console. They had
walked on and reached Piccadilly and the railings of Green
Park and stopped as if it was some sort of planned destination
or boundary. The mid-April day had grown unexpectedly
warm, the black wool coat now an unwanted impediment
and Frances had shrugged it off, willing to abandon it on the
pavement if Andrew had not scooped it up, carrying it over
his arm like an obliging lackey. Again, he had tried to stir her.
*A drink, at least. We could go to a bar. In a hotel, perhaps. You've had
nothing. Coffee if you prefer.* But Frances had looked past him
into the park where the mild weather was encouraging office
workers and bank clerks and shop assistants away from their
desks and tea trolleys and work canteens into the awkward
deckchairs and onto the grass. He had followed her gaze and
seen the woman, about the same age as Frances, sitting on a
wooden bench in the shade, a sleeping baby clasped to her in
a shawl, a sling, stroking the back of the child's head, cradling
it in the palm of her hand and bending every now and again
to kiss the fragile flesh. Eventually, he had steered her away,
wordlessly, for it had become their way, not to comment on
anything that stirred them deeply, rekindled their longing. And
now, sitting over her cooling pot of tea, her delicate squares
of toast, Frances remembered that Andrew had brought her
here, guided her along from Green Park to this place where
neither of them had ever been before, but was lodged in his
mind as somewhere safe, respectable. Somewhere where they

could both sit and order like other people – Welsh rarebit and poached eggs and tea cakes and cream horns and eclairs – and pretend that their future together was not hindered, blighted by an apparent perplexing aberration.

Frances signalled to the waitress for her bill. All of a sudden, she felt exasperated by her brief lapse of conviction. By her permission to allow doubt to hover over her when she knew it as the enemy of success.

After all, had not the past, her past with Andrew, proved this beyond doubt?

She paid, left no tip since she considered the charge to be exorbitant, the service verging on insolent, and headed to the wines and spirits department. There, a bottle of Islay single malt whisky was swiftly chosen, bought and despatched to 10 Pilgrim Square. She proffered her credit card to the biddable assistant with the air of one accustomed to such purchases and, feeling fully restored, forcefully pushed her way out through the revolving doors onto Piccadilly, causing some Japanese tourists to draw back hastily, give way to her assumption of prerogative.

Back at Willow House, anxious to act, to deflect any chance of a return to her earlier sombre mood, she knocked on Violet's door. She had bought sole fillets, enough for two, white grapes, cream, and planned Sole Veronique with a few early new potatoes and spinach. Violet had recently declared to her that she had stopped eating meat so she had chosen fish intentionally. Besides, she really needed to go over Violet's plans for the children's entertainment at the street party, confirm, in fact, that she was even going to be there to face paint and mask make. The girl was, after all, really very vague about dates. The door was opened just as Frances was about to knock again.

But not by Violet.

A tall man close to her own age, a man not too dissimilar from Andrew, in fact, open neck shirt, easy smile, stood there.

"Sorry," he said as if in response to Frances' surprise. "The lady of the house is out at the moment. Violet, that is. I presume you must be a neighbour. Unless someone else let you in." Frances looked at him blankly. "There is an intercom arrangement, surely."

"And you would be a friend of Violet's?" Frances said, irritated. She felt possessiveness over the absent Violet as if this late-middle-aged man was taking advantage over her youth, her blatantly unlined pretty face. She was not so foolish as to think of Violet as living a pure, celibate life yet nevertheless the girl suggested a certain naivety, an unchecked impetuosity that could render her vulnerable. She took a step back, tried to see beyond the man into Violet's flat. The radio was playing. The six o'clock news on Radio 4. The man held out his hand. Smiled warmly.

"Of course, you must be Violet's next-door neighbour. My neighbour, in truth. For I do own the place, after all. I'm Violet's father, Martin Lawrence. Would you like to come in and wait until Violet gets back?"

***

Beth stretched her arms above her head, stifled a yawn.

"Sorry," she said, "not used to this London air. I don't know how you keep awake all day. Or perhaps it's the wine. Have we finished the bottle?"

She was staying overnight in Miller Street, going on to see her oldest son, James, the next day, recently settled in a flat share in Hoxton. It was her first visit and however complimentary she had been, Catherine was aware how small her home must look compared with her sister's own sprawling family house. "So," Beth said, tucking her legs underneath her in the armchair, "were you surprised? About Alec, I mean."

Catherine had briefly mentioned Alec's planned marriage while she was making dinner, hoping to circumnavigate Beth's interest by moving swiftly on to the complications of the recipe, asking her assistance with red onion chopping and sauce tasting. Now, having eaten and cleared away it seemed as if Beth had saved rather than discarded the subject.

"At first, yes, "Catherine said, "if I'm honest, I was very surprised."

"And disappointed. Bereft, possibly."

"I've no right to feel that," Catherine said wearily. "Although, it did take me a day or two before I could think of the whole prospect – well, selflessly. With detachment, you could say. But now I can. In fact, I've hardly given the matter any thought at all." It was not entirely true, but after her initial reaction, she had found the idea of his marriage only peripheral to her thoughts. And certainly not distressing her in the way Beth assumed. "He's always been so against it so this radical change of heart was hard to take in, I suppose."

"Will you go?" Beth said.

"Go? To the wedding? Of course not! That's an appalling idea. Besides, I haven't been invited. It will probably be a small, private affair, anyway, just family, I imagine."

"Has Alec got any family? The few times I met him he always seemed so self-sufficient. As if he had jettisoned any annoying relatives, potential hangers-on, very early in his life."

"There was his mother, of course. But she died years ago. Leaving the house."

"Ah yes," Beth said, "the Hampstead house. What will happen to that?"

"Sold. No doubt a developer will buy it up, turn it around and sell it on for millions. I don't think Alec has applied a lick of paint to it in decades. I imagine it exists in a kind of fascinating time warp."

"So they're going to live abroad? Alec and his wife?" Such an attachment to Alec's name still sounded strange.

"Yes, I believe so. There's a child, you see."

"Ah," Beth said, draining her wine glass, "a child. I see. That does change things. Is Alec the father?"

"No, of course not," Catherine snapped. "At least – no, I'm sure he's not. He's ten," she added lamely as if the child's age precluded Alec's paternity.

"I'm just saying," Beth said, "it's possible. It would all make sense then, when you think about it. Men like Alec probably don't find being around at the baby and toddler stage terribly riveting. But once a child reaches double figures – and a boy, you say? Fatherhood no doubt becomes far more appealing. For someone like Alec. I'm surprised you didn't think of it, Cat."

Catherine stood up, went into the kitchen to find the wine bottle and returned to share the dregs between their two glasses. She knew she would regret it when her alarm went the next morning, but Beth's visit was too rare to squander on being sensible.

"How's James settling into the new job?" she asked, "and the others? Tell me everything that's going on." Beth obliged easily and at length. Catherine listened, occasionally making an appropriate response, at the same time thinking over what she has suggested about Alec. It was absurd, of course. If Alec had a child and now wanted to make him central to his life, he would have told her. Justified his sudden conversion to the idea of marriage by talking of his son. Surely. But then again, Alec had always been a discreet man, private, and might resent her knowledge of matters that were really no concern of hers. Ten years ago, she had met Eddie. No doubt any connection between that fact and the age of this boy was fanciful. Yet Beth had managed to provoke a possibility that was hard to shrug off now that it was in her mind. She looked over at her, in the middle of a long tale about one daughter's gap year travels, another's college plans, and realised that it had been years since the two of them had spent an evening together solely in each other's company. Inevitably, there had been children, husbands. Even in the last weeks of their mother's life when both of them had visited frequently Beth had always had one of her younger children with her and her time inevitably curtailed. So different in nature, in inclination, she had often wondered if it was solely the familial connection that brought them close. Now Beth, sunk back in the deep armchair, grasping her wine glass in a manner that suggested the late hour made it an illicit act, said something similar.

"Do you think we would have been friends, even liked each other, if we'd just met by chance? Of course, it's very unlikely that we would ever have met in that way. I wouldn't have stumbled over you at the NCT class or Toddler Tots or on the PTA committee. That never could have happened. When you think about it, it's terrifying the huge choices we make quite glibly. It doesn't seem like that at the time, of course, it all feels considered and inevitable. But it's not. Not at all. It's more just a stab in the dark, sticking your arm out and trying your luck without any real thought for the consequences. And there are so few chances to turn back. To have a change of heart about it all. I mean, people do, of course. Simply walk out on the whole set-up they've helped to create. Like leaving a film half way through because the plot hasn't quite turned out as they imagined. But obviously, with considerably more collateral damage, you could say."

"But you've never had doubts, surely," Catherine said, "about marriage and a large family. You've always seemed so sure from the start about what you wanted." She felt disarmed by Beth's words, as if her own understanding of her sister was entirely misconstrued. Like Alec, perhaps. Beth stretched out cramped legs, rearranged a cushion at her back.

"There's always that road not taken stuff, isn't there?" she said. "Particularly for someone like me who always appeared to be the reliable, predictable one. The one who lacked the imagination and courage to do anything other with their life than conform."

"I've never thought of you like that," Catherine said firmly. "That's nonsense."

Beth smiled, held out her hand and took Catherine's for a moment.

"Don't worry, I'm probably a bit drunk, spilling out all this stuff to you. And I'm not about to leave Henry and all the kids and our mad household. I'd disintegrate without all those ties. I'm so used to the chaos of it all. I'm just saying that things are never as straight forward as they seem. Choices, decisions. You must wonder, sometimes, what would have happened if you'd married Alec. Or not married Eddie."

"I wonder what would have happened if Eddie hadn't been killed," Catherine said quietly. "I never stop thinking of that."

Beth looked exasperated.

"That's pointless. And not what I meant at all. His accident was something out of your hands, after all."

"Was it?" Catherine said.

"It's arrogance to think you can control other people's actions. There's such a thing as self-will, you know."

Beth stood up, briskly collected their glasses and headed towards the kitchen.

"I'm putting your smart shiny spanking new kettle on," she said, "and making some tea. Tea is what the two of us need right now."

★★★

At the breakfast table in the kitchen of 10 Pilgrim Square, Charlotte Prideaux hands Andrew a large card.

"Terribly clichéd, I'm afraid, but it was either hearts and flowers or tasteful fishing scenes. I didn't think you were quite old enough yet to be treated to something so emasculating."

Andrew leans over to kiss her, slips his hand around her pale neck and strokes her skin.

"But I am old," he says, "ready to be pensioned off to the bowls club and angling society, if there is such a thing."

"Nonsense," Charlotte says, removing his hand as if the gesture is mildly irritating. "Old age is a thing of the past, didn't you know that? You're barely into your prime."

Andrew watches her as she stands up, goes to make coffee, places the pot on the table next to the basket of warm rolls. She has insisted today on sitting down to breakfast, a diversion from their normal morning routine when he drinks tea while dressing and leaves before the eight o'clock news. She pours his coffee and pushes the mug towards him. He now drinks it black, Charlotte insistent that milk is unhealthy and that the taste of the coffee is polluted by such an addition. He agrees, on the whole, although every now and again sneaks into a local café and buys a take-away latte that now tastes like a childhood treat, soothing, bland, innocuous. He takes a roll, dense and brittle in its wholemeal goodness, smothers it in marmalade. Charlotte picks an apple from the fruit bowl, cuts it carefully, evenly into eight slices, arranges them on her plate. He knows she will only eat half. He loves to watch her precision, her restraint, and matches such traits to the way she makes love, not with the supposed abandonment of one so young, so ardent (to Andrew, thirty-six-year-old Charlotte Prideaux is still very young) but with calculation as if every move is designed and controlled for ultimate success. As if she has plotted each step on a graph, a chess board, that allows for no diversion, no rash impulse. At times, it feels as if their roles are reversed and that he is the ingénue, she the sophisticate, the worldly one in their partnership.

"Has the post been yet?" he asks, suddenly wary. Charlotte looks at him, her pale eyes wide.

"Birthday boy expecting a nasty surprise? Don't worry, my darling, I'll deal with anything untoward that might arrive from a certain quarter. Which reminds me." She slips out of her chair, quarter slice of green apple in her hand and goes into the hall, returns with her large leather shoulder bag that she likes to hang over the banister. She takes out a small appointment card and a sheaf of papers which she hands to Andrew. He wipes marmalade and crumbs from one hand and takes them. Without his reading glasses, the words jumble in front of his eyes.

"You'll have to transcribe for me, the ageing process betraying me again, I'm afraid."

Charlotte retrieves the papers, leaves him with the card.

"We have an appointment," she says, in her clear, precise tone. "On Friday afternoon. To look at our options. Your options, really. To get things going. Make a start with the process."

"Process?" Andrew picks up his mug, drinks. Suddenly, the coffee is too dense, his stomach appearing to resent such an early morning assault. Charlotte smiles, takes one of his hands, separates his fingers and sinks her small even teeth into the flesh of a middle digit as if it is a particularly irresistible piece of crisp apple. He flinches. She lets go. Rubs where the imprint of her teeth still clings.

"An appointment with a solicitor," she says, "not just any solicitor either. Graham Theaker and partners. They're renowned. Graham, in particular. Ruthless, everyone says, in all matters matrimonial."

"I see," Andrew says. "Then he won't come cheap."

"He's not," Charlotte says, "but you get what you pay for. And what we want to get is …"

She stands up, stretches her arms above her head then spreads them wide and turns a slow, full circle in the middle of the kitchen floor.

"This house?" Andrew says in a quiet voice barely audible. Charlotte beams at him.

"Everything, my darling Andy, we want to get everything."

★★★

Frances sat in the café along the road from the common. It was an hour of the day she rarely chose, the place too full of women with young children and pushchairs the size of small people carriers. But it was her birthday and she intended to exercise the right to shape the day to her liking. Within current given limits. She was not going to Brighton. Her gift would speak for her today, connect her with Andrew, place her at the forefront of his mind so that when he went to bed, the taste of a nightcap of malt whisky still on his lips, he would wonder at his treachery, turn away from the arms of Charlotte Prideaux and desire only her. His lawful wife.

She ordered a large latte and an almond Danish.

Later, she was having her hair cut at a new salon she had found in Fulham. Not the expensive end of Fulham, but further north off the high road in a strip of shops that looked weary and inadequate to their postal code. She had found the leaflet in Violet's flat, one of those flyers with a coupon for an introductory offer during the salon's opening month and had slipped it into her pocket. Violet, she had heard often enough, cut her own long hair when she bothered to cut it at all so the coupon was superfluous to her. It had been the day Frances had met Violet's father, Martin. He had invited her in to wait for his daughter, had tried to make her tea then, unable to find his way around Violet's chaotic kitchen cupboards, had offered wine instead, opening the bottle he said he'd brought with him in case the flat's stocks were inadequate. He was, Frances felt, mildly flirting with her. Asking her all about the occupants of Willow House, about her *exemplary and impressive input into this street party business* as he phrased it. A big man, not overweight in any way, but the sort whose frame seemed to occupy a large space and dominated his immediate surroundings. Highly successful in business, no doubt, and just a little too sure of himself and his own ability to charm for Frances' liking. Then his wife had arrived, loaded down with shopping bags and Martin Lawrence had teased her rather patronisingly about her likely extravagance at the shops. She had ignored the gibe, but mentioned later, once Violet had joined them, that she had spent the afternoon buying more bed linen and towels for the flat to supplement her daughter's scant supply. Isabel, her name, a quiet and kindly sort of woman, who had asked Frances to join them for the take-away evening meal they were planning. Frances had mentioned her fish, the lemon sole waiting in her fridge, had finished her glass of Australian Shiraz and left, after extracting a cheque from Martin to pay for three tickets to the Miller Street party.

The gift-wrapped bottle of whisky had been sent to Andrew at the surgery. The card could be entrusted to Pilgrim Square since it was more expendable. But the Islay Malt needed to be safe from falling into the wrong destructive hands. She imagined its delivery, muddled along with numerous boxes of clinical matter and material that Andrew would push to one side, turning to the unexpected parcel to open out of curiosity. What would he think? Something along the lines of *Frances always remembers. An utterly faithful woman in every way.* And no doubt pausing a little too long between appointments, delaying the root canal procedure or the emergency extraction, racked with sudden, appalling remorse for his behaviour. Frances finished her coffee. Ate the rest of her almond Danish and found the day's paper in the café's rack by the door. Already, she was able to push away the darkness of the day that had threatened when she first woke up. Hope, she thought, faith and patience are all that are required. After all, *What God hath joined together, let no man put asunder.* And added her own dictum *and no woman neither* before turning to the paper to read of the latest rumblings in the Middle East.

✶✶✶

The passengers sit for a moment as if stupefied by endless hours in such stultifying confined space. Then they begin to gather belongings that have strayed under seats, between seats, stretch cramped limbs, search for discarded shoes. A spur of sudden and mildly frenzied activity after near comatose states.

"Quite a haul," the man next to Thomas says, yawning, "unless you're in First Class, of course. All right for them."

"Yes," Thomas says, "that would make a difference."

"Got on at Hong Kong, did you?"

"Melbourne, originally. Hong Kong was just a 4 hour stopover."

"A glutton for punishment, then. Couldn't do it myself any more. Not all in one trip. Mind you, you're young. It's different when you're young."

Thomas shrugs, switches on his phone. He waits for the aisle to clear, tries to see out of the window, but catches only the enormous wing of the plane, a square of concourse. An elderly woman struggles with the weight of a bag and he stands up, helps her and at the same time manages to extricate himself from the row. Passport control is slow. By the time he has collected his luggage, made his way through to the arrivals hall, he is drained, weary and regrets spending most of the past day and night watching films instead of trying to sleep. He heads to the coffee bar, loads a tray and sits for over an hour, watching the endless stream of passengers appear through customs, each searching faces for one that is familiar, welcoming. Irrationally, he has done the same in spite of telling no one of his return. Even his close friends in Dalston where he hopes to stay only know he is due back this month. Outside, the day looks fine, dry at least, and he reminds himself that here it is late spring, almost ready to tip over into early summer. After over two years of living on the other side of the world, he needs to adjust. Acclimatise. He glances at his phone, scrolls through messages and, as if in response, a brief text suddenly appears on the small screen. He is so relieved that, in his exhausted state, he feels foolishly close to tears. Swiftly, he stirs himself, swallows the last of his coffee, grabs suitcase and backpack and follows signs towards the underground and the Piccadilly line into London.

SUMMER
2006

17

Rowena Shaw had arrived at Harriet Howe House in the late spring. On a temporary basis, she insisted to Catherine, a secondment for six months to fill the curator post, a year at the most.

"I live mainly in Berlin, but I need to be back in England for a while because of my mother's health. I've managed to arrange a leave of absence from the university there providing I continue to supervise my doctoral students which is, of course, feasible."

Her manner of speech, cul-de-sacs of conversation, did not invite easy exchange.

"And then?" Catherine asked.

"Then?" Rowena Shaw had echoed dismissively, adjusting the narrow gold bracelet she always wore around her wrist, "I have no idea. I suggest you ask the trustees. But it's certainly not a permanent role for me. Or for the museum. I am something of a stopgap, you could say."

For the first couple of weeks, Catherine had seen little of her as she appeared to prefer working entirely on her own, either in her office with the door firmly closed or, more frequently, from home, liaising rarely, asking for scant information.

"She's a strange one," one of the volunteers said to Catherine one day in early May, "seems to pretend the rest of us don't even exist. As if what we do is of no interest to her at all."

"I think she's just anxious to get to grips with the way things work," Catherine said out of habit by now as each volunteer had expressed something similar. "Sorting out the documentation and examining – well, budgets, strategies, our vision, as she calls it."

Val Harris, one of the duty managers, was more outspoken.

"I'm not keen on that superior air she has about her. There's no mistaking it and it's quite uncalled for," she said abruptly one morning in the staff kitchen as Rowena Shaw disappeared into her office and closed her door after a cursory greeting. "Not what we're used to at all. We've always felt like a team."

"I'm sure she doesn't mean it and things will settle down once she gets to know us all," Catherine attempted to be neutral. Val paused, swallowed the last of one of her many mugs of strong tea that punctuated her day.

"Well, she's making no efforts in that direction, is she? But at least we've got a woman for the job, that's something to be said, I suppose. Old Harriet Howe would have been pleased. But you were cheated, Catherine, in my humble opinion. The job should be yours."

"She's a very clever woman. I suppose we should consider ourselves fortunate to have someone with her academic reputation and regard."

Val moved to the sink, rinsed her mug.

"But does she fit in? That's the question. Is she really what this place needs? We want the human touch, not some professor who won't give you the time of day. Now, don't delay me any longer, Catherine, as I really need to get on. I have to leave by two today, if that's all right with you as I've promised to do the school pick up for my eldest's little one. But I can give you a full nine to five tomorrow and get the gift shop sorted and ensure we're all set for the summer months."

"She's only temporary," Catherine said. "Rowena. Did I say? Evidently, she's just here for a few months. A year at the most."

"Giving us the once over and deciding whether it's worth staying, is she? I know the type."

"No, nothing like that," Catherine said, "she's very clear that she'll only be here for – well, not permanently."

Val shrugged dismissively, picked up her bag and headed down the stairs, back to the gift shop. Catherine was grateful for her lack of curiosity about matters that did not immediately concern her for she was unsure what she was supposed to say about the nature of the appointment. It was only two days before Rowena's arrival that the chairman of the trustees had rung her to say that they had come to an arrangement to tide the museum over for a few months. A close friend and former colleague, it had been explained, was at a loose end for an undefined period of time and could conveniently step into the breach. It made no sense to Catherine. Yet when she attempted to clarify why the board had not appointed a permanent replacement for Robert, she had sensed an evasiveness that was alarming. Perhaps the future of Harriet Howe House was genuinely at risk and some sort of absorption into a larger concern was intended.

Rowena Shaw's remarks during her first few days at the museum did little to alleviate Catherine's concerns.

"Quite frankly, I'm surprised the Howe has survived as long as it has," she had said in her measured tone that was mildly irritating. "In the current climate it might be seen as something of an irrelevance. As an independent body, that is. Surely its interests could be better served by an amalgamation." Catherine had felt annoyed that the woman had appeared so indifferent to the idea of jettisoning the independence of the museum before completing her first week as its curator. "I'm not saying the extensive library and the collections held here are not impressive. But part of a bigger institution could be so beneficial, a pragmatic step. Financially, this place is constantly struggling. Or at least only just about keeping its head above water."

Catherine attempted a defence.

"We survive. There's the loyalty of our Friends membership and their fundraising efforts, for a start. And our charitable status is an enormous help, of course. Then there's our staffing which is principally voluntary and even some of the maintenance is taken on by—"

Rowena had waved a hand to interrupt. She was a tall woman with the suggestion of a stoop as if she had spent years trying to disguise her height. Catherine had read some of her work, chapters in erudite titles, had even heard her talking on a Radio 4 programme about first wave feminists that had formed part of her doctoral research.

"I'm sure," she had said somewhat curtly. "And inevitably the building itself has charm, I'll give you that. But one needs to keep abreast of possibilities. That's all I'm saying. Anyway, it's of no long-term concern of mine. I'm sure the trustees know what they're doing."

And as the weeks went on, she had to admit that Rowena gave her little reason to complain. She left her alone, interfered little and even new initiatives Catherine took to her received her bland approval. She increased her time working from home so that often she would only be a presence in the museum for a few hours a week and at those times her manner was perfectly affable if a little distant. Catherine was unsure whether to be relieved by her disinterest or alarmed at what such an attitude boded for the future.

Beth, as always, was forthright.

"All this talk about being swallowed up by some bigger concern is hardly helpful. I mean, what is the woman talking about by making such comments? Does she know more than she's letting on? Would the V and A, for example, want to take you under its enormous wing? Or perhaps the National Trust. Turn you into an institution selling pictorial tea towels, preserves and potpourri?"

"I think there's a bit more to them than that. The National Trust, I mean," Catherine said. "But no, we'd be of no interest to them whatsoever. Not nearly lucrative enough to bother acquiring us."

"So why upset the apple cart with all this talk about disbanding the museum? The woman sounds like a nightmare. And don't tell me she's a huge asset to the place because she's clever. She doesn't sound very good at handling staff morale. Do tell me you've changed your mind about staying there. You ought to start looking around for other jobs in case the whole of Harriet Howe House ends up being packed into boxes and stored in some basement in South Kensington."

Catherine said, "Alec rang the other night."

"Alec? Alec Grey? I thought he'd disappeared to married life in Singapore." Beth's attention instantly, gratifyingly, shifted.

"There's been a delay. The house in Hampstead has taken longer to sell than expected. There was a buyer, but then a survey discovered extensive dry rot or rising damp or possibly both and the offer was withdrawn. It's not really surprising since the place hasn't been properly maintained for years. I believe he's having some work done before putting it back on the market."

"But what did he want? Why did he ring you?" Beth asked.

Catherine had felt confused when she had heard Alec's voice. She had assumed after their last meeting that there was scant likelihood of them ever seeing each other again. But here he was, delayed in London for longer than expected, his marriage in Singapore delayed until later in the year, and hopeful that she would meet him for dinner.

"Of course, I said no," she said to Beth.

"Good. Naturally. Although, you never know, perhaps you were too hasty. After all …"

"He just wanted me as a convenience to fill a spare evening or two that he hadn't been expecting. It annoyed me."

"But that's what you always were to each other, wasn't it?"

"What? Annoying?"

"No. A convenience. Or so you told me. I think that was the very word you used."

Sometimes, her sister's recall of past conversations was infuriating.

"Even so," Catherine hedged. Then swiftly changed the subject again so that Beth could not pursue the point. Alec had certainly seemed surprised when she had turned down his suggestion of meeting as if he failed to see his imminent marriage as a rational reason. Perhaps his feelings for her had always been even more pedestrian than she had assumed, their relationship solely that of two obliging, platonic friends. She had allowed herself at times to believe in something a little less rooted in expediency.

"I'm trying to plan a holiday," she went on now to Beth. "I've a lot of leave I need to take before the end of the year and as Rowena's in place, there's really no reason not to."

"Alone?"

"It is allowed," Catherine said.

"I was just thinking it would be good for you to have some company."

"I have company all day long at work," she said, "too much company, in fact, on days when the museum's crowded. A holiday's supposed to be different from every day."

"You know what I mean."

Catherine ignored the remark.

"Anyway, I've no definite plans, nothing booked yet, but it would be good to get away for a week or two. Last summer was so overtaken with selling Bevington and buying this place so it seems like ages since—"

"You went to Portugal last summer."

"Ah yes. Portugal. I'd forgotten."

And she had. For her snatched week in that simple single room in the enormous, anonymous hotel complex that spoke little of the country, had seemed not so much like a holiday as a place that offered her an anodyne space where she could start to heal. Or at least begin to think about healing. "It won't be for a while, anyway," she went on. "Late summer is ideal as far as the museum's concerned, September, probably, and there's the Miller Street party here in July. I can't possibly miss that after all the planning. Frances Chater would never speak to me again. Although, possibly, that would be no bad thing. And no, before you ask, Beth, I've no intention of inviting anyone else to it. I shall be quite happy in the company of my neighbours. Well, some of them at least."

"Let's hope it doesn't rain. After all this woman's planning. That would be a nightmare."

"Indeed. But I'm sure Frances already has her contingency plans in place. She's not the sort to leave anything to chance."

★★★

Barnaby Taylor collects his letters from the mat in the hall, runs up the stairs to his top-floor room, opening the envelopes as he goes. All three are rejections. *Thank you for your application. We regret to inform you that … a very strong field … not selected for the short list …* etc etc. He is not surprised.

Nor even particularly disappointed. None of the jobs was of great interest to him, but he is beginning to feel obliged to apply for something long term. An adult-sounding position with potential and prospects. A pension, even. But he is happy enough with what he has now. He likes the bookshop, enjoys the company of his colleagues, the team spirit of battling as an independent concern against the power of the chain stores. And in the evenings, the bar work is busy, regular, if not highly lucrative employment. It is enough for the time being. It pays for his room in the shared house in Kentish Town. He can survive quite adequately for a while.

And he is not unhappy, not at all.

Simply somewhat bewildered at his own ludicrous sense of loss that will not leave him.

He makes a mug of coffee, eats the last from a packet of biscuits and picks up his phone. Unusually, she answers.

"Eddie Wells is dead."

There is a slight pause then she speaks, her voice composed. The mildest of curiosity. Barnaby can hear music playing in the background.

"Is he now? Well, it comes to all of us."

"I was too late. It was only recent. Fairly recent, anyway."

"Probably for the best."

"What? His death?" Barnaby stands, goes to the window, opens it to let some air into the small room. It smells faintly of over-ripened fruit. "He wasn't even old."

"No," she says, "I don't mean that. At least I don't think I do."

"Don't you want to know how he died?" Barnaby says.

"You seem to want to tell me," she says, her voice straining now over the volume of the background music. "Although, in fact, it's of minimal interest."

"He was killed in a car crash. Killed outright."

Barnaby waits for an answer, swallows the remains of his mug of coffee. He imagines her walking across the room to the source of her music, out of obligated courtesy turning it down. When she returns, she seems softer, as if trying to accommodate his mood.

"Barnie, love, I'm sorry if it's upset you. Of course it must have been a shock to hear. But really, when you think it through, it's all of no consequence."

"It is to me. That's just – how can you even say that?"

"Well, of course, anyone's death is something to mourn. I am not dismissing the gift of life, Barnie. But if we all spent each hour counting up the daily toll of human mortality, where would we be?"

"I wanted to find him. To meet him." Barnaby is suddenly aware that he is close to tears. This is not how he has intended the conversation to go although he knows he should have predicted her reaction.

"I know you did and you know what I thought about that idea. I tried to dissuade you. I always thought it was pointless. The past is the past, Barnie. There's nothing ever to be gained by going back."

"It was hardly going back," Barnaby says, flatly. "Not for me."

"You have to make your own life. I've always taught you that, Barnie. We are all alone on our unique journeys. Nothing of mine is yours, nothing of yours is mine."

He has heard her mantra too many times to comment on it. They have argued the point endlessly over the years.

"Don't you want to know how I found out about Eddie's death?" Barnaby does not wait for an answer. "I found his address by a bit of searching on the internet, electoral rolls and stuff. A guy I know helped me. Helped me a lot, in fact. And then I went there. Looking for him."

"And found what? A funeral cortege? A mass of mourners? Eddie would have liked all that. Or at least the Eddie I remember. From all that time ago."

"I spoke to his neighbour. Or at least – anyway, in the end, I got an email address."

"Impressive."

"She replied. Eventually. And told me."

"She?"

"His wife. Or rather his widow. Catherine Wells. That's her name."

There is a silence and Barnaby is unsure whether it is caused by boredom or some stirring of interest. Then she says,

"Well, Eddie's death rather means the end of the road for your search, my love. I told you it was a fruitless task. Now, get on with the future. Push all that morbid pursuit of roots out of your way. It's holding you back, you know. There's far too much negative energy caused by such introspection. It clogs your vision, blocks the paths you're supposed to be taking."

Barnaby knows there is no point in disagreeing with her. She is stubborn, obdurate in her views, in spite of a claim to open mindedness. He will get nowhere attempting to persuade her that, for him, it is only by clarifying the past that he can move on and forge a feasible future. Sometimes, he feels as if his life is a play where the entire first act is missing and without knowledge of it the plot will continually fail to make any real sense. He sends his love, receives hers and ends the call. Lets her return to the Amsterdam apartment, her music, those few possessions and her carefully cultivated, detached life. Three floors down in the shared kitchen, he finds the remains of his loaf, sneaks a slice from someone else's and makes substantial slabs of cheese on toast, empties the last of the jar of mango chutney onto the plate and goes back upstairs to eat. In an hour he needs to be in the Holloway Road for his evening shift at the Aquarius bar and brasserie. He is unlikely to be home before the early hours by the time they clear and share out the tips and he is opening up at the book shop at nine. Conveniently, he can shelve for the time being his conversation with his mother. With Rosie. He will sleep regardless, he knows, always a sleeper of the comatose sort, and only if the shop is quiet the next day, customers few and far between, will he have a chance to go over what she has said.

And, more importantly, what she has not.

For in spite of her studied indifference, her characteristic claim to abandon always the deeds and attachments of the past, he wonders if Rosie, too, has been startled to hear his news. After all, Eddie Wells was once her partner. The man she lived with for four years.

And, of course, he was the father of her only child.

★★★

Sam Gough spoke sharply to the woman on the phone.

"It's gone midday. And no one's arrived. I'm paying for help to get my wife out of bed, wash her, dress her and get her ready for the day. It's afternoon already."

"I'm sorry, sir, but we're a bit short staffed this week. Annual leave and so on. Besides, we don't guarantee an exact time. It's just not possible. I'm sure your carer will be along just as soon as she can."

"Tell her not to bother. Whoever it is. Already we've seen four different faces this week and it's only Wednesday."

"Do you mean you're cancelling our services, sir? Because if so, we need that in writing. And you're signed up for the whole month with penalties for early cancellation of contract."

"But you haven't fulfilled the contract that I signed up to. You can't penalise me for something you're not delivering."

Sam was aware that his voice was raised. He had no intention of lowering it.

"I think you'll find that we have, sir." The woman spoke in measured, reasoned tones, robotic almost, as if the response was rehearsed endlessly. It exasperated him all the more. "I think you'll find that if you read the contract in detail, all those terms of engagement and such like, that we are fulfilling exactly what we promise. And you would have selected a package of care most suited to your needs and budget. And in your case, sir, I can see that means one of our dedicated team calling twice a day to deliver washing and—"

Sam put down the phone. Exasperated. Angry. Not only at the woman, but at himself for giving in to Polly's suggestion. It would be sensible for him to get some help, she had said firmly. There were agencies, she had pointed out, providing such services, supplying people to come in to help with practical needs. He could afford it, surely, and it would bring them both some relief. Her mother, Polly had argued, would no doubt prefer the idea if she had been capable of expressing it, of having a professional seeing to such personal care and Sam was understandably somewhat out of his depth now that her needs were so fundamental. That had been her word, Sam recalled, and was grateful for Polly's choice of the euphemism. But the system was flawed. Whilst he knew he was being unreasonable in expecting the agency to provide care at his given times – before nine in the morning, after eight at night – he was intolerant of the vagueness of the arrangement. He was appalled by Lydia remaining in bed, unwashed, unchanged, the air of the sick room too redolent in the flat when the carer did not appear until close to lunch time. Equally, the arrival of someone to prepare her for bed at five in the afternoon was unacceptable. Particularly now it was summer and the long evenings suggested a chance for Lydia to sit outside in the back garden while he attempted some desultory gardening. And then there was the intrusion of a stranger into their lives, a random individual earning scant pay to provide intimate care as part of a 'package.' As if Lydia's needs had become a commodity to be exploited by a business endeavour. No. He would manage on his own. They would manage, struggle on, his own ineptitude with handling Lydia translated into a shared joke, a source of black humour to punctuate their day. His day at least.

It was strange how he felt defeated by the garden. Always he had enjoyed growing things, approaching a mound of uncultivated, unturned earth with pioneer enthusiasm, taming acres, mulching and sewing, catch cropping and transplanting, learning by trial and error to render productive plots. In Scotland. In Cornwall.

But here.

He had never been a man for genteel weeding, pushing a rotary mower once a week to produce straight, orderly lines of perfectly aligned turf. And although he tried to feel grateful for a garden of any size, he resented the lack of privacy it offered. Frances Chater seemed to stare down at him from her back window each time he was out there, peering from behind a curtain as if to inspect and make judgement and he was aware that Catherine's small courtyard beyond her back door offered only a thin screening from their terrace. Not that he disliked Catherine Wells or resented her proximity. Far from it. He was always pleased to see her, sought out her company rather than avoided it. She was an attractive woman. An interesting woman with a certain past history of her own that suggested complexities. He doubted he would have been convinced into joining the street party committee if attending meetings had not involved seeing her. After all, Lydia's illness had changed her irrevocably and he now related to her as his patient. His needy and somewhat demanding charge. He could not look at her frail, failing body, her frightened, ferret-like expression and experience desire.

And he felt bereft by such a loss. A little less than the man he was.

Of course, there was nothing inappropriate in his response to Catherine Wells. Nor would he embarrass her, a woman some twenty years his junior, by suggesting any feelings towards her, a motive in seeking out her company from time to time.

Because in truth there was little.

Simply some consolation to be found, a satisfaction in their exchanges, a sense of his own self still vibrant, surviving.

But a suburban garden prone to neighbours' snooping was anathema to him.

The phone rang.

"It's me. Thirty-two weeks and all is well. At least for the baby. I'm enormous and have forgotten what my toes look like."

Polly. She began to apologise for not visiting for a couple of weeks, overwhelmed by school demands that she wanted to settle before her maternity leave started. Even now, she said, speaking rapidly, she was snatching a moment from her busy day to ring as there was no guarantee what time she would be back that night. Sam interrupted.

"I have a confession to make. I've sacked the carers. Or rather I've told the agency to get lost. Sitting here, all morning, just waiting for them to make an appearance – if one of them makes it by lunch time we're to be considered lucky. So that's the end of that."

There was a heavy silence. Polly rarely grew volubly angry.

"Why, Dad?" she said eventually. "This is not about you. Or rather not only about you. Mum's preferences ought to be considered. And does it matter if she's not dressed until late morning?"

"It does to me. It's so unlike her."

"Everything's unlike her," Polly said quietly. "That's the point. We're trying to come up with a plan to make life more tolerable for the situation you're both now in."

"We're fine," Sam said, "really we are." He resented even Polly's compassion, the suggestion of pity. It made him feel exposed, vulnerable and in need of others' interference. "Now tell me something cheerful. Something to brighten the day."

"The weather's good. And I'm coming over to see you this Saturday. Will that do?"

"Yes," Sam said, enormously relieved. "I'll tell your mother straight away."

"I'll try and come early and give you a break. You could go out for the day. Or at least for a few hours. Try to pretend things are normal."

"Thank you, Polly. And I'm sorry if I've disappointed you with the carer business. It's just that—"

"You're a stubborn, difficult man, yes, I know that. And I'm not giving up entirely on getting you some help, you know. Leave it with me. I've another idea. Until Saturday, anyway. About eleven."

Sam put down the phone, resenting even Polly's attempts to help. As if as a result of Lydia's illness, he was now considered incapable of running and directing his own life and required help in its management. But equally he could not deny that the prospect of her visit, of the chance for him to go out, unfettered for a few hours, brought a relief of childish proportions.

In the bedroom, he carefully helped Lydia out of bed, into a chair. He fetched water, soap, a towel and washed her face, her thin limbs with the slow, deliberate actions of the penitent carrying out a rite. Then he found her clothes. Polly was right about the weather. It was a fine early summer day with the forecasters promising real heat by the weekend. He remembered a dress Lydia used to wear in summer, yellow, he thought, or was it apricot? With sprigs of flowers around the hem or perhaps the sleeves? Or was it sleeveless? A long dress, over her knees at least, a low neck. Or was he thinking of a skirt? That royal blue skirt with spots. No, not spots, more of an overall pattern of something green. Or perhaps he was thinking of something else entirely. A photograph from years ago, Scotland or even Spain. Why had he not taken sufficient time to note these things accurately when they were living them? As if their lives were always too obsessed with the moment to step aside and look. Record. Of course, the colour of Lydia's dress, the details of flowers or frills or necklines were immaterial in themselves. But he felt now such a sadness, a vacuum at failing to recall so much about the minutiae of those days as if, lost from memory, their past was little more than a fabrication, the fragment of a dream. He will buy Lydia a new summer dress. He will go out on Saturday when he will be free to leave her in Polly's care, take time choosing something that suits her. Abandon any sensible restraint on price. Later, he will take Lydia for a walk across the common, pushing her just a little way in her chair to the first bench where they will sit in the mild air. And if it is a good day for her, a day when she can cope with some light traffic sound, bird song, the proximity of occasional passers-by, Sam will hold on to the respite, value the relief and not trade it for darker thoughts pressing to intrude.

★★★

Frances stared down from her bedroom window onto the Goughs' garden. Little was growing. There was a decent stretch of recently mown grass, but the beds were dull, offering nothing to replace the few spring bulbs – a scattering of daffodils and tulips – of recent months. Of course, the garden was private, but Frances could not help but think of it as a communal space since her back rooms overlooked it and she felt some annoyance at the apparent lack of attention it was receiving. There were some shrubs, evergreens and a considerable amount of ivy crawling over the brick wall that separated Willow House from its substantial neighbour. But Sam Gough appeared to have made scant effort beyond somewhat random planting of those early bulbs and regular mowing of the lawn. A pity. She returned to the living room, to her desk by the window, wrote out her chosen text for the next letter, *Marriage should be honoured by all,* thought of adding a comment, but decided to let it speak for itself. She had not been to Pilgrim Square for nearly a month. There had been no particular plan to halt her visits, but each time she had begun to prepare for the journey to Brighton, she had found herself suddenly resistant, lacking the resolve to see the day through. As if weary, worn out by the necessity to conjure conviction in what she was doing.

It was, after all, taking so much longer than she had anticipated.

Initially, she had expected Christmas or early New Year to reap rewards. That extravagant pale grey cashmere sweater carefully wrapped in folds and folds of soft tissue. The vigils in her burgundy coat, enduring the biting winter wastes of the square. Surely, such gestures were worthy of a response. Then there were the letters, the correspondence, precisely penned and posted twice a week intended to grind down Charlotte Prideaux into capitulation. Into swift and shamed retreat. She had also set much store on that extravagant single malt. But after their joint birthdays had passed and the following weeks had brought nothing she had felt bereft.

Entirely desolate.

For she had allowed herself to begin to make plans.

To think of the two of them, she and Andrew, taking a holiday late in the summer. September, perhaps, giving her enough time to let the flat, remove all traces of Charlotte from the house – that coat rack would go, for a start – and restore their life in Pilgrim Square. She might suggest Italy to him, the Amalfi Coast, or even Spain. Barcelona, Gaudi and the Sagrada Familia and a few days exploring Catalonia. She would embrace the organisation the way she always had, of course, the hotel arrangements, flights, arrange a locum at the dental practice, buy Andrew some new clothes for the sun in Spain. For the Italian climate. Insist on a new linen jacket, footwear suitable for sightseeing. Order the currency. Buy some travel guides. It would be nothing as clichéd as a second honeymoon, naturally, but nevertheless a chance for them both to reflect and come to the conclusion mutually that the past year had been an absurd and somewhat embarrassing aberration that was best dismissed, discarded and forgotten. The future, Frances would declare to Andrew, holding his hand firmly as they sat on a sunlit terrace – in Ravello, in Tarragona – was all that mattered. Their future together. And all would be as it always had been.

At least between the two of them.

She had abandoned all hope of resolving the other matter that she tried to leave mostly undisturbed in the recesses of her mind. After all, what could she do? Some things were beyond even her control, her ability to influence. She watched a fly crawl slowly down the window pane, negotiating the sill, with care and precision.

She went back to the bedroom to change her shoes, planning a walk down to the river after posting her letter to Pilgrim Square. Drawn back to the window, to the Goughs' back garden, she was suddenly struck by an idea and, relieved to feel a sense of energy and purpose after a desultory few days, swiftly left the flat. There appeared to be no one in at the garden flat. Catherine, however, answered her door immediately.

"Sam and Lydia Gough's garden. It's just perfect!" Frances said as if the two of them had been jointly engaged in solving a puzzle. "I can't think why it didn't occur to me before. Ideal in every way."

Catherine stared blankly and found herself pushed to one side as Frances made her way down the hall to her kitchen and attempted to open her back door.

"It's locked," Catherine said. "I was about to go out. Really, Frances, I—"

"Actually, there's no need, I know what I'll see. And you'll agree with me, Catherine, see my point entirely."

"Will I?"

"The location for the Eve of the Street Party Soiree, as I'm calling it. Just for Willow House residents, of course. And our guests. Which naturally includes Violet's parents. You've not met them? A charming couple. The real owners of her flat, of course. Did you know that? No reason why you should whereas as the immediate neighbour I've had the fortune to – they're grateful to me in their way, I can tell that, for keeping a discreet eye on things next door. Violet is, as you know, so very young!"

Her face, Catherine noticed, had turned almost manically animated.

"I had no idea there was going to be an additional event. Is it absolutely necessary?" She tried to quell the woman's effusiveness, attempt some restraint. But Frances appeared not to notice.

"The Goughs will be delighted when I tell them what's decided. So much better for them than my original idea which doesn't bear considering now. A tame drinks party in my flat is no competition, after all, for a barbecue in their back garden. This way, Lydia can be included. Do you have any idea, Catherine, how ill that poor woman is? No doubt being so busy with your job and all that you haven't had time to notice. Whereas I – well, I have a sympathetic eye for these things, you see."

Frances, Catherine saw, had begun to fiddle with a couple of cups and a plate she had left to drain, lining them up as if disturbed by their disorderliness.

"Isn't this all rather presumptuous?" Catherine said. "You haven't even asked Sam?"

Frances looked at her with surprise.

"Oh, the idea is so fresh in my mind that I haven't had a chance. But don't worry. He'll see it as I do. After all, Willow House really has been the hub, the very crucible, you could say, of the street party operation." She turned away from her rearrangement of the crockery, looked around the kitchen as if conducting an inspection. "Of course I saw this flat before you even moved in. Considered buying it at one stage. But one has to think of security, don't you think? In an urban environment? And a first-floor flat is undoubtedly the safer option." Then she headed down the hall as if suddenly aware of somewhere more essential to go and only halted when outside Catherine's front door. "A decent barbecue with a few side salads will work well, I'd say. And perhaps some strawberries for dessert. With cream, of course. I'll get a list together and let you know your contribution, Catherine. Goodness, we're already well past the middle of May so only a few weeks to go now until the party. How time flies!"

Back in her flat, Frances made coffee, sank down into a chair and drank two cups. Sometimes, she was unsure where the line lay between her adopted persona and her real self. Each encroached on the other so seamlessly that perhaps there was no line at all and this authoritarian, faintly uninviting officious character was, in fact, all there was.

18

Polly heard the noise from the kitchen.

Lydia lay on the floor, her forehead, caught on the edge of the low table in her fall, already bleeding. She stared up at Polly's appalled face, showing neither pain nor particular discomfort, but an expression of entire hopelessness. Awkwardly, Polly knelt down next to her.

"Mum! What were you doing? Why ever would you try to get up when it's just not possible for you to do that anymore? Not on your own."

She felt irrationally angry. As if Lydia had chosen to be rebellious simply to annoy. She tried to shift the helpless limbs, but her pregnant body hindered her. Lydia began to moan, soft noises at first which grew to a peal of sound that was alarming. She took a cushion from the sofa, wedged it under Lydia's head where the blood was now flowing more rapidly.

"Mum, I'll just go and see if I can find anyone to help us. Dad's not going to be back for ages and I really don't want to ring him. At least, not unless it's absolutely necessary."

Since the end of May, Polly had been relieving Sam every other Saturday, to his enormous gratitude. As soon as she arrived at the flat, he headed for the bus stop by the common and randomly caught whichever one arrived first. Or he walked the longer distance to the station, took a train to Waterloo, crossed the bridge or stayed south of the river and explored streets for little more reason than that they cropped up in his path. Every time he intended to go to a gallery, an exhibition, visit a museum, but found instead that the sheer freedom of spontaneous choice, something that he had not valued until it was absent, kept him roaming, untethered. Always he had thought that the solitariness he had craved most of his adult life was to be found only in wild, untamed places. Now he saw that the anonymity of city streets was equally accommodating and that he could spend days slipping unobtrusively, unchecked, amidst passing strangers.

Summer was suddenly evident everywhere. Cafés tipped out onto streets, the terraces of the South Bank clogged with queues waiting for outside tables at bars and restaurants as if there was a collective sense of sudden abandonment of winter hibernation for a pursuit of sunlight. Sam had forgotten how seasons had their impact, not only on rural living, but on urban habits too. How the lengthening daylight – from spring to summer solstice and for a couple of months beyond – influenced behaviour, habit, routine. A social calendar replaced the seasonal demands of the land, but nevertheless the same sense of a cyclical pattern was there, something giving a welcome shape and meaning to the endless days of existence.

But no longer for Lydia. Or so it seemed to him.

Sam had no idea how much she could now comprehend. Even Polly's pregnancy, so tangibly evident, was possibly beyond her capacity to note. Her mind was a place beyond his reach. After that Sunday when he had unloaded his qualms about that student of hers – Jezz, Josh, or whoever – he had adopted the habit of talking to her at some length about other, less potent matters, reminiscences mainly, and had found some comfort in them, hoping that Lydia too was aware. Yet still he resisted sharing with her what he really wanted to unload. The event was now so far in his past that it felt like the tale of a callous stranger. But at the same time the enormity of it, his consciousness of the part he may have played in the death of a man had failed to diminish over the decades.

Indeed, what had seemed so easy to dismiss at twenty-six had begun to load him down as the years accrued.

Polly left Lydia lying on the living room floor and went outside for help, hoping to find Catherine, but her car was gone from the forecourt and there was no answer at her front door. Miller Street was quiet. At the far end of the road she could see a few people getting in and out of cars, unloading shopping or talking by front doors, but she could not risk leaving her mother alone to go and ask for help. Perhaps she should call an ambulance although it seemed an extreme gesture. On the other hand, the fall might have caused delayed concussion, the bad graze on her forehead a symptom of something more serious. She was loath to try Frances Chater's door. She had heard her father's recent rant about the woman, his outrage at her request to use their garden for some event connected with the street party and although Polly had not listened to the details, she knew he would resent enlisting the help of this particular neighbour. She stood in the middle of the pavement and thought again of ringing her father. He had only left an hour or so before and perhaps if he returned now to help her, there would still be a sufficient wedge of the day for him to go out again. Or, on the other hand, if she managed to shift Lydia into a position where she was leaning against the sofa, support her with pillows, perhaps there would be no harm in leaving her there until his return at the end of the afternoon. Sudden movement, however, a distinct tumble and prod from her abdomen as if her unborn child was reading her thoughts, turned her away from the idea. Now that her mother's muscles were entirely dormant, uncooperative, her body felt like a solid weight in spite of her thin frame.

"Polly? It is Polly, isn't it? Is anything wrong?"

In her preoccupation, Polly had not noticed Frances Chater, looking too formally dressed for a casual Saturday as if she was heading out for a specific event. And in spite of her father's avowed dislike of his neighbour, she felt overwhelmingly relieved to see someone who might help. Swiftly, she explained the situation, feeling a little like a forlorn child in need of adult aid. Frances put a hand on Polly's shoulder for a moment then turned and headed swiftly for the open front door of the garden flat. Polly followed meekly.

In the living room, Frances discarded her bag, her green linen jacket, her cream court shoes and knelt down beside Lydia who was looking alarmingly pale.

"Should we call an ambulance?" Polly was unused to feeling inadequate.

"No need for that," Frances said, "the fuss would not be good for her. Besides, the head wound is clearly superficial. There will be a nasty bruise in a day or two, but no real damage done. Some warm water and cotton wool, Polly, and perhaps there is some antiseptic cream to hand?"

Polly dutifully followed instructions, sat down in a chair to watch as Frances bathed the graze, talking quietly to Lydia all the time. Then she managed to gather her in her arms, lifting her gently yet with impressive economy of movement onto the sofa. Lydia was biddable, simply murmuring sounds as if acquiescent to the aid.

"No bones broken, thank goodness," Frances said, inspecting Lydia's arms, legs, her ankles. Already the bleeding had stopped on her forehead. "And I don't think there's any need for a plaster. It wouldn't be good for Lydia's skin, you see."

"I'm so grateful," Polly said, "I was only gone from the room for a few moments. I'd just popped into the kitchen to make some coffee and – well, Mum must have forgotten that she can't walk. Tried to get herself up."

"I am pleased to be able to help," Frances said. "I have mentioned to your father several times that he only has to ask." Her attention was still on Lydia, checking her pulse, holding her hand gently as if to reassure.

Polly said, "I think he's too proud, feeling he should be able to cope on his own. His duty and all that. And they've always been a very private couple by nature, not sociable creatures at all." She felt a need to mitigate Sam's manner to Frances.

"Well, I would respect that, of course," Frances said, "I've never been the life and soul of the party type myself, Polly. Never like to rush in where I'm not wanted. But neighbourliness is something different and I always feel a sense of community is important. And if one can be an angel of mercy at times of need, say no more. Now, can I make you some coffee? You did say you were about to have some when Lydia fell. And it's important you look after yourself as well, Polly, in these late stages of pregnancy. Clearly, you only have a few weeks to go. Perhaps I could make you a little snack? In fact, I won't take no for an answer. A sandwich or some scrambled egg? All this has been a shock for you as well as for poor Lydia."

Frances stood up and left the room, heading for the kitchen as if she was offering hospitality in her own home. Polly called out to her to say she wasn't hungry, but Frances appeared not to hear and she dared not risk leaving her mother alone again. From the kitchen, she heard cupboards being opened, the kettle filled and cups gathered and could only imagine her father's anger if he returned to find his home so invaded. Polly, though, found herself easily compliant. If Frances Chater wanted to step in and offer some practical help, her company for an hour or so during her father's absence, she was not going to rebuff it. Besides, the woman was harmless. A little overwhelming in manner, perhaps, but nevertheless well-meaning. Sam should be more tolerant towards her. She returned to the room with a tray Polly could not remember seeing before, coffee, a stack of sandwiches and set them all out on the low table in front of the sofa.

"Now, Lydia, I believe you have particular food of your own prepared for you so I am not interfering there. We'll leave Polly to sort that. But perhaps some warm milk with a dash of sugar to offset something of the shock of your fall? That shouldn't do any harm."

Polly watched her help her mother swallow small sips of the warm liquid with the help of a teaspoon. She took a mug of coffee and the sight of the sandwiches made her realise how hungry she was.

"Were you ever a nurse, Frances?" she said.

She did not answer at first, continuing to make encouraging noises to Lydia, gently tipping her head back and wiping stray drops of milk from her chin. There was a bruise forming on her mother's ankle, another on her forehead, but otherwise she seemed remarkably unaffected by the fall and was submitting passively to Frances' care. Polly asked the question again.

"A nurse?" Frances put the empty mug of milk down on the table, seeming unconcerned that drops had spilled from the spoon onto her pale dress. "Oh, all that was a very long time ago, Polly. In my youth, you know, I did train. But of course, I looked after my late mother in her final years so the skills resurfaced, you could say. Now, did you have any plans for today, Polly? Because I think that your mother could do with a little sleep and then we could sit her out in this lovely back garden of theirs for a bit of air. We seem to be blessed with rather a good summer this year and it would be such a shame to waste a fine June day."

"But what about your day, Frances? You were clearly going out somewhere."

Frances shook her head.

"Plans easily jettisoned, Polly. I can see I'm needed here far more to lend you a hand. I'll just pop up to my apartment to change into something more sensible and then I can keep an eye on Lydia while you grab a moment or two with your feet up."

★★★

Sam held out the bunch of yellow roses.

"I'm very grateful, Frances. Polly has told me how kind you were."

Frances smiled broadly, but appeared to resist the flowers.

"Nonsense. Anyone would have done the same. I'm just pleased I could be of such help. In the right place at the right time, so to speak. Because I don't like to think what could have happened if Polly had tried to cope on her own."

Sam suppressed irritation.

"Quite."

"But as I always say, what are neighbours for if not to step in at a time of need? At least that's always been my way. And Saturday was such a time of need for both Polly and Lydia. Really, the flowers are quite unnecessary, Sam. Lovely, of course, but I'm not the sort to want a reward for what felt natural to me."

"Right." Sam started to leave then turned back. "That business about our garden. If you're still wanting to use it for this event of yours. I've had a rethink. Or rather Polly's made me see sense."

"For our Willow House get-together, the evening before the street party?" Frances took the spray of roses, sniffed into their tight buds then smiled at him as if only mildly surprised by his capitulation. "Well, thank you so much, Sam, it's a generous offer. And I know you will enjoy it as much as the rest of us. I already have numbers to hand and it's unlikely to be more than ten. Less, probably. Shall we say a seven pm start? We can liaise nearer the date about precise arrangements. I'll take it all in hand, anyway."

"Good," Sam said, already regretting his gesture, but under strict instruction from Polly. "Well, thanks again for Saturday."

She stood at her doorway, watching as he retreated swiftly down the staircase.

"Don't even mention it, Sam. My pleasure to be of help. Always."

★★★

Charlotte Prideaux looks up from the Sunday papers.

"Wimbledon," she says.

"What about it?" says Andrew.

"We should be going. It's June. That's what you do in June, go to the tennis."

"If you have tickets," Andrew says and turns to the cricket.

"We should get some. I'd like to go. I haven't been for years."

"Nor me," says Andrew. "Not since … not for years."

"Well?" she puts down the paper, lightly knocks Andrew's foot from the stool where it rests on sections and supplements.

"Well, what?" He gives up on the cricket. He knows nothing about the game, anyway, simply keeps up in a desultory sort of way in case any of his patients wants to talk test scores. He looks over at Charlotte who is wearing what he thinks is called a halter-neck top that makes her breasts look larger. Her skin, usually as light as milk, has turned palely caramel in the June heat. It suits her.

"Andy, are you listening at all, my darling man? Wimbledon! Let's get some tickets."

Suddenly, she sounds very young. A child in need of sudden treats. Or perhaps he is merely older and wiser and knows so much more about how things work. He smiles benignly, feels vaguely avuncular towards her and wonders why the sensation is mildly erotic.

"You don't just buy Wimbledon tickets," he says, "there's a ballot and you have to belong to a club. A tennis club, I suppose. Or you know someone who knows someone or you go and queue. Go in on the gate, a day pass and look at the outside courts and spend hours waiting to stand on Centre Court and by the time you get onto that it's started to rain or poor light has stopped play or all the good matches have finished. It's hard work, going to Wimbledon, I can tell you."

Charlotte stares at him, a smile on her face as if she finds his protestation predictably foolish.

"Don't be silly," she says, "of course we can get tickets. Good tickets. Anyone can get them if they're willing to pay what the seller's demanding."

Andrew picks up the paper again. He is unsure whether to be buoyed or cowed by her unflinching certainty.

"I used to know one of the linesmen," he says, remembering now, "that's how we got tickets before."

"Well, there you are then! I knew you'd think of something. Ring him now."

"Charlotte, this was all a very long time ago. I've lost touch. He might even be dead for all I know. Probably is, come to think of it." He glances up, sees her twisting her silver necklace, aligning it on her shoulder blades to lie flat. "But I'll ask around," he says, without any idea who or where he is supposed to ask. If he is honest, it is years since he has seen himself as the driving force of the household. He has grown into the habit of not so much delegating as passively watching events organised for him. It was how they lived, after all, for the years of their marriage. Frances booked the tickets, arranged the holidays, decided the destinations and wielded control over all domestic decisions. That armchair re-covered in William Morris Strawberry Thief Crimson that Charlotte so dislikes. The Victorian pine chest in the window that Frances picked up in some shop in The Lanes. Even the Pilgrim Square house, in retrospect a wise investment, but nevertheless an enormous financial step he had resisted until she told him she had offered the asking price on his behalf. At the surgery, of course, he wielded professional authority, but the running of the practice had fallen more and more into Frances' hands and he could not fault her competency. When the affair with Charlotte had started, he remembered feeling a childish sense of glee at his daring. At his ability to act subversively, defiantly, and, for a while at least, to get away with it. In many ways, it was the subterfuge that had been intoxicating. The planning of their trysts and assignations had made him feel resourceful, dominant, in a way that was otherwise remote. Guilt was a by-product, naturally, but one that he could sidestep with few qualms. For Charlotte was so decisive, so convinced that their actions were appropriate, justified by some amorous law that he easily allowed himself to wallow in, bathing in the seas of their adultery. Now he stands up, goes over to where she is sitting, feet curled under her, leans forward and kisses the tip of her nose. "I'll ask around," he repeats, "about Wimbledon tickets. Of course we must go. I'm sure I can lay my hands on some."

★★★

Barnaby Taylor reads the saved email again. It is not encouraging. If anything, it is abrupt, scant, as if the sender resents his intrusion, his attempt to find Eddie Wells. But perhaps he is reading too much into the brief message. After all, the news being shared is hardly celebratory, a reason for elaboration.

And Catherine Wells has no idea who he is.

Now he knows the facts, the raw truth about Eddie's death, he understands that neighbour's hesitation. The woman in Bevington who seemed to skate around saying too much, but with some persuasion was willing to pass on his contact details.

Now he needs to find Catherine Wells.

Another email would be unwise since the tone of hers was unforthcoming and anyway, he has no wish to announce his paternity in such a bald fashion. He needs to see her.

He wonders if his compulsion to see her, his wish to connect with Eddie's widow would be so strong if he had experienced a more conventional upbringing. Not that his mother neglected or mistreated him in any way. Far from it. But Rosie's notion on child-rearing was based on the principle of bestowing independence and self-sufficiency as early as possible. *We're all on our own in this world, Barnie,* was what he had imbibed with mother's milk. Growing up, their lives had been nomadic. A series of homes in various countries, sometimes just two or three rooms in a city, at other times a more remote, rural existence. Rosie had disapproved of schools, disapproved of the idea of loyalties and connections that would restrict her strong streak of impetuosity. In her fashion, she home-educated Barnaby, treated him more as a companion than a dependent child so often took him to work wherever she had found employment. For years, he assumed all children followed this pattern, shadowing their parents' lives, adapting to their random routines and it was not until he was nine years old and they found themselves living for an unusually extended period in the same town that Barnaby discovered he was an anomaly. Other children, the boys he met in the playground, the little girls he talked to in the park, had lives structured around an obligatory school day, curtailed by bedtimes, regular meals, household habits. And they had relations, these children, a network of family and close friends that appeared to shore up their everyday lives, provide a kind of safety net in time of need. His mother, Rosie, had friends everywhere, she claimed. Each time they arrived in a new place or planned to leave another, she would talk about her contacts who had promised work, suggested accommodation. And sometimes, these people would materialise, warmly embrace Rosie and Barnaby, take them into their homes, cook them a few meals, let them sleep on their floors, in their spare rooms. But soon enough, the novelty of a single woman and her young child appeared to wear off and there would begin to be curt remarks about the need for the space they were occupying, a reminder about the cost of food. So no, Barnaby thought, they did not have the sort of friends and relations these other children had. Normal children, apparently, that he wanted to befriend, claim and keep as his own.

And about this time, he began to need answers to questions he had not even known he wanted to ask. *Do I have a daddy? A father?* he said one day to Rosie as they sat eating at the café underneath the small apartment she'd rented for them in Trieste. She had ruffled his hair, laughed and said that surely, she provided sufficient parenting for him and that the fewer ties a child had, the better for their development. At least that was the memory he had of that first conversation, but it might have been from a later one since he began to ask such questions regularly so that, eventually, when he was at an age to probe more deeply, reject her evasive replies, he had received something tangible. Concrete. *Your father was called Edward. Eddie, to his friends. It was never going to work out between us, not long term, so I left. Besides, I didn't want all that partnership and family stuff. For any of us.* Barnaby had taken away the information, stored it, taken it out every few days to examine it, consider how such newly acquired knowledge made him feel. But there was something else he needed to ask. *Did my father know about me? Did Edward ever see me? Have I ever met him?* Rosie's clarification, however, was spent. She dismissed all further probing as if Barnaby was being unreasonable in his persistence. *The past is the past,* she would say with a wave of her hands. *Free yourself of anything that binds.* There had been, of course, transitory figures in his life to whom he had attached loosely paternal feelings. Over the years, Rosie had made friends with several men, some simply featuring among the web of people she liked to collect around her, others moving in with them in the various homes they established. Barnaby grew fond of one or two of them, was treated on the whole with mild affection or at least an easy tolerance. And he had assumed that this was enough, to have these male figures featuring from time to time, playing a temporary familial role. After all, he was trying to embrace his mother's example of spurning hooks and obligations, wanting to believe in her pursuit of living freely where an absent, entirely unknown father was the norm.

Yet suddenly, Rosie presented him with grandparents. He was fifteen when his mother decided that she wanted to travel in India for a year and that it would now be appropriate for him to spend a couple of years at school in England. She had constantly told him that all her maternal responsibilities towards him would stop the day he reached eighteen so this arrangement was perhaps something of a halfway house, a chance for her to offload him a little prematurely. Rosie's parents welcomed their only grandchild into their Hampshire home with subdued bewilderment. The three of them negotiated their way politely around each other as Barnaby, enrolled in a local school, learned to adjust to the regularity of a formal education, the culture of his peers. His grandfather, a recently retired teacher, introduced him to football and allegiance to Southampton FC while his grandmother, a librarian, cooked him regular meals and asked cautious questions about his childhood and upbringing with Rosie. Neither of them claimed any knowledge of his father. Barnaby was by no means unhappy living with these recently acquired, kindly close relations, but he felt a certain sense of detachment as if he was viewing rather than consciously occupying this new existence. And what was supposed to come next? Very soon, he found himself hedged in by careers fairs and conventions, exam targets and grades and courses and colleges that wanted to propel him in a defined direction, stitch him into a straightjacket that would shape him for the foreseeable decades. Perhaps Rosie's way was right and he had lived alongside her restlessness for too long to conform to anything other. Yet his grandparents' lives seemed more admirable in many ways. And enviable too. And he could not help wondering whether his mother, once she had reached the age of sixty or sixty-five or more, would be able to feel any of the measured contentment they appeared to embrace. Their quiet serenity, their belief in the good fortune of their lives suggested a fulfilment he doubted that his mother would ever know.

Barnaby starts with the reference library near Kings Cross.

At the beginning of his search when it had seemed hopelessly without direction, he had enlisted his grandfather's help who had patiently encouraged him towards electoral rolls and company records that had eventually led him, after a few dead ends and futile journeys, to the address in Bevington. This time, he tells himself, he has only to trawl through every recent directory for every county searching for the surname *Wells,* the initial *C* attached. But he soon abandons his search as impractical. Already he has noted down at least a dozen numbers from one directory and the thought that she could choose not to be listed at all has just occurred to him.

Besides, it is 2006. It is the 21st century.

And people no longer find people by searching through dusty directories and making chance cold calls. He rings up a friend, one of the few he has acquired since moving to London, arranges to meet for a drink that night. Dan, an aspiring photo journalist, boasts of paparazzi-like skills acquired through his media training. He will enjoy, Barnaby is sure, putting them to the test in the task of locating Eddie's widow.

In finding Catherine Wells.

19

Charlotte Prideaux lies on her back, staring up at the white ceiling of the bedroom. She pulls the discarded sheet loosely over her, fidgets a pillow into place. Next to her, Andrew tries not to doze.

"Thank you, Andy," she says, taking one of his hands, "for the tickets, I mean. We'll have a wonderful day. The men's semi-finals. I knew you could get them easily enough."

Andrew thinks of the numerous phone calls he has made, contacts he has rustled, his various attempts to use legitimate means before eventually caving in to the preposterous demands of an internet site. He had no idea that the cost of a pair of tickets for a day's tennis could rival an extravagant weekend on the Venice Lido. But no matter. Charlotte is thrilled. He is triumphant. He allows his eyes to close for a moment or two. It is close to eleven o'clock, but there is little that they must do today, a warm summer Saturday so Brighton will swell with beach-seekers impervious to the chilled waters of the channel. They will do well to avoid the crowds, stay close to home. Suddenly, Charlotte flips over onto her stomach, leans her arms against his chest, spreads out the span of her thin white hands, pressing down so that he feels their firm imprint.

"There's one more thing," she says.

He groans mockingly. He feels the flicker of her breath on his bare flesh.

"Not Glyndebourne," he says. "All that loud singing. And certainly not Henley. Those dreadful public school types in striped blazers. I might draw the line at that." Although, of course, he knows that if Charlotte wants Glyndebourne or Henley he will remove any line and do his best to oblige.

"No," she says, "it's nothing like that."

"Good," he says. "So what is your one more thing?"

He strokes the back of her neck, traces the curve of her spine down to her waist.

"A child," Charlotte says. "I would like us to have a child."

Outside in Pilgrim Square, Andrew listens to an engine turning, a door banging, a car driving off. Silence again. Then there is the peal of a door bell, once, twice, a third time, even, as if the caller is being ignored. Charlotte's heart beats against his chest. His, he is sure, beats faster.

Suddenly he is alert. Listens more acutely to the source of the sound. That ringing doorbell.

Abruptly, he sits up, toppling Charlotte so that she falls onto the other side of the bed, saying something that he misses because he is hurrying now, searching for a towel, his dressing gown, abandoning that to shovel legs into trousers instead, intent on leaving the room, escaping even, down the stairs into the hall. He stands stock still for a moment. Recovers. Flicks uncombed hair back with one hand. Then he steps forward, opens the front door wide to still the ringing.

And smiles.

"This," he says, holding both hands out to the young man on the doorstep, firmly grasping his shoulders as if to steady himself, as if to prove that it is no mirage, a figment of imagination, "this I was not expecting. Thomas, come in. Come in!"

★★★

Frances stood in front of Willow House, her hands sifting through flyers for delivery to each home in Miller Street. Even those households that had shown little interest in the street party needed to know the arrangements for the day, in order to follow the instructions for alternative parking, abide by road closure notices that would operate for a twelve hour period. Violet was supposed to be helping her with this particular job, but there had been no sign of her for over a week and Frances had already wasted ten minutes of her morning knocking on her door in vain. The young woman lacked structure and discipline in her life. That was her trouble. As a consequence, her idea of commitment was based solely on enthusiasms that waned rapidly. She behaved more like an adolescent which these days seemed prolonged as if the generations born into the final decades of the 20th century had awarded themselves some sort of licence, shrugging away any idea of sober, industrious living as if it was an impediment to their liberty.

Which, of course, in a way, it was. So perhaps they had a point.

She looked down at her bundles of flyers, flicked away a wasp that hovered near her arm.

"Frances? It is Frances, isn't it?"

A woman she initially failed to recognise approached her from the end of the road bordering the common.

"Yes, for my sins," she said, immediately regretting her phrase. It sounded like something her mother would have said. Then she realised it was Violet's mother. "It's Isabel, isn't it? How nice to see you again. I didn't realise you were staying with Violet at the moment. I mean, I've heard people coming and going, of course, not to complain of, you understand. It's only that being such close neighbours one is aware. Of people in residence. Arrivals, departures, that sort of thing." She felt too warm, sweating in the increasing heat of the morning so

that her shirt was already clammy against her skin. She regretted
the polyester skirt clinging to her legs. Isabel Lawrence wore
a long, loose, light blue dress, open sandals that managed to
look appropriate as well as fashionable. Espadrilles, they were
called, a sort of rope and canvas construction that Frances had
always thought rather foolish. Unlike her, however, Isabel was
accommodating the hot day with ease. Her hair, pale straw in
colour with random streaks of grey, was pulled back from her
face with a clasp that exposed her neck freely to the air. On
anyone else the style would have been ageing and too severe.
On Isabel, it managed to look flattering.

"We're not staying with Violet," she said in the quiet,
measured voice Frances remembered from the evening when
they had first met. "At least we're staying in the flat, but Violet
is away at the moment so it's just me and Martin."

"Away?" Frances said somewhat sharply. "Well, that would
explain things then. She was supposed to be helping me, you
see, with a delivery." She held out a sheaf of flyers as if for
verification. "We only arranged it at the beginning of the week
and she said nothing to me about going away. But no doubt
something last minute cropped up and she simply forgot to
mention it." She knew she sounded proprietorial over Violet's
movements, but pressed on. "She has such a wide circle of
friends, of course, and she's at that age when invitations
just keep pouring in. One wouldn't want to criticise her
for thoughtlessness. Towards me, I mean." Isabel appeared
unmoved. Instead, she looked up and down Miller Street as if
assessing the challenge.

"Well, I'm free at the moment," she said, "I'm sure we
could do the road between us in fifteen minutes or so? It
doesn't look like a particularly arduous task."

"But I couldn't possibly – I mean, it would be such an
imposition to expect you to cover for Violet."

"Hardly," Isabel said dryly. "I'm simply here and available. And anyway, it's too good a morning to spend inside the flat."

"In that case, I accept your kind gesture." Frances said, dividing the pile and handing over half, feeling inexplicably disarmed by the offer and wishing too late she had refused it.

"Odds or evens?"

"I beg your pardon?"

"Odd or even numbers?"

"Oh, you mean which side of the street do I want you to do? Well, it's not quite that simple, in fact, as a couple of the larger places are divided into flats – not properly like Willow House, of course, but even so there's some sort of division into multi-occupancy."

"I'll do the other side of the road, Frances, shall I? That would seem simple enough. I'm sure I'll work it out." She smiled, Frances thought, the way she herself used to summon a smile for some of Andrew's awkward, nervous patients. Tolerant, impartial. She watched the way Isabel's pale blue summer dress – light linen, probably, or lawn cotton – draped airily and tent-like around her small frame as she crossed the street and felt perspiration gathering into two unsightly wedges under her arms, thought of the stain it would cause, the possible odour if anyone drew too close. Purposely, she took some time with her delivery, grabbing any opportunity for a brief chat with anyone she saw, engaging some children in a one-sided conversation about their scooters, stroking cats sunbathing in flower beds, picking up random strands of litter. Out of the corner of her eye, she could see Isabel efficiently despatching her pile of flyers, negotiating squeaking gates, calming barking dogs. On the way back, she stopped pointlessly by the lamppost displaying the street party poster as if checking for some sudden irregularity that had appeared in the text and was gratified to see that she had caused Isobel to wait for her in front of Willow House. Isabel silently returned the few surplus flyers.

"So sorry to keep you, but one can't help being stopped by some of the neighbours asking questions," she said with an exaggerated shrug. "You'd think there would be enough information already circulating, but I really think people have lost the art of reading and absorbing detail these days, don't you? Of course, we're all on the same page, so to speak. Everyone simply wants a wonderful occasion, something truly to remember so it's understandable they like to check with me. They assume I have all the answers!"

"Of course," Isabel said, turned away and found her keys in a deep pocket. Frances followed her into the house, up the stairs and then pushed her way ahead as they reached the landing in front of the two flats.

"Now, coffee, Isabel. I really must insist," she said, "after all your help. On such a hot morning as well, positively humid."

Isabel smiled. Again, Frances thought, that smile, bland, neutral, hiding as much as it displayed. She found the woman's self-possession, her composure, an irritant, as if designed to beguile.

"No, thank you. That's quite unnecessary. Besides, I've only come back inside to fetch a book. I intend to spend the rest of the morning sitting somewhere shady on the common. I enjoy, you see, being somewhat solitary."

"Of course," Frances said, "don't we all? But I wanted to ask you about Violet."

"Violet?"

"Yes. You say she's away. But she will be back in time, I presume?"

"In time?"

"For the Miller Street Party. It's getting quite close now, you know."

"Oh that," Isabel said, "well, I'm not at all sure of her plans for the summer, but I shouldn't think so. I can't imagine she's particularly bothered about it, can you? Not really her sort of thing at all."

The few remaining flyers dropped from Frances' hands. She let them remain in a muddle for a few seconds in the space that lay between Isabel's slim feet in their white espadrilles and her broad, bunion-accommodating navy shoes. Then Isabel bent down, swiftly retrieved them, presenting them to her in a neat pile. She smiled again as if with summoned reassurance. "But Martin and I are coming. In fact, we're both very much looking forward to it so you can certainly count on us, Frances."

★★★

The pub is emptying now, the afternoon lull between lunch time and early evening drinkers. Their glasses are empty too and there is an awkward pause in the piecemeal conversation of the past couple of hours. Charlotte looks from one face to another. Waits for someone to speak. Decides to take control.

"Well?" she says, "there's a lot I need to get done this afternoon. And no doubt you – you'll want to get back to London, I expect? If you leave it too late on a Saturday, you'll find the trains can be murderously crowded." She stares blatantly at Thomas, turns it into a brittle, fixed smile. Thomas avoids her eye. Shuffles enormous trainers under the table. Fiddles with the neck of his grey T-shirt. And Andrew looks across the table at him and sees not the six-foot-tall self-possessed young man who has spent the past two years in Australia, remote from him, estranged. Or not only him. But also the toddler faltering on first stumbling steps. The young child waking inconsolable, lost in night terrors. He sees the five-year-old on his first day at school, his hand hesitant to let go. There's the ten-year-old too, shivering from an early morning summer sea swim, skittering across the sharp pebbles to his father's side, his lankiness faun-like. And even the awkward teenager, groping his way to articulate words in his new-found, uncertain voice, is there for Andrew as he watches his son, feeling close to weeping at having him once more near enough to touch or embrace. Andrew turns to Charlotte.

"You get on with your day," he says, not unkindly, "I'll see you later. Tom and I might just go for a walk, spend a bit of time together."

Charlotte starts to say something, her hand reaching out to his as if in objection. Then she lets it fall to her side. A gesture of rare compliance. She stands, kisses Andrew's cheek, keeps her hand on his shoulder while she says something indefinite to Thomas about visiting again. She kisses Andrew once more and leaves. They watch her go. Then Andrew gets up.

"Come on," he says to Thomas, "let's get out of here. I think we could both do with some sea air."

They walk. At first they are both quiet, but their silence is not heavy; more a relief at being freed from the strain of the trite conversation in the pub. The afternoon's heat has drawn the crowds to the beach and they find their pace slowed through the traffic of pedestrians along the front. They reach the West Pier and stop as if by tacit agreement to lean against the railings and stare at the disintegrating shroud of a structure.

"You'll be used to more spectacular beaches than our tame south coast ones," Andrew says. Thomas nods, watches seagulls scratching over a discarded hot dog on the pebbles below. "No sharks, I hope? People always talk about sharks. In Australian seas, I mean. And snakes, of course. See any of those?"

He shrugs. "One or two."

Andrew is aware of how much he needs to say and yet at the same time how very little really matters. He wants to suspend time, occupy only this moment, with his son standing so close to him that he could save him from any freak, frantic calamity that might arise. Protect his body with his own from the target of any stray armed madman. A family walks past, a young father with a small, dark-haired boy, no more than three, riding on his shoulders, and a girl, taller, older, her arms twisted tight around her mother's waist like a belt. The man stops close to them, lifts the child down with a mock groan at the burden and the boy stamps a foot so that his sandal flies off and the girl, his sister, no doubt, leaves her mother's side, scuttles to collect it, solemnly buckling it back into place. Then the boy is lifted high again, gleefully resumes his shoulder ride, and they walk on. Thomas watches them for a moment then shifts his gaze back to the beach, the sea and the horizon.

"When did it happen?" he asks. His voice is flat. The teenager Thomas again, Andrew thinks. Protesting indifference out of awkwardness.

"What?" Andrew says. "The West Pier? The fire? You remember."

Thomas bangs his hand on the railing several times.

"Not the pier. You and Mum. Her. You and Charlotte. No, not so much that – when did Mum leave?"

Andrew feels suddenly weary. His elation of only a moment or so ago is deflated entirely. He tries to recall how much Thomas knows. He remembers writing to the only address he had for him somewhere in East London, Dalston, he thinks, where Thomas had stayed until he had left for Australia. The friend – Charlie, was it? Oliver, perhaps? – was supposed to be joining Thomas out there and he had hoped the letter would be forwarded. He had sent a couple of emails too with scant facts, assumed they had reached Thomas although there had been no reply. At the time, he had been so consumed by Charlotte, overwhelmed by her need of him, her willing, surprising surrender, that nothing else had particularly registered. Frances had left. Removed herself swiftly to her late mother's house in Worthing. Later, she had supplied him with a new address somewhere in south London and he had duly delivered the information to Thomas in another brief email out of some vague sense of obligation, like giving required details of a next of kin. Perhaps he had even harboured some resentment at the way Frances had appeared to deal with the marriage breakdown so efficiently, coldly, negotiated herself the sale of one home, the purchase of another. But the time line of it all is now muddled to him so his answer to Thomas is vague.

"A year or so ago, I suppose. No, a bit more. Quite a bit more, in fact."

Thomas turns to his father. He has put on dark sunglasses so Andrew is unsure of his focus.

"It was my fault," he says bleakly.

Andrew thinks he has misheard.

"Your fault? What are you talking about, Tom? How could any of this be your fault?"

"I left. There was that huge row. Not just the one, but all that stuff about … it was all such a mess. I did want you both to understand, but it was so hard and so I just went."

Andrew tries to think, to hollow his way back and sequence events. Thomas is entirely wrong, of course. The appalling arguments of that summer, by autumn drifting into tense, resentful silences, had no connection to the break-up of his marriage to Frances, his affair with Charlotte. There was absolutely no link at all. Yet even as he stands there, shifting his gaze from Thomas and out to the horizon, he wonders if this is entirely true. After all, when Thomas had left, nothing had ever felt quite the same again. It was as if bereavement hovered over their lives in Pilgrim Square, a grief that both of them shared, but neither was willing to express. Each, he suspected, blamed the other, but by then even accusation, heated argument seemed out of reach. As if they were too worn down by conflict and no longer knew whether there was a moral high ground to occupy. Brittle, functional exchanges replaced conversation. Andrew remembered feeling that the sense of absence was similar to the time before the birth of Thomas. When their difficulty in conceiving had made their lives seem vacuous, each month confronting them with their own failure, teasing them with their inadequacy. But then, of course, eventually, blithe fortune had intervened, the chance miracle of their child that had united them again.

Only this time, there was no such respite.

And as the year turned, shifted through seasons, it seemed that Thomas' departure, his declared determination to sever himself permanently from his parents was absolute. Andrew remembered one day, looking across the room at Frances as she sat with a book, apparently absorbed, detached, and wondering quite objectively if he loved his wife any more. If, in fact, he even liked her sufficiently to tolerate living with her in their house in Pilgrim Square.

It was about this time that the affair with Charlotte had started.

And initially, his actions had felt not so much illicit as compulsory. He had wanted to be overwhelmed, to capitulate, the victim of a physical desire that dulled all other senses. Guilt had seemed irrelevant. Charlotte had presented him with what seemed like a legitimate alternative to the void of an existence with Frances. And she had, after all, been so obdurate, entirely unyielding with Thomas. But equally, he had been spineless, inadequate in failing to defend his son.

Andrew puts his hand on Thomas' shoulder, feels the warmth of his skin through the thin cotton of his T-shirt.

"Let's walk on a bit and then go and find somewhere to sit and talk. Now it's just the two of us. You're not in a hurry to get back to London?"

Thomas shakes his head, falls into step beside his father.

★★★

Polly said, "Once the baby's here, I'm not sure if I want to go on living in a small flat just off the A2."

Sam, thinking every time he picked up the phone and heard Polly's voice it was to announce her departure for hospital to give birth, relaxed.

"I thought you liked it there."

"I do. At the moment."

"So?"

"We could both sell. Buy somewhere a bit further out."

"Sell? We've just got here, Polly. Anyway, I didn't think you wanted us living in the middle of nowhere." He felt mildly irritated as if she was being either playful or perverse.

Polly said patiently, "I mean we could buy somewhere together as a family. A bigger place with space for all of us. A house. With a large garden for you, land, as you like to call it. Not anywhere remote. But not just off the A2."

Sam said, "Is this a joke? I would drive you mad."

"Possibly," Polly said with equanimity, "but that's a chance I'm willing to take. And anyway, with the proceeds of our two flats and moving out of the city – nowhere remote – we could afford a house where we could be apart as well as together. It makes sense."

"That's a lot to think about," Sam said, trying to curb expectation, dull the prospect in case Polly changed her mind.

"And this way I'd be closer to Mum. And she'd see the baby. Get to be a grandmother for at least a while. It's actually selfish of me, if you think about it. I've a lot to gain. But if you don't like the idea—"

"I didn't say that," Sam said swiftly. "It's all so sudden, that's all. Your idea. And what about in the long term?"

"I'm not thinking in the long term," Polly said calmly. "Not decades ahead. I'm thinking what would work now. For all of us."

Sam looked out at their rectangle of garden with its neat patch of lawn, narrow borders. Polly's blithe ability to remove obstacles never failed to astound him. She was talking again. "Anyway, must go now, I have an antenatal appointment in an hour. See you next Friday evening. About 6?"

"Next Friday?"

"This event in your garden. Eve of the street party get-together? And I'll stay over if that's all right. You'll need me for Saturday to keep Mum company."

★★★

Catherine put the phone down from speaking to Rowena Shaw, stared out of her office window onto the street outside. She had been insistent on arranging a meeting within the next week. Preferably after museum hours so they could be sure of talking without interruption. *After all, during the day you are always so preoccupied with the guides or visitors,* she had said as if this was a neglect of duty of sorts, *and I really want this to be a private conversation between us. There is a lot I need to discuss with you.* The following Thursday at 5, was agreed, the call ended and only then did Catherine wish she had pressed Rowena for more detail. There had been something almost furtive in Rowena's tone that had alarmed her as if it was confirmation that the museum's future was in doubt. It was hard to think of anything else that would require such a clandestine approach since all other matters they talked of were essentially practical and routine. There was the new exhibition about to start, focusing on the philanthropy of some of Harriet Howe's female contemporaries, and the plans she had outlined sketchily to Rowena for a more radical and original project the following year, but neither of these were matters that could possibly require any sort of discretion. Catherine's thoughts were interrupted by one of the duty managers coming to find her to help with a tour.

"So sorry, Catherine, but things are already difficult with so many guides away. Usual perennial summer holiday absences, of course. And now a group who'd booked for six have arrived at least twenty-six strong. Or as near as. They didn't seem to think it would make a difference to us. Should I simply turn them away or could you possibly come and help out?"

Catherine willingly went and sorted out the problem of the amassing party of Canadian tourists, led one of the tours and then picked up another, dovetailing through the next few hours and extending a little beyond the usual closing time to accommodate them all.

With the house eventually empty of guides and visitors, she was about to go back to her office to pick up on some work she had left earlier when she caught sight of someone hovering outside on the pavement, staring up at the house, absorbed by it in some way. The young man then took one step up towards the front door, looking as if he was about to push it open when he stopped abruptly, glanced at the side window and briefly met Catherine's eye. Then, with a sudden movement, he turned, skipped back down the step and hurried towards the end of the road. He had, perhaps, mistaken the place or confused the address for another in the scattering of similar side streets in the hinterland between Bloomsbury and Clerkenwell. Back in her office, sorting out the agenda for the next trustees' meeting, she tried to focus her mind away from the conversation with Rowena Shaw. Speculation, however irresistible, was pointless, after all. And the hot July day, now sliding into a warm, soft evening, was consoling. She was meeting her niece, Beth's oldest daughter, Emily, in Covent Garden with an overdue birthday present to hand over and had promised her a meal if Emily could spare the time. Catherine was well aware that, where familial connections were concerned, the young allocated their free time with frugality and caution. Encouraged, however, by the thought of Emily's sweet, gentle face, a startling echo of Beth's at twenty-four, she abandoned concerns with both the fate of Harriet Howe House and her own position, left the agenda midstream, turned off the computer and left in good time to meet her niece.

Turning the corner of the street, she came close to colliding with someone who seemed uncertain about the direction in which he was walking. After a flurry of apologies on his part followed by an awkward sidestepping, his head held down as if in embarrassment, he crossed rapidly to the other side of the road and disappeared.

★★★

Charlotte Prideaux stands naked by the basin in the bathroom, rubs cream into her face with slow, deliberate strokes. Andrew, already tired after a restless night, shrugs into clothes, tries to think about the day ahead. Routine, mainly, unless there are any emergencies waiting on the surgery answer phone. Voices consciously strained thin with pain to gain swifter attention. Charlotte comes into the bedroom, takes a slip of a dress from the wardrobe and steps into it, her small breasts flattened by the fabric, her stomach concave.

"Nice colour," Andrew says, "very … vibrant."

She smiles. "Orange is the word you're looking for, Andy. Very orange. Too hot for a bra. Too hot for knickers, actually. But I suppose one must. The knickers, anyway."

He yawns. "I need a holiday. Or at least a break. A chance to make the most of this weather."

"September. That's what we decided."

"What?"

"We're taking two weeks in September. You can't have forgotten." Charlotte pulls a swift comb through her hair. "Have you booked that place yet? The one you were talking about."

"Was I? What place was that?"

"Really, Andy, you're hopeless! You must remember."

"Actually, Charlotte, I don't. I mean we talk about all sorts of places that we'd like to go to."

"Italy. Lucca. Half way up a mountain or – do they have mountains in Tuscany? Well, a hill anyway. You said there was this incredible small hotel, kind of a converted old farmhouse or a convent or something and that it was just my sort of place. You know, luxurious, but authentic at the same time."

Andrew opens a drawer, finds one sock, searches for its other half. His socks, he recalls, used to appear in his drawer already paired. He wishes fervently he had not talked of that place in Lucca. He cannot imagine what had prompted him. No doubt it had been after a bottle or more of wine or in bed, Charlotte's elfin chin perched on his shoulder, her slim legs knitted around his. He hedged.

"It's never a good idea to go back to places. Probably gone to seed and run-down. It was a very long time ago, after all."

"You can look it up," Charlotte persists, sitting down on the bed next to him as he slips on socks, now united with a match. "Give them a ring and see how it sounds. Check the website if they have one. The guide books. For all we know, it's become the most sought-after hotel in the whole of Tuscany."

"We could go somewhere else."

"What?"

"Not Italy, I mean. Greece. Or even Turkey. Everyone's talking about Turkey these days."

Charlotte takes one of his hands, presses it deliberately between her legs.

"I would like to conceive our child in Italy," she says. "I like the idea of that."

Andrew sits very still. He can feel the warmth of Charlotte's bare leg against the flesh of his trapped hand. Eventually, he says, "Ah. The child." And can think of nothing else to say that is adequate. Charlotte appears not to notice his silence, jumps up suddenly saying something about the time, goes back to the bathroom to find her wrist watch and heads downstairs. He stays sitting at the end of the bed, feeling as if an enormous effort is required to propel him upright and into the required motions of the day. It would be so much easier simply to sink down into a kind of lethargic existence where nothing is expected of him, little demanded.

After all, he has not prepared himself for this.

Charlotte speaks of having a child in an abstract way as if progeny is an experiment, a curiosity of human experience best approached in a pragmatic, systematic style. Organised, clean, controlled.

Whereas he knows the truth of it.

He hears her now downstairs, moving around in the kitchen, pouring water onto ground coffee, chopping up raw vegetables, her portion of almonds and walnuts, those dried apricots, a cube of low fat cheese, to fill her square lunch box that she will slip into that blue tote bag of hers. He sees her rinse her hands swiftly under the running tap, shaking them dry, turning to the cafetiere and pressing down firmly to release grounds from liquid. In a moment she will move to the door, call along the hall and up the stairs to him, and he will go down, spend five minutes or so drinking coffee, eating a slice of dry toast, looking across the room at her, still startled by her desire for him. Always it has seemed so simple with Charlotte. So effortless, satisfying a mutual need with rapt absorption. As if they had cut through the complications and complexities that hinder and plague other lives.

Until now.

Now, sitting on the end of the bed, staring at the swathes of cream carpet at his feet, Andrew feels as if he has just woken from a long coma of denial. Of contrived forgetfulness. He imagines his state to be like someone who is slowly recovering their memory, synapses vigilant again, connections alert. He has been existing in something of a parallel universe, an alternative reality that has cushioned him from the rigours and persistent anxieties, the grubby, grinding compromises of living. Now the past begins to crawl over him again, reminding him that it is not possible to wipe the slate clean, unfettered by hooks and scars as if he is somehow immune to guilt and memory. To responsibility. Yet for a while he thought he was. Brazenly, he had walked away from his marriage, exultant in his daring, as if the gesture in itself was admirable, a feat worthy of praise.

For there had been nothing left for the two of them.

He and Frances had been spent, a husk of a couple that was better sundered than persisting in a sunless arrangement that served neither of them.

Or so he chose to think of their marriage at the time.

Now he is far less sure. And he thinks inevitably of Thomas, of his startling, glorious arrival on the doorstep a few days earlier. And realises that the only thing he knows for

certain any more, the sole truth that he can swear, is his love
for his son.

His unconditional love.

Nothing else endures with such adamantine certainty.

Charlotte calls him from downstairs. He calls back, says
something vague, something evasive about needing the
bathroom again. He has not moved from his place at the bottom
of the bed as if the moment he stands some decisive action is
required of him, a choice that he is incapable of making. The
only impulse he has at all is of a mad, frantic desire to go up
to London and collect Thomas, absconding, just the two of
them, to some remote island or distant region where they can
live in blithe contentment for six months or more. A simple
existence, father and son, free from recrimination, with time
to talk, to confess remorse and culpability. He sees them
fishing, making camp fires, sleeping in rudimentary tents or
huts under star-studded skies, living humbly, richly.

The desire to run away is potent.

And he understands now so easily what propelled Thomas
to leave. Charlotte had asked him once with casual, transitory
interest, what had caused the *family rupture* and he had flinched
at the implied violence of her phrase, had been oblique. He
told her the bald facts alone. Thomas had abandoned medical
school half way through training, had discarded his hard-
won place and potential career with apparent impetuosity
and had arrived home one day with no warning to deliver
the news. At that point, Charlotte's interest in the matter had
waned so Andrew had felt no obligation to expand. His relief
had been overwhelming. For even now, he found it hard
to view the ugliness of the day when Frances had raged at
their only child, responding with such inflated fury as if his
decision had been engineered solely to wound her, to deprive
her of a prize long cherished. And, as so often in the way of

these things, the heat of disagreement had ignited, licked dry
kindle of past squabbles and irritations until it was no longer
solely Thomas' impetuous abandonment of medicine that
had stood divisively between mother and son. Their words
to each other, spiteful, malicious even, had shocked Andrew
and he had waited anxiously for a retreat from hostilities, a
return to equilibrium.

But he had said nothing.

His lack of protest over that day and the next had been
baleful, he knew. And his attitude of cowardly reticence must
have spoken to Thomas in a way that he had never intended
and regretted profoundly.

He pushes himself onto his feet with the weariness of a
man decades older and moves to the window. Outside, the
traffic warden is doing her first round of the morning so
already it must be past eight. He needs to leave. But he is
reluctant to shift onto the practicalities and routine of his day
and lets his mind focus again on Thomas.

The idea had come from his son.

In fact, it was presented not so much as an idea, but as
an urgent, heartfelt request for Thomas had no wish to go
alone. Automatically, Andrew had turned him down. But now,
thinking again, he sees the merits of the thing.

And besides, he wants inordinately to please Thomas. To
do something solely for him.

He looks around the room for his phone, finds it next to
the bed and is about to ring the number Thomas has given
him when he decides a text will be more discreet. Charlotte,
after all, is downstairs and there is no need at the moment for
her to know of their plans.

Thomas, you're right, he taps out with the methodical
slowness of an older generation, *it's a good idea, let's go together.
Can't do this Saturday, but next, perhaps? July 15th. I have the address.*

See you around noon at Victoria station? People always meet under the clock, they say. Until then.

He has no intention of contacting Frances ahead of time. That would make the visit seem too significant. Portentous, even. So there is a good chance that she will be out. Even away. But at least if the two of them together make their way to her door, estranged husband, prodigal son, Thomas can see that he is trying.

That his father is at last, belatedly, doing his best to support him and to redeem himself in his eyes.

★★★

Barnaby Taylor, in the middle of a quiet midweek shift at the bookshop, the front door open to encourage some breeze and relief from the sultry summer day, scans a copy of an A to Z map of London. He is not as familiar with areas south of the river and it takes him some time to work out a route to Miller Street. Underground, the northern line, probably, then a bus. He is wary of appearing uninvited on Catherine Wells' doorstep, but on the whole it seems preferable to haunting her place of work like an unfortunate stalker. When his photo journalist friend had first produced her contact details it had seemed enough simply to covet the possibility of meeting her. He had felt no urgency to act upon the information. Perversely, it had been a phone call with his mother, with Rosie, that had prompted him to want more. *I do hope you're not still obsessed with Ed Wells, Barnie,* she had said unexpectedly. *Whatever are you after, anyway? The man's dead. End of it. Is it a photo you want? An image of your biological father or something sentimental like that to stick into your wallet?* Barnaby had denied it at the time, cut the call short since he was due for a double shift at the restaurant and was already running late. But he had woken in the early hours around three, remembering what his mother had said. And the idea of seeing a photograph had suddenly became so compelling that it had been impossible to go back to sleep.

Of course.

This would justify approaching the widow, Catherine Wells, provide him with a rational explanation for arriving at her door. All he wanted, he would say, apologetically, all he needed to go away and leave her permanently in peace, was a photograph of her late husband. Of his father, Eddie Wells.

Barnaby checks his work rotas for the shop, the restaurant, sees he is free the following Saturday, July 15th, his only entirely free day for a month. He thumbs the appropriate page in the A to Z again.

Makes a groove firmly along Miller Street.

20

S am stood at the window, as if looking out at a party to which he was not invited. Of course he could open the doors and bring something of the gathering into the room with him, but he chose to remain remote as if the event was of little relevance. Which just about summed it up, he thought, his concession to Frances to use their garden being the extent of his willingness to take any interest. He watched Martin Lawrence, Violet's father, fussing with a portable barbecue at the edge of the narrow terrace, saw Frances setting up a trestle table and unpacking a cardboard box of glasses. Catherine Wells arrived then quickly retreated back the way she had come, returning a few minutes later with a large bowl. Polly, he could see, was talking to a fair woman he thought he vaguely recognised, but could not place. Violet's mother, perhaps. He saw her find a chair for Polly, insisting she sat down, perching on the grass beside her so they could continue to talk. Frances had assured him that the evening was solely for Willow House. Already, however, he could count close on a dozen cluttering the lawn, grasping glasses and wine bottles and people were still arriving. There were even a couple of children darting between adult legs, attempting a game of hide-and-seek with limited success given the insufficient space.

And really, the event was so unnecessary in view of the entire following day given up to the street party.

He turned away from the window, went and sat next to Lydia on the other side of the room, aware that he was as close to sulking as a grown man could be. He took one of her hands from where it was folded neatly, redundantly, in her lap.

"I'm a miserable old fool, Lyddie, bad tempered and curmudgeonly. You should be ashamed of me," he said. "You probably are, come to think of it. Inside that head of yours, you are probably thinking all sorts of dark thoughts about me. You should have expressed them when you could, you know. I bet you're thinking that now. Why on earth didn't I shout at the old man, put him in his place when I had the voice to do so?" He held onto her hand for some moments before letting it go, replacing it carefully beside its partner in her lap. Her nails, he noticed, needed cutting.

At least he had made an effort with her clothes today. Dressed her in the sort of thing he imagined her wearing if she had been going to Frances' garden event. Just because choice now eluded her there was no reason not to exercise it on her behalf. So he had flicked through the rails of her dresses that he generally dismissed, finding buttons and zips and hooks too onerous a way to start the day, and had found something that required just that. He had even opened a drawer in the bedroom and found a necklace for her to wear. Now she sat next to him on the sofa with the air and manner, he thought, of someone expectant of company. But attempting to take her out into the garden, with its random assortment of people and sudden bursts of sound and laughter would be unwise. Increasingly, contained, prescribed situations suited Lydia, the company of few.

Polly opened the garden door widely, allowing in the drift of noise and smoky smell of sausages and barbecued burgers. Sam insisted on her closing it.

"I don't want your mother bothered by it all," he said as she settled herself in the large armchair and pushed her feet up onto a stool. She looked flushed, he thought, glowing yet drained at the same time if that were possible. She pushed her hair from her forehead with one hand, placed the other at the base of her back.

"If I had enough energy, I'd argue that it was you just as much as Mum who is bothered by harmless socialising going on just feet away from you. How are you going to cope with the entire street celebrating all day tomorrow?"

"Ah, that will be easier," Sam said, "I can get lost in the crowd. In other words, lurk in the front hall and just make a brief appearance for propriety's sake. Not that I care particularly about propriety."

"Well, I'm here to relieve you now. I'll stay with Mum while you go out into your own back garden and eat and drink with your neighbours."

"It's not necessary, Polly."

"Oh, but it is," she said, wedging herself even more firmly into the armchair and arranging the cushion behind her. "I'm full of aches and niggles today. Entirely at odds with anything other than a quiet room. And one of us needs to be out there, surely, just to show support."

Sam stood up. However much he resented the invasion in the garden he felt stifled by the closed rooms of the flat on the warm evening.

"I don't understand where all these people have come from," he said, hovering somewhat reluctantly by the garden door. He would have preferred to sneak out the front and walk on the common for an hour or so. "On the last count, I thought there were only four flats in Willow House."

"Frances thought it only right to invite a few of the others who've worked hard for tomorrow's event. You know, the woman who's in charge of the catering, the guy who's sorted out all the legal bits. And their families, of course. And then there's— "

"Spare me," Sam said curtly. "Simply an excuse to let more people run roughshod over my lawn."

"You don't care about your lawn," Polly said calmly. "You're not the sort to be precious about a few grass turfs. And if you'd taken more interest in the arrangements for tonight, I'm sure you could have influenced the guest list. But as you left everything to Frances – well, you have only yourself to blame."

"I know, Polly, no need to remind me. I'm only too aware of my failings, I can tell you. But before I go out into the fray, prepare me a bit. Who should I talk to?"

"Everyone seems perfectly pleasant so there's no need to be difficult. And you know Catherine Wells, of course. And Martin?"

"The man wielding the barbecue tongs – yes, think we've talked over the rubbish bins once or twice."

"And his wife seems a lovely woman. Isabel. The one in the lilac dress. So you can talk to them if you're intent on avoiding Frances."

"I am," Sam said, "at all costs."

"In spite of—"

"In spite of the fact that according to you she's actually an angel in heavy disguise. Kindness itself."

"People are complex."

"Your tolerance puts me to shame, Polly."

She waved her father away. "Off with you now and we don't want you back until the whole thing's over. No sneaking home to hide in the kitchen before it's finished and everyone's gone home."

Catherine saw Sam come out into the garden and was on the point of going to speak to him when Frances stopped her, saying something about the need for more plates. When she looked up again, he had moved towards the barbecue and appeared to be talking to Martin and Isabel Lawrence with a drink in hand. She would catch him later. Yet her news would really be of little interest to him, however significant to her. People, beyond closest friends and family, were on the whole indifferent to others' fortunes, their own lives generally of sufficient concern. Beth was different. She had not managed to reach her since talking to Rowena on Thursday evening and it was a phone call she needed to make.

Sam found himself with a bottle in each hand, courtesy of Frances who instructed him to replenish emptying glasses. About to protest, he realised that since the party was in his own garden he might as well take some ownership of the occasion and obliged. As he toured the lawn, topping up glasses, he realised with surprise that he was enjoying himself. His resentment, residual and instinctive towards Frances, had waned and he relaxed in the agreeable tone of the summer evening as if giving himself permission to be gregarious. The neighbours he spoke to were undeniably pleasant although he failed to grasp any names and only spoke to them in the most general of terms. Yes, the urban foxes could be a bind, couldn't they, litter strewn over the forecourt of the house. The parking congestion in the road was getting no better and the air traffic noise was an undeniable blight on the area. But still, they agreed, with a faint sense of complicit guilt stemming from complacent lives, that Miller Street was by and large an agreeable place to live. And then there was the street party, of course! The very fact that everyone was coming together for a day in mid-July to celebrate their very own centenary was testament to the fact that they were a real community! Sam agreed, showed suitable and appropriate enthusiasm. And as he went on drinking steadily, lulled by the mood as well as the alcohol, he began to think that perhaps Frances Chater and his neighbours had a point. That the party was rather an inspired idea and that it always took a person with an enterprising and forthright manner to carry off such a coordinated social event. Already, it was well past eight o'clock yet he felt no temptation to chivvy anyone to leave. On the contrary, he found himself looking around the crowded garden with pleasure, wanting to urge everyone to stay rather than curtail such conviviality. It had been a long time since he had felt warmed and comforted by the company of others. He excused himself from a man who was talking about the original property owners that Catherine's research had uncovered, went over to find another bottle of wine to open. With Polly staying the night and therefore shared responsibility for Lydia, he felt justified for once in some licence. He wondered if this notion of Polly's about them all sharing a home together would offer him a similar freedom and worried for a moment if he was in danger of exploiting her good, affable nature for his own selfish benefit. But no, he reassured himself through the increasing haze of alcohol – he had forgotten to eat anything from the barbecue and now only a few wisps from the salad bowl and a reject burnt burger remained – the idea had been hers. She was driving it, seeing it as serving her needs as much as his. As Lydia's. Sam looked around him now, at a group talking animatedly about something. He saw Catherine Wells with Martin, the two of them sitting on chairs that he thought he recognised vaguely as ones from his kitchen. He must have brought them out earlier in the afternoon when Frances Chater had been fussing around him, asking him to help. And now he saw her coming from the direction of the flat, heading straight towards him and he smiled, held out the bottle of wine he had just opened.

She waved it away. "No thank you, Sam. I'm teetotal tonight with the thought of tomorrow's event to handle. A clear head will be needed. I just wanted to tell you that Lydia is in bed."

"What?"

"Lydia. I popped in. I noticed it was getting late and of course knew it might be a strain for Polly to manage on her own. What with her time being so near." She made it sound biblical. For some reason, Sam thought of the Angel Gabriel, a stable and manger. "But you're not to worry," she went on. "You can relax. You're not needed. Polly is anxious for an early night herself. These last days of pregnancy are very tiring, you know, and she needs to prepare herself. I mean, labour is called labour for a very good reason."

"I suppose so. I had never really thought about it."

"Men," Frances said, "usually don't. Anyway, you're off duty tonight, Sam. I thought you would like to know."

Sam said, "Thank you. Thank you, Frances. That's so very kind. Most considerate." Polly was right as always. The woman did possess, among other traits, qualities of goodness.

"Just going to have a word with the Maxtons," she said.

"The Maxtons?"

"From number 8. Lucille and John. You'll remember them from the committee meetings. Auburn-haired woman? She's been tremendous in providing the celebration centenary cake for tomorrow. Not baked herself, naturally, it's through one of her patisserie contacts. You know how these things work."

"Not really, Frances. It's not my world at all. Cakes."

Sam found himself alone as Frances slipped across the lawn to a woman he assumed was Lucille of centenary cake importance. Suddenly, he felt a need to sit down. He had no intention of relinquishing his glass or the bottle, but some support was required if he was to last out the evening which suddenly seemed pleasantly endless.

Isabel Lawrence was sitting alone on the small bench at the end of the garden.

They had brought the bench from Cornwall, a present years back from Lydia, for an anniversary or was it a birthday? Their silver, possibly, or even his fiftieth.

"Hope you don't mind if I join you," he said as she made room for him. "Not used to all this standing around and drinking. Socialising is a remote activity for us these days."

"Of course," she said, "I can see that your wife is gravely ill."

Sam was taken aback. People generally orbited the fact of Lydia's illness rather than addressed it directly. As if it was something of an embarrassment that he might not have noted so was best ignored. He was tempted to place his hand on Isabel's knee to show his gratitude, but even in his drunken state suspected the gesture could be misread. So he poured more wine into his glass instead and offered to replenish hers which sat empty at her feet. She shook her head.

"Our daughter's about to give birth," he said to fill a silence which hovered between them although it did not feel awkward. He simply found that he wanted to talk to this considerate woman, hold onto her company, but had no wish to delve further into Lydia's illness. "No partner involved, you see, and now she has this idea of us all living together," he went on. "Would you say that's a mad scheme and doomed to failure or something to cherish? To embrace wholeheartedly?"

After a pause, Isabel said, "Family life can be very complicated. Difficult to navigate. But I would trust your daughter's instincts. She must have considered it very thoroughly."

"Polly always does that."

"Then I would see it as an opportunity."

"Of course it means more upheaval. Another move. After all, we've only been here two minutes. Longer than Violet, but even so."

"Have you always lived in London, Sam?"

"God, no," he said instinctively, "I'm a countryman at heart. Lyddie and I have always lived in rural, out of the way sort of places. Up until now."

"I see." Isabel looked across the garden as if searching for someone. Her husband, Martin, perhaps, Sam thought, and found himself anxious to retain her. He offered to fetch a soft drink, water. Some strawberries, for a large bowl had appeared from somewhere and people were helping themselves. Isabel shook her head again. She untied a light cardigan from around her waist and shrugged arms into it.

"It was to be near Polly, you see. The reason we moved to London," he went on.

"Of course. Family is essential at testing times."

"And you?"

"Me?" Isabel turned to face him directly as if she was discarding any interest in the rest of the activity around them. Sam was foolishly flattered. He felt drawn towards her, not in any physical or sexual way, but in a fraternal sense. A sympathetic sibling, a wise friend. He needed to prolong the comfort of her conversation as if she provided the role of a confidante that his life lacked. He sipped steadily from his glass.

"Where do you live now? When you're not here in the flat, I mean."

"We're in Cheshire near the Welsh border. In quite an isolated area, in fact. A little like you used to be, perhaps? But that has not always been the case. My childhood and early teenage years were very urban, you see. I grew up in the London suburbs."

"Like me, then," Sam said. "Something we have in common. Until I had some choice in the matter, that is. As a young man, I lived abroad for some years, took work that would let me travel, footloose, I suppose. There were such opportunities then if you were willing to grab them. And I was. All too willing. And of course then there was Lyddie and Polly, and the three of us just drifted for a while until we decided to come home. Couldn't ignore the pull any more. We took ourselves to Scotland first of all."

"But where?"

"In Scotland? Or do you mean where overseas?" Somehow Sam knew that Isabel was asking him something else.

"No. Where did you grow up?" she said in her quiet, even tone. Isabel was sitting close enough for him to be able to see her face, the genuine curiosity that he knew he would find hard to elude.

"Oh, somewhere very forgettable," he said out of habit. "I don't even remember the name of it now. So long ago and all that. One's past is so out of reach, don't you think?"

"No," Isabel said. "Not at all. Places and the events attached to them inevitably shape us, even if for negative reasons. They stick."

Sam paused then said, "Commuter territory. North West of London. I lived there with my parents until … it used to be home. One of those notches along the metropolitan line." Sitting on the bench next to Isabel, the light of the summer evening slowly waning, soporific on wine, he felt close to the state just before sleep when thoughts are in free-fall, dulled yet perversely acute. And he found it was easy simply to slip down, to let go. "Edgewood," he said. "A place called Edgewood."

"Me too," Isabel said calmly, "I lived with my family in Edgewood until I was fifteen. Until my father died. Then we left."

"I'm sorry," Sam said, "for your father's death." He felt little surprise at the coincidence. As if, in fact, he had spent the past forty years waiting for it, knowing that one day, chance would play its hand. It even felt like something of a relief to arrive at the moment. He poured the last of the dregs from the wine bottle into his glass, waited for Isabel to go on.

"My father was a troubled man, you see. A very bewildered and unhappy person. And in those days help for mental health issues was woefully inadequate, of course. The outcome might well have been very different in another era."

"I'm sorry," Sam said again because Isabel's account was confusing him, as if she was now the one trying to be evasive, distort the truth. He had come too far now to want any subterfuge, needed clarity. "But your father died?"

Isabel said, "Yes. He killed himself. He had tried before, but this second attempt – well, he made sure. He had no intention of failing again." Sam said nothing. He took Isabel's hand and this time the gesture felt entirely appropriate and understood. After a moment she went on. "After that, his suicide, my mother didn't want us to stay in Edgewood. Entirely reasonable, really. All the associations of the place – the neighbours talking – and, anyway, the house had to be sold. She couldn't afford to keep it on. Not without my father's income to pay the mortgage. So we moved soon after. Me, my younger brother and our mother went to live with family in Derbyshire. It was probably the right decision for all of us, an attempt at some kind of new start, however much the past has its hooks into you. As, inevitably, it does."

The party had thinned to only a few. A slice of moon had appeared, waning. Catherine and Frances and Martin Lawrence were collecting discarded glasses from the grass, picking up stray bottles, talking quietly between themselves. Sam watched them as if from some enormous distance of space and time. He let go of Isabel's hand where his had still been resting.

"When was this? If you don't mind me asking, Isabel, when did this terrible thing happen?"

"My father's suicide? That's easy to remember. It was the night before the Aberfan disaster. Remember that? Everyone does, of course, anyone who was alive then. The evening of Thursday October 20th. 1966. Although, of course, he was not found until the next day. My father was discovered in the woods in that road running down from Edgewood station first thing in the morning."

"A dog walker found him," Sam said dully. Isabel looked at him in surprise.

"Yes, that's right. You must have been living in Edgewood at the time if you know that."

"Someone told me about it," he said. "My mother, in fact. She wrote to me."

"He had hanged himself. He had said he was just going out to walk the dog. We had a large Labrador at the time, you see, a beautiful black Labrador. And it was quite normal for my father to take her out late evening for a walk so there seemed nothing particularly unusual or worrying about that. He had always liked to be out alone at night. Something about the darkness, I suppose."

"And the dog?"

"The dog?"

"What happened to the Labrador?" Sam said.

"She was found the next morning too. People said she must have run into the main road in a kind of frenzy and got hit by a car then run back into the woods because she was near him. Near the tree. Badly injured, but still alive. Just. She only lived for a few days."

Sam said, "There must have been an inquest."

314

"Of course," Isabel said, "but a straight forward verdict of suicide. No doubt about that. My father had left a letter, you see. He knew exactly what he was going to do that night."

Martin Lawrence crossed the lawn towards them.

"End of celebrations for one night, I think," he said jovially. "We've a full day ahead of us tomorrow, after all. You two look as if you've been deep in conversation. Nothing too serious, I hope, no sex or politics or religion or anything like that?"

Isabel took Martin's outstretched hand and let him pull her up from the bench.

"Nothing at all like that," she said. "Sam and I have simply been getting to know one another a little."

"Right, I see. Gossip about the neighbours, no doubt. The appalling domestic intrigues of Miller Street!"

Sam felt too tired to stand. He wondered if anyone would notice if he simply fell onto the grass, crawled into a convenient flower bed and slept until morning. He was saved from doing anything immediate by a sudden flurry of movement in the garden, someone clearly arriving and voices escalating swiftly. Frances appeared to be taking charge.

"Does anyone have any money on them to pay a taxi fare?" she called across the lawn. "Can we all chip in? It's for Violet, you see. She's just arrived back from her holiday. Isn't that lovely? In time for the street party tomorrow."

In the fading light, Violet was caught in outline against the house, a cluster of bags and a suitcase at her side.

"I'd run out of money for the train," she said, "even my card wouldn't give me any. So I thought a taxi would be easier. Because you pay at the end instead of the start of the journey. So it's the fare from Gatwick. Can anyone help?"

21

Miller Street SW22.

Saturday 15th July 2006. Seven in the morning.

It could have been mistaken for the same place a hundred years earlier. Empty of cars – the last recalcitrant resident just hurrying his to one of the alternative spaces arranged – peace settled on the road, something of the mood of its Edwardian antecedent. Or so Frances liked to think.

There was nothing to do before eight.

No one would be setting up tables, festooning balloons, portioning the road into areas for the children's games, face painting – thank heaven for Violet's return – and the whole event did not formally start until noon. She felt redundant. And suppressed a rising sense of panic at what the following weeks and months would hold. A void threatened. The street party had provided a purpose to the past year, after all. She had been needed. She had mattered. Wielded a certain significance. Now, once the trestle tables had been returned to the church hall, miscellaneous spoons and plates and platters reclaimed, notices about road closures unpinned from lamp posts, the treasurer's report received and signed off, nothing remained. Her role was relinquished.

And what then?

Back to the letter writing, she supposed. Back to vigils in Pilgrim Square which she had let slide for the past month or two. Perhaps she should try and get a job. She could not survive much longer on the little money left over from the settlement of her mother's estate. Yes, a job was not only sensible, but a necessity.

The thought, however, was bleak.

After all, she had no idea if her skills were adequate for the current work place. She had run Andrew's practice with efficiency for years, but she had applied her own system, a somewhat individual way of doing things that had worked for the two of them, used, as they were, to each other's method of operation. The idea of entering a job market that demanded sophisticated, jargon-heavy work practice, an instinctive embracing of advanced technological skills, was terrifying.

Still, it was no day for introspection. For self-doubt.

In fact, the success of the street party, given the extensive preparations, the fortuitously fine summer and the general sense of good will from the neighbours, was ensured. And her role in that success was undeniable. She was the catalyst, the brains behind the whole endeavour and could afford to bask a little in any praise that might come her way at the end of the day. She turned away from the window, headed for the bathroom. She liked to think that even Violet's late, last-minute return to fulfil face-painting duties had been out of loyalty to her.

Sam had woken too early. At first he thought it had been some disturbance from Lydia that had interrupted his sleep and he looked across at her in case she was distressed in some way, but she had been sleeping soundly. Then he had remembered. And in spite of the headache that he immediately attached to the unusually large amount of wine he had drunk the evening before, he had felt clear-headed. Expansive in his sense of well-being as if graced with a kind of weightlessness. For he had, he knew, been exonerated for his past which, in fact, had not been his past at all. He felt pardoned, a man in receipt of absolution as if the victim of some miscarriage of justice. At some point in the early hours, he had woken, heard Polly moving from the spare room to the bathroom and back again and had tried to stay awake long enough to do what he had spent decades resisting. Now he could freely recreate that night, nearly forty years before, when his old car had collided not with a man, but with a desperate, frantic animal that had disappeared back into the cover of the evergreens and had lain there, stunned, unconscious.

He had been responsible for the injury of a dog, not for the death of a man.

If only he had known.

But he had fallen asleep again too swiftly to let his thoughts roam where now, in the early morning, they decided to settle. To wonder how different the past years would have been if he had found the courage to confront fully the incident in the days and weeks following it. If he had not run away, and kept running, from the truth of that one single night.

The past, it appeared, was not fixed, but malleable. Open to revision.

Again, he heard Polly, in the kitchen this time. Water filling the kettle, a window blind lifted. The consoling noise of someone else awake and active that had become unfamiliar to him.

"Making tea?" he said. "I'll do that. It's early, you know, barely seven."

Polly relinquished mugs and tea, pulled out a chair, sat on it cautiously.

"Sorry for being asleep when you came in last night," she said. "Enjoy yourself? It seemed to go well in spite of your grumpiness about the whole thing."

Sam was filled with an absurd desire to tell Polly about his conversation with Isabel Lawrence. Mariner-like, he felt compelled to share his story as if only in the telling of it did it remain true. Instead, he opened the fridge door. Found the bottle of semi-skimmed.

"It wasn't bad. Drank far too much, though. Forgot to eat, I think. Did you sleep well?"

"Not really. I just couldn't get comfortable for long enough. But it's been like this all week. What with the hot weather and having a small elephant strapped to my stomach."

He placed two mugs on the table, sat down opposite Polly.

"I know this is your due date, but don't first babies always come late? Not that I know anything about such things. Just what you hear people say." He thought how inadequate he was, blatantly out of his depth whereas Lydia would know how to support. To say the sort of things Polly clearly needed to hear. She looked strained suddenly, her normal composure subdued. He was so used to Polly's equanimity that anything else was mildly alarming. "How are you feeling this morning?"

"Strange," she said, adjusting her position on the chair, "different, but don't worry, I don't feel as if something definite is going to happen just yet. Like an actual birth."

"What does that feel like?"

Polly said, "How do I know? I've never done this before. I've been to all the classes and read the books, of course, but even so it's not really until you get to this point that it becomes rather frightening. I think it's the unpredictability of it all."

Sam got up, switched on the radio. The weather and early morning news seemed the best way to maintain some sense of normalcy.

"Frances Chater is certainly rewarded with fine weather for this centenary business of hers."

"Not just hers, surely. It seems to have found favour with the whole street."

"Perhaps. And she has a point, I suppose. Nothing wrong with getting to know one's neighbours every once in a while."

Polly looked surprised. "That's quite a statement from the most unsociable person I've ever come across. Urban living's done something for you, it seems."

Sam said, "Breakfast, Polly? While your mother is still asleep perhaps."

She nodded.

"A bit of toast, thanks. And then I think I might go and lie down again for an hour or so as it's early. Try and catch up on some sleep."

"Good idea," Sam said, finding bread, plates. Marmalade. "After all, it's going to be quite a busy day. Are you sure you're up to this, keeping an eye on your mother while I go out and join the throng later? The Chater woman has me down for a few jobs on one of her numerous rotas, of course."

"I'll be fine," Polly said firmly. Then added, "but I think I'll give my midwife a ring in an hour or two. Just to check if what I'm feeling is …"

"A sign of something significant?"

"Something to be expected. No more nor less than that. All things considered."

★★★

Charlotte Prideaux rubs a towel over her head. Bends over and shakes her hair, finger combing it.

"You're still going up to London?" she says. "When was all this arranged, anyway?"

"Oh, very last minute," Andrew says vaguely, reaches for his wallet and slips it into his jacket pocket. "Thomas rang on – can't remember now – but it's just something to do with him, that he needs to get sorted. I won't bother you with the dull details."

"And it has to be today?"

"Yes. That's what we've arranged. Today. The two of us."

"Tell you what," Charlotte says, "I'll come with you." She moves towards the wardrobe, begins to pull out clothes. "We could drive up and I'll go and do a spot of shopping while you're seeing to stuff with your son and then you and I can meet up and have dinner somewhere. Or take in a show, perhaps. We could even find a hotel and do an overnighter. Make a bit of a weekend of it."

"No," Andrew says, far more sharply than he intends. "No, it's pointless to drive. Train is the only thing that makes sense."

"All right," she says, "train it is." She is moving swiftly now, something mildly frenetic in her compulsion to dress, fill a bag with a few necessities.

"No," he says again and this time does not even attempt to lighten his tone, "I need to go alone, Charlotte. Without you. It's something only me and Thomas can do. Together. In fact," he adds, his conviction growing as he hears the certainty of his voice, "I should have done it a long time ago."

Charlotte drops the clothes she is holding, stares at Andrew for several moments, then silently picks up the white jeans, a pale primrose shirt that sit pooled at her bare feet. Andrew slips coins from the chest of drawers into his pocket, fastens his watch around his wrist.

"Actually, I won't even bother with breakfast," he says with his back to her, slipping feet into shoes, "I'll just get going and grab a coffee at the station. Have a good day, won't you? Won't be late, I don't expect. But I'll ring you when I'm on the way back. Just so that you know."

At the bedroom door he stops, turns to go towards Charlotte for a brief kiss. But she has gone back into the bathroom.

Closed the door firmly behind her.

★★★

Catherine joined Frances by the low platform at the end of Miller Street. At noon, the party was to be declared open by the resident of longest standing, a woman in her late eighties who had moved there in 1946, and houses had begun to empty, small clusters of neighbours gathering in readiness. Violet, in a sudden spurt of enthusiasm, had arranged her face-painting table under the protection of a large umbrella and was already vividly decorating young faces with an eager queue swiftly forming. Frances had tried in vain to restrain her.

"There is a timetable for a reason," she complained to Catherine. "She's not due to start for another couple of hours. Look! It's all there on the blackboard. Children's games followed by face painting."

Catherine, disposed to be genial, put a hand on Frances' arm.

"Just be pleased that Violet has turned up. Besides, everyone's already enjoying themselves so it doesn't really matter when things happen, does it?"

Frances seemed about to disagree then smiled, turned to Catherine.

"You are absolutely right, of course. I can be a bit of a stickler about organisation, you see, and just a little controlling. I have been warned about that in the past."

Catherine said, "You must see this entire event as a wonderful testament of your skills, Frances. It's an extraordinary achievement and without you it simply wouldn't have happened."

For a moment, Frances looked confused as if unsure how to accept the compliment. Then her attention was drawn to a couple of young boys who had mounted the platform, heading towards the microphone.

"Excuse me, Catherine, but there's only ten minutes to go and I really need to be in a hundred places. But I'll catch up with you later. Unless, of course, you have invited a guest to share the day with you?"

Catherine shook her head, was about to speak, but Frances was already heading towards the recalcitrant young boys.

Beth had asked her the same question when they had talked late the previous night. But it had been easy to divert her. Her sister had been elated by her news.

"About time too! That's wonderful to hear. If you're sure, of course, that it's what you want."

"Of course it is. It's the job I applied for, after all."

"So at long last they've made you the curator?"

"No, that's rather the point for the delay and the trustees are still working out what I should be called. House Director, possibly. After all, it's been decided that Harriet Howe doesn't actually merit a curator."

"But it's a promotion, surely. There'll be more money?"

"Some increase, yes. But there's nothing in writing yet."

Catherine had spent the days leading up to her meeting with Rowena preparing herself for the news that the museum was to close. Or to be subsumed into a larger concern, essentially reduced to no more than a small department, her own role negligible. Instead, Rowena had begun with an apology, admitting that the past few months had seen something of a covert operation to allow her to assess on behalf of the trustees the most effective staff structure to ensure the secure future of Harriet Howe House. And it had become clear to her, as already suspected by the chairman of the trustees, that the role of curator was redundant. No more than an inherited title of old that had little relevance to the nature of the place in the 21st century. Catherine, as House Manager, had proved herself in the months since Robert's departure more than equal to meeting all that he had embraced and, in addition, Rowena said her eye for innovation, for sympathetic development of the museum's provision, had been noted. Harriet Howe House would be more than safe in her hands. Provided, of course, Rowena had added somewhat cautiously as Catherine had said little, sitting silently opposite her in the top office, she was happy to accept such a position in the new structure the trustees planned to put in place. Her willingness to move forward with the idea was what Rowena was initially seeking before new contracts were drawn up. Catherine swiftly reassured her and then tried to take in more of what Rowena was saying, about the necessity to provide her with a permanent part-time assistant and the thought that perhaps one of the present duty managers would be interested in such a position.

"It's just the best news," Beth said.

"Yes, I can't quite believe it even now. I feel I've been living in a kind of limbo for far too long where work was concerned."

"Not just work," Beth said. "Ever since Eddie went it's as if you've felt you were undeserving of happiness. Of ever being free of his loss and moving on."

She started to protest, but then swiftly decided to change the subject. Beth was too fixed in her opposition to Catherine's sense of accountability to accept the fact that she would always feel in some way implicated. Hitched irrevocably to the man as well as to the manner of his death. Love was stubborn. That was the truth of it. Even when worn down to a shell of what it had once been, a residue of responsibility was indelibly left, impossible to shift.

"It's street party weekend," she said instead to Beth. "Frances Chater's moment of glory."

"Invited anyone?" Beth said.

"Who would I invite?"

"Exactly. My point entirely."

"It's a neighbourly affair with no interest for anyone outside Miller Street," Catherine said. "Hangers-on simply not required. And actually, I find I'm quite looking forward to it."

★★★

Barnaby Taylor stretches out on the grass of Clapham Common, shuts his eyes to the strong sunlight. Perhaps he will just stay here for the afternoon. Abandon this foolish and rather bizarre idea of his to track down his birth father's widow, confront the poor woman on her own doorstep. It would have been different if he had started all this business a year or two earlier. If he had felt the same compulsion for clarity while Eddie Wells was still alive. Typical, Barnaby thinks, of his own arrested development as he now sees it, asking crucial questions too late to gain from the garnered information. Maybe his mother is right. Does it matter who provided his paternity? Rosie clearly felt no link to the man who had fathered her only child even though there had been a history between them of some years. But then Rosie's perspective always shunned sentiment or any sense of obligation. In the warmth of the early afternoon, Barnaby drifts off into a light doze. Distantly, he hears cries of children playing, dogs barking, sirens from the road skirting the common. An hour, maybe more, pass by. Then he sits up suddenly. He pulls out the bit of paper from the pocket of his jeans with details of the address, the bus routes that will take him close to – what is it called? – Miller

Street. To Flat 2, Willow House, Miller Street. He stands up, brushes dried grass from his T-shirt, his hair, and heads back towards the main road. Chance, Barnaby decides, will play a role in this whole matter and at the bus stop he waits to see which number will arrive first out of the half dozen or so due. There's a long wait, an impatient queue before anything appears at all. Barnaby feels like a gambler with his money only on one horse. Eventually, there's one in the distance. As it draws close, he resigns himself with a slight shrug at the way the dice have fallen, fumbles in his pocket for his fare and gets on, taking a top deck seat.

And stares out of the window as the bus heads him slowly, but deliberately towards Miller Street.

***

At Victoria, Andrew waits for Thomas, beginning to wonder at the wisdom of this impromptu visit. Nothing else, however, seems a sensible alternative. And it is crucial to resume communication. For Thomas and his mother. And for Andrew too, in a way, for it has been far harder than he had imagined to dismiss his estranged wife entirely from his concern.

The past was insistent, grasping in its refusal to recede quietly.

And Thomas needs to see his parents together, to reassure him that their separation is cordial, devoid of bitter recrimination, and can be handled with mutual respect.

At least he hopes it can.

He pushes from his mind the knowledge of those letters Frances sent to Charlotte, the alarming vigils. He looks around him at the crowded concourse, at the destinations board, the queues at the ticket machines, and feels suddenly an overwhelming desire to step on any train and head mindlessly for somewhere else. A variation on his earlier fantasy about Thomas and himself for this is a step further, unencumbered, blissfully alone, disappearing to a place where he is unknown, a stranger amongst strangers who will be entirely disinterested in him and his obligations.

His trailing past deeds.

He sees himself taking a ferry to the French coast then finding a room at some cheap hotel, a pension, in a faintly dull town, spending his days reading, walking, perfecting his inadequate schoolboy French. Eating simple meals along with the locals, drinking carafes of vinegary wine, gaining affection for pastis. The sort of life the young are supposed to live, Andrew thinks, yet in truth is only relished when out of reach. When it is too late. And he wonders why there seems such a compulsion always to belong, to attach oneself to hooks and ties that, once gained, are so hard to shrug. Would it not be so much easier to live singly, lead an existence governed only by selfish choice and some sort of evolved moral compass to serve conscience?

Then he sees Thomas.

That loping stride of his, a head taller than the rest of the crowd and he is pulled back, burns only with the desire to envelop his son in his arms.

"Sorry, am I late?" He bends down to retie his trainers. When, Andrew thinks, did my child's feet grow to such enormous proportions?

"There's no hurry," he says, "We've got all day."

"In that case, can we eat first? I'm starving."

"Of course. A bit late for breakfast, early for lunch. What do you want?"

"Both," Thomas says.

They find a small Italian café in Buckingham Palace Road. Stare at large plastic menus.

"I did speak to her, you know," Thomas says not raising his eyes. "To Mum."

"But we agreed not to warn her."

"Not now. I mean I rang her at Christmas. Well, Boxing Day actually."

"Your birthday?"

Thomas nods. "From Australia so of course the timing was a bit all over the place. I suppose I just wanted her to know I was ok. Alive."

"How did she sound?"

"All right. I don't know, really. I think it was a bit of a shock to hear from me. Probably neither of us knew what to say."

"It won't make today any easier. Even if we manage to find her at home."

"I know," Thomas says. "But I want to see her. I really do."

Andrew says, "Me too."

And is surprised to find how much he means it.

★★★

Catherine cheered enthusiastically when a little girl with an expression of steely determination on her round face won first place in the children's obstacle race. Sitting on a low front wall halfway down the street, she wondered if Frances would notice if she went back to the flat for a couple of hours, returned once proceedings moved on to evening events. It was only four o'clock and, knowing few of the neighbours who mostly seemed to be on close terms with each other, forming in effect small parties of their own, she felt self-conscious at being alone. Violet had disappeared, having run out of face-painting customers and she had not seen Sam since earlier that morning when she had helped him set out a table for Willow House. Frances was a fleeting figure, constantly pre-occupied, and Martin and Isabel Lawrence were nowhere in sight. Unintentionally, she caught the eye of a woman she recognised as a vociferous force at the street party committee meetings and found herself being rapidly approached.

"You must be someone's guest," the woman said suspiciously, looking down at the clipboard she held with the manner of an officious night club doorman. Her voice bore the faint trace of a Scottish accent long supressed. "Which household are you attached to? A guest, I presume. Just checking, you understand."

"I'm not," Catherine said bluntly, "someone's guest, that is. I live here."

The woman was unembarrassed.

"It's my responsibility to ensure no intruders, you see. People who may have sneaked in from a neighbouring road without paying the party fee. And I simply don't know your face. You're not by any chance the new family at number 20 where all that work is going on? Loft extension, isn't it? In which case, I've already met your husband and oldest daughter so that's all right."

Catherine corrected her. The woman – Helena Harris, she now remembered – abruptly appeared to lose all interest in her and began to move away, apparently to check others' validity.

"I'm the one who wrote the booklet," Catherine doggedly called after her. "Or rather collated the information. The Miller Street centenary history? I think Frances has ensured that every house has a copy."

Helena Harris stopped for a moment, looked mildly irritated.

"Oh that. Possibly. Or possibly already lost amongst family paraphernalia – you know how it is."

"Quite," Catherine said and, anxious to end the conversation, turned to look down the street to see if her attention could be caught by something in particular.

And immediately, it was.

Sam, looking ill at ease, stood on the forecourt of Willow House, Polly at his side. Catherine began to negotiate her way around deckchairs and sunshades to reach them, but Isabel and Frances were there first, Isabel slipping an arm around Polly's shoulders and Frances relieving her of a large bag.

★★★

Andrew pulls out the scrap of paper with the address. Thomas fiddles with the raw edge of a finger nail, looks out through the window.

"Why here?" he says. "What made Mum buy a place here?"

Andrew shrugs. He has no idea. And unfathomably feels ashamed of such ignorance. He is beginning to feel he knows very little about anything. Anything that really matters, that is.

"It's respectable enough, isn't it?" he attempts. "Nothing wrong with the area. Quite pleasant, really."

"No. I didn't mean …"

"Of course not. It's all right. I understand." Another five minutes and Andrew stirs, stands up as the bus approaches a stop. "Best get off here, I think. Miller Street is not far."

Only one other passenger gets off the bus, colliding unintentionally with Thomas so that the two young men step over each other's feet on the pavement. Half mumble apologies. Regain their balance and separate. And find, after fifty yards or so, that the three of them appear to be heading in the same direction. Crossing a main road, skirting a common edged with large houses and then coming to a sudden halt as a block at the end of a street prevents further access.

Miller Street Closed, the three of them read, *Emergency access only – Party in Progress.*

"So that's that," Andrew says and is surprised to feel deflated. But Thomas is already slithering around the barrier, Barnaby over it, the two of them apparently unfazed by such restriction. Andrew stands watching their progress up Miller Street then, with mild apprehension, rapidly follows in their wake.

***

Lydia Gough in the garden flat, sitting in her chair by the window, stares down at her hands, into her lap and sees only sky.

"Such a pretty colour, that blue," someone says. Not Polly. Not Sam. "Your dress, Lydia. It really suits you. Sam tells me it's new."

The voice reaches her, but she is still looking down and sees more sky. And white patches and shapes that her fingers try to touch, but refuse. Her eyes too. Like a baby's. Isn't that what they say? At birth the baby's eyes only focus on objects close. A mother's face. The baby finds its mother's eyes. Like Polly. Polly's face, only hours old, pressed close to her breast, small nose flattened against the fullness of flesh. Then lifting away for a moment, new-born eyes finding hers. She remembers. Love. There is a word for it, the love of one's child, but she has lost its syllables, sounds slipping out of grasp like a cup spilling milk. Words are slippery, blobs of dissolving jelly, that no longer hold together even in her head. Like thoughts, an unstrung necklace of those poppet beads her mother used to wear. That voice again, here in the room. Too close to her. Not Polly. Not Sam. They went somewhere else. They said. There has been some noise, a fuss, something happening, people

331

leaving, arriving. And Polly's kiss. She remembers that, her skin against her face. She always knows Polly. Now another voice or is it the same one? Asking her something. Repeating a question. She stares up at the face. A kind face, smiling. She smiles back. At least she thinks she does. She tries. But suddenly feels too tired to bother since nothing seems to be of concern to her anymore. She is remote even from herself. Displaced. Lydia closes her eyes. Then opens them again, looks down, searching for that sky. Spreads thin fingers against its enormity. A hand is placed on one of hers. Startling her. But the voice is quiet. Calm.

"Lydia? It's Isabel. My turn to keep you company now. Until Sam is back."

★★★

Outside, Frances found Helena Harris.

"I've had to be vigilant, you know," the woman greeted her, "already caught some teenagers from another road trying to gate crash."

"I suppose it's inevitable," Frances said.

"I explained that it's a stringently controlled ticketed event and entirely restricted to the residents and sent them packing."

"Except for guests, of course. Partners, parents, boyfriends, that kind of thing."

"What?"

"We did extend an invitation to appropriate other halves."

"Well, yes, naturally. Of course we did. But there's very few of them and I have them all listed and accounted for." Helena indicated her clipboard with some pride. "So rest assured, Frances, there's no chance of anyone slipping through the net on my guard."

Frances looked at her watch.

"Cake!"

"Pardon?"

"The cutting of the centenary cake was supposed to be at four and it's closer to half past. I was going to relieve you, Helena, from your post for a while, but really I'm going to have to chase things up, announcements, the knife and … now who was going to be responsible for the knife?"

"I expect it's with the cake," Helena said curtly.

"Of course."

Frances swiftly headed away, disappearing through the open door of number 8 where the cake was waiting in the cool of the kitchen. Helena watched her go then let her eye idle over the children's Edwardian costume competition occupying the middle stretch of the street. A certain licence appeared to have been taken where authenticity was concerned. Genuine, painstaking attempts at parlour maids, cooks and kitchen skivvies vied with Spiderman and Superman where clearly last-minute raids on dressing up drawers had been made.

Then suddenly Helena's attention was caught.

Two young men – early twenties, younger than her own son, surely – and an older man, looking out of place. As if unfamiliar with their surroundings. Detached. Clearly removed from the camaraderie of the party.

She had not noticed them before. Possibly they had eluded her when she had been chastising the teenagers, slipped through her cordon undetected. Now they appeared not so much to be attempting to join in with the party as sidling along the pavement, inspecting front doors. It was possible, Helena thought, that they were thieves. House-breakers intent on crime at a time when occupants' attention was elsewhere, security lax.

It was, after all, a London street.

One must remain alert to that. Possibly there was an entire network of crime working such events, exploiting community occasions for their own invidious gains. Convinced now of the idea, she began to move towards them furtively, dodging around the trestle tables and garden chairs cluttering the pavements, tracking their tentative progress as the three of them moved down the street. Clearly, they had a target in mind and Helena increased her pace.

Outside Willow House, Andrew stops, suddenly alarmed by the idea of intrusion. Supposing Frances is no longer alone.

He realises that he has never considered this idea, the possibility of some infidelity of hers intended to match his. Thomas looks at his father, questioningly.

"Flat 3? I think the door's round the side." Then he turns to Barnaby. "Are you following us or something? Who are you looking for?"

Barnaby, seized suddenly with apprehension, mutters something about it all being a mistake, turns to head away and is abruptly stopped.

A hand is on his shoulder. Fingers firm through his thin T-shirt.

22

Helena Harris stared at the three of them.

"Clearly, you are not residents," she said crisply and looked down at her flip board. "And all guests are already accounted for. Would you care to explain yourselves?" She turned to Andrew as if his seniority rendered him most culpable. There was a pause. Barnaby and Thomas shifted from one foot to another evasively, as if reverting to childhood with the prerogative of allowing the adult to take the blame. A loud megaphone pierced the air. People were being instructed to gather near the platform for the ceremonial cutting of the centenary cake. Andrew, smiling and touching Helena Harris' arm fleetingly the way he had cultivated for nervous female patients, said,

"Let me explain. There's really no problem. My name is Chater, Andrew Chater. I am Frances Chater's husband. And this is our son, Thomas. So yes, we are quite legitimate, no worries on that score."

He waited for her apology, for some embarrassment on her part.

"As I thought," she said eventually, lowering her voice as if anxious not to cause disruption to the party mood although by now most were heading to the top of the street for the cake cutting. "Trespassers. Would the three of you kindly leave – now?"

"Look," Andrew said, abandoning charm. The visit to Miller Street promised to be wrought enough without the contribution of this tiresome woman. "If you would just let me and Thomas find Frances all this will be sorted. I have to say I can't speak for this other young man. But no doubt he has his genuine reasons for being here too."

Barnaby felt himself blush in a way he had not known since he was fifteen. He began to look around him for ways of surreptitiously slipping out of the street, but at the same time felt irritated by this woman's accusations. He reached into the back pocket of his jeans, pulled out a snatch of folded paper.

"I've come to see Catherine Wells," he said, shoving the grubby pencilled scrap towards Helena. "Although, of course," he added deprecatingly, "she doesn't actually know me. Not like these ..." Barnaby waved a hand towards Andrew and Thomas. "Not really the same thing at all. Although actually, we are related. Kind of."

Helena said firmly, "Frances Chater is the steering power behind today's events. And the chairman of our street party committee. I know her well. And I can safely tell you that the woman is unmarried. Single and childless. So your story is ludicrous. Pure fabrication." She folded her arms across her chest, unintentionally wedging her clipboard which began to slip awkwardly down, finishing at her bare sandaled feet.

But attention was suddenly elsewhere.

Further down the street, Barnaby saw a woman holding an enormous cake on a large tray, a silver knife somewhat precariously balanced next to it, standing as still as if instructed at gunpoint. She stared at them, like she might stare at something that belied her understanding. Then she looked down, as if the weight of the tray in her hands reminded her of what she was holding and bent down carefully, placing the tray and its contents in the middle of the road. She began to walk towards them, cautiously at first before picking up her pace with such intent so she did not so much arrive as collapse at their side. No one spoke. Or at least not with any clarity for Thomas let his mother hold on to him so tightly that any words either of them might have been saying were muffled by the strength of their embrace. After a few moments, Andrew gently pulled the two of them apart and said,

"Perhaps there is somewhere more private for this. After all, we don't want to intrude on the party."

Frances looked at Andrew as if she had only just noticed him, with curiosity rather than the wonder with which she looked at her son. She said something about her flat, but did not move as if worried that the reality of Thomas would dissolve if they left that spot. Catherine, who had been sent in search of the absent cake, passed Helena who was scurrying rapidly away, her head held down. Frances turned to Catherine and said, smiling,

"I seem to have lost it. The cake, that is. Sorry. I know I put it down somewhere."

Barnaby stepped forward, eager to seize the chance to become more than an onlooker in the proceedings. Within moments he had retrieved the large tray with its imposing cake from the middle of the street and presented it to Catherine. Frances said,

"Perhaps you could take over from me, Catherine, on the platform? You see, I have some unexpected visitors. Important visitors." And she waved her hand towards Thomas.

"Of course," Catherine said, attempting to take the cake from Barnaby. He clung on. Stared at her intently. She returned his stare, trying to summon the memory of someone else whose face this stranger reflected.

"I'll carry it for you if you like – weighs a ton." And he followed Catherine to the top of the street, to the platform where people had already grown impatient with the wait and had started to drift away. Somewhat hastily, therefore, the cake was cut without the formality Frances had intended and whisked away to someone's kitchen to be portioned. Catherine waited for the young man to move away, but he seemed resistant to leave her side.

"Excuse me," she said eventually, "I'm going back to my flat for a while. Perhaps you could re-join your family? Or whoever you are with today."

"Actually," he began, "I think it might be you who I've come to see. That's if you don't mind seeing me."

Catherine looked at him closely and again sensed a remote similarity, a faint imprint or echo of someone she could not define.

"Do I know you?" she said and for a moment thought wildly of the friends of one of her nephews. She tried to think of any she had met when staying with Beth and her family, someone to whom she might have rashly issued an open invitation. The young man looked suddenly embarrassed and hesitant, his brief assertiveness gone.

"I just thought you might want to know," he said eventually, staring into the front garden of the nearest house to avoid her eye, "that my name is Barnaby. And although I don't use my birth father's surname, by rights I could call myself Barnaby Wells."

★★★

Thomas talked. At first, the three of them had been mute, suddenly shy of each other, hesitant to spoil the elation of the initial reunion in the street. Frances had offered tea, trivialities about the party, to fill the breach that each in their own way was unsure how to negotiate. Then Thomas mentioned something about the climate in Perth. Frances asked him which Australian cities he had seen and after a hesitant start he launched into a long account of his travelling, regaling them with anecdotes, with numerous incidents so that anyone listening to the three of them, Andrew thought, would never have known what lay beneath the surface of their conversation. Frances looked well. Her hair was longer – or was it? Perhaps he had merely forgotten, so used now to Charlotte's cropped bob. And the flat was clearly comfortable, accommodated to her needs in a way that he found faintly disquieting. He had no idea what he had expected or why the thought that she had organised her life so effectively away from him should be a surprise. She had always been, after all, a resourceful woman. He looked at the two of them now, Thomas's long legs and wiry body spilling over the armchair while Frances sat forward on the sofa as if desperate not to miss one word he shared. For the time being he knew he was redundant. He was not sure they deserved this, he and Frances, the foolishly intractable parents absolved, seemingly, by their child. And surely, his part in the breakdown of their marriage, his adultery, rendered him beyond easy forgiveness.

Even his own.

All his life he had been a man absolute in his sense of responsibility, intolerant of others with an indifferent moral code. Until Charlotte. The idea that he could behave with such flagrant disregard for his own convictions still astounded him.

Through the open windows of the flat, they could hear musicians warming up, a tenor sax, a clarinet. Someone testing for sound. Frances glanced at the clock. The jazz band would be starting soon heralding evening events. Andrew said something about it perhaps being time for them to leave, that intruding on such a day had not been their intention.

"Not yet," Frances said, "please. Surely you don't have to go so soon. Either of you." Then she turned to Thomas. "I am so sorry," she said, "I am sorry beyond words. For the way I behaved. The things I said. I can't imagine now why I thought such a thing mattered. You had just changed your mind. As reasonable as that."

Thomas said nothing at first. Then muttered something about it all feeling so long ago now, the rows, the disagreements. They had all probably said things that they didn't mean. And there had been a chance for him to think too, to understand just a little of what she had felt at the time. He looked at Andrew.

"Are you in a hurry to get back, Dad? I'd like to stay a bit. If that's all right with you."

Andrew said, "My time's my own. Nothing important to get home for."

Frances stood up, looked at the two of them and felt for a moment such unclouded joy that it was impossible to speak. Thomas went to the window, looked out.

"So can we join in? With this party that seems to be going on outside? Music sounds good."

Andrew looked questioningly at Frances. "According to some woman, it's only guests of the residents. And neither me nor Thomas were considered ... appropriate, shall we say?"

Frances looked at him blankly for a moment then simply smiled, waved a hand as if dismissing the problem.

"Oh that business," she said. "Don't worry. Easily sorted. Of course you must come. As my guests. It's the highlight of the year in Miller Street, after all."

★★★

Catherine said, "Of course, being Saturday night, you've probably got all sorts of plans. I wouldn't want to delay you."

"Not really," Barnaby said, "I'm usually working at the

restaurant, but I've got today off. But will it be all right?" He remembered the officious Helena Harris with her clip board and glanced a little nervously out of the window.

"I'm allowed a guest," Catherine said, "to take to the party and you can be mine." It was not so much that Barnaby resembled Eddie facially. There was no immediate matching of identical features between father and son. Eddie's eyes had been blue, Barnaby's were brown. But each was indelibly in the other as if the younger man had inherited the older's demeanour, shape, absorbed his bearing. Now he shrugged broad shoulders, turned his head towards the clock on the wall and Catherine struggled with the catch in her throat. There was absolutely no doubt at all that this was Eddie's son.

"Ok, then," he said, "I'd like that. If you don't want me just to disappear out of your life forever. I wasn't sure, you see."

"I don't," Catherine said, "want you to just disappear. It's the last thing I want you to do."

Barnaby nodded. Smiled. Again that faint flicker of familiarity. But where to start getting to know him? Catherine felt there was both so much to ask yet so little that Barnaby might feel inclined to supply. That he might consider of interest to her. She had shown him a photo. He had stared at it for some time, saying nothing, a silence that had become awkward so she had said something about there being more and that she could dig several out to give him to keep and eventually he had said that he would like that. He would like it very much. Having a photograph of his father would make him real, he said. Even though he was too late to meet him. And then she realised that it was not the time for her to learn about Barnaby. That could come later. Instead he needed her to talk endlessly about Eddie. To bring his father alive for him.

But it would have to be for another day.

Already, Catherine felt overwhelmed by Barnaby's arrival and she wanted only to absorb the truth of his existence. To cherish it, in fact, this extraordinary, quite unexpected gift that had presented itself to her.

"I suppose," Barnaby said as they left the flat to join the party, "you're kind of my stepmother. Is it all right if I think of you like that? I never thought I'd get one of those."

Catherine found herself capable only of smiling. Nodding her head in agreement.

The street was at its most crowded. Every house had emptied as people congregated around tables, eating and drinking, whilst others gathered near the platform with some impromptu dancing to the band. The mood of the perfect summer's evening seemed to encourage conviviality and even those who had been staunch opponents to the party had mellowed and stood with glasses in hand, chatting to neighbours. On the forecourt of Willow House, Isabel and Violet had brought Lydia out in her wheelchair so that she could at least share in something of the mood of the evening for a short while. Distanced from the centre of noise and activity further down the street, she was placid, content.

Violet said, "Who are those people with Fran? She's even dancing with the young one."

"I believe it's her son and husband," Isabel said evenly.

"But she doesn't have a husband. Definitely not a son. Not Fran."

"I think you'll find," Isabel said, adjusting the shawl around Lydia's shoulders, "that she has both."

Violet stepped into the street to peer down towards the dancing figures, picked out now by spotlights in the fading light of the summer night.

"Well," she said, "you think you know everything about someone and then they go and surprise you."

342

"Oh Violet," Isabel said, "surely you realise by now that most of us are an entire mystery to each other."

★★★

Sam drove back from the hospital wondering how it was possible to feel both exhausted yet imbued with more energy than he had known in a long time. He was certainly hungry, could remember only too many cups of indifferent coffee and very strong tea, a bar of chocolate, perhaps a bun, since breakfast. But there was no time to stop and eat now. He needed to get back to Lydia. Remembering to park several roads away, he headed at a pace to Miller Street, the sounds of music and voices pulling him there even if he had not known the way.

To find Lydia, with Violet and Isabel, watching events from the forecourt of Willow House.

"I'm so sorry to be away all day. I was just going to drop Polly and get back here, but then things started happening." He moved to Lydia's side, took both hands in his and she looked up at him as if in some way anticipating the news he was about to share. "A baby girl, Lyddie," he said, "a beautiful granddaughter for us. Eliza Florence. How about that? Polly's used your middle name. Eliza Florence Gough."

And although he suspected that tiredness was masking the clarity of his perception, Sam was sure that Lydia increased her grip on his hands. And smiled.

POSTSCRIPTS

Letter on the kitchen table at 10 Pilgrim Square addressed to Andrew.

Andy darling,

It's better this way. I'm not the type for melodramatic scenes and really there is so little to say. I have taken all my things although if by chance I've forgotten anything, just donate it to a charity shop. My resignation as dental nurse at the practice will be sent under separate cover. (I'm owed holiday, anyway, and intend to take that right now in lieu of notice)

Andy, the trouble is – you. You're the problem. You're a better man than I gave you credit for and I am not at my best with good men.

Nor am I tolerant of being in second place. To anyone. Ever. And anyway, it was never going to be forever, was it? We were always more of a salacious short story than a saga novel.

And what fun we had!

Charlotte XXX

Andrew reads the letter several times, waiting to register how he feels. Perhaps it is the hour – gone midnight after catching a late train home from London – but he is finding it difficult to summon heartbreak. Instead, a curious sense of relief, a reprieve almost, as if granted a freedom that he had no idea he had lost, embraces him. And in the morning, when he wakes to a silent house, potters downstairs to the emptiness of the rooms, he senses something that has felt long out of his grasp.

The gift of choice.

~~~

Sam scans the details of the house. Good sized rooms, an extension on the ground floor providing a form of annexe. A sizeable garden.

"Good value," he says. "Compared with prices around here. You get so much more for your money a little way out, don't you?"

"Not a rural retreat, though. Hardly that. So a compromise really," Polly says, shifting the baby from one shoulder to the other.

"A compromise? What do you mean?"

"Between your ideal of living in remote countryside and inner-city life. A halfway house, you could say."

Sam watches Polly's dexterity with handling this frighteningly small bundle of humanity. How is it possible to feel this intense and unconditional love for his grandchild, for Eliza Florence who he has known for only three days? Even Lydia, when Polly had first placed her cautiously, carefully in her arms had felt, he was sure, the enormity of such love.

"Oh that," he says dismissively. "I don't seem to have a need to live remotely any more. You could say I've come in out of the cold."

Polly looks at him quizzically. Then says,

"So shall we go and see it? This house. It could be ideal."

Sam stands up.

"I'll go and ring the agent now. Get things going as soon as possible."

~~~

Thomas Chater says to his mother,

"I'm thinking about graphic design. I need to make a decision about – well, the future. What I really want to do."

Across the table of the restaurant near Waterloo, Frances says, "You must take your time. You're still so young. And congratulations on getting the job."

"It's only a stop-gap," Thomas says. "Office boy, really, in this architectural firm. I do a lot of photocopying and making tea. But I like it. And it's just about paying the rent."

"As long as you're happy. And you're not planning on rushing off anywhere again like …"

Thomas smiles, looks down at his menu.

"No. I've done with all that stuff. Australia at least. Quite fancy a weekend in Paris, though."

"Paris," Frances says, "sounds ideal."

They order.

"Have you heard from Dad lately?"

Frances says, "We spoke last week. He's coming up to London soon for an annual conference. We'll probably meet for dinner. Nothing arranged yet, but he said he'd be in touch."

Thomas says, cautiously, "So you've heard?"

"Yes," Frances says, "I understand that Charlotte has moved out."

The waiter brings wine, bread. Lager for Thomas. And Frances thinks of how she had greeted Andrew's news calmly. As a matter of interest rather than as victor over conquest. The future is unmapped, in limbo, and she is content for the time being to leave it so.

All that essentially matters is sitting opposite her in this small, unremarkable restaurant, sharing a meal, conversation. And thus her happiness is complete.

"Sometimes," she says, more to herself than to Thomas

although she knows he will understand, "it's possible to look back and hardly recognise ourselves. How easy it is to get things so very wrong."

After a pause, he says, "I certainly got the idea of going into medicine wrong. Turned out I couldn't stomach hospitals all day long. Or being around ill people."

"Something of an occupational hazard, I would imagine," Frances says, "an unavoidable combination."

And for some reason impossible to explain, they find her comment hilarious, ridiculously funny so that when the waiter places their food in front of them, they are still recovering from the mild joke, still bursting into sudden laughter at the memory of it.

~~~

Barnaby says, "I spoke to Mum. Told her about meeting you."

Catherine had remembered the name, Rosie. There had been two or three girlfriends Eddie had spoken about, but he had mentioned Rosie more often than the others in faintly disparaging tones. It had always made her think that she had been the one to leave him.

But nothing about a child.

"It must be awkward for her," Catherine says as they walk along the Regent's Canal in the light of the early August evening.

"Not really," Barnaby says. "My mother compartmentalises her life. Once she's left one bit of it, she discards it with no backward glance."

"Sensible woman," Catherine says.

"I don't think so. After all, if I had done that, I wouldn't have found you."

Catherine is pleased to have the diversion of a runner who crosses her path. This is the first time they have met since the day of the street party and still the knowledge of her sudden inheritance moves her to tears. She wants to throw her arms around this tall twenty-year-old young man, play substitute father as well as step mother, but knows she must be cautious. They must both take their time, negotiate their way to find the appropriate place in one another's lives.

"There's just one thing I've always wanted to know," Barnaby says, "and my mother refuses to tell me."

Catherine says, "I'll tell you all I know about Eddie. But your mother must have left him over ten years before we even met."

Barnaby says, slowing his pace, "Did he know about me? Did my father know Rosie was pregnant, that he had a son?"

Catherine has anticipated the question.

"I have no idea for certain, but in ten years of living with

Eddie, of being married to him, he certainly never mentioned it."

It is sufficient, Catherine has decided, for Barnaby to know. What is the use of loading this young man with pointless speculation about Eddie's declared choice to be childless?

"One thing I can say for sure," Catherine goes on, as they pick up their pace again, "if he was here this evening with us, no doubt striding far ahead, disappearing into the distance to beat us to the nearest canal side pub, he would be the proudest father in the world. Justly proud, Barnaby, of his son."

Barnaby fiddles with his hair, the fringe that flops over easily into one eye. Then he says,

"You said something about a pub, Catherine. Shall we find one?"

 Matador

For exclusive discounts on Matador titles,
sign up to our occasional newsletter at
troubador.co.uk/bookshop